Love WITHOUT DEMANDS

THE BOUVIER FAMILY SAGA

book 3

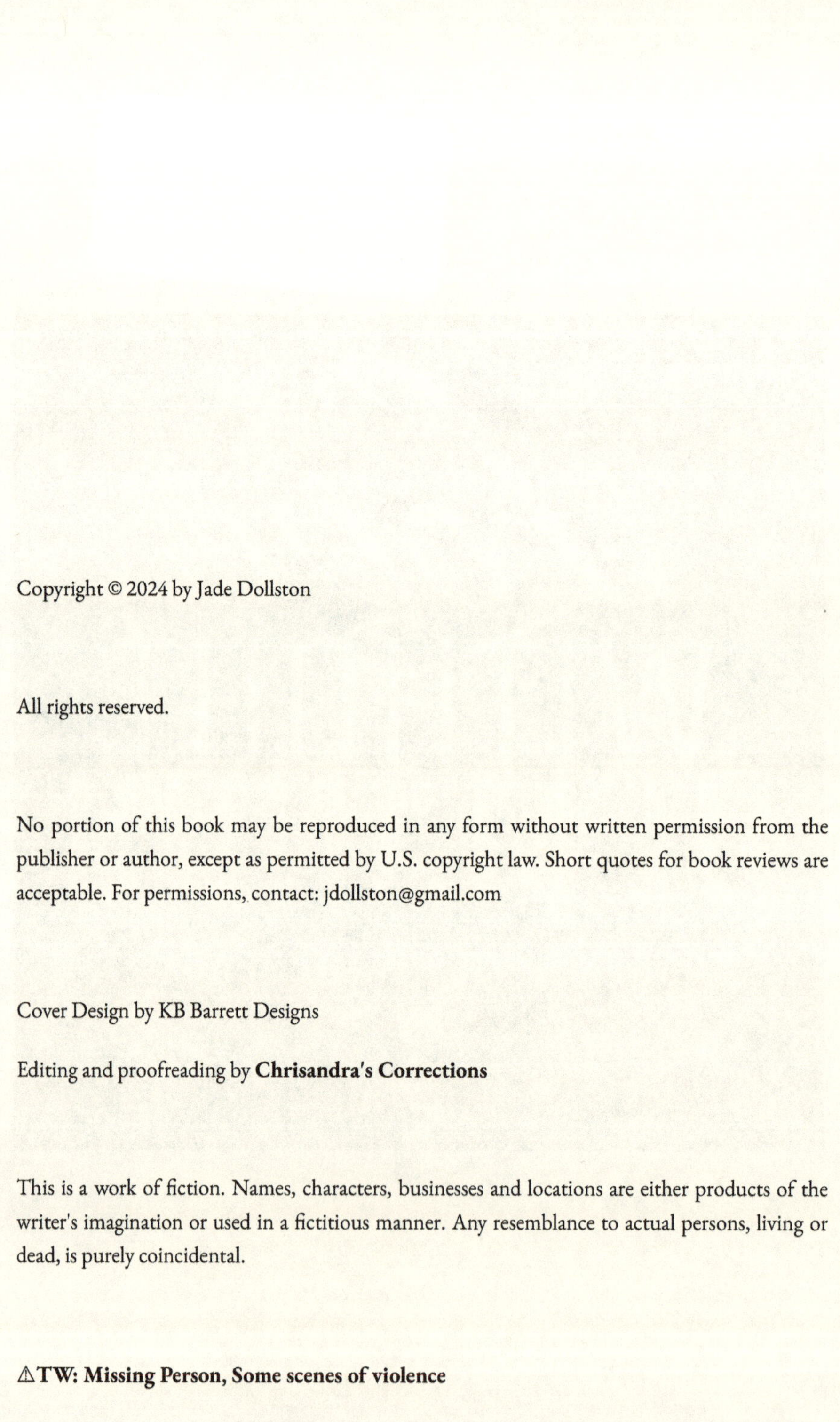

Contents

Author's Note:

A few things here.

First, if you have an original copy of **Love Without Influence** (book two in this saga), you may notice an inconsistency with how Cruz was hired when compared with this book. When I started writing **Love Without Demands**, the story began to take shape in a slightly different way.

It's a small thing (one sentence) that didn't really affect book two, but it would affect how my entire timeline progressed in book three. So I made the decision to change it. Like I said, the original version will still have that sentence in it, and I apologize if that bothers anyone, though I figure most won't even notice. But I felt the need to address it for those eagle-eyed, detail queens. (I'm one too!)

Second thing, since this is a work of fiction, I took a few liberties with the structure of Cruz's weekend job. I purposely never mentioned exactly which department Cruz worked for, though I'm sure you could infer that information from where he lives. I researched a lot of SWAT teams for various police departments in different locations and formulated what worked best for my story.

Last thing, there are two prologues in this book. Yeah, I know. Kinda weird, right? But just wait... it gets even weirder! The prologues are also not told from the point of view of this book's main characters.

If you read book two, you probably remember the patriarch of the family, Paul Bouvier, and his heart-rending story. He fell in love with a beautiful, young nanny named Estrella. That entire story has a direct effect on this book in a huge way, and I thought their voices deserved to be heard.

Paul and Estrella's narrative has been rambling around in my brain for a long time, and I wanted to share parts of their stories with you from their points of view since this book would not be possible without them.

Okay, that's about it. I hope you enjoy reading **Love Without Demands** as much as I enjoyed writing it.

Playlist

Drink You Away by Justin Timberlake

Someone Like You by John Legend (Adele cover)

Landslide by Fleetwood Mac

I Can't Make You Love Me by Bonnie Raitt

Stay With Me by Sam Smith

El Mundo by Banda Caio Rodriguez

Just the Way You Are by Bruno Mars

Burning Love by Elvis

Can't Help Falling in Love by Elvis

Fireball by Pitbull

He's a Pirate – Pirates of the Caribbean Soundtrack

PROLOGUE 1

PAUL BOUVIER - AGE 33

"Paul, I just wanted to let you know the divorce papers have been served to your wife in Vermont."

Clutching the phone to my ear, my teeth ground together when my attorney said that word. *Wife.* Chloe Bouvier had been my wife for over a decade, but recently, the title was in name only. There was absolutely no love left in our marriage.

"Thanks, George. Keep me updated," I said before hanging up.

Chloe had always been a selfish woman, but it hadn't bothered me that much. Not until our son was born. I smiled at the thought of Auburn, my five-year-old, with his dark hair and big blue eyes. He was a good boy, quiet and thoughtful, but with a ready smile whenever I came home from work each night.

A smile that he lacked whenever his mother was around, however. It hurt me to the depths of my soul that the woman I'd married was so cold and unfeeling toward our boy.

And toward Evelyn, or Evie as Auburn liked to call her. I picked up the photo on my desk, and my lips crooked up at the corners. My baby girl and Auburn were sharing my lap, and three sets of matching blue eyes stared back at me. Evie's hair was a few shades lighter than mine and my son's, but otherwise, the family resemblance was obvious.

How the hell can Chloe's heart not melt when she looks at these two precious children? They were my world. My wife was too, in the beginning, but after

Auburn had come into our lives, Chloe's narcissistic personality had been shoved to the forefront. She was cold and unfeeling, bordering on cruel.

I knew she was jealous of our son since she was no longer the sole center of my universe, but that's how it's supposed to be, right? When you have children, you make room in your lives and in your hearts. We should have been drawn closer as a couple, but the opposite happened.

Chloe and I hadn't shared a bed in a long time. Well, except for that one night months ago. Fuck. I hated myself for giving in to the temptations of the bottle.

Reminded of my vice, I stand and pour myself two fingers of bourbon before walking to the huge windows and looking out over Manhattan. I'd built the *Bouvier* fashion empire here, and I hoped one day I could hand over the reins to Auburn and Evie.

Chloe had left for a retreat in Vermont the day after I'd allowed her into my bed all those months ago, and I can't say I was saddened by that. The guilt of sleeping with my wife ate at me, and when she announced one day later that she was going away for a while, relief tore through me like a freight train.

Why did I feel guilty about sleeping with my own wife? This is going to make me sound like a total asshole, but here we go. I'd begun to develop feelings for someone else. Someone I couldn't and shouldn't want. But I did.

So many times I'd drowned myself in a bottle of bourbon, and when Chloe appeared in my bedroom that night in June, offering herself to me, I took the opportunity she was giving. It had been about a year since we'd last had sex, probably the night Evie was conceived.

With liquor sloshing through my veins and sexual neglect hardening my cock, I'd ripped Chloe's negligee off and tossed her on my bed. Our joining that night wasn't gentle. It wasn't filled with sentiments or thoughts of reconciliation. No, it was a hard, rutting fuck from behind, meant only to satiate a biological need.

I cringed at the memory and slugged back the contents of my glass as my eyes caught on an orange leaf floating on the September breeze. I loved fall in New York.

My little girl was six months old now. Her mother had been gone for three months. Three fucking months! She'd just abandoned her infant daughter and five-year-old son, and on the rare occasions Chloe would call, she didn't even ask about them.

That only solidified my decision to serve her with divorce papers. There was absolutely no chance that this marriage could be saved. I'd tried for years. I'd spoiled her, showered her with attention, flowers, and gifts, but the more I gave, the colder she became.

Because I wasn't giving her *everything*. I wasn't giving her my undivided adoration. Chloe was incredibly jealous of my relationship with my kids. I didn't neglect my soon-to-be-ex-wife, not by any means, but any time I spent with Evie and Auburn drew more and more derision and contempt from her.

So I finally did it. I called my attorney and got him to draw up the divorce papers. It was a fair settlement, giving Chloe much more than our prenup allowed, but I didn't care, and I was pretty sure she would be amenable to it as well. She was wealthy before our marriage, and with the amount of money I was offering, it would only increase her monetary worth. All I asked was that I be granted custody of the kids. Hell, she didn't want them anyway; that much was obvious.

The phone on my desk buzzed, and I turned from the window and hit the button to connect to my personal assistant. "Yes, Carol?"

"Mr. Bouvier, Franklin is pulling the car around."

"Thank you. I'll head down now."

I set down the empty glass and pulled on my suit jacket. Checking the mirror in my personal restroom, I brushed down the stray locks of my black hair and straightened my tie, transforming myself into Paul Bouvier, the composed and stylish CEO of a major fashion house.

Appearances counted in my industry, and I didn't want my employees to see the man I'd become. A broken man with a dependency on alcohol just to get through the miserable days and nights.

But, hopefully, that misery would be alleviated soon.

I entered my grandiose red brick home through the front door, my shoes squeaking across the cream marble floor. My nose led me to the kitchen, and I paused in the arched doorway.

Estrella Acosta was standing with her back to me, Evie on her hip, while she sang a low tune in Spanish. Her dark hair hung down her back in a long braid, and I noticed a bead of sweat drip down the tawny brown skin of her neck.

Estrella had been our nanny since Auburn was a baby, and I'd always been fond of the woman. She was kind and gentle, a true nurturer.

With Chloe gone, I was solely responsible for the children once Estrella got off work at six. But recently, she'd started staying much later, helping me with dinner and putting the kids to bed. Our employee/employer relationship had developed into an easy friendship, and my fondness eventually turned into more.

So much more. I'd fallen in love with my children's nanny. I kept my shameful feelings to myself until one night, she'd broken down in tears and confessed her love for me. God, the way my heart had almost burst from my chest at her admission.

And suddenly, my feelings weren't quite so shameful. They were good and pure, and I admitted to her that I felt the same. Absolutely nothing physical had happened between us since that evening a few weeks ago, though I longed to touch her, hold her hand, kiss her rosy lips.

When Estrella turned to find me staring, her beautiful face broke into a smile. "Paul…"

"Hi, Estrella." I crossed the room, fighting the urge to tuck away that stray piece of hair that always seemed to escape her braid and curl in front of her ear.

Her shy brown eyes blinked up at me as she stroked Evie's caramel hair. "Your daughter has been asking for you."

As if on cue, Evie babbled, "Dadadadadaaaaa."

"Come here, my princess," I said, taking the little one and cuddling her to my chest. Evelyn Bouvier was a happy baby, constantly enjoying the sound of her own voice.

Auburn burst into the room then, and I bent to scoop him up with my other arm. He patted Evie's head and kissed her sweetly on the nose. My boy adored his baby sister, and I loved the affection between the two.

"How was school today?" I asked him, and he beamed a smile up at me.

"Good. I drawed a picture of our family." He points at a drawing on the refrigerator. "See? It's me and Evie and you and Straya." He couldn't quite pronounce Estrella's name.

My heart broke a little at the fact that my son didn't even include his mother in a family drawing. If he already neglected to realize that she was part of his family, what kind of influence would her coldness have on him as he grew up?

For so long, I'd been reluctant to file for divorce because I thought that would be damaging to my kids, but now I knew I was doing the right thing. Growing up in a loving household is more important than anything.

I kissed the top of his messy hair. "That's such a pretty picture," I told him. "You're my smart boy, aren't you?"

"Uh-huh," he said with a nod. "Straya said I can put the pepperonis on the pizza."

"Good boy." I set him on the counter beside the sink and instructed him to wash his hands.

"Let me take this little peanut while you get changed," Estrella told me, taking Evie. Her hand brushed my arm, and I felt a jolt of electricity. Our eyes met, and I knew she felt it too.

After dinner, we worked together to get the kids ready for bed. I watched from the doorway of Auburn's room as she read a book to him, and then she bent to kiss his forehead when he drifted off to sleep. My heart almost exploded with love at the tender gesture. Estrella was more of a mother to my children than Chloe ever dreamed about being.

I went downstairs to my study and poured myself a drink, sipping it slowly until I heard soft footsteps on the stairs. Then I leaned against the doorframe, waiting for her to come say goodnight.

With her purse over her arm, she came down the darkened hallway, and I grew aroused at the easy sway of her hips. Estrella had a gorgeous body, all soft curves and subtle sensuality.

"Can I speak with you in my office, please?"

Her eyes flashed with worry as she entered, and I directed her to the leather sofa. She sat primly on the edge as I sat inches from her, not daring to touch her.

"Is something wrong, Paul?"

"No, not at all. In fact, I haven't felt this good in a long time." Inhaling a deep breath, I held her brown eyes with my blue ones. "I filed for divorce from Chloe."

Estrella sucked in a breath, and her hand went to her chest. "Oh." Her voice was a soft squeak.

"I know how you feel about divorce, but there's no way I can stay in this situation any longer."

Her eyes lowered and she nodded. "I understand."

My finger crooked beneath her chin, and her eyes went round when I lifted her face. I'd never touched her in this way before, but I needed her to understand. "I meant it when I told you I was in love with you, Estrella. I want us to be together."

Tears filled her pretty eyes, and one escaped down the curve of her cheek. I wiped it away with my thumb, and she bit into her lower lip. "I don't want to be a homewrecker, Paul."

"You're not," I assured her. "You know my marriage has been over for a very long time, and this house isn't a home without you in it. Did you mean it when you said you love me?"

"I did," she breathed, and I reached for her hand, pressing a kiss to the back of it. The skin was soft and smelled like Evie's baby shampoo.

"I know you're worried about how things will look, so we can wait an appropriate amount of time after the divorce is final, and then... then I want you to be my wife, Estrella."

She closed her eyes and shook her head. "You don't want to marry me, Paul. I'm not... in your league."

Cupping her pretty face with both hands, I obliterated the physical barriers we'd both maintained. "Estrella, you are so far out of my league. I don't deserve you, but that doesn't mean I don't love you."

She looked up, blinking away the tears that were threatening, before returning her gaze to my face. "I love you too, but—"

"No buts. If we love each other, we should be together." I tilted my forehead against hers, inhaling the cinnamon scent from the snickerdoodles she'd made for dessert. "You are the most incredible woman I've ever known, my beautiful star. You are kindhearted and warm, the type of mother my children deserve, and the type of wife I want."

Her hands rose to rest against the backs of mine, and the gentle touch almost undid me. "I want that. God help me, I shouldn't, but I do."

"Then be with me," I whispered, my chest tightening when she nodded. "May I kiss you?"

She angled her head and rested her lips against mine. "Yes."

I closed my mouth over hers, and her hands slid up my arms to wrap around my neck. She parted her lips, and I dipped my tongue into her mouth, tasting her for the first time. It was so goddamn sweet, my cock hardened in an instant.

We started out slow and tender, and our mutual need came to life with every stroke of our tongues. I hadn't kissed a woman other than Chloe in over ten years, and my veins were instantly ablaze with desire. Estrella tasted new and familiar at the same time.

The kiss quickly became more passionate, her hands twisting in my dark hair. "Estrella, I have to tell you something," I told her, dread slipping down my spine.

"What?" she asked, leaning back on the couch and pulling me down with her.

"I—I slept with Chloe the night before she left. About three months ago." She stilled, and the tear that dripped down her soft cheek cut me to the bone. "I'm so sorry. I was drunk, and she walked into my room with a condom, and... I just did it. I've never felt worse about anything in my life."

Her eyes darted away for a long moment before she returned them to mine. "She's your wife. You have every right to..."

"No, don't make excuses for me. I had no feelings for her whatsoever, and I've felt guilty about it ever since."

"Because you didn't want to hurt her?"

A tear dropped from my eye and landed in her hair. "No, Star, because I didn't want to hurt *you*. I'd already started developing feelings for you, and even though we hadn't even discussed it, I felt like I was being disloyal to you."

Estrella dragged the backs of her fingers down my cheek. "If we're going to be together, you've got to get your drinking under control."

"I will," I promised with a resolute nod. "If I have you, I won't need the liquor to numb me."

"Make love to me, Paul. Show me you mean what you say."

And I did.

Prologue 2

ESTRELLA ACOSTA - AGE 25

I spent the entire night in Paul Bouvier's bed. Our lovemaking was gentle yet passionate, with whispered words of love every time he was inside me.

Even with my limited experience with men—Paul was only my second lover—I could tell he was skilled. *Very* skilled. He made my body sing in a way I didn't know was possible. Probably because there was true love thrumming between us.

I had an IUD, so we hadn't bothered with protection, a decision we made together before the first time. And there were many times that night. Dios, the man was a machine.

I rose early and dressed before kissing my sleeping man's cheek. "I'll be back in about an hour," I whispered, and he smiled a lazy, sated smile up at me as his hands gripped my waist.

"Can I tempt you for one more round?" he asked in a sexy voice filled with morning grit.

Pulling away with a laugh, I shook my head. "No, I have to go to my apartment and change clothes so I can be back in time for you to go to work."

He groaned and swiped a hand through his deliciously messy hair. "One day, you'll live with me and won't have to leave." His thumb traced a lazy line against my cheekbone. "Is that still what you want?"

I was surprised the thudding inside my chest didn't wake the children. "I think so," I teased. "You were pretty impressive last night, Mr. Bouvier."

A grin full of mischief curled his lips up at the corners. "Glad you approved, Ms. Acosta. Why don't you pack a bag so you can stay with me again tonight?"

"I can't," I told him, sweeping a lock of hair from his forehead. "I have to leave right after work to help my sister with her immigration papers. I was born here, but she's a few years older than me and was born in Cuba. We're trying to get her citizenship."

He pulls me to him for a soft kiss. "Okay, but I'm going to miss having you in my arms all night. I think I'm addicted to you, Star."

I loved that nickname, which was my name in English. "I'm addicted to you too," I admit.

"I love you, baby," he said, and my breath caught in my chest, exactly how it had every time he'd told me that last night. "Make plans to stay with me on Friday night. I haven't had nearly enough of you."

Heat flushed my face and then seeped down my body as I caressed his handsome face. "I love you too."

As soon as I walked into my tiny apartment, I found my sister sitting on the couch with her arms crossed over her chest. *Oh shit.*

"Maya, hi!" I said, way too chirpily, which only deepened the frown on her face.

"Where. Have. You. Been?"

"I, uh, stayed over at the Bouvier house. I'm so sorry I didn't call, but I got... distracted."

Her eyebrows pinched so close together, they were at risk of becoming a unibrow. "By your boss's penis?"

Dammit. Maya can read me like a book. I never should have told her about our love confessions.

"That's none of your business," I said airily, heading to my bedroom, but my sister followed.

"So that's a yes. What are you thinking, Estrella, sleeping with a married man?"

"He's getting a divorce, and we're going to be together."

Maya scoffed in disbelief. "Honey, there's no way that man is going to leave his wife. That's just something rich men say to get in your panties."

"You don't understand," I snapped. "Paul really loves me."

"Billionaires don't marry women like us," she shot back, and my stomach dropped to the floor.

She doesn't know what she's talking about.

My voice softened. "Look, Maya, I need to shower and get back to work. I appreciate your concern, but we know what we're doing."

She stepped forward and ran her slim fingers through my hair. "Honey, you are so sweet and naive. He's eight years older than you, and I just don't want you to get hurt."

"I know," I murmured, "but trust me on this. He's already sent her the divorce papers."

"Did he show them to you?"

No.

"I need to get to work in time to take Auburn to school," I deflected. "I'll be home this evening to help you with your paperwork."

Maya's lips tightened into a thin line. "Just be careful, okay? I love you and I worry about you."

"I love you too," I told her, giving her a hard hug before making a shooing motion with my hands. "Now let me get ready." I needed her out of here so she didn't see the love marks Paul's mouth left all over my body.

With a reluctant nod, she left the room, and I headed to the small bathroom. Removing my shirt, I traced my fingers over the hickeys my man had sucked onto me each time he'd proclaimed me as *his*.

And I would be Paul Bouvier's. Forever.

As soon as I was done with work Thursday, I headed home to help Maya, but not before Paul gave me a long kiss at the door and told me he loved me. I was pretty sure my feet didn't even touch the ground until I arrived at my apartment.

The immigration paperwork was long and confusing, but we finally wrapped it up and went to bed without speaking of our argument that morning. Thank god. I hated fighting with my sister.

On Friday, I took an overnight bag with me to Paul's house since he wanted me to stay the night again. Auburn was at school, and Evie had just woken from her nap when I heard the garage door open about noon. With the baby on my hip, I looked up from where I was spooning mashed bananas into a bowl.

To my utter shock, Chloe Bouvier strutted into the kitchen, and I swallowed hard, instantly eaten up by guilt. As horrible as the woman was, I *had* slept with her husband.

"M-Mrs. Bouvier. Welcome home."

"Hmmm, soooo nice to see you, Estrella," she said in her trademark catty voice.

"Yes, ma'am. It's been a while." *Since you basically abandoned your husband and children*, I thought but didn't say aloud. Instead, I injected faux cheerfulness into my voice. "Evie has two new teeth. Would you like to take her?"

The bitch from hell barely glanced at her baby and shook her head. *Good lord, she hasn't seen her child in three months, and she's not even going to hold her?*

"No, I'd like for you to put the baby down so we can have a little… chat."

The way she said that last word made my stomach roll over, but I nodded. Carrying Evie to the living room, I placed her in her playpen and returned to the kitchen.

Chloe was dressed in a pristine camel-colored wool coat, looking like a million bucks as she leaned against the counter with her arms crossed over her middle. "How long have you been sleeping with my husband, Estrella?"

I practically choked on my own tongue as I felt heat stain my face bright red. "I, uh, I don't…" Dammit, I was such a shitty liar.

"You might as well tell me the truth. I already know."

What? How?

"I'm not sure what you're talking about," I managed to say, unable to meet the woman's eye, which I was sure only made me look more guilty.

She let out a laugh that would put the Wicked Witch of the West to shame. "Let me guess. He told you he was going to marry you, right?" Then she made a tsking sound as she pushed away from the counter and strolled toward me until she was right in my space. "Oh, you poor, dumb girl. Men like Paul Bouvier don't marry… *the help*." Her perfectly glossed lips made a popping sound on the last word.

Biting the inside of my cheek to stave off the impending tears, I simply shook my head. I had no words.

"I'm going to need you to vacate my home immediately. Your *services* are no longer needed." The snide curl of her mouth was laced with derision and bitchiness.

"Mrs. B-bouvier, I don't know what you mean."

One of her eyebrows arched high on her smooth forehead. "You see, I have some very happy news," she said, unbuttoning her coat, "Paul and I are expecting another baby." Her hands rested on the barely there bump that was obvious on her normally thin frame.

No, no, no. That can't be right.

But he did say he slept with her before she left... and used a condom... which she provided.

"Congratulations," I heard myself squeak, though that was the furthest sentiment from my mind. In fact, the mere thought made me nauseous.

"Thank you," she said in a cultured, superior tone. "Paul was thrilled when I told him. He's hoping for another girl. You know how much he adores Evelyn."

"Yes," I whispered, staring at the floor because I simply could not look at her for one more second.

"So, like I said, we would like you to leave our home."

My eyes snapped to hers. *This couldn't be right. Paul wouldn't abandon me. He loves me.*

"I can see you're questioning me, Estrella, but I assure you this is what my husband and I want. In fact, Paul said to give you this for your... troubles."

She stuffed something into my purse on the counter, and I glanced over to see stacks of hundred-dollar bills sticking out the top.

"I don't want your money," I insisted, humiliation thrumming through me.

"Trust me, you're going to need it. *My husband* and I decided it would be best if you left New York altogether." It wasn't lost on me that she kept emphasizing the *my husband* part. Chloe took another step forward until I could feel her breath on my face. Her voice was low and dangerous. "Otherwise, immigration services might receive an anonymous phone call." Her smile could have belonged to Satan himself.

Panic rose up in my throat even as I lifted my chin. "I was born in this country."

The horrible woman tilted her head to the side and smiled smugly. "But your sister wasn't, was she?" She proceeded to rattle off my sister's name and date of birth before her smile turned into a feral baring of straight white teeth. "Be gone by Monday night, or I'll have your sister deported. And trust me, I can do it. Power and money can buy pretty much anything."

Except a soul.

"I want to speak with Pa—with Mr. Bouvier," I corrected, and her brows narrowed.

"Paul. Does. Not. Want. You. Maybe he enjoyed getting between your legs for a bit, but now, with our new addition, he wants to make our marriage work for the sake of our children." To drive the point home, she rubbed her belly. "You will not contact him, now or ever. Am I understood?"

Tears spilled down my cheeks, and I started to protest, but she grabbed my chin in a harsh grip, pure evil glowing in her eyes.

"I want you gone, you little slut." She shoved, and I stumbled back a few steps, catching myself on the counter behind me. Picking up my purse, Chloe crammed it into my hands. "I think my husband has been more than generous. I would have sent you packing with absolutely nothing, but he's too goddamn soft for his own good. There's plenty of money here for you and your illegal sister to go back to Texas to be with your family. If you ever contact my husband again, having your sister deported will be the least of your worries."

The ferocity on her face put a fear into me like I'd never known, and I clutched my purse to my chest and backed away, never turning my back on her until I was in the foyer.

And then I ran.

Four days later, the unending tears were still streaming down my face as we passed through Houston and headed south on Interstate 45 to Galveston.

"I'm sorry, Estrella," Maya said for about the millionth time, clutching my hand in hers. To her credit, she hadn't said *I told you so* a single time.

My heart was shattered. I missed little Auburn and Evie. I loved them so much, and god help me, I still loved Paul, despite his betrayal.

We arrived at my parents' small home, where Maya and I would live until we found a place of our own. I stayed holed up in my bedroom, not speaking and barely eating. I'd never felt more broken.

And two months after that, I stood in the bathroom and stared down at the stick that informed me I was pregnant with Paul Bouvier's baby.

A baby he could never know about.

Chapter 1

If vaginas had emotions, mine would currently be... disappointed.

Attempting to find a better angle, I pulled my knees back and shifted my hips upward. *Almost... if he would just...*

"That's it, Lehra. You like Dwight's big man stick in your lady hole, don't you?"

And that's when I lost it.

For the record, I don't mean I lost it in terms of falling over the cliff of pure bliss and directly into a pool filled with orgasms and twitching thighs. No, as an off-key Tom Cruise once crooned, I lost that lovin' feeling.

Because my boyfriend was officially the worst dirty talker in the history of sex. *Sigh.*

He tried; he really did. But since I'd told him a few months ago that I wanted him to talk dirty to me during intimate times, he'd taken that to mean I wanted him to discover more and more creative ways of referring to his manhood.

Gone was all the *cock* and *dick* talk I'd hoped for, only to be replaced with things like man stick, trouser snake, and my personal favorite: skin flute.

Yeah.

And don't even get me started on the whole talking in third person situation. I'm not sure how I expected to get off when he moaned things like, *Dwight loves poking his pepperoni peen into your beaver box.*

In case you were wondering, my beaver box was not all aflutter the night he said that.

Rotating my hips in little circles to get the stimulation I craved, I buried my fingers in Dwight's blond hair. "Baby, do you like how my pussy feels around your cock?" I purred, hoping that would give him some inspiration as to the kind of naughty things I wanted to hear.

"Shit. Yes," he groaned, speeding up the pumping of his hips.

"Tell me how much you love stretching my pussy with that big dick of yours."

His eyes closed, and his jaw clenched hard. "You know I do," he panted out.

"Dwight, can you..."

"Yeah, baby. I can come for you."

Not what I was going to say, but the familiar jerk of his man stick—er, cock—inside me told me he'd found his release. I inwardly sighed as Dwight slowed his movements and eventually stopped.

With a grunt, he rolled off me and flopped onto his back with one arm flung over his dark-blue eyes. "Wow, babe. That was awesome."

Was it, Dwight? Really? For everyone involved in the proceedings?

Then he turned his handsome face toward me with that sweet smile of his and said softly, "I love you so much, Lehra."

My heart melted. "I love you too, Dwight."

After tossing the condom in the trash, he wrapped an arm around me and pulled me against him. I rested my cheek on his chest, and his heart tha-thumped rapidly against my ear, gradually slowing as his hand on my waist fell away and plunked softly onto the bed.

With a quiet kiss against his chest, I extricated myself from his hold and slipped from the bed and into his en suite. While the shower warmed, I pulled my curls on top of my head with one of the alligator clips Dwight kept here for me and stepped inside the glassed-in space.

After wetting myself beneath the slanted spray, my eyes fell on my very best friend: the Seventh Heaven Attachment Head. And yes, you heard those capital letters correctly. And no, that's not the actual name of it, though it damn well should be.

The Seventh Heaven Attachment Head—or SHAH for short—was smart enough to remove heavy metals, chlorine, and any other contaminants from the water, leaving your hair and skin glowing, but that wasn't the best thing about it. My absolute favorite feature was dial setting number three—and yes, I whispered that reverently in my head.

With two simple twists of my wrist, the Holy Grail of showers was in my hand. I had no doubt in my mind that setting three had been developed by a woman. Perhaps by a woman whose boyfriend called his penis a *love snozzle* and couldn't quite seem to master the precise amount of pressure her clitoris needed to orgasm.

The central stream of water on this setting was round, less than an inch in diameter, and powerful without being harsh. Approximately a million needle-thin jets surrounded it in concentric circles and were somehow the most gentle streams of water I'd ever experienced. They delivered soft caresses against needy flesh, and the combination was absolutely phenomenal.

"Come to mama," I whispered, and in my brain, SHAH whispered back, "You're the one that's going to be coming, baby."

One of my fantasies—and there were many—took shape in my mind. A large beast of a man stood before me, a brawny version of Johnny Depp. His skin was darkened by years at sea, and he was finally home to see the woman he'd left behind but had never forgotten.

And the big pirate couldn't wait one more second to plunder that woman—*which is me, if that wasn't obvious.*

"Turn around," he grunted.

I did, of course, and he immediately raised my simple tunic to find me wearing no undergarments. I was going for *medieval era slut* vibes in my fantasy, and I seemed to have hit the mark because in the next moment, I was being bent in half and entered from behind.

Bringing the silver head of the shower head between my legs, I bit back a groan of pure rapture when the center found its target. "God yes," I whispered. My hand found the slightly transparent wall as the fantasy continued in my head.

My pirate plundered me like it was the last time he'd ever fuck. He was hard. Rough. A goddamn beast in leather as he railed me.

The streams of water between my legs hit me in all the right places and then trickled down my thighs as my orgasm approached. It never took long with SHAH.

One hand tightened on my hip and the other fisted in my hair as the fucking turned almost brutal. I welcomed it. No, I reveled in it.

As his hips slapped against my ass, the pirate leaned over my back and whispered rough, guttural words in my ear. In contrast to the ferocity with which he took me, his utterances were sweet and possessive.

He'd missed me. He loved me. I was *his woman.*

With the softest of cries, I came, my fingers curling against the shower wall. "Holy fuck," I mumbled, my breaths leaving my gaping mouth in brisk pants as I pressed my forehead against the damp coolness.

I jiggled SHAH a little, extending the orgasm as long as I could as warm fingers of water stroked my swollen flesh. When I was finally done, I thanked the shower head for her service and replaced her back in the holder.

My eyes roamed around the luxurious shower space, but there was no pirate in there with me. For some reason, it always surprised me because these little scenes came to life so vividly while they were going on.

Turning off the shower spray, I stepped out and dried off before going back to Dwight's bed.

"Nice shower, baby?" he asked sleepily as he pulled my freshly sated body against him. He usually woke up after my showers, and I was sure he thought I was some kind of clean freak or something, though he was too polite to ever say anything about it.

"Very nice," I murmured.

I'd felt guilty the first time I got myself off after being with Dwight, but goddamn, I'd been needy that night. Now I viewed it as a necessary evil. Women deserved satisfaction just like men did, and I'd come to grips with the fact that the man I loved wasn't able to get me there. And that was okay. Setting aside the sex, Dwight was everything I needed in my life. Kind. Loyal. Honest.

I tried not to feel remorseful about my fantasies. Everyone had them, right? And it was something I enjoyed. Though I have always wished I could find a guy that was into the same things.

But I'd learned that those things were better enjoyed in private.

After all, no one wanted to indulge in my silly little role playing games.

"I'll miss you, honey," Dwight said, holding my face and kissing me in the middle of Detroit Metropolitan Airport. He always insisted on parking and coming inside with me. I protested each time, letting him know I didn't mind being dropped off at the curb, but I secretly loved that he wanted to spend those last few minutes with me.

"I'll miss you too," I replied. We hugged for a long while, and I inhaled the scent of his woodsy cologne. "But I'll see you next month."

"As soon as I make my flight arrangements, I'll send them to you." We reluctantly separated, and Dwight held both my hands. "I'm still working on getting transferred to the New York office, but it's going to be a while. There are a lot of projects I'm involved in here."

"I know," I assured him with a watery smile. "I'd better go so I don't miss my flight." Grasping the handle of my tiny suitcase, I blew him one more kiss and headed toward security.

As soon as I reached my gate, my cell phone rang, and I looked down at the display before answering. "Hey, Tony! You're up early." *It's five in the damn morning. Doesn't he ever sleep?*

"Hello, lovely Lehra. I have a surprise for you."

"Ooh, is it Captain America?"

Tony Moschella's laugh was warm and deep. I loved this guy. He was the personal assistant to Auburn Bouvier, the CEO of one of the largest fashion companies in New York City, and I was the downstairs receptionist in the *Bouvier* building.

"Unfortunately, no, but I think you'll be pleased. Bouvier is driving himself today, so I texted his driver to pick you up from the airport."

"Are you serious? Screw Captain America. You, Tony, are the real hero here. That will save me a fortune in Uber fees."

"I know, dear, and I enjoy taking care of you. You're like my surrogate daughter since my Gianna lives in Texas."

My heart went out to him. Tony talked about his daughter all the time, and I knew he missed her terribly. "Maybe she'll come to visit soon," I consoled.

"She's got to finish school first," he insisted. "She's so smart, Lehra. Did I tell you she's working on her master's in accounting?"

I laughed and teased him a bit. "I think you may have mentioned it. *About forty times.*"

"Right," he said, and I could hear the chagrined amusement in his voice. "Well, have a good flight, and I'll look forward to seeing your smiling face in a couple hours."

"Thanks, Tony, and tell Smithson I'll meet him outside Terminal B."

"Terminal B, got it. Oh, and remember, Smithson is retired as of Friday. The new guy has been helping out and learning the ropes the past few months, but he just took over full-time. I don't think you've met Cruz yet."

"Apt name for a driver," I quipped. "Thanks again, Tony."

"No problem, dear."

That man is a saint, I thought as soon as we hung up. I wasn't sure how he put up with Auburn Bouvier on a daily basis.

Walking out of the terminal, I glanced around for the black Bentley and spotted it a couple dozen steps away. The wheels of my suitcase made a clacking sound as they bumped over the cracks in the sidewalk when I headed in that direction.

That's when I noticed the man standing beside the fancy car, and my feet faltered to a stop. *Dear god in heaven!*

He was around six foot three, in my estimation, and built like a brick shithouse with a chest that could only be described as *expansive.* Well, and maybe *delicious* wouldn't be a bad descriptor.

The driver was standing ramrod straight in a black *Bouvier* suit with a crisp white shirt and black tie. One thick finger reached up and tugged at his collar, and I got the feeling he wasn't accustomed to wearing a suit.

His skin was deeply tanned, like maybe he was Italian or Latino. He sported coal-black hair that was cut short, but I could tell it would curl if he let it grow out. To top off the look, he had absolutely the most perfect mouth I'd ever seen on a man. A well-defined Cupid's bow topped lips so full I wondered if he'd had lip injections. *Do guys get lip filler?* I mused. I didn't see why not.

The man I assumed was Cruz lowered the tugging hand to clasp its mate in front of his crotch, and if he wasn't wearing a custom-tailored suit jacket, I knew the fabric would have bunched over those broad shoulders. I couldn't see his eyes because they were covered by classic Ray-Ban Clubmaster sunglasses, but based on his appearance, I assumed they were brown.

As soon as I talked my feet into walking, his head swiveled instantly in my direction. "Hi," I said as I approached. "Are you Cruz?"

"I am, and are you, um, Leer-a? Did I say that correctly?"

"Close. It rhymes with Sara."

He pronounced it again, correctly this time, and the sound of his voice reminded me of s'mores. Sweet marshmallow and warm chocolate melting onto a crisp graham cracker.

Oh jeez. Poetic much, you weirdo?

"I'm Cruz Estrada." He held out a hand, and I placed mine in it, instantly feeling like a child shaking an adult's hand. Then he smiled and pushed his sunglasses up, giving me his eyes and showing off his... dammit, *dimples*.

Well, that was just too damn much. Someone stop the Earth's rotation and let me climb off because it's not fair that I should have to live on the same planet with a man who possessed so many gorgeous features. The audacity of him!

A current of something hot and indistinct pulsed between us as our gazes held. His eyes were blue, not brown like I expected; a thick ring of navy surrounding a shocking azure toward the middle.

Stop staring at the pretty man's eyes, Lehra. Abort! Abort!

To distract myself, I looked back down at his lips. "Do you get lip injections?" I heard someone ask and glanced around to see who had asked such a presumptuous question.

Yeah, it turned out that was me.

Someone. Anyone. Please. Stick a dirty, dirty sock in my mouth to shut me the hell up.

For fuck's sake.

Chapter 2

A LAUGH STARTED DEEP in my chest and rumbled up my throat at her question. "Not since I was four."

Lehra's big eyes widened, and she blinked those long lashes a few times in surprise. I had the strangest urge to feather my thumb along the tips to see if they felt as soft as they looked. *Dude, that would be weird.*

"Oh, well. Okay." She appeared confused by that revelation.

Leaning toward her a little, I caught the scent of summertime and wondered if it was her as I pointed to my bottom lip. "I was running when my mama told me not to and busted my lip open. I got a numbing shot and two stitches."

She craned her head closer and inspected the tiny scar. *Yes, that's definitely her fragrance. Something light and breezy with a hint of... pineapple?*

"Wow, the scar perfectly bisects your bottom lip and turns it into two pretty pillows." Then a scowl formed on her pretty face, and she shook her head. "Are you carrying a firearm?"

I couldn't quite keep up with this chick, but I shot a surreptitious glance around at the people filing past us. No one seemed to be paying us any attention. My gaze came back to her because it was difficult to look away from her for very long.

A heart-shaped face was set off by her ash-gray eyes, which were framed by long, inky lashes. Her skin was a few shades lighter than her blonde hair, which fell below her shoulders in bouncy curls.

"I am," I whisper.

"Good. Could you shoot me in the mouth so I'll stop saying embarrassing shit?"

A quick bark of laughter popped from my lips before I could stop it. "Afraid not, Lehra, and don't worry about it. I appreciate honesty."

"There's a difference between honesty and saying everything that pops into your head. I just called your lips *pretty pillows*," she informed me, propping her hands on her slim waist. That gesture drew my eyes down, and my tongue instantly found my bottom lip, working forward and back over the scar in the center.

This girl is fucking breathtaking. I'd been so focused on her perfect face that I hadn't noticed the body, but I'll be damned if I wasn't noticing it now.

Lehra was probably five seven, with long legs and curves in all the right places. She was dressed for work in a fashionable black-and-white dress that showed a hint of cleavage. I had to force myself not to stare at the tits that were just big enough to almost fill my large hands.

Working my way down, I found shapely legs, slender ankles, and flats on her feet, though I could see a pair of heels sticking up out of the white bag she had slung over one shoulder. She'd probably change into her work shoes once we arrived.

Which we never will if I don't stop staring and start doing my fucking job, my brain reminded me.

"That's not the worst thing that's ever been said about me," I assured her as I reached for her suitcase. "You just keep on saying whatever pops into your head." *I want to hear it all.*

Lehra's lips curved up, and my heartbeat seemed to swell until it was thumping my entire torso. I really liked her smile. She had the slightest of overbites, which caused her perfectly straight white teeth to rest against her lower lip. Undeniably sexy.

I was staring again, and I really needed to get my shit together here. I'd never been struck like this by a woman. I had seen my share of beautiful ladies, but no one had ever made me want to drop immediately to my knees and beg her for a date.

Yanking my eyes away, I took her suitcase and placed it in the trunk before going back to her.

"Let's get you to work, Miss Lehra," I said, reaching for the back door, but she stopped me with a hand on my arm. A beam of pure energy traveled up my arm and set off a round of fireworks in my brain. Our eyes met, and Lehra's mouth dropped open like she'd felt it too and was just as surprised as I was.

"I, um, do you mind if I ride up front? Or would that be uncomfortable for you?"

"Not at all," I assured her, trying to temper my tone so I didn't sound like a giddy schoolboy as I opened the front door for her. *Could she be interested in me? Does she feel this pull I'm feeling?*

As she slid gracefully into the seat, I caught a glimpse of creamy thigh before she adjusted her dress. *That little spot would look stunning coated in my saliva as I work my way up to...*

Cutting off that thought, I rounded the car and dropped into the driver's seat, the interior now filled with the scent of Lehra. *A pretty name for such a pretty woman.*

"I don't remember seeing you when I was given a tour of the building a few months ago," I told her. *I would definitely have remembered you.*

"Was it September?" she asked, and when I nodded, her face scrunched up. "That's probably when I was out with the stomach flu. Oh my god, it was the grossest thing ever. Have you ever puked so hard the vomit came out your nose?"

"I have," I assured her with a smile. "Worst thing ever."

"All I could smell was puke, even three days later. I was so self-conscious it was me and took, like, five showers a day, but I think it was seared into my nostrils. I finally had to get one of those Neti Pots and clean out my sinuses."

My chest shook with laughter. "I'm so sorry you were sick, but that's hilarious."

"I know. Sorry I got gross there for a second. I'll change the subject," she said as I pulled away from the curb. "How's your first full day been?"

"Good. Still getting accustomed to the New York traffic."

"Oh, are you new in town?"

"I am. I moved here from Galveston a few months ago, though I've been in the military since I was eighteen, so I've lived in a lot of places."

"That's exciting," she said, and from the corner of my eye, I could see her blonde curls flowing over one shoulder as she tilted her head. "I moved here a few years ago from Missouri. That's the only other place I've lived."

"I spent some time there during SRT training. It's a beautiful state."

"It is. What's SRT?"

"Special Reaction Team. It's kind of the Marine Corps' version of a SWAT unit."

"Wow, Cruz. I didn't realize I was in the car with a bona fide badass," she chirped. Lehra really had the perfect voice. Very feminine, but she wasn't one of those girls who practically whispered everything she said in an effort to sound sexy. I hated the whispery chicks.

"Well, now you know," I teased, making my way out of the airport. "What brought you here from Missouri?"

"I had my heart set on being a model, but I was told by everyone that I was too short. Especially for runway work. You have to be at least five ten for that."

"Well, I think they were ridiculous for turning you down. You're very beautiful." The words came out before I could stop them, but it was absolutely true. Even with my eyes firmly on the road, I could see the prettiest flush of color stain her cheeks.

"Thanks, Cruz. When I interviewed at Bouvier, they were looking for a receptionist and offered me the job." She twisted a little in her seat. "What made you get out of the military? Did you get injured?"

"No, a couple years ago, I was trying to decide whether to stay in or not, and then my father died. That made my decision for me. I needed to be there for my mother."

Her hand rested lightly on my shoulder, and I felt that zap of something electric again. "I'm so sorry you lost your dad. That must have been hard. What brought you to New York?"

Well, that was a loaded question I didn't care to discuss right now, so I stuck with a partial truth. "My sister, Quinnie, is here. Her husband is a surgical resident at Sloan Kettering, so he works long hours. It's nice to be close to her and my niece, Noelle."

"How old is Noelle?"

I could feel my smile widen like it always did when I talked about my niece. "She's four and a total ball of energy. She believes she's a princess but she refuses to wear dresses."

"That's okay. If she's a princess, she can wear whatever the hell she wants."

"That's what I told her," I said with a chuckle, flicking on my blinker to change lanes.

"Did you say your sister's name is Winnie?"

"Quinnie," I corrected. "It's short for Quintessa."

"Is she your only sibling?"

Such a complicated answer...

"We have a younger brother named Eli. He's twenty-two but still lives at home. I don't think Mama will ever get rid of him." I said that last part on a chuckle. "What about you?"

"No siblings. I'm completely boring."

"I doubt that."

"Is your mother doing okay now?"

"She is. Otherwise, I wouldn't have left. It's still hard, of course, but she has Eli, and she's started going to a book club and making more friends."

"That's good. Okay, enough sad stuff," she said, clapping her hands once. "Tell me a happy thing."

Startled a little at the change of subject, I glanced at her and questioned, "A happy thing?"

"Yep. Whenever anything sad or upsetting happened when I was little, my mom said we had to counteract it with something nicer. So she made me tell her a happy thing."

"Oh, um, let me think." *I just met the most beautiful girl who makes me smile more than I have in years.* But I couldn't exactly say that to her, so I said, "I got accepted as a reserve officer for the police department."

"Really? That's so awesome, Cruz." She touched my arm again, just an encouraging squeeze, but I fucking loved it.

"Yeah, I want to join the unit that does SWAT work. I'm actually meeting with the guys from one of the teams this week to see how we get along. Just for drinks, nothing formal."

"You'll be great. I'm sure they'll love you," she said as her phone began to ring. "Oh crap, I forgot to call Dwight when I landed."

Who the hell is Dwight?

"Hi, honey. Sorry I forgot to call," she answered into the phone, and disappointment shoved my heart down to the vicinity of my stomach.

Honey. She has a boyfriend. Or a... I checked her hand and was pleased when I didn't see a ring. I'm not sure why it mattered. Boyfriend, fiancé, or husband... it was all the same to me. I would never touch another man's girl, no matter how attracted I was to her.

"Okay, that sounds good. I'll see you then," she was saying. "Love you too." Lehra hung up the phone and smiled over at me. "Sorry about that. What were we talking about?"

"Oh, I was," I scrambled to think of something, "about to ask you to tell me a happy thing."

She tapped her bottom lip with a french-tipped finger. "Hmmm, my happy thing is that it's only a week till Christmas, and it's my second favorite holiday behind Halloween."

"And are you spending Christmas with your... with Dwight?"

Lehra laughed, and the sound was like a melody, sweet and high. "No, he and his family have a tradition of going to Aspen for Christmas. I'm going home to Missouri for a week."

If I had a woman like you, you'd be included in my family's traditions, not excluded, I thought.

"How long have you two been together?"

She cocked her head to the side. "Let's see... ten months. We met when he was in town for a meeting. Dwight is an architect."

Of course he is, I thought with a hint of bitterness. "And he doesn't live here?"

"No, he's in Detroit, but he's trying to get transferred to his company's New York branch. We only get to see each other once a month. What are you doing for the holidays?"

Once a month? What the actual fuck?

"I'll go back to Texas for Christmas Eve and fly back late Christmas Day. I'm too new to ask for much time off from work."

She shifted and leaned a little closer like she had a secret. The slight movement had her intoxicating scent swirling around me. "What's it like working with Sexy Shrek every day?"

"Sexy what?" I asked, unable to hold in my laughter.

"Sexy Shrek. That's what I call Auburn Bouvier because he's an ogre but a very good-looking one. Most of us in the building only see him briefly each day. I couldn't imagine being trapped in a car with him." She shuddered. "So, are you scared of him?"

I grinned and shook my head. "No, I'm not scared of Auburn Bouvier. On the few times I've driven him so far, he's been nice enough to me. A little quiet. He mostly works while I drive him to meetings and stuff."

"And do you serve as his personal security too like Smithson did?"

Nodding, I turned right, toward the *Bouvier* building. "I do. When Smithson was off a couple weeks ago, I drove the boss to a lunch meeting, and when we got to the restaurant, there was some kind of protest going on out front. I told him I didn't feel it was safe for him to go in there, and he didn't even question me. He called the man he was meeting, and we met him near the side door of the building. I drove them both to another restaurant a few blocks down."

"He trusts you," she said softly.

"We're getting there," I said, not mentioning that I'd parked down the block while Auburn was at lunch and watched the protest turn violent. The Emergency Service Unit had to swoop in and de-escalate things. I'd had a feeling that was going to happen just by reading the mood of the crowd.

Thank goodness my new boss had listened to me. He was a stubborn fucker, but he wasn't stupid.

Lehra began changing her shoes as we neared our destination. "I can't thank you enough for the ride, Cruz."

"It was my pleasure," I told her honestly, pulling up to the curb and hopping out.

"You didn't have to get my door for me," she protested when I opened it.

"Of course I did. Would you like me to drop your suitcase off at your apartment building?"

Her cute nose scrunched up. "No, that's okay. I don't have a doorman or anything at my place. The bag is small enough to fit in the closet behind the reception desk."

I unloaded the case from the trunk and pulled the handle up for her before sliding it toward her.

"Thanks again, Cruz. It was nice to meet you."

"You too, Lehra. Don't let Sexy Shrek get you down."

She laughed that melodious laugh and turned to walk inside the building. With my hands in my pockets, I enjoyed the view of her retreating form. Tiny white bows winked at me from the backs of her sky-high black heels, and her blonde curls bounced merrily as she walked. Not to mention that truly outstanding ass of hers.

This woman ticked all my boxes, including some I didn't even know I needed ticked. She was smart, funny, gorgeous, and adorably sweet.

And taken, Estrada. Don't forget that one.

Just before Lehra entered the *Bouvier* building, she glanced back, and the sun glinted off her pretty smile as she wiggled her fingers at me. I returned the gesture, one I was pretty sure I'd never done before in all my thirty-one years.

As soon as she disappeared, something heavy settled in my chest. Something I recognized.

Regret.

CHAPTER 3

As soon as I woke on Tuesday morning, blonde curls and a pretty smile were at the forefront of my mind. *Lehra*. Maybe I'd dreamed about her, but I couldn't remember any specifics.

Getting ready for work, I pushed her from my thoughts and reflected on my dinner meeting last night. These dinners had been a weekly thing for the past month, every Monday, and I had begun to actually look forward to them. Last night was very informative.

Checking my tie in the mirror, I stared at the man looking back at me, deciding I looked pretty damn sharp in the black suit and tie. The Bouvier company provided all employees with their clothing for work to promote the brand or some such shit. I guessed it made sense. It wouldn't look good for employees to wear their competitor's clothes.

To my surprise, it didn't bother me to wear a suit each day. The fabric was luxurious and breathable, and the shoes were like goddamn butter on my feet. A helluva lot more comfortable than combat boots, that was for sure.

My phone chimed with a message from my boss.

Auburn: Come up to my penthouse. Your key card should give you access.

That was weird. I usually brought the car around and waited for him in front of the building. Striding through my apartment, I marveled at the view of Manhattan from the tall windows. I still couldn't believe my housing was a benefit of being Auburn Bouvier's driver. He said it was for convenience since he lived on the top floor of this lavish building, and I was his personal security guard.

It was a two bedroom, two bath and very spacious. I'd heard rumors about New York apartments, so I was pleasantly surprised the first time I'd walked in here a few months ago. This was way more than I would have ever been able to afford, despite my generous salary.

Tucking my gun into my holster, I headed up to the penthouse and knocked on the door. Auburn Bouvier answered in his shirtsleeves and gave me a tentative smile, something you didn't see from the man very often.

"Come on in, Cruz. If you don't mind, I thought we could have breakfast together."

"I, uh, of course, sir."

His smile turned wistful, and I got the feeling he was... sad, maybe? "When it's just us, you can call me Auburn, if you want." He sounded hopeful, and his smile turned genuine when I nodded.

"All right, Auburn. Do I need to go pick up some food?"

"No, I cooked." I guessed my face registered my surprise because he chuckled and said, "Don't look like I just told you I'm the pope. I can cook."

My sharp eyes took in everything as we walked through his expansive living room. If my apartment was big, his was absolutely fucking enormous. The well-appointed kitchen looked like it had every high-end appliance known to man, and Auburn gestured for me to take a seat at the breakfast bar.

"I grew up with a full staff in our house. Chefs and housekeepers, all that," he explained, "but I always found it annoying to never have any privacy. So I taught myself to cook and clean." He lifted his shoulders in a halfhearted shrug. "I don't really like people in my personal space."

"Understandable," I said, wondering why I was here as he dished up the food and placed a plate in front of me.

"It's just eggs and bacon."

"My favorite breakfast," I said. "It looks good."

He visibly relaxed and took the seat next to me.

I'll be damned. I think Auburn Bouvier is lonely.

I waited out front of the *Bouvier* office building a little before noon. Auburn had a lunch meeting across town. A flash of green caught my eye, and I inhaled a deep breath when Lehra exited the building and walked swiftly toward the Bentley.

She looked like a million bucks in a grass-green dress and heels, her hair pulled back on one side, and she was carrying a small pink box. I rolled down the window, and she filled the December air with her summery scent when she leaned through.

"Hey, I made you some cookies as a thank you for the ride yesterday. You're not allergic to almonds, are you?"

"Not at all," I said, unable to control the upward curve of my lips.

Opening the box, I found a stack of misshapen beige blobs with some kind of red filling on top of each. Popping one into my mouth, I chewed. It was awful.

"Mmmm," I feigned, grabbing my water bottle and taking a long pull to try and moisten the sawdust forming in my mouth.

"They're almond-cherry," she announced proudly, and I nodded, the sawdust now a wet paste that I valiantly managed to swallow.

"This is so sweet of you," I croaked, taking another drink. "Thank you."

"You're welcome," she beamed. "I better get back to work. Don't eat all of those and spoil your lunch."

"Oh, I definitely will not. Thanks again, Tink."

Her brow creased for a second, and then she laughed in realization. "Oh, like Tinkerbell because of my dress." *And your pretty little face.* "See you later, Cruz."

My eyes followed her, and the blustery wind whipped her hair into a frenzy as she retreated back into the building. Auburn exited a few minutes later, and I hopped out to open the back door for him.

Once back in my seat, I fought a smile as I picked up the pink box and stretched my arm back. "Want a cookie?"

He eyed the box suspiciously. "Did Lehra make those?"

"Yep."

"Noooo, thank you," he drawled out with an eye roll. "Thank god that woman is beautiful because she won't be winning any awards for cooking."

I burst into laughter. Bossman got jokes. "So you've had her cookies, I assume?"

Auburn shuddered. "I have. And just a warning. Do not, under any circumstances, eat any cakes that she makes."

"Duly noted," I said, reaching for my bottle and draining the rest of it.

That evening, I walked into Flannery's Pub where I was supposed to meet the SWAT guys. A tall, burly, bald man stood near the front.

"Estrada?" he asked, and I nodded, holding out my hand and receiving a firm shake.

"I'm Cruz Estrada."

"They call me Curly," he announced, leading me to a table in the back where four other men sat. "Guys, this is New Fucker."

I laughed at that and introduced myself. "Cruz Estrada."

In response, everyone lifted their drinks and called, "New Fucker!"

Okaaaay, guess my name is New Fucker. I could roll with it. Curly sat, and I slid into the only open seat, on a long bench facing the three chairs on the other side of the table.

Curly continued the introductions, pointing out a burly brunette with a healthy dose of gray. "This is Maverick. We call him Grandpa Fucker."

"Because of my age, not because I fuck grandpas," the man clarified. "We leave that to Chris." He jerked a thumb at the blond man who appeared to be the youngest of the group. He had a baby face that seemed incongruous with his huge frame.

"I like older men," Chris said unashamedly. "They're more stable."

"Sugar daddy," another man fake-coughed, and everyone laughed, including Chris. I liked these guys already. I could tell their teasing was done good-naturedly and with affection.

Curly sighed as if he was dealing with a group of children and pointed out the last two guys. "That's Kai. He's the quiet one." The Asian man gave me a wave. He was smaller than the rest of the men, but he had well-defined muscles that were obvious beneath his long-sleeved black T-shirt. And his dark eyes looked like they could cut you quicker than a razor slice.

"And Jayden here is an asshole, so we call him Motherfucker."

"That's what your mom calls me," the Black man retorted with an easy grin. He had thick arms that told me he spent a good amount of time in the gym.

Curly simply rolled his eyes, obviously having heard this insult before. "There are some other guys, but most of them are married so they don't come to these Tuesday night gatherings."

"I'm married too," Maverick stated, "but my wife is on duty tonight. She is a firefighter." His ruddy face beamed with pride.

"That's cool," I replied.

"So tell us about yourself, New Fucker," Jayden piped up.

I didn't really like talking about myself—though I'd had no problem doing so with Lehra yesterday—but I wanted to play nice with these guys.

"I'm thirty-one. Grew up in Galveston, Texas, but went into the Marines right after high school."

"I'm from Houston," Kai said quietly, holding up a fist for me to bump. "Nice to see another south Texas guy."

"Same. How long have you lived in New York?"

"Six years. I was a sniper in the Army before that."

"Kai here can shoot a booger out of a fly's nose from a thousand yards," Maverick commented.

"Do flies have noses?" Jayden asked, and we all chuckled as the waitress approached.

"Another round, fellas?" Everyone nodded, and she turned to me. "What can I get for you, New Fucker?"

I grinned and shook my head. They even got the staff in on their little game. "Beer. Whatever you have on tap is fine."

"You have a woman?" Curly asked me, and I shook my head.

"No. So you're all single except for Mav?"

"Yep, I'm holding out for Curly's mom," Jayden commented, his lips curling into a mischievous smile when the bald man flipped him off.

The server brought our drinks, beer for everyone except Mav, who was drinking soda. "Sober for fifteen years," he informed me as he took a sip.

I really liked these guys. They razzed the hell out of each other, and it felt good to just hang out again. I hadn't done that in a while, not since leaving the military. Besides work, my family had been my focus the past couple years.

At the end of the night, Curly slapped me on the shoulder and said, "Same time next week, New Fucker. See you then."

Pleased, I went home with a smile on my face.

Chapter 4

I RUSHED INTO THE Butterfly Martini Bar on the Friday night before Christmas, walking beneath the hundreds of multicolored butterflies suspended from the ceiling. This place was gorgeous and had such a fun vibe.

"Hey, sorry I'm late," I said, dropping into a chair. My friends Artie and Nicolette were already waiting for me.

"No biggie," Artie said, kissing the chill from my cheek with a smack. "We just got here. They have a special menu featuring Christmas martinis." He handed me a leather-bound card.

"I'm getting the cranberry one," Nicolette informed me, pushing a loose strand of dark, wavy hair behind one ear. My friend was gorgeous, with the most striking green eyes I'd ever seen, but she hid herself behind thick black glasses and prim buns.

"Hmmm." I perused the selections and made my decision just as Charmaine, our regular server, approached.

"Merry Christmas, y'all," she said. Charmaine was originally from Arkansas and still retained most of her adorable accent. "Did you see our specials?"

"Merry Christmas," I told her, stripping off my black wool coat and hanging it on the back of the chair. "We saw them. I'm going to try the peppermint one. Vodka, not gin."

"Oooh, that's a good one, honey. Very snappy. What about you, Nicolette?"

"Cranberry Chill."

"I like that one too." She placed a hand on her hip and turned to Artie. "Are you trying something new tonight?"

"No, I'll have the regular. A dirty martini." He stroked his closely shorn red beard and lifted an eyebrow. "Very dirty. I'm talking, I want it to be *anal sex with a hobo* dirty."

We all cracked up. We lived to hear how Artie was going to embellish his standing order every time we met.

"Got it, you crazy freak," Char teased, tapping him on the head with her butterfly-shaped order pad. "Be right back."

"How did your weekend with Dwight go?" Nic asked, resting her chin in her hand.

"It was fine. How about yours?"

"No, no, miss thang. You're not deflecting," Artie said. "Did you get lucky?"

"Once," I admitted, and he shook his head.

"I can't believe he's not all over you the entire weekend like a socialite on a Louboutin purse."

"It's fine," I defended out of loyalty. "We had fun. Watched some movies and went out to some nice restaurants."

They both looked at me with sympathy, not falling for my whole *it's fine* routine. "Is he still trying to do the dirty talking?" Nicolette asked. "Oooh, did he call his penis a love pickle again?"

A fit of giggles took over me. "No, he didn't use that one, but yes on the creative dirty talk."

"If a man ever called his dick a love pickle with me, I'd bite the motherfucker off," Artie declared loudly just as Charmaine showed up with our drinks. She barely raised an eyebrow, accustomed to our insane conversations by now.

A small frisson of guilt seeped down my back. I didn't want to bad-mouth Dwight to my friends. I loved Dwight, but I needed someone to talk to about my sex struggles. Wasn't that what friends were for?

"Is it bad that I used the shower to get myself off afterward?" I whispered, taking a sip of the pink froth. It was delicious, the peppermint gently nipping at my tongue.

"Girl's gotta do what a girl's gotta do," Artie said wisely. "Thanks for the recommendation on the shower head attachment, by the way. I got one installed last week, and you bitches are lucky I'm even here." He held up his well-manicured hand and studied it. "I was in there so long, I wasn't sure the pruniness would ever go away."

"I wish I could get one for my apartment, but with my lack of water pressure, a treasure like that would go to waste," I lamented before arching an eyebrow at Artie. "Did you enjoy setting three?"

"Actually," he drawled as Nic and I took a drink of our beverages, "setting five was better for me. Really tickles the ole man clit, you know?"

Liquid spewed from mine and Nicolette's mouths at the same time, forming a pool of sheer pink on the white tile table. My friend slapped at her chest to alleviate her choking.

"Well, now you've killed her with your man clit comment," I scolded with a laugh, mopping up the mess with a couple cocktail napkins. "Are you happy with yourself?"

Artie leaned back in his chair and crossed one ankle over his opposite knee, taking a leisurely sip. "Not as happy as I was in that shower. I actually considered having a mini-fridge and toilet installed in there so I never had to leave."

Clearing her throat, Nic dabbed at her lips. "If anyone could make it work, it would be you."

Our friend was an interior designer who could make any space shine. "Thank you," he replied, tracing a finger down the perfectly pressed seam of his burgundy trousers. He'd completed the look with a stormy-gray V-neck sweater that made his brown eyes pop.

Nicolette, on the other hand, was dressed in her trademark black, but I could see her white lab coat hanging on the back of her chair.

"I'm not sure I could get off with a man named Dwight," Artie announced. "All I can think of when I hear that name is the guy from *The Office*."

"So you want me to have Dwight change his name?" I asked dryly.

"No, but maybe you could get him to dress up as Thor. That would be a sexy name to moan."

The thought of straitlaced Dwight in a costume made me grin, but my inner freak couldn't help thinking that sounded like a fine idea. *Is there something wrong with me? Probably.*

"Names are important," Artie mused.

"Your name is Arthur," I deadpanned, and he pretended to pop the top off his middle finger and put on lipstick.

"But Artie is a totally hot nickname," Nicolette assured him.

"Thank you, deary." He leaned forward, his brown eyes bright as he folded his forearms together on the table. "What's the hottest guy name you've ever heard? Don't think. Just say the first thing that pops in your mind. Nic, go!"

"I crushed on this guy named Dante in high school, so that name has turned me on ever since," Nicolette said, her eyes going dreamy. "What about you, Artie?"

"Liam," he purred. "Liam calling me a good boy with a sassy accent while he strokes my—"

"If you say man clit, I'm going to throw my shoe at you," I warned.

"Please do. Those taupe *Bouvier* booties are fucking fabulous, babe."

"They are, aren't they?" I asked with a grin, lifting my right foot and tilting it to get the full effect of the suede in the dim light.

"Utterly divine. When are you going to introduce me to that fine-ass piece you work for? He could invite me to his home to redecorate, and I'd suggest we start in his bedroom. Then I'd—"

"Jesus," Nic groaned, "don't get started on your Auburn Bouvier fantasies again. The man is not gay. Besides, Lehra hasn't told us her sexiest name yet."

Then both looked expectantly at me, and I blurted out, "Cruz."

Cue the record scratch...

Fuck. Where did that come from?

Nicolette nodded, and Artie fake-fanned himself. "Hells bells, that is a hot one. I need me a Cruz in my life."

Downing the rest of my minty martini in one gulp, I changed the subject before I could think too much about what I said. And why I said it.

"Nic, how is work going for you?"

Her sigh was long-suffering and dramatic. "I love my work, but I'm sick to death of my boss. Joyce is so unimaginative and set in her ways. She never lets me stretch my wings and develop new products."

"That's a shame," Artie replied. "You're a brilliant biochemist, Nic. Why did they hire you if they just want the same old shit day after day?"

"No clue, but Joyce turned down my idea for a men's line of cosmetics last week."

"Oooh, intriguing," Artie said, drumming his fingertips against his dark-red beard. "Tell me more."

Nicolette expounded on her idea and the reasoning behind it as we listened. It did sound like an untapped market. My sweet—and slightly nerdy—friend had two doctorate degrees and was the smartest person I knew. Like seriously genius-level smart.

"Anyway, I just wish I could work somewhere else."

"What about Hale Cosmetics?" Artie asked. "They seem to be a very forward-thinking company."

"They are, but their headquarters is in Houston."

"I'll come visit you if you move to Texas. I'm not a country boy by any means," Artie began, wagging one finger in the air, "but Wrangler butts are fine as hell. They have entire Instagram pages dedicated to showing the virtue of cowboy asses in those jeans."

I laughed even as my stomach knotted at the thought of one of my friends leaving New York. These two were my lifeline, and I would be so lonely without them.

"I'll think about it," Nicolette said thoughtfully. "Hale really is a much better company than Aquarius Cosmetics."

I forced a placid smile on my face and signaled for another round of drinks as I felt Artie's astute gaze on the side of my face. "Why do you look constipated, baby girl?"

"I don't look constipated," I argued, putting indignation into my tone.

"You look like you haven't dropped a poo in two weeks. You always get that look when you're making yourself smile."

Rolling my eyes, I sighed, "Fine, I was getting a tad melancholy at the thought of Nic leaving." I reached across the table and grasped her thin hand. "But I would support you a million percent. I only want you to be happy."

"Thanks," she replied, squeezing my hand. "I don't want to leave, but I actually dread going to work every morning, and I shouldn't. I love biochem and cosmetics, so this should be my dream job."

"You're right," I said, internally scolding myself for being selfish. "You deserve to be happy as a clam."

"Speaking of clams," Artie broke in, staring at the food menu. "Should we split an order of fried clams? Their dill tartar sauce here is the bomb."

And just like that, the subject of Nicolette leaving was put aside.

As we shared a basket of crispy clams and french fries, the conversation turned back to men. "I have a date tomorrow night," Artie informed me. "He's the brother of the client I just wrapped up."

"Ooh, tell us," I said, swirling a fry through the spicy ketchup.

"He asked me out a month ago, but I had to turn him down since I was still working for his brother. I may not have many standards, but mixing business with pleasure is one of them."

"But he asked you again after you were done with the job?" Nic asked, and he nodded with a pleased look on his soft lips. "That's so romantic. He thinks you're worth waiting for. I wish I could find a romantic guy. All the men I work with are science dweebs and wouldn't know romance if it bit them on the dick."

"Speaking of biting dicks," Artie said, leaning forward with a gleam in his eyes, "let me tell you about the date I had last weekend."

Nic and I burst into laughter. I really fucking loved my friends.

CHAPTER 5

JANUARY BLUSTERED INTO NEW York City like an invading army, coating everything in its path in pure white. Which lasted all of three minutes before the pristine snow was transformed into piles of muddy sludge as life—and traffic—carried on.

Seated behind the reception desk at work, I looked out at the passersby bundled in their hats and coats. I was feeling wistful this Monday morning, the dreariness matching my mood.

Dwight had flown in Friday night to spend the weekend with me, and we'd fought. I'd summoned up some bravery and asked him if he wanted to role play a little bit, and he'd initially agreed.

When I suggested that we play naughty nanny, he wanted to know where the hypothetical children's mother was in this scenario, and I made up something on the fly. *Maybe she's out of town.*

And that's when the fighting began. Dwight blew up, accusing me of condoning cheating. I told him he was being ridiculous and that it was all just a bit of fun, a little forbidden romance scene. He'd shot back that maybe some things were forbidden for a reason.

He made me feel small, and I hated that. Not for the first time, I wondered if there was something wrong with me for wanting to engage in naughty fantasies. I'd never cheat in real life. Hell, I abhorred cheating.

"You all right?" Anita asked beside me, and I lifted a shocked eyebrow. Anita rarely spoke unless spoken to, and she certainly never showed any concern or hint of friendship toward me. We worked together. That was it.

"I'm okay. It was just a stressful weekend."

"For me too," she said with a sage nod, which caused her perfect black pageboy hairdo to bounce. "We moved recently, and my son is having trouble sleeping in his new room."

Color me surprised. I didn't even know Anita had a child. "How old is he?"

"Colby's six. You want to see a picture?" Her brown eyes looked hopefully over at me.

"Of course."

She held out her phone, and my heart melted. Anita's little one had her dark skin and black hair, though his was a mess of curls that hung around the most adorable chubby face.

"Oh. My. God. He is freaking darling, Anita." I gave her a sad smile. "I feel like a shithead because we've worked together for two months and I didn't even know you had a kid."

She returned my smile. "I'm not exactly the easiest person to get to know. And to be honest, maybe I'm a little intimidated by you. You're so pretty."

"Me?" I practically shrieked. "You look like a damn supermodel. I feel like if I touch your cheekbones, they'll cut my hand off." She let out a laugh, making her even more attractive. "And you have to be at least six feet tall. Why aren't you a model?"

Her slim nose scrunched. "I hate the spotlight. I'd rather die than be on a stage in front of people. I have to take Xanax just to do this job. When I interviewed here, I asked for a back office position, but this is all they had available. It's why I let you do most of the talking when guests approach. You're so confident talking to people."

"Yeah, my mama always said I could have a conversation with a pine tree. I know it doesn't come that easily for everyone, but you're doing a great job, Anita." I patted her arm encouragingly. "You learned all the floors and offices within two days of being here. It took me a week to get everything straight. And you're excellent on the phone."

Her smile was appreciative and brilliant. "Thanks, Lehra. I don't mind talking on the phone. It's just the face-to-face interactions that make me nervous."

The phone rang, and I bobbed my eyebrows at her. "Do your thang, lady."

Anita laughed and picked up the phone. "Bouvier. How may I direct your call? Oh, hi, Tony... Of course, I'll let Lehra know... Okay, you too." She hung up and pointed upward. "Tony said Mr. Bouvier is buying lunch for the entire staff, but the restaurant just called and their catering van broke down. He asked if you could go with Cruz to pick up the food."

"Oh. Well, that's nice of Mr. Bouvier. When?"

"He said about five minutes."

I glanced up to see a flower delivery person approaching and put on my brightest smile. "Hi, can I help you?"

"Delivery for Miss Kincaid." He squinted at the card. "Um, Lora? Leera?"

"Lehra. That's me," I said, accepting the bouquet of a dozen red roses. Opening the small envelope, I found a typed card with the words, *Sorry. Dwight.*

My forehead creased and I checked the back of the card, but there was no *I love you* or anything else. Disappointment flooded my system, and I instantly felt ungrateful. Dwight had been thoughtful enough to send apology flowers, and here I was, trying to read too much into the wording on the card.

It's fine. He was probably just in a hurry when he talked to the florist.

"Those are pretty," Anita commented, and I plastered a smile on my face.

"They are very pretty. My boyfriend sent them."

Anita's eyes flashed toward the front of the building, and she said, "I think your ride is here." My gaze followed hers and found one of Bouvier's black delivery vans at the curb.

"Crap, I better go." Placing the flowers on the center of the desk so everyone could enjoy them, I stuck the card in my purse and grabbed my coat from the hidden closet behind us.

I shrugged it on over my ice-blue pantsuit and rushed to the door, my low-heeled boots tapping across the black marble floor. Cruz was waiting beside the passenger door, and his face brightened when he saw me.

"Hey, Lehra. I heard you're cruising in elegance with me today."

He instantly made me smile, and I said in my poshest voice, "Who needs a Bentley when you can ride in a van?" For the record, it was a very fancy van, a sleek black vehicle with *Bouvier* in the brand's signature font down the side.

Cruz opened the door for me and then closed it when I climbed into the passenger's seat. He was in another finely cut black suit and black leather driving gloves, looking like danger and sin, but I couldn't help but notice he wasn't wearing a jacket.

"Aren't you cold without a coat?" I asked when he took the driver's seat.

"Nah, I run hot."

I bet you do, my wayward mind said, and I mentally slapped myself. Rock music played softly on the radio, and I stared out the window, lost in thought as Cruz drove down the block and took a right at the next corner.

"You're quiet today," he noted, and I pulled my head around to face him.

"Just tired, I guess."

"Are you okay?" The concern in his voice melted me a little.

"I'm fine." But that wasn't entirely the truth. I was still upset about this weekend and a little confused at the curtness of Dwight's note.

Cruz stopped at a red light, and his lips tipped up on one side. "Tell me a happy thing."

My heart did a stutter step because he remembered that little thing I mentioned to him weeks ago. "It's supposed to snow again this weekend, and I plan to go to the park on Saturday with my friends, Artie and Nicolette."

"Sounds fun," he said, returning his attention to the road when the light turned green. "We didn't get to see much snow in Galveston."

"You're welcome to join us," I said without thinking. "I mean, you probably wouldn't want to do that. We plan to act like children."

His smile was so warm, I could practically feel it radiating through the cab of the van. "I'd love that." Then his face fell. "Oh never mind. I'm supposed to babysit my niece that day."

"Bring Noelle along. I love watching kids enjoy the snow. We can make snow angels."

"You sure? She's a handful."

"Of course. Your sister and brother-in-law will thank you for wearing her out so she'll sleep like a log on Saturday night."

Cruz nodded toward his phone in the console. "Put your number in there and then send yourself a text so you'll have my number. My code is 0204."

"Oooh, trusting me with your code? What if I change all your predictive text to crazy things when you're not looking?"

A wicked smirk crossed his lips. "Then I'll have to punish you."

It seemed as though the freezing weather outside had turned into a balmy ninety degrees because the back of my neck was suddenly sweating.

Jerking my head down to hide my heated cheeks, I put my name and number into his phone and said, "Then I'll have to make sure to be a good girl."

Fuck me sideways. Did I just say I'll be a good girl?

"That's... I mean... not like *that*," I said, trying to backtrack, but Cruz simply chuckled.

"I heard what I heard, Lehra. Now you just sit over there and put your number in my phone like..." he wiggled his eyebrows, "a good girl."

Oh for fuck's sake. Why is that so hot?

"Are you *trying* to embarrass me," I scolded, laying his phone back in the console as the heat of a thousand suns reddened my face.

Cruz grinned like Satan himself. "Look at you blushing. I bet your face gets all pink when Dwight calls you a good girl in bed, doesn't it?"

"I don't, um, he doesn't..." *Jesus, shut the fuck up, Lehra.* "Why don't you tell me your happy thing?"

His brow furrowed, and he cast me a glance before schooling his face into a smile once again. "My happy thing is that I have plans to play in the snow on Saturday with my niece and my friend Lehra."

If there was a sweeter answer, I couldn't imagine what it would be. "It will be fun. I look forward to meeting Noelle."

"We're here," Cruz said, double parking in front of a gourmet sandwich shop. "Tony said we're supposed to park out front, and they'll load the food for us."

Workers began filing out with hundreds of gold boxed lunches, and a few minutes later, the back of the van was full.

"Does Bouvier do this often?" Cruz asked as he headed back to our office.

"A couple times a year. It's a nice treat. I'm not sure why Tony asked me to ride along. I wasn't much help."

"Of course you were. You were an excellent sidekick."

I brushed imaginary lint from my shoulder. "You're right. There's no way you could've driven those five blocks without me."

Cruz smiled warmly. "I could have, but I'm glad you came anyway."

"Me too," I said, feeling a lot brighter than I had a little while ago.

"You look so cute," Nicolette said on Saturday when I found her and Artie in the park. I was wearing a red puffer jacket with a baby-pink pom-pom hat and matching gloves, along with jeans and black snow boots.

"You look like Cupid," Artie cooed.

"So like a chubby baby with a weapon?" I joked, lifting a sardonic eyebrow. "That scarf is gorgeous, Artie."

He flung the tail of the chunky teal scarf dramatically over his shoulder. "Thank you. My granny made it for me."

"I hope you guys don't mind, but I invited someone to join us. It's Mr. Bouvier's driver. He's keeping his niece today, and I thought it would be fun for her to get to play in the snow."

"That's cool," Nicolette said. "What's the driver's name?"

I opened my mouth to speak and then froze. *Mother of all fuckers.* When my friends and I were discussing sexy names, I'd stupidly blurted out Cruz. No way they wouldn't remember that.

But I was granted a brief reprieve when I spotted a large man holding hands with a little girl in a purple coat. "Oh, there he is."

My friends' eyes shifted in that direction and then widened. "Dear heavenly father, bless me, for I have sinned," Artie breathed out before doing the sign of the cross.

I slapped at his hands and hissed, "Cut it out. You're not even Catholic."

"That big ole man looks like he could snap my spine in half, and I'm here for it," he shot back, his eyes still on Cruz.

"He is really hot," Nic said quietly.

Cruz Estrada was dressed more casually than I'd ever seen him, and he had a bit of scruff on his normally clean-shaven face. It still allowed those damn dimples to show through, while also giving him a more rugged look.

He was wearing a forest-green cable-knit sweater and faded jeans that fit in all the right places. His only concession to the freezing weather was a black jacket and gloves.

The little girl, on the other hand, was bundled up like she was hiking to Antarctica. Her coat was poofy and made her look like an adorable blueberry. The hood was pulled over her head with a ring of white fur framing her cherub's face.

Every few steps, she'd stop and hop a few times, obviously fascinated with her own footsteps in the snow. Her uncle stopped and let her do her thing each time with the utmost patience.

They finally reached us, and Cruz flashed me a big grin. "Hey, Lehra."

"Heyyyy, you," I said, avoiding the use of his name. "These are my friends, Nicolette and Artie. Guys, this is... Mr. Estrada."

I know, I know. I had to at least try.

Cruz looked at me strangely before holding out his hand to shake Artie's and Nicolette's. "You can call me Cruz."

I refused to look at my friends, but I could literally feel their eyes shift to me. *Dammit.*

"Cruz? That's a nice name," Artie drawled, and I wanted to find a snowdrift and bury myself in it.

"Thanks. And this is my niece, Noelle."

Ignoring the amused glances from my friends, I squatted down and smiled at the little girl. She was absolutely precious with her baby face and what looked like dark curls peeking out from the fuzzy hood.

"Hi, Noelle. I'm Lehra. Are you ready to play in the snow?"

She pressed her lips together and nodded bashfully, her brown eyes bright and playful. It didn't take long for that shyness to wear off. Within minutes, Noelle was giggling happily, tossing handfuls of snow at Artie, who delighted her by falling to the ground each time with the most drama he could muster.

All of us made snow angels and then ran around like kids, hiding from flying snowballs we threw at each other. "Ceasefire," I finally called from behind a tree. "I need hot chocolate."

Cruz tirelessly continued chasing his niece around while the other three adults went to the nearby food truck for cocoa and cookies for all of us.

"Someone's been gatekeeping the hottie," Artie chastised after we placed our order.

"I have not!" I insisted. "I only met him about a month ago, and this is the only time I've seen him outside a work situation."

"Hmmm," he hummed, glancing back to see Cruz pretending to search for Noelle, who was giggling at him from behind a bush. "I'd like to have a work situation with that man. I wonder if he dabbles in the ways of sphincterism?"

Nic and I screamed out a laugh, and she bumped Artie with her shoulder. "You are deranged, mister. Besides, my gaydar is not picking up a signal. I think Cruz needs a lady science nerd in his life." She gave a fake toss of her hair because, of course, her dark locks were pulled back into a low bun beneath her charcoal-gray beanie.

Artie directed an arched eyebrow at me. "Is Blue Eyes single?"

"I have no idea. He hasn't mentioned a girlfriend."

As we were walking back, we found a crying Noelle with Cruz kneeling next to her. We stopped and watched the interaction.

"I losed my glove and m-my hand is c-c-cold, Uncle Cooz."

I heard muttering and turned to Nicolette, who had her eyes closed and was chanting. "You're too young, and you don't have a husband. You're too young, and you don't have a husband."

"What are you saying that for?" I asked in confusion.

"I'm trying to talk myself out of getting knocked up and having a little cutie of my own. Dear god, she is adorable. Uncle Cooz? Gahhh!"

As we watched, Uncle Cooz took his niece's tiny hand in his big ones and lowered his head to blow warm air against her pink fingers. "There. Is that better, baby girl?" Then he tucked her hand inside the neck of his sweater to lie against his skin.

"Annnnnd, my ovaries just exploded," Nicolette hissed, and Artie nodded.

"Mine too."

"You don't have ovaries," I pointed out, and he shot me a glare.

"I spontaneously grew some brovaries, and then they exploded, thank you very much." He circled a long finger toward niece and uncle. "But not before this little scene got me pregnant. I think I'd like the theme of my baby shower to be baby woodland animals. Make it happen."

And with a saucy snap of his fingers, he strutted off, leaving Nicolette and I laughing in his wake.

We found a couple benches arranged perpendicular to each other and brushed off the snow. Artie and I sat on one, and Nic claimed the spot beside Cruz, who had Noelle on his lap on the other.

He pulled the little girl's hood down and brushed a hand affectionately over her dark riot of curls. "How did you get chocolate on your forehead, baby girl?" he asked, swiping the offending smudge with his thumb and sucking it off. Noelle shrugged, unconcerned, and continued eating her chocolate chip cookie.

"Dear god, if I dropped my cookie on my lap, do you think Blue Eyes would lick it off?" Artie asked me from the corner of his mouth.

"Would you stop it?" I attempted to glare at my friend, but I couldn't help the grin spreading across my face. Artie was always a good time.

Digging in the pocket of my coat, I pulled out a small bundle and tossed it to Cruz. "I always carry a spare set of gloves. They're the stretchy ones and will be way too big for her, but at least she won't get frostbite."

He blessed me with a grateful smile before unfolding the gloves and pulling one onto Noelle's bare hand. The knit material flapped off the ends of her fingers, which seemed to delight the little girl.

"What do you say?" Cruz prompted, and she grinned at me with tiny white teeth between rosy lips.

"Tank you, Lehra."

And yeah. There may have been some ovary detonation inside my own abdomen at that point.

Chapter 6

As August dawned, I realized I had been in New York for almost a year. Things were going well at work. I was quiet, respectful, and damn good at my job as Auburn Bouvier's driver and personal security agent.

I smiled at the thought of him. The past few months had been pretty eventful in his life. Auburn met a woman, and it wasn't that horrible girlfriend he'd dated on and off for years, Magdalena Lewis. I'd driven her a few times, and she was a complete shrew. I was so glad he was done with her.

Auburn's new lady was much younger than him, an intelligent woman named Gianna Moschella who didn't take one bit of his grumpy shit. And the billionaire was head over heels in love with her. They were still keeping their relationship a secret because Gianna's father was Tony, Auburn's personal assistant, but it was only a matter of time before he locked her down and made her Mrs. Bouvier.

I only wished I could find a woman like that. Well, I had, but she was taken. Yes, I was still harboring a crush for Lehra Kincaid, even though she was still dating that Dwight character. I knew I should move on, but I couldn't bring myself to find interest in any other woman.

Changing out of my suit, I dressed in a royal-blue polo shirt and jeans in preparation for my Monday night dinner. My eyes found the shoebox on the top shelf of my closet, and I pulled it down, feeling the weight of it in my hands.

I opened it and stared at the letter on top, noting the slight yellowing of the envelope, which wasn't surprising, given that it had been written over two decades ago.

As my fingers brushed lightly over the faded writing, I flashed back to last year when I'd accidentally come across this box in my mother's home.

"Thank you for doing this, mi tesoro," my mother says, kissing my cheek. "I didn't want to have to call a plumber."

"No need, Mama. I'm perfectly capable of changing out a hot water heater. I stopped by Home Depot and bought one on the way."

"Give me the receipt, and I'll pay you back," she insists.

"Make me a few dozen tamales, and we'll call it even. The guys in my unit love them." I'm a member of Houston's Special Weapons and Tactics detail, better known as SWAT, and my teammates live for Estrella Estrada's tamales.

Correction: Stella Estrada, which is what she's gone by since marrying my father because she said her full name sounded estupido.

"I'll make them this weekend. Now, do you need me to get the tools out for you?"

"Mama," I said sternly, "I know where everything is. Go to work. You have a business to run."

My father was a private investigator, and my mother worked with him for many years. After he died from a heart attack last year, Mama had gotten her P.I. license and took over the business. I was so fucking proud of her.

Once she's out the door, I flip the electrical breaker and turn off the water going to the old hot water heater. Then I drain it before disconnecting the hoses and electrical conduit. Using a dolly, I wheel the leaky heater out of the small closet and load it into my truck.

Deciding to clean the floor before I install the new one, I grab the broom and mop from Mama's pantry. While I'm mopping, I notice a couple loose floorboards and pull the hammer and some nails from my father's old red toolbox, intent on hammering them back in place.

I'm not sure what makes me drop to my knees and lift the floorboards, but I do, peering down into the hole by the light of a flashlight. A blue shoebox rests inside the opening.

"What the hell is this?" I mutter, lifting the box and setting it on my lap.

There are letters inside, hundreds of them, addressed to Benjamin Estrada, my father. All of them have a return address in New York, from someone named Paul Bouvier.

Who the hell is Paul Bouvier? *I think, opening the envelope on top and reading the handwritten words on the enclosed page.*

Benjamin,

I can't tell you how grateful I am that we could come to an agreement. I wish Estrella would be more flexible, but I never want to cause any upheaval to your family. I promise you that's the last thing I want.

All I care about is that Cruz is happy and healthy. I appreciate you allowing me to play a part in his life, even from afar.

Thank you for sending the pictures of him on the bike I sent. You said blue is his favorite color, so I hope he likes it. I also hope that damn horn doesn't drive you too crazy.

Regards,

Paul Bouvier

I frown at the letter and read it again. Who is this guy? Some friend of my dad's? Or maybe an estranged family member? From the tone, he's obviously someone my mother doesn't approve of.

And the bike... I remember my dad coming home with a blue bike for my sixth birthday, and it had a silver horn with one of those big black rubber bubbles I could squeeze to make it honk. It was loud as hell and sounded like an old car horn. I absolutely loved it.

Flipping through the rest of the envelopes, I notice they were sent to a post office box and not to my parents' address. Was my dad hiding these letters from my mom? Is that why they were concealed beneath the floorboards in the water heater closet?

I rub a hand over my lips as I stare down at the multitude of letters. Would it be wrong to go through these? I mean, my dad's been dead for over a year, but does death negate your right to privacy?

My brain wars with itself. On one hand, my father wouldn't have kept these letters for so long if they weren't important. The first one dated back to when I was six, and I seemed to be the subject. But on the other hand, he wouldn't have hidden them if he wanted anyone to look at them.

Fuck. I'm so torn. Huffing out a breath, I close the lid and carry the box out to my truck. I have to get this heater replaced and then get to work. I'll sort through all this in my mind and decide what to do later.

"Hey, Mama. How is the hot water heater working?" I ask when she picks up the phone the next morning.

"Fantastic. Thank you again for being such a good son."

"It's what I'm here for, Mama. I want to take care of you."

"I know you do, mi hijo, but I'm doing okay now. I still miss your father every day, but I feel like the fog is lifting a little. Like the world has finally started turning again. So you can stop fussing over me so much like a mother hen."

I chuckle. *"Is that your way of telling me I'm getting on your nerves?"*

"Never, but I worry about you, Cruz. You never do anything with your friends. You're young and handsome so you shouldn't be sitting at your mama's house every weekend."

"Some of the guys invited me out for Friday night. I was thinking about joining them," I say thoughtfully.

"You should. But don't drink and drive," she adds quickly. "You call me, and I'll come pick you up. Day or night. No questions asked." That was exactly the same thing she used to say to me when I was a teenager.

I fight back a snicker. "Okay, Mama. Or I could just call an Uber like a normal person."

"It's not nice to tease your mother," she scolds.

"Just pointing out that I'm thirty years old and fully capable of finding a ride home."

"I know how old you are. I gave birth to you, remember? Almost ten pounds. In labor for twenty-seven hours."

Before she could retell the entire story of my birth—because that was where this was headed—I break in. "Mama, did you know the floorboards were loose in the water heater closet?"

She gasps. "Nooo, there weren't mice in there, were there?"

I chuckle. My mother hates rodents of any kind. "No, there weren't any mice. I just didn't know if you were aware that the boards were loose."

"No, I never go in that closet. Your father—God rest his soul—took care of all that stuff. Do I need to call a handyman?"

"No, ma'am. I nailed them back down."

"Oh, okay. Well, thank you, son."

She seems completely unconcerned about me finding the hidey hole with the letters in it. I'm pretty sure that means she knows nothing about it.

We say our goodbyes, and once home, I reach beneath my bed for the shoe box. I'll just read a couple more to see if I can figure out who this Bouvier man is in relation to my father and why he sent me a bike.

Papa was a Marine for two years before he was discharged due to an injury. Maybe Bouvier served with him.

Opening the second letter in the stack, I begin reading.

Benjamin,

Thank you for your most recent letter and the photos of Cruz in his baseball uniform. He is getting so big.

I hate that I can't be a bigger part of his life, but I'm trying to respect Estrella's wishes. I can't say it doesn't hurt though, knowing my son is growing up without knowing me. I feel like part of my soul is missing.

So I remind myself it's not about me and that Cruz is being cared for by parents that love him. But I love him too, so very much. As long as he's happy, I can bear it, only getting these small glimpses. It's not easy, but I know it's what's best for him, and that's the most important thing.

Thank you again for everything, Benjamin. You're a good man.

Regards,

Paul

My gaze goes back to the second paragraph. I read it seven more times before those two words sink in and begin to make sense.

My son.

Only, it doesn't make sense at all. I'm not this man's son. Benjamin Estrada is my father. Though I've always wondered why I have blue eyes and the rest of my family has brown eyes.

But no. It can't be. Dread seeps into every bone in my body, making them feel soft. My legs barely hold me up when I stand and find my computer, and my hands shake so badly, I have trouble typing the name into my search engine.

Paul Bouvier.

Articles flood my screen. Apparently this man's famous in the fashion world, and that's when I remember the fancy suit Papa had given me for my high school graduation. It was a charcoal-gray Bouvier suit.

Fuck.

I click on the images tab, and photos of the man spread across the screen. He appears older than my parents, and he has salt-and-pepper hair and...

Goddammit.

The bluest eyes I've ever seen. But in actuality, I have seen those eyes. Many times.

Every time I look in the mirror.

I stood outside the restaurant and peered into the window. I always had to do that before my Monday night dinners, simply to ground myself before meeting my dinner companion. It was easier than it was the first time, which was almost a year ago.

Leaving the heat of the August evening behind me, I entered the cozy bistro, my face cooling from the blast of air conditioning that met me. The hostess looked up and smiled.

"He's already here," she informed me.

No surprise. He was always here before me. I made my way to our regular table nestled in the back, out of view of most of the other diners.

He stood with a huge smile on his face, and I walked toward Paul Bouvier.

My biological father.

CHAPTER 7

"HI, SON." PAUL PULLED me into a hug, and I returned the embrace before we took our seats across the table from each other. He greeted me the same way every time, and it was beginning to feel more natural, him calling me son.

I wasn't quite ready to call him Dad yet—and I wasn't sure I ever would be—so I replied in my usual manner. "Hi, Paul. It's good to see you." And I meant it. I really liked Paul Bouvier. Was he a perfect person who'd never made any mistakes? Absolutely not. But was he one of the most genuine people I'd ever met? A million percent.

It's why I tolerated his affections and no longer cringed when he called me his son. He'd been so fucking kind and understanding with me and the way I struggled with all this new information. He answered every question I had for him, even the things that were difficult for him to discuss.

"How is work going?" he asked.

"Very well. Both jobs. I got to work with the team this past weekend. Not much exciting going on, mostly serving high-risk search warrants."

His face was solemn as he nodded. "I'm very proud of you, Cruz, but I worry."

"You don't need to. We're the most highly trained officers on the force, so we're prepared for anything."

"I don't doubt your abilities for a second, but I know what you do can be very dangerous. I just keep telling myself that your training will keep you safe." His head tilts to the side. "Did I tell you I came to your boot camp graduation?"

My eyebrows lifted in surprise. "No. Really?"

Paul stares at his plate for a moment, and when he looks back up, his blue eyes are filled with tears. "Of course I did. I came to so many of your events and hid in the back. Your high school graduation. All your playoff games your senior year."

My mind was blown. "You came to my baseball games?"

His smile broadened. "That walk-off homerun you hit over the left field wall in the state finals almost hit me in the head. Luckily, the guy beside me was wearing a glove, and he caught it." He inhaled a deep breath and then blew it out. "I still have the ball."

"Wait. What? You said the guy beside you caught it."

"I bought it from him." Paul reached beneath the table and pulled out a cardboard box with my name written in marker across the top. His eyes were wary when they met mine. "Do you want to see my Cruz box?"

My already blown mind practically detonated. "You have a Cruz box?"

His jaw trembled with emotion and then clenched hard and firm as he nodded. "It was the only thing I had of you. I couldn't have my son, but no one could take away my memories."

Damn. It was difficult to see the raw pain on his face. It told me what I already knew from our discussions. I was never some illegitimate bastard child he'd been happy to get rid of, which was my initial thought. No, I was the son who had been kept from him but who he had never forgotten.

"I'd love to see it," I told him, my voice sounding huskier than usual.

Paul's smile could only be described as prideful when he unfolded the lid and opened the box. "Here's the ball." He handed it to me, and I turned it over and over in my hand, my fingers finding the familiar bite of the laces.

"I can't believe you have this," I said, the sweet memories of that home-run infusing my veins with nostalgia. The resounding crack of the bat, the rise of the ball, the velocity of a perfect hit that I didn't even have to watch to know it was gone. But I'd watched it anyway and then lost sight of it as I rounded first base.

"I was wondering if… if you'd sign it for me. You have no idea how much I wanted to march down onto that field after the game and ask for your autograph, but I didn't want to take away from your big moment or upset your mother."

"Sparkling water and a whiskey sour," the server, Kenzie, said, setting down our drinks before we'd even ordered them. We'd been coming to this place for almost a year, and we got the same beverages every time.

Paul informed me on our first visit here that he had given up drinking years ago, and when he told me why, I was shocked by his honesty. It was a story he hadn't even shared with Auburn and Monty, though he said he planned to when the time was right.

"Do you have a pen I could borrow?" I asked Kenzie, and she pulled one from her pocket. I took it and signed my name on the baseball before handing it back to Paul. "There you go. I think this is the first time I've ever signed a ball."

"Thank you," he breathed, holding the small sphere in both hands like it was made of gold.

I passed the pen back to Kenzie, and she used it to write down our orders, pasta primavera for both of us. Paul began pulling items from the box, narrating their history for me.

"They sold these as souvenirs at your graduation," he said, holding up a maroon tassel. The strands rippled as he gave it a little jiggle. "I was so proud of you for being the Salutatorian. Your speech was really good."

"I was nervous as hell," I admitted with a chuckle. "I'm not exactly the *get up and talk in front of people* kind of guy."

"I couldn't tell. Now this? I could tell you were nervous in this Christmas play. You kept shifting around."

I took the folded program and busted into laughter. It was from when I played the esteemed role of Wise Man Number Two in third grade. "I had to pee. That's why I was so antsy," I admitted, and Paul grinned across the table at me.

"Well, good job on not peeing on the stage. That's something."

"You really came to all this stuff?" I asked, sorting through the paraphernalia he'd collected over the years.

"I did, and for what I couldn't make it to, Ben sent me pictures and programs." It no longer startled me when Paul referred to my papa with such familiarity. The two men had forged a kind of friendship, with their love for me as the cement that held it together.

"Thank you for being there. I mean, I know I wasn't aware of you yet, but it really means a lot to me now."

Paul graced me with an affectionate smile and a pat on my hand. "It was my pleasure. I wish I could have done more."

We cleared the table as Kenzie approached with our dinners. "I hate that I didn't even know you existed until you were six," Paul said once she was gone. "I still remember the first time I ever saw you in person. You were playing in the front yard, and you gave me the cutest little snaggle-toothed grin."

I'd heard this story before, but I sat quietly and ate as Paul told it again. It seemed to bring him some kind of comfort to talk about.

"I had gotten a private investigator to locate Estrella for me. I still thought about her all the time, and I had to know why she'd run. He found her in Texas, and I took a flight down the next day and found the address to your house. When I saw you playing with your dump truck, you looked up at me, and as soon as I saw your blue eyes, I just knew. You looked exactly like your brother, Monty."

I knew from my research and from Paul's stories that Monty was his third child, with me being three months younger than him. Paul twirled some pasta around his fork and took a bite before continuing.

"My heart was beating so fast. All I wanted to do was scoop you up and hold you, but I didn't want to scare you, so I asked to speak to your mother. You ran inside to get her, and as soon as she saw me, she sent you back inside."

"And she cussed you out in Spanish," I filled in as he took a drink of his water.

"Right in the front yard," he said with a chuckle. "Then she took off her shoe. I'm pretty sure she was going to throw it at me, but your papa pulled up just then and defused the situation."

"He was the only person that could calm her down when she got riled up," I remembered. "I got a shoe thrown at me once when I was seventeen. Completely deserved though. I stayed out all night without calling. Luckily, it was only a fuzzy slipper, but the intent was there."

Paul gave me an amused shake of his head and rolled his eyes. "Teenage boys. Auburn gave me the most trouble. Monty was pretty quiet. He had a girlfriend named Kassie, so he spent most of his time with her."

"You told me Monty is single, so I guess they broke up?"

Paul's lips thinned and turned down at the corners. "That's a story for another time. Anyway, after your father got Estrella—sorry, Stella—calmed down and in the house, he came back outside. Demanded to know what the hell I wanted."

I took a bite of my excellent pasta and listened to the story I'd heard at least three times already. "I assured him I didn't want any trouble, but that I thought I deserved to know if I had another child. He didn't admit it then, but he offered to get together and talk with me the next day."

Paul took another drink of his sparkling water. "We planned to meet at a small pub, and I was almost shocked out of my shoes when he actually showed up."

"If Papa said he was going to do something, he did it," I said, and Paul smiled.

"He really was a good man, Cruz, and I'm sorry you lost him too soon." He looked away for a long moment, his voice soft. "I can never tell you how grateful I am that you had him in your life. I couldn't have asked for a better father for you."

This was the thing I appreciated most about Paul Bouvier. From the first time we'd met face-to-face last year, he'd spoken about my papa with nothing but respect. There was never a hint of awkwardness or bitterness in his tone, only gratitude. And he never once tried to use his position as my biological father to usurp Benjamin Estrada's position as my real dad.

Paul dabbed at his mouth with his napkin and smiled wanly. "Do you want the old man to shut up? I know I've told you this story before."

It seemed to bolster him to tell it, so I indulged him as Kenzie refilled his water glass. "Not at all. Continue."

"So I met with Ben, and he told me Stella wanted nothing to do with me. She was being tight-lipped, but he said she seemed afraid." He pulled at the back of his neck. "I'm assuming that had something to do with Chloe." His top lip curled into a sneer at the mere mention of her name.

He'd told me before about his wife's blackmail scheme against him, and I was happy I'd never met the bitch.

"I'd gotten a hotel room and thought about the situation all night. Didn't sleep a wink. You seemed so happy and well cared for, and I didn't want to disrupt the only home you knew. Once your papa knew I meant no harm," Paul continued, his voice taking on a musing quality, "he agreed to keep me in the loop regarding you. In return, I wouldn't try to get custody of you."

"Papa related to you as a father," I stated.

Paul nodded. "He was very kind and understanding about it. Your mother was already pregnant when they met, so he knew you weren't his biological son. We came to a mutual agreement. It was the hardest decision

I'd ever made in my life, but disrupting the life of a child with two parents and a stable home would have been cruel. I never wanted to hurt you, Cruz."

Sincerity rang through every syllable, even as a tear slipped down one cheek.

"I know, Paul, and I appreciate it so much. I know that was a huge sacrifice on your part, but you were right. It would have been traumatizing for me."

He nodded and swiped away the tear with the heel of his hand before picking up the box he'd set beside his chair. "There are letters in here from your father. I know you've read mine to him, but I thought you might like to read the story from his perspective."

Slugging back the rest of my drink, I attempted to rein in my emotions. "I'd love that."

"You can keep them, but I'd like to have the mementos back when you're done looking at them."

"Of course," I assured him.

Paul left some money on the table, and we rose. Setting the box on my empty chair, I pulled him into a hug. "Thank you," I said quietly. "You mean a lot to me, Paul."

It was the first time I'd initiated any kind of affection with him, but it felt good and right. He'd given me the gift of hearing my father's voice through those letters, and I couldn't have been more grateful.

"You keep this," I said, pulling the baseball from the box and placing it into his hand. "I'm sure it's worth at least five cents now that I've signed it."

His face creased into a smile. "It's worth everything to me, Cruz. More than you know."

And before my emotions could get the best of me, I picked up the box and walked from the restaurant.

CHAPTER 8

I. Am. So. Stressed.

My landlord just informed me that she wasn't renewing my lease because her niece "needs" my apartment. I have to move out by the end of October, which is in exactly twenty-eight days.

Shit.

She did offer to let me move into the apartment her niece currently resides in, which is in the same building, so I headed up to the fifth floor to take a look.

"Here it is," Clara said, opening the door with a flair.

I was immediately struck by the darkness. Reaching for the light switch, I found that it was already on, and yet blackness stretched as far as the eye could see. Which wasn't very far because this was literally the smallest apartment I'd ever seen.

The reason for the darkness became apparent. Everything in the entire room was painted black. The floor, the walls, the ceiling, the furniture. Hell, even the refrigerator.

And... I squinted, attempting to decipher the shapes in the corner. Was that the toilet and shower? Also painted a dark ebony? Yep, it sure as hell was.

"W-why is it like... this?" I asked, waving my arm around.

"Genesis went through a goth phase, but she's tired of it now."

"So you're giving her my apartment? Are you at least going to re-paint?"

"No," Clara said flatly. "It will be leased as-is. You can paint if you want to though."

"It will cost me a fortune to re-do everything in here. Are you going to pay for it?"

"Sorry, I can't. Take it or leave it."

Leave it! my mind screamed. I'd be depressed as hell within a day of living here. It was a single room unit with only one small window, and it was little more than a closet. If my tiny apartment was a shoebox, this was a bar of soap. I'd be living in a black bar of soap.

"I'm assuming there's a cut in rent since it's much smaller than my place?"

"Actually, it will be the same," she informed me without an ounce of apology.

"What? That's ridiculous, Clara."

"Take it or leave it," she repeated, "but I need to know by the end of the week so I can lease it to someone else."

"Oh, I'm sure people will be lining up down the block to live in the room of gloom," I retorted, a heavy bite of sarcasm in my tone. Then I puffed out a tired sigh. "I'll let you know."

Looking at the apartment had thrown my morning routine off, and I dashed into the *Bouvier* building ten minutes late. "Shit, sorry," I rushed out to Anita. "I've got housing woes."

She winced. "That sucks." Her eyes darted to the switchboard, and she lowered her voice. "Tony called a few minutes ago and wants to see you immediately in his office."

Panic surged through me. "Crap, do you think I'm getting fired for being late?"

Anita shook her head. "I covered for you. Told him you were in the bathroom."

Awesome. He probably thinks I have the poops.

"Thanks," I breathed, stashing my purse in the closet and brushing my hands down the front of my black pantsuit. "Do I look okay?"

"You look great. Go," she replied, pointing a finger toward the gold elevators.

I was nervous. Tony was a sweetheart, but I'd never been called up to the fiftieth floor before. Was I in some kind of trouble? Inserting my key card into the slot, I pushed the button for the top floor.

Tony Moschella stood as soon as the elevator doors opened and thank god he had a smile on his face. "Lehra, come in and take a seat."

Forcing my face to look pleasant and not panicked, I sat in the chair across from his desk. "Did I do something wrong?" I blurted, and Tony chuckled.

"Not at all. This is a good thing. At least I hope you'll think it's good." He rounded the desk and leaned his butt against the edge, crossing his arms over his chest. Tony was a good-looking man in a dad kind of way, and he dressed the part of an executive assistant to a tee. His gray suit fit to perfection, and his salt-and-pepper hair was nicely styled.

"Okay, hit me with it."

"I'm considering retirement."

My heart sank. "Oh. That makes me sad, Tony. I'd miss seeing you all the time."

"It's not imminent, but maybe in a couple years. I called you up here because I wanted to see if you'd be interested in taking my job when I leave."

If my eyes had popped out of my head and rolled across the floor, I wouldn't have been surprised. "Me?" I stupidly pointed at myself with both thumbs, even though we were the only two people in the room.

"Yes you, Lehra. The benefits and pay are fantastic, and..." He dropped his voice and glanced at the closed door behind him, Auburn Bouvier's private office. "Mr. Bouvier can be a difficult man, but recently, he's been different. Much more pleasant."

"Hmmm, I've noticed that too. He seems looser or something. More smiley."

"I've put together some numbers for you," Tony said, sliding a folder across the desk.

As soon as I opened it and saw the salary, my eyes were once again at risk of exiting my body. "Holy shit," I breathed, and Tony chuckled.

"Yes, it's very impressive. Not quite what I'm making now, but I've been here over a decade. I think this would be a good move for you, Lehra. A career and not just a job."

And with this kind of money, I could afford a place in a nicer building. It wouldn't happen right away, but eventually, right?

Looking up at him with a gigantic smile on my face, I slapped my palm against my leg. "Sign me up."

"I was hoping you'd say that. I'll talk to Bouvier about it, but I'm sure he would agree with me that you'd be the best fit. I wanted to see if you were even interested before I mentioned it to him."

"I'm so excited about this, Tony," I said, rising and giving him a big hug. "Thank you for thinking of me."

He patted my back before I pulled away. "You'll have to start training with me, the sooner the better. There's a lot to learn."

"Of course. Just let me know what I need to do."

"There is something you can do for me today. I've got to look over this stuff the finance department sent up," he said, tapping a knuckle on the top of an intimidating stack of papers on his desk. "But I'm also supposed to pick up the invitations for the staff Christmas party. Can you go get them for me?"

"Of course," I said eagerly, and then my face fell when I wondered how I was going to carry boxes of invitations by myself. "I don't have a car though. I ride the subway to work."

"Cruz will drive you. Now look, I need you to look over the invitations and make sure everything is correct. They've sent me two proofs with Bouvier spelled wrong." He rolled his eyes. "The last one they sent looked fine, but please check it over thoroughly for any errors before you accept them. Here's the info." I took the hot-pink sticky note he held up.

"Okay, I'm an excellent proofreader," I assured him. "I used to charge three dollars a page to proof papers back in high school. I made a fortune off the football team."

Tony laughed and patted my shoulder. "Very entrepreneurial of you. I'll call Cruz and tell him to be waiting at the curb."

"Hey, Lehra," Cruz said, waiting beside the car to open the door for me. His dimples popped as his lips turned up at the corners. He really had the best smile.

"Hi, Cruz. Thanks for hauling me around today."

"It's my pleasure," he said, flashing me a wink as I settled in the front seat. *Jesus, why is he so damn cute?*

I suddenly remembered that I had no idea where the printer was located. *Great, Lehra. That would have been important information, don't ya think?*

"Do you happen to have the address?" I asked meekly when Cruz climbed in behind the wheel.

"Got it in the GPS already," he assured me, pulling away from the curb.

As we drove, I watched the apartment buildings pass by and daydreamed about living in one of them. *One day…*

"You're awfully quiet," Cruz commented, and I turned away from the window I'd been staring out of.

"Sorry. I just found out that I'm losing my apartment at the end of the month. The replacement one the landlord showed me is hideous. Everything in it is painted as black as night. I mean, everything. Walls, floor, ceiling, furniture. It's so depressing."

"Can you move to a different building?"

"I'm going to have to try and find something. The new apartment isn't much bigger than the Bentley. Hey, do you think our boss would let me live in one of his cars?"

Cruz chuckled. "That bad, huh?"

I gave him a flat stare. "It's a single room, the couch is in the kitchen, and the toilet and shower are less than a step from the bed. I guess I could use the toilet as a nightstand."

"If you find something, let me know. I can help you move." He whipped the car into a parking space as soon as another car pulled out. "That's the place right there," he said, dipping his head toward a storefront.

"Be back in a jiffy." I climbed out and walked into the printer's office with the sticky note held between two fingers.

"How may I help you?" a lady with a stern face asked when I approached the counter.

"I'm supposed to pick up some Christmas party invites for Mr. Bouvier."

Her chilly demeanor instantly warmed at the mention of his name, and she practically gushed. "Of course. Just let me grab them."

Five minutes later, I had checked the sample over multiple times, referencing the note to make sure the time and date were correct. The invitations were gorgeous, a deep red with a translucent vellum overlay that was affixed by a tiny white satin bow.

"Is everything satisfactory?" the woman asked, and I went over everything once more before nodding. I didn't want to screw up my first task from Tony.

"It looks fine. Thank you."

She smiled and called to the back for someone named Atticus to come and carry the box for me. A man appeared. He was short and plump, with gangly arms that looked like they were made for someone else's body. I was afraid they were going to snap in two when he lifted the box, but he managed to get it outside and placed safely in the trunk.

Cruz was on the phone when I re-entered the car, and he wrapped up with a, "Sounds good. Thanks," before placing his phone back in the console.

"Tell me your happy thing," he prompted as we headed back to work.

My teeth sank into my bottom lip, and I tried to camouflage my smile. "I have something, but I'm not sure if I'm supposed to say anything about it yet."

"Is it about taking over as Auburn's PA?"

I blinked in surprise. "How did you know that?"

"Tony mentioned it to me."

My shoulders shimmied in excitement. "That's it. I think I'm going to go for it."

"You should."

"I hope I can do it. Tony's job is complicated."

"You'll be great," he said, smiling encouragingly at me and nudging me with his elbow. "You're very bright, Lehra, and I think you could get along with anyone. Even Auburn Bouvier."

Warmth spread through me at the simple touch and his sweet sentiment.

We arrived, and Cruz lifted the invitations from the trunk before I could grab them. "I'll carry these up for you." He hefted the box on one shoulder, and I watched with rapt attention as the sleeves of his jacket threatened to pop right open as his biceps bulged.

"What's your happy thing?" I asked once we were in the elevator.

He smiled shyly at the floor and then lifted his eyes to look at me from beneath his dark fringe of lashes. "I got to see you today."

"Well, I'm sorry you don't have anything better than that," I teased, and he laughed.

"Trust me, it's been the highlight of my day."

I couldn't deny the flutter in my belly at those words.

Tony rose as soon as we entered. Cruz set the box on the desk, and I watched nervously as Tony looked over the sample invitation taped on top of it with a speculative eye.

"They're perfect," he announced, and I felt the tension drain from my shoulders. "Good job, Lehra."

Cruz winked before leaving.

"Anything else you need from me?" I asked Tony, and he shook his head as the door behind him opened.

"Lehra, can I see you for a moment?" Auburn Bouvier asked, and my nerves ratcheted up to level one hundred. Did he want to talk to me about the job? Or being late this morning? Shit, it could be anything.

"Of course."

Tony gave me a bolstering pat between my shoulder blades as I followed our boss into the inner office where he closed the door and gestured for me to sit. He took his high-backed leather chair and folded his hands in front of him on the desk.

"I understand you're thinking of taking Tony's position when he leaves."

"Yes, sir. I would love to."

Pursing his lips, he nodded. "I think you'll be a good fit. Where do you live?"

"In Queens."

Bouvier sat back in his chair and stroked a finger over his lips, his enigmatic blue eyes meeting mine. "That's too far. I'd like you to move to Manhattan. There's a one-bedroom available in my building."

Ummm, do what? I forced a smile onto my face. *How to say this delicately...*

"That's really nice, Mr. Bouvier, but I don't think I could afford an apartment in your building. Not that my salary isn't great," I assured him, "but you're... you know..." *A freaking billionaire.* I stumbled over my words, feeling like an idiot, but he smiled patiently.

"Tony also requested a raise in pay for you since you'll be training with him and inevitably taking on new responsibilities in addition to your receptionist duties."

"Oh, that was very nice of him."

"Instead of a raise, I'd like to offer you the apartment. When you take over for Tony, your salary will be increased to the one he presented you with earlier today, and you can still keep the apartment. You're welcome to come by this evening and see if it's to your liking."

If it's to my liking? I wanted to scream. *Would you like to hear about the dreary bar of soap I was considering living in this morning?*

I knew the building Auburn Bouvier lived in, and it was extravagant and way more than I would ever be able to afford in this lifetime. Free housing would save me thousands in rent every month. This was like a dream come true.

I was pretty sure I looked like a starving catfish, my mouth gaping open and then closing. "I'll be there," I said, trying to sound cool and not like I was about to bust at the seams.

Two weeks later, with Cruz's help, I moved into the nicest place I'd ever lived.

"It's so spacious," I gushed, spinning in an ecstatic circle. "Look at these hardwood floors! They're so shiny, I can almost see my reflection in them. And the windows! They're so clear." I flung an arm out to indicate the floor-to-ceiling windows.

"That's a good thing for windows to be," Cruz replied with a smirk, obviously amused at my excitement.

"Smartass," I shot back, giving his shoulder a shove. "I'm going to order us a pizza as a thank you for helping me move."

"You don't have to—"

I facepalmed him. "Shut it, Estrada. You're eating pizza with me."

When the food arrived, we sat together on my couch and ate like the starving people we were. "I can't believe this place came furnished," I said, bouncing my butt on the soft cushions.

"Mine too," Cruz replied. "It's cool that we're neighbors now."

Bumping him with my shoulder, I smiled up at him. "Thank you for helping me move."

His responding smile was sweet and made my breath hitch a little. "Anything for you, Lehra."

CHAPTER 9

I KNOCKED ON THE door to apartment 302 with a pink box in my hand.

"Hang on," a voice came from inside a second before the door swung open. "Lehra, hey."

But I couldn't respond because Cruz Estrada stood in the doorway in only a pair of sweat-stained gray shorts. Dear god in heaven! I didn't think men like this existed in real life.

Sweat dripped down his slick tan chest, the droplets tangling with just the right amount of hair, which arrowed down over a spectacular set of abs and into the waistband of those damp shorts. Beautifully done tattoos covered his upper arms. *Dammit! Why does he have to have tats?*

His right bicep featured a large ornate cross with dark-red roses as the background, and on the other arm was an arrow alongside an intricate feather.

"Lehra, did you need something?"

I realized I was awkwardly gawking when he spoke, and I lifted guilty eyes to his. "Hi, I came over to…" My addled brain couldn't quite remember why I'd come over here. *To ogle? No, that couldn't be it.* Then I realized I was holding a box and held it before me in triumph as I remembered. "I brought you more cookies."

"You didn't have to do that," he said, swiping sweat from his face with a white towel. "I just finished a workout. You want to come in?"

Yes.

"No, that's okay. I better get back to my place." I gestured vaguely toward my apartment which was across the hall and two doors down.

"Okay. Well, thanks for the cookies."

I turned to walk away and then realized I was still holding the box. "Oh, sorry," I said with a forced laugh, handing over the snacks.

Good grief! What is wrong with me?

As soon as I got back to my apartment, I checked my phone on the glass-and-chrome coffee table, and guilt instantly sank into my pores when I saw a missed call from Dwight. *Ogling another man while your boyfriend is calling? Not cool, Lehra.*

I immediately curled up on the couch and dialed him back. "Hi, babe," he answered.

"Hey, I saw you called."

"Yeahhhh." The way he drew out the word had a sliver of dread inching down my back. "About this weekend, I'm not going to be able to make it, babe."

My hand clenched into a fist against my thigh, and my voice thickened with sadness. "Why?"

"My mom is having a garage sale in a few weeks, and she wants me to help her price things."

"Can't you do that next weekend? We only get to see each other once a month. Plus, it's Halloween, and I got us some costumes." I thought of the Superman costume I'd rented for him and my sexy Lois Lane outfit.

"This is how long-distance relationships work, Lehra." His tone was patronizing, and it grated on my nerves.

"Oh, I thought they worked by both parties following through and showing up when they said they would. You skipped August too."

I heard a long sigh trek down the phone line. "I should have known you were going to be immature about this."

Ouch.

As the anger and hurt rose, my knuckles pressed so hard into my leg I would probably have little circular bruises tomorrow. "You're right, Dwight. I guess I'll see you when I see you."

"All right, babe," he said easily, like he hadn't just upset me. "Let me know your flight information for November, and I'll pick you up at the airport."

"I will." My voice sounded defeated, and I was tempted to tell him I was too busy in November, but that would be *immature*.

"Love you, Lehra."

"Love you too," I mumbled before hanging up.

Needing wine, I got up and poured myself a glass of pinot grigio, leaning against the marble-top counter and taking a long gulp of the crisp white. I heard my phone ping from the living room and smiled over the top of my glass. That was probably Dwight messaging to apologize for insulting me.

I crossed the light hardwood floor and picked up my phone, seeing a message from Cruz.

Cruz: Thanks for the cookies!

A picture accompanied the text, one of Cruz holding up one of the cookies with a goofy grin on his face. It made me smile.

I honestly didn't like those almond-cherry cookies. They were dry and brittle to me. But Cruz seemed to love them, so I'd keep making them for him.

Christmas came around fast this year. I was at the annual Bouvier office holiday party wearing an adorable strapless red dress with beading at the top and a flirty hemline. I'd pulled my hair up on top of my head, allowing the springy curls to drape down around my ears.

"You look ah-maziiiing!" Gianna sang as she approached me at one of the many food tables. The lobby of the *Bouvier* building was decked out in bright reds and snowy whites, with sparkly snowflakes draped from the thirty-foot ceilings.

"You do too," I gushed. Auburn Bouvier's new fiancée was decked out in a fitted red cocktail dress and sky-high heels that showed off her long legs. "We're rocking the red dresses tonight."

"We are. Let's take a selfie." She held up her phone at the perfect angle, and we smiled. Our smiles turned into laughter when Auburn Bouvier himself photobombed us with a cheesy grin on his handsome face.

I was so damned happy for these two. Gianna Moschella had swept into the billionaire's world and turned it upside down. After dating in secret for a while, they'd finally told Gianna's dad, Tony, about their relationship. I'm sure that was awkward at first, but he seemed to be coming around.

"You two look gorgeous tonight," Auburn said. It was nice of him to include me, but he only had eyes for Gia.

"Thanks, boss. You're looking mighty suave as well." He was wearing a charcoal-gray suit, no tie, and a red pocket square that precisely matched his fiancée's dress. No doubt coordinated by Devereaux, the head designer here.

"He is," Gianna said, looking adoringly up at him.

He pressed a kiss against her neck and whispered something in her ear that caused her to giggle and smack at his hip. I was still getting used to seeing my boss acting playfully. He'd been so stoic for years.

"How are the kids?" Gia asked, and Auburn's face melted into softness like a popsicle in Arizona.

"I just checked on them. They're with Abby. Jane is eating every sweet she can find, and Jaxon is flirting with all the models."

We laughed. Jaxon and Jane were the twins the couple planned to adopt, and they were freaking precious.

"Where are they? I need to go say hi to my little buddies," I said, glancing around the crowd of people for the five-year-olds.

"That means you're going to give them candy, right?" Gia asked flatly.

I waved a dismissive hand. "They know they can always count on Auntie Lehra to come through with the goods."

"They're over there with Abby. She's one of the teens from the children's home," Auburn explained, gesturing to his left. "We hired her to come help us with the twins for the evening."

"We wanted them to be able to come and have fun, but my fiancé needs to do his duty and *mingle with everyone*, right?" she asked pointedly, lifting her eyebrows at him.

Auburn Bouvier put on a grimace of a smile. "Yay. Mingling is my favorite." Then he stroked a hand down Gianna's arm and gave her a look that said he'd be doing some horizontal mingling with her later tonight.

Jealousy spiked through me, and I wished Dwight looked at me like that. With the kind of desire that radiated heat and wanting with every glance. Shoving that feeling away, I said goodbye to the couple and detoured to the reception desk, which was covered with a red cloth and dotted with elegant flower arrangements in white vases. Carefully lifting the back edge of it, I located the drawer that held my stash of candy I kept for when the twins visited.

Assuming the kids would be dressed up, I took a hard pass on the chocolate, instead opting for a couple Blow Pops, red for Jane and purple for Jaxon. Then I went to find them.

Jaxon was wearing a suit that perfectly matched his soon-to-be dad's, except his pocket square was white to match his sister's dress. He had both hands in his pockets and was speaking with a leggy brunette, obviously one of the models.

"You are the most beautiful woman in this room," he told her, and I bit my bottom lip to keep from laughing out loud. *The boy's a little player.*

The woman, whose name was Angie, I think, laughed and ruffled his hair before heading to the drink table.

"Heeeey," I chirped when I drew near, and both kids waved exuberantly. I squatted to their level and handed over the candy. "I brought you both something."

"Thank you, Auntie Lehra," they replied in unison while unwrapping the suckers.

Jaxon pointed his at me and waggled his eyebrows. "Have I told you you're the most beautiful woman in this room?" I stifled a snicker.

Leaning forward, I pressed a kiss to his cheek, leaving a lip print there. He already had two on the other side. "Thank you, Jaxon. That means a lot coming from you." I straightened the lapel of his little jacket. "You look incredibly handsome in this suit."

"Thanks, babe." *Oh my god, this crazy kid.*

I turned to his twin in her wheelchair. "Janie, that dress is so pretty." She was wearing white on white with a small faux fur shrug. Brilliant snowflakes danced across the shiny material of the dress.

"Thank you. Lolli made it for me."

"Did I hear my name?" a voice sing-songed from behind me, and I stood and turned to find Tora and Tony approaching with matching smiles on their faces. They had recently come out as a couple, and I couldn't have been happier for them.

"Lolli! Pops!" Janie squealed before accepting hugs from her soon-to-be grandfathers.

As the guys visited with the kids, I introduced myself to Abby, their babysitter for the evening, and learned that she wanted to be a pediatrician one day. She had long hair braided into cornrows and the emerald dress she was wearing set off her smooth, dark skin.

"That dress is stunning," I told her, and she beamed.

"Mr. Auburn brought it for me." Her eyes widened. "He said I could keep it. And he and Ms. Gianna bought a new Christmas tree for the home and got presents for everyone."

My heart was full, and I'd never been prouder to work for *Bouvier*.

"Merry Christmas, Tink." I would have recognized the voice even without the nickname.

Twisting my head, I found Cruz standing beside me at the canapé table. "Merry Christmas," I said, lifting my glass of wine in a toast. "You look nice."

Actually, *nice* wasn't exactly the right word for how he looked in a solid black suit and shirt, the first two buttons open at the neck to reveal a masculine smattering of chest hair, but I figured he might not take it as a compliment if I called him dark and dangerous.

"And you look... wow." He patted his chest. "I think you gave me palpitations in that dress."

I laughed and elbowed him. "Stop teasing."

He gave me a once-over that made my skin flush before turning to the table and picking up a canapé with some kind of creamy spread and a rosette made of a thinly sliced meat. Studying it, his brow creased.

"I need man food."

"Man food?" I scoffed, and he nodded.

"These are tiny. Just big enough to piss me off." He popped it into his mouth and chewed. "It's tasty, but they need to make them bigger."

"They're canapés. They're supposed to be cute and small," I argued.

Giving me a mock scowl, he said, "Cute is not something I look for in food."

I stacked four of them on top of each other and handed them to him. "There ya go. Manly canapés." He crammed them into his mouth, and I laughed. "Are you satisfied now?"

Swallowing the enormous bite, he crooked his lips up on one side in a sexy half-grin. "Not quite, but it's a start."

Oh. My. Was that statement filled with innuendo or what?

I drained my wine in a single gulp, and Cruz looked down at my now-empty glass. "You want another drink?"

"That would be awesome. I'm drinking the chardonnay."

"Be right back," he said, heading for the elegantly decorated bar in the corner.

Picking up one of the tiny snacks, I ate it and had to agree with Cruz. It was barely enough to whet the appetite. My eyes scanned the room, and I had to do a double take when I saw who was walking toward me with a big smile on his face.

"Dwight?"

"Hey, babe," he said, jogging the last few feet and wrapping me in a hug.

"I'm... what are... oh my god!" He set me down, and I rested my hands on his shoulders and smiled happily at him. We were the same height with my heels on. "I can't believe you're here. I thought you were headed to Aspen."

"I was about to, but I wanted to stop by and—"

Surprise me by telling me you packed me a bag so I can go with you? I thought hopefully.

Dwight was interrupted from finishing when Cruz returned with my drink. "One chardonnay for the lady," he said before noticing the new-comer and holding out his hand for a friendly shake. "Hey, man. I don't think I know you. I'm Cruz Estrada."

"Dwight Jones."

"Oh, Lehra's boyfriend. Nice to meet you."

"And who are you? One of the servers?" Dwight asked, and his snooty tone instantly annoyed me, though Cruz just smiled easily.

"No, I'm Auburn Bouvier's driver and personal security."

Embarrassed by Dwight's arrogance, I said, "Cruz is also a reserve police officer. He works with the Emergency Service Unit."

"You're like a paramedic or something?"

Cruz shook his head and took a sip of the brown liquid in his glass. "No, though we are trained in medical and rescue operations. We serve as the city's SWAT team."

"Oh," Dwight said with a fake smile. "I could never do that. I abhor violence."

Cruz's smile showed all his teeth before he responded with a curt, "As do I, *Dwight*. We're tasked with *preventing* violence, not causing it."

Oh, eek! The look on Cruz's face said he might reconsider causing a bit of violence just then, and I broke in. "Dwight surprised me tonight. He was just about to tell me why he's here." I linked my arm with his and gave him a warning squeeze.

"I was just about to reveal the big surprise," he said, taking my glass and handing it to Cruz before leading me to the center of the room.

What is he doing? I wondered, still hoping he planned to invite me on his family's Christmas trip. My mouth fell open when Dwight dropped to one knee and took my hand. *Oh. My. God.*

The crowd slowly caught on and spread out, every eye on us as the room was bathed in silence.

"Lehra," Dwight said with a huge smile on his face and a ring box suddenly in his hand, "you are the bright spot in my life, and I love you more than anything. Please honor me by being my wife."

I was sure my face was as red as my dress while I processed what he'd just said. *He's proposing? Now?*

We'd talked vaguely about marriage a couple times, but I never expected him to do this now. We didn't even live in the same city.

I loved Dwight, but I wasn't ready for this. *Was I?*

"Lehra?" he prompted, his smile faltering a little, and I felt like a million tons of pressure had landed directly on top of my head. Everyone was looking at me expectantly, so I forced out the only words I could say in this situation.

"Yes, of course."

Everyone clapped as Dwight slid the ring on my finger before standing and wrapping me in his arms. "I love you," he whispered.

"I love you too," I replied, meaning every word, but I was still conflicted about getting engaged without more discussion about our future.

Someone handed us each a glass of champagne, and everyone came up to congratulate us as we sipped. I showed off my ring, which was huge and a little busy for my taste, but I couldn't deny it was a beautiful piece of jewelry.

The well-wishers finally drifted off, and I squeezed Dwight's hand. "Can we talk for a second?"

"Yeah, sure," he said easily. "Let's go outside." Linking his fingers with mine, he stopped at the security desk and grabbed his wheeled suitcase before leading me out the front door. He took off his jacket and hung it on my shoulders when I shivered from the cold.

"Well, that was a surprise," I started as Dwight looked down and tapped on his phone.

"Good. Glad I could surprise you. Do you need a ride home?"

"I, uh, what?"

"I'm calling an Uber to take me to the airport. I was wondering if you wanted me to drop you off or if you're staying a bit longer."

"The airport?" I asked stupidly, like I'd never heard the word before.

"Yes, I'm taking a late flight to Aspen."

I blinked. We'd just gotten engaged a half hour ago. "And you're not taking me?"

He tilted his head to the side, an apologetic smile on his face. "Babe, we've talked about this. My mom only allows family on these trips. It was the same with my brother. Tiffany didn't start coming with us until after she and Daniel got married."

"Oh, I guess I just thought…" My voice trailed off.

Dwight gave me a soft kiss on the lips and then returned to his phone. "Don't worry. As soon as we get married, you can come with me. It's really fun. We all ride snowmobiles up into the mountains, and then at night we relax in the hot tub with drinks."

"That does sound fun," I murmured. *Too bad I'm not invited.*

"The car is only a minute away," he said, wrapping his arms around me and holding me close. "I'm so excited to marry you, Lehra. I'll make you the happiest woman in the world."

The chill inside me thawed a bit, and I nuzzled my lips against his neck. "I wish you could stay."

"Me too, but you know I can't. My mother would be so disappointed if I missed Christmas."

What about me? I wanted to ask but didn't have time. A Hyundai pulled up to the curb, and after another kiss, Dwight pulled his jacket from me and slipped it back on.

"Bye, fiancée," he said with a wink as the driver loaded his suitcase into the back.

And then he was gone, leaving me feeling very, very alone.

Chapter 10

"Surprise!"

I widened my eyes as Dwight's mother walked past me and into my apartment.

"Mrs. Jones," I said, attempting to put some enthusiasm into my voice as I shot my fiancé a look of panic. "I didn't know you were coming. Here. To my apartment." *Which is a complete mess right now.*

I waddled toward her with toe separators between my toes since I'd been giving myself a pedicure.

"We thought it would be a nice treat for me to visit," she simpered, pressing a kiss to my cheek. Then she looked down my body and blinked rapidly. "I can see you weren't expecting company."

Well, I was, but I was expecting Dwight. And only Dwight. As evidenced by the tiny red negligee I'm currently rocking.

"Oh. Yes, um, let me just go get my robe." I immediately crossed my arms over my bosom and then penguin-walked down the hallway, cursing under my breath the entire trip.

Shit, shit, dammit to fuck. Way to impress the mother-in-law, Lehra.

I'd only met Dwight's mother once in the two years we'd been dating. She was a rail-thin woman with a brown bob and a face like a fox. She'd been distantly polite, and I had the feeling she didn't like me very much.

Slinging on my robe, I tied it tightly around my waist and hobbled back to the living room. "I'm ba-a-a-ack," I announced, spouting out a nervous giggle. "And decent now. Hi, Dwight."

"Hey, honey," he said, giving me a peck on the cheek. I hadn't seen him since our engagement, and I'd hoped this little reunion would be... different.

"Let me just move this stuff. I was doing my toes." I picked up the towel from the coffee table and placed all the polish bottles back in the small basket before setting them on the dining table. *God, she's going to think I'm such a slob.*

"You really should find a good pedicurist," Mrs. Jones advised, glancing down at my freshly painted toes. *Harlot red to match my naughty nightie.*

I hadn't grown up with money, and therefore, had never had a professional pedicure in my life. I could definitely afford it now, but I had gotten pretty good at it, so I continued doing it myself.

"Okay, I'll think about that. Can I get you anything to drink?"

"A sparkling water would be divine," she replied with a smile.

"I don't have any sparkling water. I have regular and can add some Sprite to it," I said with a chuckle.

Mrs. Jones was not amused, and my own smile faded. "Tea is fine."

"Coming right up. Dwight, why don't you help me in the kitchen?" I requested in a sweet voice that contradicted the daggers I was shooting at him with my eyes. I also needed to check on dinner. "I made that Mexican casserole you like."

"Sure, babe, and that sounds good."

As soon as we were in the kitchen, I whirled on him and hissed, "Why didn't you tell me you were bringing your mother? I was wearing lingerie for fuck's sake."

Dwight winced. "Sorry, I thought you'd be surprised."

Oh, I was surprised all right. I wrapped my arms around his waist and laid my cheek on his chest. "It's okay, but some warning would have been nice."

He kissed the top of my head and smoothed his hands up and down my back. "For the record, I liked the lingerie."

"Maybe you can see it again later, if you're a good boy," I purred, snuggling a little closer.

"Probably not," he said with a tiny laugh. "Unless you want Mother to see it too."

"After she leaves," I whispered, kissing my way up his neck. "Did you book her a hotel close by?"

"Yes," he said and then hesitated. "I got us each a room at The Langham."

I halted my kissing and looked up at him. "So I'm staying with you at a hotel? I thought we could christen my new apartment since you've never been here before." I wiggled flirty eyebrows at him.

Dwight stepped back and looked down, running a finger along the forest-green countertop. "This is a really nice place. Even better than the pictures you sent me."

"You didn't answer me, Dwight. Should I pack a bag to stay at the hotel?"

His nose wrinkled as he shook his head. "No. Mother wouldn't approve of us staying together."

I blinked in confusion. "Where does she think you sleep when you come to visit?"

He lifted one shoulder and then let it fall. "I tell her I get a hotel room when I come here."

I gawk at him and shake my head slightly. "That's just weird, Dwight. You're thirty-three years old."

"Do you need some help in there?" Mrs. Jones called from the living room, startling me into action.

"Crap, the tea," I whispered before calling out, "Just a minute."

I rushed to put some water in the kettle and set it on the stove to heat while I found the chamomile tea bags I kept for when I had trouble falling asleep.

Then I searched through my cabinets for a nice teacup. I wasn't exactly fancy. I drank my coffee from a mug Artie had given me that read, *Blow Me... I'm Hot*. Somehow, I didn't think Mrs. Jones would appreciate that.

I finally found a pretty cup that had a matching saucer and no chips. It had been my grandmother's before she passed. Pouring the hot water in it, I placed the teabag on the saucer, and questioned Dwight.

"How does your mom take her tea?"

"Cream, sugar, and one lemon wedge."

"Crap, I don't think I have any lemons." I searched the refrigerator, frantically waving my hand around like I could conjure one from thin air but still came up empty. *This right here* is why some notice would have been appreciated. "Take that out to her, and I'll get the cream and sugar," I hissed after closing the fridge.

I'm sure Mrs. Jones expected to be served from a cream and sugar set, but I didn't have one. I always poured my creamer from the carton and added sugar with the little scoop in my canister. *Fucking hell... why can't I be fancier? This is nerve-racking!*

I located a little white bowl and scooped enough sugar into it to give the entire building diabetes before placing it on a wooden tray along with a teaspoon and the carton of vanilla creamer. Oh well, she'd just have to deal with my basic-ness.

Before returning to the living room, I checked the casserole and determined it needed a few more minutes.

"Here we go. Sorry I didn't have any lemons," I apologized, setting the tray down on the coffee table.

"I'm sure it will be fine." My future mother-in-law picked up the creamer and stared at it like she'd never seen an actual carton of the stuff before.

And maybe she hadn't. Dwight once mentioned that his mom had house-hold staff.

She poured in a dash and added approximately three grains of sugar before stirring it around. Feeling the need to break the silence, I sat on the chair adjacent to Dwight and asked, "How was your flight?"

His mother took a sip and answered, "Simply dreadful." I wasn't sure if she was talking about the flight or the lemon-less tea with cream crudely poured from an actual carton. "They let people from coach use the first-class restrooms."

"That is… unimaginable," I managed to say, putting on what I hoped was a sympathetic smile. "How was the traffic? It can be hell coming from the airport in early evening."

Mrs. Jones's back stiffened, and Dwight reached over and patted my hand. "Honey, Mother doesn't approve of cursing."

What the hell did I say? Oh… I said hell.

"I apologize. New York traffic is enough to get a saint to curse," I said with a kind of high-pitched giggle that gave away my nerves.

"I'm sure it is," the woman replied before setting her cup down, apparently finished with it now. "I wanted to come see you so we could get started on the wedding planning."

"Oh, that's… great. Thank you, but we have a while. We'll have to wait till Dwight is able to move here."

"The wedding will take place a year from now, next February. It was the only date available for the club in the next two years. We got very lucky because someone canceled."

"The club?" I questioned.

"The country club," she replied, like I should frigging know that. "Our family has been members since the Roosevelt administration."

"Which one?" I had no idea why that seemed a relevant question, but I was still processing that our wedding date and location had already been set.

"Which what?"

"Which Roosevelt?"

"Oh, Theodore."

"Did you know that the teddy bear was named after Teddy Roosevelt?" I asked. *Again... is this a relevant tidbit of information? No, no, it is not, but this woman had me on edge.*

"Yes," Mrs. Jones replied shortly. "Anyway, moving on." She pulled a white calendar with *Bride* printed across it in a flourished font. "Here's your calendar with all the dates we have so far. I'll keep you abreast of any additional events for you to add."

"Can we just go back to the location for a second? I always wanted to get married in Missouri. In my hometown."

Dwight's mother looked like I'd just told her I wanted to travel to another planet and marry Marvin the Martian.

My fiancé spoke up with a patronizing pat to my hand. "Honey, Mother has already put down the three-thousand-dollar deposit."

"My church only charges a hundred dollars for members, so that would save a lot of money," I said brightly. "Maybe your mom can get a refund."

"We're not religious," she said with a tight smile. "And there are no refunds at the club."

"Then maybe you should have asked me before putting down the deposit," I argued as gently as I could.

"I asked my son," she said, tilting her chin up a bit. "He gave me the approval."

My eyes went to Dwight, and he smiled and nodded. "It will be great, Lehra. I promise. The club is beautiful. Very classy."

"Well, are the dates flexible? I always pictured a summer wedding."

"I already said that's the only date available for the next two years," Mrs. Jones said with an edge to her voice. "Besides, summer would be too hot."

Sensing an impending argument, Dwight broke in. "Mother, aren't you tired? We should probably go ahead and check in at the hotel."

"Yes, we can grab dinner there."

I didn't even mention the casserole I'd prepared because, to be honest, I was ready for them to get out of my apartment. I was overwhelmed and needed to get my thoughts together.

"Morning, Mrs. Jones."

"Good morning, dear," she said brightly as she swept into my apartment the next day with a large white book beneath one arm.

Dwight trailed in after her and stopped just inside the door to press a kiss to my cheek. "Hi, honey. Did you sleep well?"

"Not really," I said in a low voice. "I'm already stressing about all this."

His eyebrows furrowed. "Don't stress, babe. My mother is here to help, so you have nothing to worry about."

Yeah, that's exactly the problem.

Glancing over my shoulder, I saw her setting the book on the coffee table and taking a seat on the couch. I'd thought about this all night and knew I needed to enlist my fiancé's help in dealing with his mother.

"Dwight, I really need you to have my back with all this wedding stuff."

"Of course, Lehra. Why wouldn't I?"

"I don't know, but you didn't last night. Not at all."

He huffed out a long sigh. "The venue is already set, and there's nothing we can do about it now, so just move on."

Gritting my teeth, I closed my eyes and counted to ten. When I opened them again, Dwight was standing behind the couch, looking over his mother's shoulder.

"Come along, Lehra," Mrs. Jones said. "We have a lot to get to today."

Trudging toward the couch where she was patting her hand on the seat beside her, I felt like I was heading to my own execution. *Do all brides feel like this? Isn't this supposed to be fun?*

I sank down and took a look at the thick book in front of me.

"This is your bridal bible," she explained. "I've taken the liberty of making some selections for you so you don't get overwhelmed by all the choices."

"I think I'll be fine," I said patiently.

"Of course you will," she said in a patronizing tone. "I've made myself a duplicate of this book, so if you have any questions, you can call me and just refer to the page number."

Wanting to make a sarcastic comment, I bit my tongue and flipped open the first page. There were several selections of bridesmaid dresses that were actually a very pretty style, though they were all in the palest of pinks.

"These are nice," I said, pointing to one. "This one would look great in a darker pink or purple."

"I think the blush color would work better for a February wedding."

"Well, I like brighter colors."

"Of course you do," Mrs. Jones said, looking up at her son. "Dwight dear, why don't you go get us some breakfast? Egg white veggie omelets, please." Then she winked at me. "Lehra and I have to watch our figures for the wedding."

"Actually, I'm good with where I am. I'm a size six."

"Multiple experts have determined that size four is the perfect size for a wedding dress."

"The only expert I need is Dwight," I said, matching her faux-sweet tone and looking up at him with raised brows. *Time to put up or shut up, buddy.*

His eyes darted between his mother and me, and he swallowed nervously. "I, um, I think Lehra looks fine."

Not exactly a resounding endorsement, but at least it was something.

"I'll have a side of bacon with my omelet," I told him, a tiny bit out of spite, and he nodded before scurrying to the door.

"Be right back."

"We'll come back to the colors at a later time. Let's discuss cakes," Mrs. Jones said, flipping to another section, which was marked with a blue tab. "What do you think of these?"

To be honest, I liked all of them, but after studying the photos for a few moments, I decided on an elegant, tiered cake with pearl embellishments.

"We probably don't need four tiers though. That will be entirely too much cake," I noted, and Mrs. Jones frowned.

"Actually, I was planning to ask the baker to add an extra tier. We have four-hundred and thirty-three guests to invite from our side. Do you have an estimated headcount for your people?"

"Four-hundred and... uhhh, that seems like a lot."

She smiled indulgently. "Yes, well, we have lots of business associates and other important people that *must* be invited. How many do you expect from your side?"

"Maybeeee, sixty? I was picturing more of an intimate wedding with friends and family."

"The friends and family will still be there," she reasoned. "Now, what flavor of cake do you prefer?"

Guess we'll come back to that too.

We miraculously agreed on cake flavors. A classic white cake with buttercream frosting was my favorite. I adored the moist, fluffy cake blended with the creamy sweetness. Red velvet was a close second, so we decided to use that for the groom's cake.

"Do you know how many bridesmaids you'd like?" my future mother-in-law asked.

"Three," I said firmly. "My friends Nicolette, Artie, and Gianna." I smiled. "I'm also going to be in Gianna's wedding in May."

If Mrs. Jones hadn't had so much Botox, I'm sure her forehead would have wrinkled. "Artie?"

"Yes, he's one of my best friends."

"He?"

"Yes, Artie is a guy." I let out a little laugh. "I told him we would call him a bridesman."

The woman winced and shook her head. "No, that just won't do. He wouldn't match."

"It will be fine," I assured her. "I thought he could wear a tux or suit with accents of the bridesmaid colors in his tie and pocket square."

"But that would throw off the aesthetics, dear. Think of the pictures." She literally shuddered like I'd suggested we have a troop of gorillas in the wedding.

Dwight returned then and his mother instantly started in. "Dwight darling, tell Lehra she can't have a *man* as a bridesmaid."

"A bridesman," I corrected, fixing my eyes on my future husband. "I want Artie up there with me."

His eyes left mine, and he audibly gulped. "I think that would be..." We waited for his answer, and when it came, it boiled my blood. "Weird. Maybe Artie can be an usher or something."

"No, I want him as part of my bridal party. I'm pretty sure that's my decision."

"But not at the expense of the aesthetics," Mrs. Jones inserted. "Aesthetics are very important in a wedding ceremony."

I could feel my face heating. *She could stick her aesthetics right up her...*

"Oh, then I should get some say in who the groomsmen are, right? Because I'm assuming you want to ask Chad."

"Yeahhh," Dwight drew out, placing the food down on the low table in front of us and eyeing me warily.

"Well, I think he's way too tall. He wouldn't *match*," I snarked, throwing Mrs. Jones's words back at them. "And besides, you've told me he cheats on his girlfriend all the time. That's definitely not the type of *aesthetic* I'm looking for at our wedding."

He blanched. "Yes, but Chad is one of my best friends."

"And Artie is one of mine," I replied smartly. "So either they both stay or they both go."

His mother's mouth tightened into a thin line. "We can circle back to it." *How did I know she was going to say that?* "I think I'd like to take my food back to the hotel and eat. This has worn me out."

Yeah, well, you've worn me out, lady.

Mrs. Jones came to New York with Dwight for the next three months, and I was supposed to travel to Michigan in June to look at the venue. Luckily my bridesmaids and bridesman agreed to go with me because, honestly, I needed a bit of backup.

I certainly wasn't getting it from Dwight. He agreed with his mother on every single point of contention, and I was so damn annoyed with him.

In March I was told that my idea to have the groom's cake in the shape of a golf ball was tacky. I'd truly thought they would like that one since Dwight loved golf and the wedding was being held at a country club with a golf course.

In April, Mrs. Jones informed me that the florist agreed with her on the flowers and that bright colors simply wouldn't work for a February wedding. So we were going with something called blissful blush. That would also be the colors of the bridesmaids' dresses.

And in May... well... that one really pissed me the fuck off.

"When you're here to look at the venue next month, we'll go to Tremblay's to shop for dresses," Mrs. Jones said.

"I saw that on the calendar and have been meaning to talk to you about it. I'm getting a Bouvier dress. Since I'm an employee there, I can get a custom-designed dress for next to nothing."

Her nose scrunched up and she glanced at Dwight before looking back at me. "But all the brides in our family shop at Tremblay's." She said the name of the store like it was the eighth wonder of the world.

"That's nice, but I'll be the one wearing it, and I want a *Bouvier*."

If eyes could pierce holes in a person, I would have been swiss cheese right then. "You *must* get your dress at Tremblay's. Tremblay's is the best. It's where our family shops."

I pictured myself with a big ole gun, à la Samuel L. Jackson in *Pulp Fiction*, pointing it at Mrs. Jones while I growled, *Say Tremblay's again. I double dare you, motherfucker.*

Instead I smiled, a kind of feral thing that crept across my lips like an angry snake. "Well, I'm not part of the family yet, am I?" *As evidenced by the Aspen trips*, I almost said but didn't.

"It won't hurt to take a look. I booked the appointment months ago, and it would be rude to cancel now."

"But—"

Dwight interrupted with a soft hand on my shoulder that I barely restrained from shaking off. "Honey, it's like a tradition, and it would mean so much to Mother."

What-the-fuck-ever. I would go and pretend to look, but on my wedding day, I was showing up in what I damn well pleased. "Fine," I muttered, dreading my trip in June like I'd never dreaded anything in my life.

CHAPTER 11

IT WAS A STEAMY Monday night in June, but I walked to the restaurant where I always met Paul. I needed time to think.

He wasn't pressuring me to tell my mother I'd discovered the truth about my paternity. He was letting me make that call regarding when and if I shared that with her.

He was, however, very anxious to tell Auburn and Monty that I was their brother. Paul was in the process of divorcing Chloe—about damn time—and that was helping to heal old wounds with Monty. He talked about it a lot with me. And also about his daughter, Evie, who had gone missing over a decade ago.

God, it was fucking weird to think I had another sister out there somewhere. Was she still alive? I somehow felt drawn to this woman I'd never met, and I wished there was something I could do to find out what happened to her. I could read the pain in Paul's eyes and hear it in his voice every time he talked about his only daughter.

Maybe I should let him tell Auburn and Monty about me. How would they feel hearing I was their brother? Would they think I was some crook trying to scam a wealthy family? Because that was the absolute last fucking thing I wanted.

Checking my phone, I saw that I still had thirty minutes before I was supposed to meet Paul, so I bought a Diet Coke from a vendor and settled on a park bench a couple blocks from the restaurant. The first sip went down cold and refreshing, the carbonated bubbles adding just the right amount of burn.

It had been around two years since I'd found those letters, and I stared up at the fading sky as I let my mind drift back.

My father wasn't my father. I allow that realization to roll around in my brain for a while.

I haven't read all the letters in the box; there are more than twenty years' worth, after all, but I've read enough to learn that Paul Bouvier is the man who gave life to me. Allegedly.

For two weeks I scour online articles and Paul's Wikipedia page.

That still blows my mind. The man I think is my father has a goddamn Wiki page!

I find that he's married to a woman named Chloe and has sons named Auburn and Montague. There's mention of a daughter, Evelyn, who went missing years ago. That sparks my interest, and I spend hours one night poring over what is apparently a cold case. The young woman vanished without a trace.

Paul was head of his company for decades, and his oldest child, Auburn, took over a few years ago. There's a shit-ton of info on that guy, including lots of pictures of him at events, always with a beautiful woman on his arm.

There's not much on Montague, or Monty, as I've seen him referred to a couple times. But I do find a couple paparazzi photos from around the time the sister went missing. He and Auburn both have the same eyes as me.

Fuck.

Pacing around my apartment in League City, which is between Galveston and Houston, I try to figure this out. I have the basics from my research, but who the hell is the real Paul Bouvier?

I could ask my mother, but I don't. I'm not sure how I'd even go about bringing it up with her. "Hey, Mama. I found a secret stash of letters that

Papa received from a man named Paul Bouvier. Quick question... is he my dad? And can you pass the carrots?"

Yeah, not doing that.

She's been through enough with losing Papa, and besides, the letters were something he didn't seem to want her to know about.

No, the only way to get answers is to go directly to the source. But how do I get access to him? The man's net worth is in the billions, so I'm pretty sure I can't just waltz up to his door and announce that I have paternity questions for him.

The answer to this conundrum appears later that night when I'm researching the Bouvier fashion company. There's a "Join Us" tab on the website, and when I click, a list of job openings appears. Right at the top, I see it.

"Driver and Personal Security - Executive Level."

As I stare at that link, I tap the flat of my thumbnail against my top teeth for so long, I'm concerned I may chip the enamel. And then I click on it.

My fingers tap across the keys as I fill out the application and hit "Send."

"Whew," I say on a long exhale and stare at the screen.

Two days later, I receive a reply asking me to come in for an interview.

Quinnie picks me up at the airport, and I give her a bone-crushing hug as she laughs. "I'm so happy you're here. Noelle is going to freak when I pick her up from preschool and she sees her Uncle Cooz is in the car."

"I can't wait to see her," I say as we climb into the car.

"What made you finally come for a visit?"

I hesitate for a moment before saying, "Actually, I have a job interview. But don't tell Mama yet. I don't want to worry her if I don't get it."

"Okay, I won't say anything. What's the job?"

"Corporate security. The pay is great, and I'd get to be near you."

"Oh my god, Cruz. Are you serious? You really might move to New York?" Her eyes are wide as she turns on her blinker and enters traffic.

"I probably won't get it. I'm sure it's very competitive."

"They'd have to be stupid not to hire my big brother."

It turns out Quinnie wasn't far from the truth. I make it through the first interview with a guy named Tony, and it goes really well. The next day, I'm invited back for an interview with the big man himself, Auburn Bouvier.

Walking into his office, I watch him intently. Does he know about me? Or am I a dirty little secret that's never spoken of?

When I see no flash of recognition on his face, I don't know if I'm relieved or disappointed. During the interview, I find him intelligent and a bit serious. He's not friendly, but he's not a dick either. He's just... straightforward.

I have to force myself to focus because the entire time we're talking, one question keeps popping into my mind. "Are you my brother?"

"Do you have any questions for me?" he asks when we're nearing the end.

"I was wondering about weekends. As you saw on my resume, I've done police work, and I'd like to apply to be a reserve officer on the force."

He sits back in his chair and crosses an ankle over his other knee as he flips through my paperwork with one hand. "I think that would be fine. I'll mostly need you for workdays. Occasionally for weekends if I have an event to attend, but I can give you advance notice."

"That sounds good."

He puffs out a sigh that makes him sound older than his thirty-seven years. "For some reason, the damn press finds me interesting, so I like to have a driver that can also serve as security. Your background is very impressive and exactly what I'm looking for."

"Thank you," I reply.

When he stands, I do too, and we shake hands. The unspoken question runs through my head again. Are you my brother?

Two days later, I'm offered the position. The first thing I do is call Mama to talk with her about it. I tell her the job is security for a corporate bigwig, the pay is excellent, and housing is included.

She assures me she will be okay and is actually excited that I'll be near Quinnie and Noelle. She worries about my sister living in the big city since her husband, Flynn, works such long hours at the hospital.

Thank god my mother isn't a clinger. She's always said that she never wants to keep her little birds cooped up in her nest. She wants us all to fly.

So I take a chance and accept the job with the man I'm pretty sure is my brother.

Only a few weeks into my training, I'm working solo when Bouvier calls me on the phone. "Cruz, I'm meeting with my father in my office today. I need you to go pick him up and bring him here. Tony has the address."

"Yes, sir," I say as my heart tries to pump out of my chest. This is it. I wasn't sure it would ever happen, but I'm finally going to meet Paul Bouvier.

I find the address after making only one wrong turn and pull up to the security gate. They check my credentials and allow me to pass through. The house is like a damn palace, and I steel myself as I pull into the circular driveway.

Getting out of the car, I leave it running as I round the back. Before I can approach the house, the front door opens, and I instantly recognize the man who exits. My feet forget how to work, stopping my body near the back door of the Bentley.

Paul has a smile on his face as he walks down the steps in a perfectly tailored light-gray suit. Then he meets my eyes.

I can see instantly the way his face changes. It's teeming with shock but he doesn't look angry. He takes another two steps and stops a few feet away from me, his eyes never leaving mine.

A lump rises in my throat, and I swallow it down. "Do you know who I am?" I ask, and he nods.

"Yes, Cruz. I know who you are."

Christ. He recognizes me. Is this really happening? Wetting my lips, I ask the question that's been burning through me since I first found those letters.

"Are you my father?"

A tentative smile pulls the corners of his lips upward, and he nods once again as his eyes shine with unshed tears.

"Yes. I am."

Tonight's dinner was going well. Paul brought up the idea of talking to Auburn and Monty again, but he dropped it when I said I wasn't ready. It was one of the things I admired about him. He never pressured me. Plus, I think we both enjoyed our secret dinners together, just talking and learning about each other.

"Is something bothering you?" he asked in that intuitive way he had.

Poking my salmon with my fork, I chewed on the inside of my cheek before speaking. "I like this girl, but she's off-limits."

Paul chuckles. "I've been in that situation before."

I knew he was referring to my mother, and I smiled. He'd always been completely honest with me about falling in love with her.

"It's not exactly like that. She's getting married to someone else, so I know it's a no-go. But I still really care about her, and…" I searched for the words. "I'm worried about her, Paul. For the past few months, she's been different. She rarely smiles anymore, and god, she has the best smile. I've missed seeing it."

"Have you asked her what's wrong?"

"I have, and she says it's nothing. I can tell something is bothering her though, and it looks like she's lost weight." I shrug. "I guess I'm at a loss as to what I should do next. She's so withdrawn, and I don't know how to help her with... whatever."

His lips pressed together in sympathy. "There's not much you can do until she's ready to talk about it. I'd say just be there for her. Don't pressure her to tell you what's wrong because that may drive her farther away."

"You're right," I said, taking a bite of my fish. "She lives near me, so maybe I'll drop by more often, just to say hi or whatever."

"That's a good idea. Let her know she has a friend if she needs one." Paul's eyebrows lifted infinitesimally. "She's *just* a friend, right?"

"That's all it can ever be," I told him, trying not to let the disappointment of that show on my face.

I was still thinking about our conversation when I exited the elevator on my floor and paused beside Lehra's door. Maybe I should see if she wants to go get ice cream or something.

As I raised my hand to knock, I heard something from inside her apartment. *What the hell? Was that a sob?* Listening closely, I heard it again. Yes, she was definitely crying.

"Lehra?" I called, knocking on the door in a panic.

"Y-yes?" The raw misery in that stuttered word was gut wrenching

"What's wrong?" I asked gently.

"N-nothing. I'm fine." It sounded like she was right on the other side of the door.

"You're not fine. Open up and talk to me."

"No, it's... I'm fine," she repeated, and I felt as though I was about to bust out of my skin. She was obviously the furthest thing from *fine*.

Putting some force behind my words, I called out, "Open the fucking door right now, Lehra, or I swear to god, I'll break it down."

CHAPTER 12

I HADN'T MEANT TO sound so harsh, but I was really worried about Lehra. And my bossy tactic worked. The door creaked open, and a red-rimmed eye peeked out.

Her words came out in little hiccuping gasps. "Did... you... need... s-something?"

Pressing gently on the door until she allowed it to open, I stepped inside and closed it behind me. "I need you to talk to me, Lehra. You weren't at work today. Are you sick?"

"No, it's other shit." Ash-gray eyes blinked up at me, causing a couple tears to spill over the rims of her bottom eyelids.

Those tears hit me as hard as if I'd shed them myself, and I reached for one of her hands, needing the contact with her. She must have needed it too because her slim fingers closed around me.

"Why don't you talk to me about it? I'm a good listener."

Her bottom lip trembled as she whispered, "It's the wedding and Dwight's mother." The way she said that last word told me what I needed to know.

"Do we have a Mom-zilla situation going on?"

"Yes!" she practically shouted, and my understanding seemed to fuel something inside her. "That woman is driving me fucking crazy." Lehra's tears, which seemed to be ones of despair, were now driven by anger.

Yanking her hand away, she flailed her arms wildly and began ranting. "It's every damn thing. She's in charge, and I'm just supposed to let her run everything, despite the fact that it's my wedding. It's like I'm nothing but a prop."

She was in full fired-up mode now, pacing and shaking her head with her arms crossed over her stomach. I couldn't help but notice how loosely her gray T-shirt hung from her frame, and it worried me.

"Have you talked to Dwight about it?"

Lehra whirled, and her eyes blazed with a fury that surprised me. "Ohhh, yesss," she hissed. "He takes her side on everything. Ev-er-y-thing! So it's two against one, and I get outvoted."

My own fury rises up that a man wouldn't support the woman he's planning to marry. What a fucking douche. "It's not her wedding, Lehra. She doesn't get a vote."

"Right?" she snapped, but I was aware her anger wasn't directed at me. "I had all these hairstyles pinned on my Pinterest board, but she didn't like any of them. I want an updo, but she wants my hair down. Of course Dwight agrees with her. And they're not mean about it. They turn every-thing into a compliment." Her voice turns mocking. "Oh, Lehra dear, you have such pretty hair. It would be a shame to hide it."

"So they're gaslighting you."

"Yes," she fervently agrees, poking me in the chest. "They *are* gaslighting me. I've tried to stand up for what I want, but when they gang up on me, what can I do?"

She turned and paced away, and I couldn't help but notice how matted her hair was in the back. I wished I could run my fingers through it and soothe her like I used to do with my sister when she was little. When Quinnie would get scared in the middle of the night, she would come and climb in my bed, turning her back to me and asking, "Will you rub my hair, butter?" She had trouble pronouncing brother, so that's what she called me.

I didn't have an answer for Lehra, other than me committing homicide against Mrs. Jones and her pussy-ass son, so I simply let her talk.

"It's not just the hair thing. It's also the venue, the bridesmaids, the wedding colors." She spun around to face me again. "And if I hear the word *aesthetic* one more fucking time, I'm going to scream. Do you understand me?"

I answered the rhetorical question with a quiet, "Yes."

"I'm supposed to go to Michigan this weekend with Gianna, Artie, and Nicolette. Mrs. Jones said she would arrange the flights, but when she sent the tickets, there wasn't one for Artie. She said, 'Oh dear, the airline must have made a mistake,' but I know she's lying. We've had several arguments about Artie being my bridesman, and she hates the idea, so she's trying to freeze him out."

"That's fucked up," I replied. "That should be your decision."

"I know, and now I'm worried she's going to railroad me into getting a dress I don't want. There's this shop where everyone in her family gets their wedding dresses, but I want Devereaux and Tora to make mine. They've already done some sketches, and I've fallen in love with one of them. It's what I want."

Her eyes pleaded with me, and goddammit, she was going to have me on her side, even if her dickhead fiancé wasn't. "I think you should get whatever fucking dress you want, Lehra. Can your mom help?"

With a softening expression, she said, "My mom is awesome, but she works as a nurse and can't take off work for all these *meetings*. I'm... all alone."

A large crack forms down the center of my chest at the despair in her voice, and I mentally go through my weekend schedule. I'm not supposed to work, so I made the snap decision to take a little impromptu trip to Michigan.

Lehra stomped to the coffee table, which was littered with what looked like wedding invitations, and picked up two hands full. "I hated all the invitations Mrs. Jones sent, so I told her I would pick them out from here. I decided I wanted to control at least *one thing*, so I went to that printer where we picked up the Christmas party invites. They gave me all these samples."

She waved them wildly around, and her tears were back, ones of frustration and hurt this time. "But now I'm second-guessing everything. What if I pick the wrong ones? What if Dwight hates them?" She threw them up in the air and watched as they drifted down to the rug and table. "What if they're right, and I'm just stupid?"

Her voice broke, and that was fucking it for me. These assholes have broken her down to the point that she doesn't even feel confident picking out an invitation to her own wedding.

Crossing the room in two strides, I yanked her into my arms and pressed her face against my shoulder. And I let her cry. The sobs shook her body, and I could feel them emanating from her slight frame and piercing directly in my bones.

"Shhh," I soothed, finally allowing one of my hands to go to her hair and gently smooth out the tangles. "You're not stupid, Lehra. They've gotten into your head, but I won't let that happen anymore. You're not alone, sweetheart. I promise you're not."

She sobbed and sniffled, and I could feel the dampness of her pain seeping into my shirt. My heart wanted me to tell her to call off the whole fucking wedding because any man who treats her like this doesn't deserve her. But my mind was telling me that wasn't what she needed to hear, so I wrapped both arms around her and held her tight, loving the feel of her against me and wishing she was mine.

"You give the best hugs," she murmured, and I lowered my lips to the top of her head.

"That's what Noelle says, but I think she's biased."

That earned me a small laugh, and I pulled back a little to see a slight smile on Lehra's blotchy face. "Noelle is a smart girl. If they gave out Nobel Prizes for hugs, I would nominate you."

I wanted to punch the hell out of everyone who had taken that smile from her face the past few months, and an idea hit me.

"Go change into some workout clothes."

Her eyebrows knitted together. "Why."

"Just trust me, Tink," I said, and she nodded as she backed away.

"I do trust you, Cruz." *Music to my ears.*

As I watched Lehra walk down the hallway, her shoulders were still way too tight for my liking. If she were mine, I would have another way I could relieve her stress. I would be on my knees, and she would be loose and sated within minutes. But she's not mine, so we'd have to go with plan B.

Lehra stared down at the pale-blue boxing gloves I'd strapped onto her and then looked back up at me. "Are we going to fight?" she asked skeptically.

"Hell no. I don't want to get my ass kicked," I teased. "You're going to punch Dwight's mother."

Her gray eyes widened. "Trust me, I'd love to, but I don't want to sleep on a cot and share a cell with some woman they call Hattie the Hammer."

I busted out laughing and shook my head as I led her to a punching bag in the training gym I'd brought her to. "You're not actually going to hit *her*. You're going to picture her face right here," I drew a circle on the black leather, "and hit that."

Her teeth sank into her bottom lip, and I caught the hint of a smile. She liked this idea. After showing Lehra how to throw a proper punch, I rounded the bag and held it.

"Ok, Tink. Let her have it."

She pulled back her arm and hit the bag. Her form was correct, but she didn't put any weight behind it. "Come on, Kincaid. Is that all you got?" I taunted, and her next punch was a little harder but not much.

Letting go of the bag, I walked toward her and fixed her with a scowl. "You're supposed to be working out your frustrations, Tink, and you can't do that with these weak-ass hits. I need you to knock the fuck outta that bag. Pour everything you've got into it." Her shoulders pulled back, and she nodded. "What is Mrs. Jones's first name?"

Lehra smirked before answering, "Bambi."

A chuckle left my lips, and I tapped my knuckles against the bag. "Give me a good punch right here, and say *fuck you, Bambi*. Can you do that for me?"

She appeared to be fighting a smile, which I planned to fully pull from her by the time we were done here. "Okay, I can do that."

Taking my place behind the bag again, I said, "Come on, Lehra."

I could see the fire in her eyes now as she pulled back her arm and punched the bag. "Fuck you, Bambi."

"Good girl! Louder now."

"Fuck you, Bambi!" Another solid punch.

"You got it, Tink. Show 'em who's the goddamn boss."

Her arms moved so fast, they blurred before my eyes as she threw punch after punch. I was having to put some serious muscle behind holding the bag for her, and a trickle of sweat dripped down my back.

"Fuck you, Bambi! Fuck you, Bambi! FUCK YOU, BAMBI!" she screamed as leather met leather over and over.

Lehra was breathing hard, and her body was covered with a fine sheen of sweat when she finally stepped back and shook out her arms. But she was smiling. A big, upward curve of her pink lips that creased the corners of her eyes. A real, genuine smile.

Then she reared back and gave one final hit, the strongest one yet. "Fuck you, Bambi!" she sneered through gritted teeth.

That's when we both noticed a woman with closely shorn black hair standing beside us, her eyes wide in apparent horror.

"Oh, um, my mother-in-law," Lehra explained, "not the Disney deer."

The woman's mouth turned up into a smile, revealing that her canine teeth had been filed into sharp fangs. "Right on," she said, holding out her own red boxing gloves for Lehra to pound. "Give her hell, killer."

Lehra laughed, and it sounded so fucking good to hear that again. "I definitely will."

The other woman leaned closer, her eyes darting side to side before whispering, "And if you need backup or an alibi or something, you just let me know. My name's Hattie."

Then she strolled off, leaving Lehra and I staring at each other with wide-eyed amusement on our faces.

"I say we wrap up this evening with some ice cream," I tempted as Lehra tugged her T-shirt on over the black sports bra and tight shorts she was wearing. I was trying not to stare, but fuck, she was beautiful.

Her lips twisted to the side like she was unsure, but she nodded. "Okay."

We strolled down the street side by side. The sun was down, so the muggy evening air had cooled a bit.

"You feeling better?" I asked, and Lehra flashed me a smile.

"Much. Thank you." She was silent for a few seconds before speaking again. "If I ask you a question, will you tell me the truth?"

"Always."

She inhaled and exhaled a loud breath. "Do you think I look okay? I mean size wise?"

Stunned out of my head, I stopped in the middle of the sidewalk, and Lehra turned to face me, her eyes wary. "Did someone say something to you?" My voice was dark, low, and demanding, and she stared at the traffic passing behind me and shrugged. "Answer me, Lehra. Did that bitch say something to you?"

"Just a comment a few months ago. Something about the perfect size for wedding dresses, and that I needed to watch my figure. Then a couple small comments since then."

My blood, which had been on a low simmer all night, threatened to boil right the fuck over. "Is that why you've lost weight? To please her?"

She shook her head. "No, not at all. I've just been too stressed to eat, I guess. I don't think I look bad when I look in the mirror, but those comments keep coming back to me inside my head." Her chin dipped, and she scuffed her toe against the concrete. "I just wanted an unbiased opinion."

Well, you've come to the wrong place, sweetheart, because I'm very biased when it comes to you.

"Did Dwight have anything to say?" I asked, the name tasting bitter on my tongue.

"He said, 'Lehra looks fine.'"

I wished I was back in the boxing gym so I could work out some of my own frustrations with Dwight Jones's head on the receiving end. Instead I took a step closer and cupped her face, lifting it so she had no choice but to meet my eye.

"Fine? You are way more than fine, Tink. You are hot as fuck."

Her cheeks flushed, and she tried to look down again, but I didn't allow it. "I drove a limo full of models to a location shoot last week, and none of them... none... of... them..." I reiterated slowly, enunciating each syllable, "held a goddamn candle to you."

Our eyes locked, and the air around us turned magnetic as I held her face in my hands. I'd never wanted to taste another person's lips as much as I wanted to taste hers. I wished I could take her home and bury myself inside her to show her how perfect her body was. If only I could stand her in front of a mirror and run my reverent hands over every inch of her until she could see her own worth. Her own beauty.

Our mouths were so close, I could practically taste her, and she smelled so fucking good. Even through the sweat and grime from the gym, she still smelled like pineapples and sunny days. It was intoxicating.

I was treading into dangerous territory here, and she looked as though she wanted to follow me down that perilous path. But she wasn't mine, and I needed to remember that, so I backed away and forced a smile onto my face.

"Did that answer your question?"

She huffed out a breathy, nervous laugh. "Yeah, I think I got it."

"Great," I said, forcing my voice into one of teasing as I placed my hand on the small of her back and guided her down the sidewalk once again. "Anytime you want me to come over to ogle your body and tell you what I think, just let me know."

"You're a true humanitarian, Cruz."

"Well, I was nominated for a Nobel Prize in the hugs category," I said with false modesty.

She giggled. "True."

This entire situation was worse than I thought. Bambi Jones wasn't just fucking with the wedding stuff. She was getting inside Lehra's head, making her doubt herself, and I wasn't going to have it.

"You know, my mama is pretty awesome, so dealing with a horrible mother figure may be a bit above my pay grade." I pulled out my phone and dialed as Lehra looked questioningly at me. "But I know someone who can help."

"Who?" she asked, and I answered her question as soon as the person on the other end of the phone picked up.

"Gianna, I need your help with Lehra."

"Anything," came the quick reply.

"We're dealing with a bitchy mother-in-law-to-be."

"Oooh, now that's my jam," she drawled, and I could practically see her rubbing her hands together in glee. "I'll be right over."

"Give us about an hour," I requested. "I'm about to buy Lehra a triple scoop of ice cream."

CHAPTER 13

"I BROUGHT WINE AND nachos. Let's take a bitch down," Gianna announced, marching into Lehra's apartment with her hands full of bags.

"Well, alrighty then," I deadpanned. "Thanks for coming over on such short notice."

"You're welcome," she said, plopping the bags on the coffee table. "What's going on?"

"She had a major meltdown earlier, and I didn't know what else to do," I told her quietly. "I took her to the gym and let her punch some shit, and it helped, but I think she's going to need support."

"So you decided to call in a professional?" she asked with a smirk, and I nodded.

Lehra came out from her room, rubbing her hair with a maroon towel. While she'd been in the shower, I'd cleaned up the invitations she'd tossed earlier and stacked them neatly on the table.

"Gia, you didn't have to come over," she protested.

"Of course I did. I have a master's degree in dealing with bitchy mothers-in-law. Chloe Bouvier is the most evil woman on the planet, and since she's no longer in our lives, I could use the practice. Don't want my skills to get rusty."

Lehra smiled, and the two women settled onto the blue-and-white striped couch while I sat in the matching chair.

I spoke as Gianna pulled wine glasses and a corkscrew from one of the bags and proceeded to open the bottle of white. "Lehra's future mother-in-law and Dwight have been gaslighting her to get their way with the wedding," I said in explanation. "She can give you the details."

Gianna paused, her mouth agape, and then waved the skewered cork at Lehra. "Let me get this straight. Your *fiancé* is allowing her to boss you around?"

"Yes, they team up and outnumber me."

Gia's head shook from side to side, making her raven ponytail bounce. "Oh hell to the naw. You don't just have a mother-in-law problem, honey. You've also got a fiancé problem." *Damn right she does.* She placed a comforting hand on Lehra's knee. "The first time I ever went to Chloe's house, she was a complete bitch. As soon as she disrespected me, Auburn told her off and dragged me from the house. We've never been back."

Lehra's eyes widened. "Wow, that's amazing. I can't see Dwight ever doing that."

"Then you need to set his ass straight. Otherwise, you'll be stuck forever with his mother running your lives. There's a whole section on Reddit about atrocious mothers-in-law. Some of those stories will blow your wig off. Why don't you tell me what's been going on?"

For the next thirty minutes, Lehra explained the situation while we ate and drank. Flopping against the back of the couch, she groaned. "Dwight's mother is one of those people who says everything so nicely, you're not sure if she's insulting you or not."

"Ohh, the fake sweet. Yeah, I can go toe-to-toe with her on that shit," Gianna replied with a confident nod.

"Like she keeps referring to my family as 'your people.' *Your people can stay at the hotel, Lehra. Do your people eat seafood?* But she smiles when she says it, so I'm not sure if she's being offensive or not."

"*Your people*?" Gia asks. "Yeah, that definitely feels offensive. What else do I need to know?"

"Um, let's see. Her first name is Bambi, and she hates cursing."

"Bambi," Gianna repeated with a roll of her eyes. "Social climber, I assume?"

"For sure. Their family has money, but she acts like they're the Rockefellers or something."

"Or the Bouviers," Gianna replied, a sneaky grin crossing her full lips, and I could see her brain formulating a plan. Then her voice turned high-pitched and daringly sweet. "Golly, I hope I don't accidentally curse while we're there. I wouldn't want to offend *Bambi*."

Lehra let out a laugh. "What are you up to, Gia?"

She waved a hand. "Let me take care of the mother-in-law. The only way to handle a haughty woman is to out-haughty her. I've learned a thing or two since I met Auburn. I have to put up with pretentious assholes all the time."

"You're awesome, Gianna. You too, Cruz. I feel so much better after bitch-punching the imaginary Bambi at the gym tonight."

Gia ate her last chip and tilted her head to the side. "I'm just sorry I haven't been around more to be there for you. I hate you've been going through this alone."

"You had your own wedding stuff to deal with and then the honeymoon," Lehra told her.

Gianna pulled out her phone and tapped her thumbs against the screen. "Well, I'm back now, and I'm your ride-or-die. Now, who all is coming this weekend?" She looked up from her phone, waiting for a response.

"You and me. Nicolette and Artie."

"And me," I piped up and two sets of eyes snapped to me. "What? I figured five against two couldn't hurt." I smiled softly at Lehra, and she returned it. "I told you I would support you, Tink."

Her lips rolled between her teeth as we locked eyes again. "Thanks Cruz. And Dwight won't be there Friday and most of Saturday. He's involved in some kind of project for work in Chicago."

"Five against one then," I corrected. "I like those odds."

When I pulled my gaze from Lehra, I found Gianna staring speculatively at me, her finger tapping against her top lip. "Cruuuuuz."

Shit, did she notice the way I was staring at Lehra?

"Yes, Giannaaaa?"

Her lips formed a wicked smile. "How do you feel about ascots?"

"I love that movie," Artie said as we exited the plane.

"*Bridesmaids* is my favorite," Lehra agreed before elbowing me playfully. "I can't believe you've never seen that before, Cruz."

"I didn't know what I was missing. Melissa McCarthy was hysterical."

Gianna slipped on a pair of big, dark sunglasses as she descended the last step and pointed us toward the waiting limo. I'd driven Auburn's limousine many times, but the only other time I'd been a passenger in one was my senior prom.

We all climbed in, and the driver took off. Gia had insisted that we leave New York at the ass-crack of dawn on this Friday morning, and we pulled up to the Jones house four hours earlier than Bambi was expecting us.

When Dwight's mother answered the door, she was in a battleship-gray bathrobe, had some kind of mud mask on her face, and was sporting huge curlers in her hair. The look of shock on her face was worth getting up before the sun this morning.

"Wha—Y-you're here," she stammered, looking around at all of us in confusion while fingering the curlers. Good. We'd thrown her off. "Your flight wasn't supposed to land until noon."

Gianna took over and strutted—literally *strutted*—past the woman and into her large house. The rest of us followed, stopping in the high-ceilinged foyer.

"Yes, well, with the *unfortunate mix-up* with the airline, we decided to just come in my private plane. I do hope that's okay," Gia finished sweetly, still wearing her movie-star sunglasses.

"It's, um, you... private plane?" The woman patted at the crust on her face, and her neck flushed. "But I sent tickets."

Lehra spoke up, her saccharine tone matching Gianna's. "I'm sure you can get a refund, since it was the *airline's* fault that Artie didn't have a ticket, right?"

God, I was so fucking proud to see her standing up to this woman. All she needed was friends at her back to stand strong. And isn't that what we all needed?

Our entire group looked like a billion bucks. Gianna had *styled* us, whatever the fuck that meant. Artie was wearing a classy black suit with velvet lapels, and the ladies looked like a force of nature in power suits. Nicolette was in black and white, Gianna in blood red, and Lehra was looking fine as hell in Barbie pink.

And me? Well, I was wearing a goddamn ascot with my ivory double-breasted jacket and pants in a material Gianna called *summer linen*. I felt a bit ridiculous, but Gia said she wanted me to look, and I quote, "like a fancy pants." She hadn't detailed her plan, simply told us to follow her lead.

"These are my bridesmaids, Artie Baker, Nicolette Bell, and Gianna Bouvier," Lehra introduced. "I know you've been looking forward to meeting them."

"Oh, yes, of course," Bambi gushed fakely, her ambitious eyes straying to Gia. "M-Mrs. Bouvier, I didn't realize... when Lehra said she had a bridesmaid named Gianna, I didn't know it was you. I saw photos of your wedding online. It was simply stunning." She looked like she was about to get down and lick Gianna's stilettos.

"It was," Gianna said airily. "Some have called it the wedding of the decade."

I knew she was acting, putting on a good front for the woman who had been bullying Lehra. Gia didn't give a hoot about the trappings of wealth. A year ago she'd been fresh from graduate school and had next to nothing. Now, after marrying Auburn, she had more money than she knew what to do with. She may be playing the part of a snooty bitch, but in reality, she was the kindest woman in the world, one who would bend over backward to help her friends or anyone in need.

I hadn't thought about it before, but I suddenly realized she was technically my sister-in-law, and that made me smile. Then she looped her arm through mine and tugged me closer.

"And this is Marvolo. He's the wedding planner who helped me, and I couldn't have done it without him." She pressed a hand to her chest like she was getting emotional. "He was invaluable to me, and we're so lucky to have him with us today."

Marvolo? What the fuck kind of name is Marvolo?

"Oh, uh, how lovely," Bambi said through gritted teeth. "I didn't realize we were hiring a wedding planner. I've been doing fine on my own."

"Hmm, I'm sure you have," Gianna replied with an edge of condescension in her tone. "But Marvolo here has coordinated some of the finest weddings from all over the world, including for royalty." She looked up at me and batted her eyelashes.

I'm going to murder you, I told her with my intense gaze. I knew nothing about coordinating weddings.

"Royalty? Is that so?" Bambi's appraising eyes snapped to me, and I gave her my full-wattage smile.

"Ahhh, yes. Queens and princesses and such," I intoned, putting on an accent of indeterminable origin. I sounded like a cross between Arnold

Schwarzenegger and Antonio Banderas. I attempted to think of something else I could say, but the only thing that popped into my mind was a name from the movie we'd watched on the plane. "Zee last was Princess Melissa of zee McCarthy Islands."

Lehra camouflaged her snort with a cough, Nicolette covered a smile with her fingertips, and Artie turned his back, suddenly becoming extremely interested in an ugly painting on the wall of the foyer. Gia simply gave my arm an encouraging squeeze.

But Bambi bobbed her head up and down. "Oh Princess Melissa. Yes!" Her voice was almost a squeal. "The princess is stunning and such a kind-hearted soul. She does all that work with the, um, the…"

"Zee Pygmies?" I suggested.

Christ, Estrada. What the hell?

CHAPTER 14

CRUZ WAS CRACKING ME the hell up. Every time he used that ridiculous accent, I couldn't even look him in the eye without laughing. And the white suit and ascot were the icing on the cake.

Okay, admittedly, he was actually pulling that look off with his fit body and deeply tanned skin against the light fabric.

And Gianna was rocking the snooty bitch act to a tee. She actually had Bambi Jones flustered. She patted my future mother-in-law's arm and said, "You go do whatever you need to do to get ready. I've hired a car and driver for the weekend so you don't have to worry about a thing. We'll just shit in the living room and wait for you."

I had to literally pinch my lips between my finger and thumb to keep from barking at the look on Bambi's face. "You'll… what?"

"I said we'll sit in the living room and wait for you," Gia said, blinking innocently. Now I understood what she was talking about when she said she might *accidentally* curse in front of Bambi.

A little over an hour later, we were at the country club to check out the site. It was nice and would provide a lovely backdrop to the wedding, but it wasn't somewhere I would have chosen.

"I guess this will do," Gianna said, unimpressed, "but I do wish you'd consulted with me and Marvolo before locking yourself into this place, Lehra."

I barely caught her subtle wink. "The decision wasn't mine. I was *informed* that the wedding would be here after it had already been rented," I replied, finding it easier to speak up when I wasn't being tag-teamed by Dwight and Bambi.

Gianna knew this but she acted shocked, turning narrowed eyes on the other woman. "Why wasn't the bride consulted about the venue? That's highly irregular."

Bambi stumbled over her words, "Well, you see, there was a, um, a cancellation, and it was a really urgent matter to, well, to snap it up before someone else did." She snapped her fingers in the air to demonstrate. "And I do love the club so much."

Gia gave her the most syrupy smile I'd ever seen. "How sweet. Maybe you should get married and have your ceremony here. Perhaps a vow renewal ceremony?"

And for the rest of the day, every time Bambi gave an unwanted opinion, Gianna would reply with some version of, "Fantastic. You should do that at your ceremony, Bambi. But let's ask Lehra what she thinks about it for *her* wedding."

I'd never felt so heard. So supported. Nicolette and Artie spoke up several times as well and backed up everything I wanted. And dear, sweet Cruz, with his ascot and crazy accent, declared everything I requested *magnifique!*

When we dropped off Bambi at the end of the day, she looked so defeated, I almost felt sorry for her. But not quite. The woman needed to be taken down a peg or two.

Besides the groom's cake, the completely ridiculous headcount, and the location—which I had resigned myself to—I'd gotten pretty much everything I wanted. The boring menu had been replaced with a vibrant selection of foods, and the wedding colors were now springy and bright rather than blissful fucking blush.

The color choosing had almost made me bust a gut. After I'd whispered what I wanted to Cruz, he'd gone into full Marvolo mode, pressing his fingers into his temples as he closed his eyes.

"I am tinking... I am tinking... of zee rejuvenation of life. Zee approaching of spring. Zee blossoming of love." He'd opened his eyes and clapped twice before shouting, "And voila! We will use zee spring colors."

He was seriously the best.

At the hotel last night, Nic, Gianna, and I checked into our room, and then congregated in Artie and Cruz's room across the hall. We laughed, drank, and ate everything on the room service menu before calling it a night.

Today we went back to the Jones house to pick up a subdued Bambi in the limo before heading to a couple bakeries to taste the cake flavors we'd chosen.

"Mmmm, this one is so good," Artie said, swallowing a mouthful of the wedding cake. "I think pricking out cake has been my favorite part so far."

I managed to keep a straight face even as Bambi's cheeks flushed a dark crimson at the pricking comment. My friends had been dropping "accidental" curse words every chance they got. Cruz even mentioned the almond-cherry *cockies* I liked to make.

Bambi tilted her chin up and smiled at me, and I braced myself. I'd come to recognize the expression that said she was about to say something snarky. "Lehra dear, maybe that's enough cake. You're trying on dresses today and don't want to be bloated."

Cruz's hands balled into fists, and I gripped his knee beneath the table to keep him from leaping across the table.

In a calm but firm voice, I said, "No worries. I've already chosen my dress and been measured for it this week."

Bambi's face went apoplectic, and I was afraid she was going to pop a blood vessel in her temple. "B-but we're getting your dress at Tremblay's. We already decided."

Cruz's hand found mine with a tight squeeze, and it filled me with strength and bolstered my resolve.

"No, *you* decided. I told you I already had plans to have Devereaux design my dress."

She opened her mouth to speak, but Gianna broke in. "Tremblay's? I think they applied to carry one of the *Bouvier* lines but were rejected. We have very high standards." Her smile was laden with sugary sweetness. "I mean, I'm sure it's fine for... *your people*, Bambi, but not for our Lehra. Auburn and I think of her like a sister."

She reached over and took my other hand, and my heart was so damn filled with the love and support of my friends.

Bambi spluttered out a weak protest, but Gianna said, "If you have a problem with it, you can take it up with my husband," before taking another bite of cake. And that shut my future mother-in-law right the fuck down.

"Well, I haven't had that much fun since I dated that clown in college," Artie quipped as we re-entered the hotel where we were staying.

Cruz chuckled. "I thought Bambi was going to faint when Nicolette said you'd picked out the bridesmaid dresses with the *slut* up the thigh."

My friend brushed imaginary lint off her shoulder. "That was a good one. Now what are we doing for the rest of the day and night?"

"I'm taking these damn heels off and propping my feet up for at least two hours," Gianna stated. "Then after dinner, we can hit the hot tub."

"I'm down for some hot tub time," Artie said, raising his hand like a third grader asking permission to go to the bathroom. "What are we having for dinner?"

"I could go for a burger," Cruz said.

Nicolette tapped her mouth with one fingertip. "Me too. I wonder if they have tater twats?"

We all burst into laughter.

Yep, I love my friends.

We were spread across the two king beds in the room, wearing comfy shorts, tank tops, and no shoes.

"God this bed is comfortable," I groaned, staring at the ceiling as the air conditioning cooled us off.

"Mmhmmm," Nicolette said, half asleep.

Gianna turned on her side and propped up on her elbow. "What do you think Dwight is going to say about the changes to the wedding stuff?"

I shrugged. "I honestly don't think he gives a crap what color the brides-maid dresses are or what kind of chicken we serve at the reception. I think he just hates conflict with his mother and didn't want to argue with her. Now he doesn't have to because we handled it." Reaching out a hand, I gave hers a squeeze. "Thank you again for everything. I have the best friends in the world."

"Well, you were an awesome friend to me when I first moved here and barely knew anyone." Her eyes filled with emotion. "I'd had a horrible day with the lost luggage and rude people, and you were the first friendly person I met."

I was about to respond when we heard a knock at the door. "Probably the guys," I said, rising and donning one of the hotel robes. "I'm going to put this on so I don't give them a nipple display."

"Yeah, you're a little pointy. Might scare Artie, but I don't think Cruz would mind," Gianna said with a smug smile.

What the hell is that supposed to mean?

But when I opened the door, it wasn't the guys from across the hall.

"What the hell is going on, Lehra?" Dwight asked, storming into the room.

Nicolette popped awake with a little squeak from Dwight's volume, and I glanced back to see her and Gianna scrambling from the beds.

"We're just gonna, um, go across the hall," Gia said, grabbing shirts from her suitcase and tossing one to Nic.

"Hi, ladies. Sorry for the intrusion," Dwight mumbled, but his angry eyes were still on me.

As soon as they were gone, I lifted my eyebrows and stared him down. "Problem, Dwight?"

"Yeah, I've got a problem. You and your friends have spent the past two days bullying my mother. She called me in tears."

"No one bullied your mother," I said in what I hoped was a placating tone and not the pissed-off one that was bubbling inside me. "We simply made choices, and she was outvoted." *Like I've been outvoted on everything since we started this.*

"She said you changed everything."

"Not the location," I shot back.

"I won't have my mother treated like this," he growled, tossing his hands up and pacing away, giving me his back, which I suddenly had an urge to throw something at.

"But you were fine with me being bullied and stressed out to the point that I've cried almost every night for the past few months. And when I tried to talk about it, when I cried on the phone to you, you didn't give two shits. Not once did you stand up for me, Dwight."

He whirled back and glared at me. "But she's my mother."

"And I'm going to be your wife, Dwight!" I yelled. "Your fucking wife! I should get some say in my own damn wedding."

"I just want you two to get along and be close," he argued, his voice slightly quieter than mine.

"I'll play nice on the holidays and when we come for visits. One day, when I've had time to get over all the snarky comments she's made to me, then maybe we can forge some kind of decent relationship."

"It's going to be a lot more than just holidays," he muttered, and I took a step closer to him as dread rose up in my throat like a hot-air balloon.

"What's that supposed to mean?"

Dwight closed his eyes and let out a long-suffering sigh. "Just that she'll be our neighbor."

"A-are your parents moving to New York?" Then I added quickly, "I don't think there are any apartments available in my building." I'd talk to Auburn and beg him not to rent anything to the Joneses since he owned the building.

Dwight's hands pushed through his hair as he avoided my eyes. "I've been meaning to talk to you about this. I'm not getting transferred to New York."

I was beginning to understand, and the dread in my throat turned into full-fledged panic. "So what does that mean?"

Still not looking at me, instead choosing to stare out the window at the tall buildings beyond, he said, "It means I bought the house next to my parents." He finally brought his eyes back to mine and smiled. "For us."

"Without talking to me?" I shrieked in a tone that was probably nearly inaudible to human ears.

"It was going to be a surprise," he said weakly, still fucking smiling at me, even though he was turning my life upside down.

"You expect me to move? That wasn't the deal, Dwight. You said you've always wanted to live and work in New York. And I'm training for my dream job at a company I love."

"There are plenty of secretary jobs in Detroit," he argued, and I felt like my head had suddenly turned into an active volcano.

Secretary jobs? I was going to be the personal assistant for one of the most powerful men in New York City. It was a hell of a lot more than a *secretary job.*

I looked Dwight over as everything began to shift. I'd thought if we could just get through the wedding, we could start our lives together and be happy. But now he was changing everything and without even discussing it with me. Was this what my life was destined to be like?

And living next door to Bambi? Hell. Fucking. No.

"I'm not moving, Dwight," I told him with finality.

He gritted his teeth and glared at me. "So you want to continue doing the long-distance thing after we're married? I want to share a bed with my wife."

"Maybe you can go share a bed with your mommy since you'll be right next door," I snapped, letting my anger get the best of me.

"Don't be ridiculous, Lehra. Just get a fucking job in Detroit and stop making everything so difficult."

"Why don't you apply for jobs in New York so we can live there *like we planned*?" I said pointedly. "There are lots of architectural firms in New York besides the one you currently work for."

He shoved his hands onto his hips and directed his gaze at the corner of the room, and that's when I knew. He didn't *want* to move. Or maybe mommy dearest wouldn't allow it.

"Look, we can decide all this after the wedding, okay?" he muttered. The eyes that I'd loved for so long came back to me, and I was almost bowled over at the realization that... I wasn't in love with Dwight anymore.

While I was still reeling and trying to sort through my feelings, he went on. "We'll switch everything about the wedding back to how it was before, and you'll be nice to my mother and stop being a bridezilla."

I was snapped out of my self-reflective stupor at those words, and every cell in my body vibrated with anger. "Bridezilla? Have you lost your fucking mind?" Taking a few steps forward until I was right in his face, I gritted out, "I've been the farthest thing ever from a bridezilla. I've acquiesced to every damn thing *your mother* wanted, even though this wasn't her goddamn wedding. I've dealt with her bitchy comments and your pussy-ass mama's boy shit until I'm blue in the face."

Dwight's eyes widened in what looked like fear. "Lehra..."

"No, don't you use that tone with me. I'm done, Dwight." Pulling the ring from my finger, I shoved it into his hand and drove the point home. "*Done.*"

Chapter 15

Dwight looked down at the sparkling ring in his palm, and his eyes lifted to mine in incredulity. "You don't mean that."

But I did. I'd been carrying a heavy weight, like a thousand pound blackbird roosting on my shoulders, and I hadn't even realized he was there until my words gave him wings. Forced him to fly away and leave me light and free.

"I do mean it. I'm not going to live like this."

"But we can get through this. I love you, and you love me." I stared wordlessly at him, and his head cocked to the side. "Don't you?"

"I did love you, Dwight, but..." I heaved all the air from my lungs before taking a fortifying breath. "You've been chipping away at it until there was only a thread left hanging."

"But there's a thread," he cajoled. "We can rebuild what we had around that."

"That thread was snipped the second you called me a bridezilla."

His hand dragged down his face, and he suddenly looked very tired. "I didn't mean that. I know you're not, Lehra. You've been nothing but sweet and accommodating. I should have... I should have supported you."

"Thanks for saying that, but the damage is done." My thumb and forefinger stroked one of the soft robe ties as I gathered my words. "For future relationships though, you need to think about your priorities, Dwight.

Your family will always be your family, but you have to make room at the top of your heart for the person you love. They need to come first."

He swallowed hard. "I'll work on it," he said, and I liked to think he actually would. But probably not. "Can I kiss you goodbye?"

"You haven't kissed me for months, Dwight. Why would you want to kiss me now?"

"But it would have been uncomfortable since my mother was always with us."

"Think about that statement, and you'll see exactly why you're now single," I retorted, walking to the door of the hotel room and opening it in an invitation for him to leave.

Two people fell into the room, one landing on her knees. *Nicolette.* Gianna helped her up, and their guilty eyes darted to each other and back to me as they stood side by side.

"We were just going to get some, uh, ice," Nicolette muttered, jerking a thumb over her shoulder. I looked pointedly at the eavesdroppers' empty hands, and apple-red bloomed on their cheeks.

"But we realized we forgot the bucket," Gianna said, grabbing Nic's hand. "We'll just go get that." And they sprinted across the hall and knocked furiously on the guys' door. "Let us in. Now!"

Once they slipped inside, I allowed my slight smile at their antics to fade away and turned back to my former fiancé. "You can go now."

He trudged like his feet were made of lead and stopped beside me. I looked up at him, and he seemed to find the finality in my gaze because he nodded. "Goodbye, Lehra."

"Bye, Dwight."

As soon as he walked out, I closed the door behind him and leaned my back against it, waiting for the tears to come.

But they didn't.

I wasn't sure why. Maybe I was in shock that my relationship of over two years was over. Or maybe I was a bit relieved that I'd dodged a bullet.

Nonetheless, once I was sure I wouldn't be a blubbering mess, I slipped the room's key card into the pocket of my robe and went across the hall to the guys' room.

Before I could even knock, the door opened, and I was yanked inside and directly into Nicolette and Gianna's arms.

"Oh, honey. We heard," Nic cooed. *I knew these bitches weren't getting ice.* "I'm so sorry."

"Me too," Gianna sniffled. "Just let it all out. We're here for you."

I laughed and gently pushed them away. "I'm okay. I promise."

Two sets of green eyes peered expectantly at me like I was going to collapse into a heap at any moment. "You're sure?" Nicolette asked, and I nodded. "How do you feel?"

"Would I sound like a total bitch if I said I feel a little relieved and a lot hungry?"

"Not at all," Artie assured me, rising and kissing the top of my head. "You've been going through a lot, so I think it's normal to feel relieved that all that stress is off your shoulders."

"I say we go get the lady some greasy food," Cruz suggested from his perch on the chair in the corner.

"I'm ordering tater twats in honor of Lehra finally getting rid of that twat she was engaged to," Artie announced, making us all laugh.

After a long dinner at a dive bar, where we'd gorged on bacon-cheese tater *twats* and burgers, we all settled into the large hot tub on the second floor of the hotel with plastic glasses of wine.

"Oh yeah, that's right. Rub mama's tootsies," Gianna groaned, holding her feet over one of the lower jets.

We talked and drank for a while, with Cruz getting out to refill our glasses twice from the bottles we'd left on the table. I tried not to stare at the droplets of water dripping down a perfect set of abs every time he rose.

I was feeling so relaxed and grateful as I glanced around at my friends, Artie and Nic across from me, Gianna on my right, and Cruz on my left.

"I just wanted to say thank you for coming this weekend, and I'm so sorry I wasted your time."

"You didn't waste our time," Nicolette insisted. "Why would you say that?"

"Because you went above and beyond for me on all this wedding stuff, and then I called it off."

Artie rolled his eyes. "Honey, we're glad you broke up with Dwight. Nic and I never liked him."

"Really? You never said anything."

"We didn't want to mess up our friendship by badmouthing your boyfriend," Nicolette said quietly.

Artie added, "The few times we met him, we both thought he was a bit of a pompous douche." He lightly splashed water at me. "Not to mention the sex stuff."

"Artie!" I scolded, splashing him back.

"Ooh, what sex stuff?" Gianna asked. "Did he have a teeny wienie?"

I giggled and took a sip. "No, his wienie was... fine, I guess. And can we please talk about something besides my sex life?"

"Baby doll, that was no sex life. You had a better relationship with the shower head."

"You can stop talking now," I warned as everyone laughed.

"It wasn't the actual peen. He just didn't know how to use it," Artie kindly informed everyone. "His motto was good guys finish first."

Cruz smirked into his glass before taking a drink. "He looks like the type."

"And what's your motto, Cruz?" Artie asked sweetly, and I noticed I wasn't the only one whose eyes kept drifting to the man beside me.

Cruz chuckled. "My motto is *good girls* finish first, and the *right guy* finishes at least third."

Well then...

Artie fanned himself dramatically. "Good lawd! Why did this hot tub just get a thousand degrees hotter?"

"Cruu-uuz!" Gianna whined. "Now I miss Auburn." She stood in her white bikini and reached for a towel. "I think I'll go call him."

"Make good choices," Cruz called as she wrapped the towel around her and slipped into her sandals. She flipped him off.

"I don't get it. Why would you come third?" Nicolette asked in a quiet voice before widening her eyes. "Ohhhh, are you talking about being with two women at once?"

Artie and I locked eyes, sharing a smile. Nic may be a brilliant bio-chemist, but she could be a little ditzy where sex was concerned.

"Honey," Artie said patiently, bumping her shoulder with his, "he means he makes his woman come twice before he... you know..."

"Oh." She looks Cruz up and down. "You can really do that? I thought men like that were a romance book myth."

"Cruz Estrada... the man, the myth, the legend," Artie said in a movie announcer voice that made us all crack up.

"I'm really glad you invited us," Nicolette told me, polishing off the rest of the wine in her glass. "I needed to get away."

"Work still driving you crazy?" I asked sympathetically, sinking into the water a little and finding a jet that shot the most delicious stream of water against my lower back.

"Yep," she said on an exhale and then yawned.

"Welp, time to go," Artie proclaimed, standing and pulling her up by the hand. "I don't have the upper body strength to carry you upstairs, Nic."

Bet Cruz could, I thought, admiring the breadth of his chest and shoulders from the corner of my eye.

"Probably right," she said, rubbing at one eye. "Wine always makes me sleepy."

"I'll be up in a little bit," I told them, my voice sluggish. "I just found a jet of water I may date now that I'm a single woman."

"Lehra! You're cheating on the shower head?" Artie exclaimed, pressing a dramatic hand over his chest.

"Haha, asshole. It's hitting my back, not... *down there*."

"I'll stay with her and make sure she gets back to the room okay," Cruz told him before twisting his head toward me with a slight frown. "Unless you wanted to be alone for a while?"

Closing my eyes, I tilted my head back against the edge of the tub. "No, stay and become a prune with me."

"Bye, kids," Artie sang before leading a yawning Nicolette from the pool room.

I sensed Cruz shifting beside me, and then he let out a low groan. "Mmmm, I think I just found one of those jets you were talking about."

"Nice, huh?"

"Hell yeah. Feels soooo fucking good."

Those words and the deep timbre of his voice sent my imagination on a fast train to inappropriate thoughts. *Is that what he sounds like when he's fucking? Can he really make a woman come twice? How big is his dick?*

Also, can I see it?

Then it was like the Earth paused its rotation for a brief second, causing everything to shift, and I became very aware of Cruz, of my shoulder pressed against a large bicep. I mean, I knew he was seated right beside me, but suddenly the moist, chlorine-filled air seemed to sizzle around us.

He must have felt it too because I could feel his gaze on the side of my face. Opening my eyes, I found his face only inches from mine, and an unbidden sound whimpered up from my throat.

"You okay, Tink?" he asked, and I nodded. "You need anything?" Again, I nodded, inching my face closer. Cruz looped his arm around my shoulders until the side of my body was snug against his.

The only sound was the bubbling of the water as he brushed a damp piece of hair behind my ear before settling his hand on the side of my neck. Our eyes held like they had been bound together by invisible ropes as his thumb drew a slow circle around the hollow of my throat. The move was intimate, a lover's touch, and I wanted more. So much more.

Cerulean eyes dropped to my lips and then made a slow inspection of every inch of my face before rising once again to mine. He must have found the answer to his unasked question there because he closed the distance between us, angling his mouth over mine.

My body came alive quicker than a flash of lightning, tingles alighting my skin. I'd never had such an instantaneous response to a kiss, and when his tongue made an unhurried trek across the seam of my lips, they parted like he was Ali Baba uttering *open sesame*.

Our tongues met, and I knew immediately that this man knew how to kiss a woman. He licked into my mouth, circling and caressing my tongue with strokes of warm velvet.

My body became heated, the water around me feeling suddenly tepid, though it had to be over a hundred degrees. This man was so sexy he could make a nun hike up her habit and spread her legs.

And speaking of spread legs, how did I end up straddling his lap? I wasn't sure, but I damn well liked it. Our torsos were pressed tightly together, and Cruz's hands slid up and down my thighs before settling on my hips. His every touch was confident and sure, the simple strokes of his thumbs against my hip bones promising that he had the ability to take me to heights I'd never before reached.

With a mere tightening of his fingers, he urged me to move, and I did. It took a second for my kiss-addled brain to figure out what I was feeling between my legs. *Is that his friggin' penis?*

Another rotation of my hips told me that yes, yes, it was indeed. His cock was a thick, hard rod nestled against my pussy, and I couldn't have stopped moving if I wanted to. Which I most assuredly did not.

One of Cruz's hands slid up my spine and cupped the back of my head, holding me in place while he deepened our kiss. We devoured each other's moans as I rocked against him, an orgasm already on the horizon.

I was so damned wet, I was surprised I didn't overflow the hot tub as Cruz blazed a trail of kisses across my cheek and to my ear. "Goddamn, baby. Does the rest of you taste as sweet as those pretty lips?"

"Yes," I managed to say as he tongued the lobe of my ear. "I taste like Skittles."

His low, dark chuckle raised goosebumps all over my body. "My favorite candy. You gonna let me taste the rainbow, Tink?" he growled before biting down on my earlobe.

Sweet lord have mercy! If he hadn't been holding me up, I would have flopped back into the water and drowned at the mere thought of that gorgeous mouth of his between my legs.

"You can taste anything you want," I panted, gripping his shoulders when his mouth made its way down my neck and to my chest. His skin was like fire beneath my fingers, every muscle bunching as he guided me in a slow roll over his length with all the control of a puppet master.

His own hips lifted, grinding that long erection against my clit, and my body shuddered with my impending orgasm. I hadn't come with anything other than some very handy vibrators in so long, but now I was right there. On the edge of beautiful bliss.

All I needed was...

As if reading my mind, Cruz's mouth closed around my nipple through my bright-purple swim top, and I clutched his hair.

"Yes, Cruz. Please," I begged, my voice a desperate sob.

"Use my cock, Tink. Come for me." It wasn't a request but a sweet demand, and when his teeth sank into my nipple, I willingly complied.

Throwing back my head, I came. Really fucking hard.

"Yes, god yes! Cruz!"

My hips bucked wildly, and the man beneath me held on tight, his moans vibrating through my breast and shooting directly to my pussy. Water sloshed from the tub, and the pungent scent of chlorine combined with sex was like a sensual drug shot directly into my veins.

I'd never had an out-of-body experience before, but *fuck me*, it was like I was watching us from above, envisioning every movement of our bodies as I fell apart.

"Oh my god," I croaked, my voice hoarse as I floated back to Earth on a lust-filled cloud. "You just blew my mind, Cruz."

When I looked down at him, his smile had those wicked little dimples popping, and I pressed a hard kiss to his lips.

"I'm about to blow something else," he said, "and I'd prefer not to do it in a public hot tub."

That made me laugh, but it was cut short when the door to the pool room opened. Cruz instantly had me off his lap and seated about a foot away when an older gentleman with a gray mustache poked his head in.

"Hey, guys," he said in a thick midwestern accent. "Pool area closed fifteen minutes ago."

"Thanks, sir," Cruz answered. "We were just leaving."

I stifled my giggles until he was gone. "Do you think he knew what we were up to?"

Cruz groaned and shook his head. "I don't know. Your face is all flushed, but maybe he didn't get a good look." He winced. "Sorry, that probably wasn't a very smart thing to do. In public, you know?"

"I know," I agreed, but I couldn't bring myself to regret it. Not even a little bit.

<h1 style="text-align:center">CHAPTER 16</h1>

"GOOD JOB WITH THAT jumper today, Estrada," Curly said as we stripped off our gear at the station. They no longer called me New Fucker, so that was progress.

"Thanks. I'm glad I was able to talk him down. Poor guy's been through a lot lately."

"But threatening to jump off the Brooklyn Bridge? Damn," Maverick said, pulling a gray T-shirt over his head. "Mentioning his kids was a good idea though. I could see it the second those words hit home, and I knew he'd back away."

"You stinky fuckers go clean up, and we'll meet at the pub in an hour," Curly ordered before picking up his black bag and heading for the exit.

An hour later, my hair was still damp when I took a seat on the booth side of our regular table.

"Ordered you a beer," Chris said from beside me.

"Thanks, man."

"Didn't you go out of town last weekend? Was it a romantic getaway with a special lady?" His voice was lightly teasing.

"It wasn't for me. It was for a friend who is getting married. Or was. She ended up breaking off the engagement while we were there."

Eyebrows lifted all around the table.

"You don't sound exactly broken up about it," Kai mused.

I took a long draw of beer and swiped the back of my hand over my mouth. "He doesn't deserve her. Guy's a prick."

Jayden's eyes sparkled as he leaned forward. "Sounds like you think a certain blue-eyed Latino deserves her instead."

I measured how much I wanted to say and finally thought, *fuck it.* "I would treat her like a goddamn queen."

"You down for just some fun or is this something you want long term?" Curly asked.

"Long term," I said, with assuredness.

"Hmmm." He glanced around the table, and the guys seemed to be having some kind of unspoken conversation.

"What?"

Curly blew out a breath. "You want to be careful you don't become Rebound Guy."

"Or Revenge Guy," Mav added, and they all bobbed their heads in agreement.

My eyes shifted between them. "Who are they?"

Jayden pointed at me. "You know, when a woman gets divorced or breaks off a long relationship, she finds Rebound Guy to get over the last one."

"And that guy *never* lasts," Chris advised. "I've seen it twice with my sister. And then you've got Revenge Guy. They usually get with this one after they've seen their ex with another woman. They find the hottest dude out there and bang him for a while to make the ex jealous. Even if she doesn't want the ex back, she still wants him to see what he's missing."

"Agreed," Mav said with a nod. "If you actually want a relationship with this woman, you do not, under any circumstances, want to be these guys."

"I was Rebound Guy once," Kai added. "Only lasted three months."

Curly rubbed a hand over his bald head. "I'm always Revenge Guy. Don't get me wrong. Being that guy is a helluva lot of fun, but she wants him for a good time, not for a long time."

I took it all in, fascinated, as I sipped my beer.

"There was this one woman though... I wanted more. And it could have gone somewhere if I'd just fucking waited," Curly said, stroking his fingers over his square jaw. "She's the one that got away. She married Friend Guy."

"Wait, there's another guy?"

Jayden chuckled. "Yep. And some women also go through the Wild Guy stage."

"This is getting confusing. I feel like I need to take notes. What's the deal with Wild Guy?"

Kai twirled his beer glass on the table. "There are several scenarios with that one. Maybe she's been with only her man since high school. Or maybe she's been in an oppressive relationship and when she finally breaks free, she wants to sow her wild oats."

"She starts thinking how she's never been with a man who rides motorcycles or has a dick piercing. Or she's never had a threesome," Mav added. "Whatever. She just desires the adventure she's never been allowed to have. That's when she finds a guy like Jayden." He bobbed his head toward the man across the table, who grinned like the cat that ate the canary.

"I have a bike and a piercing. I make an excellent Wild Guy," he said, his white teeth a sharp contrast against his dark skin. "I'm down for it because I'm not looking for anything serious, and no woman wants to marry Wild Guy."

I thought of my own piercing and decided I definitely didn't want to be Wild Guy. Or Rebound Guy. Or who-the-fuck-ever those other temporary ones were.

"If I'm serious about her, who do I want to be?"

Curly looked across the table. "Mav, you wanna take this one?"

Maverick downed the rest of his soda and signaled for another before pointing a thick finger at me. "Based on personal experience, you definitely want to be Friend Guy." I lifted my eyebrows as he continued. "My wife, Pam, was married before. We were acquaintances, kinda hanging out in the same circles. I never liked the way her husband treated her. Just his tone of voice when he spoke to her rubbed me the wrong fucking way."

"Understandable," I said, thinking of how Dwight had railroaded Lehra into getting what he wanted. Or what his mother wanted.

"So she finally wised up and divorced his ass. I'd had a low-key crush on her for years, but she was married so I couldn't do anything about it, you know?"

I nodded, knowing all too well. "How did you two end up together?"

"I became her friend, a shoulder to cry on. I didn't plan it or anything. It just happened. I was fighting my own demons, and we bonded over some stuff." He closed his eyes and grimaced. "I watched as she went through Rebound Guy and Revenge Guy. It was so fucking hard because I was harboring these secret feelings for her. She even had a Wild Guy at one point, but she broke it off after one date because he smoked."

Mav let out a soft chuckle. "This went on for about a year. I could see the changes in her. I watched her heal before my very eyes. And the entire time, I was there, supporting her through everything."

"A year?" I practically yelled before slugging back the rest of my beer. Fuck, I didn't want to wait a year.

Mav smiled patiently. "Trust me, Pam was worth the wait. She finally saw that what she wanted had been right in front of her the whole time. We've never looked back."

"Those two are like a friends-to-lovers romance book come to life," Chris said with a grin. "And yes, I read romance books. Fuck off."

I laughed and held up both hands. "No judgment here, dude. I started one of my sister's books while I was babysitting and my niece was napping. It was so good, I asked her if I could take it home to finish."

"I have a couple friends-to-lovers books that might interest you. I'll text you the titles and authors."

"Okay, if the Hallmark boys are done talking, let's move on," Curly said gruffly.

As I was headed home an hour later, I sat in the back of a cab and thought about what the guys had said. Had I already fucked up any chance I had with Lehra that night in the hot tub?

Knowing that her previous sex life had been less than stellar, watching her come apart on top of me had been the most satisfying thing I'd ever seen. She needed to know she deserved to have her needs taken care of and that I was the man who could get the job done.

But when I'd walked her back to her room and she stumbled a little, I realized how tipsy she was, and the guilt crept in. *Did I take advantage of her?* Because that wasn't me at all.

So I'd kissed her on the cheek and returned to my room with an enormous erection that proved to be quite persistent. Nothing I thought of could make the damn thing go away. I was still frustrated the next morning and told Artie to go downstairs to breakfast without me. Once he was out of the room, I'd stepped into the shower and taken care of business with my fist.

It hadn't taken long. All I had to do was picture Lehra riding me in the hot tub, her head thrown back and the tips of her long, blonde hair dragging the churning water as she found her sweet release.

Goddammit, now I'm getting hard again just thinking about it.

Tugging my phone from my pocket, I read through the text thread with Lehra from Monday.

> **Cruz: Hey, just checking on you. Sorry I haven't been around much. Auburn's schedule has been crazy.**

> **Tink: I knowwwww. I'm helping Tony with scheduling, and it's been wild. And I'm doing good.**

Cruz: I'm glad. Also, I wanted to apologize about Saturday night. You were a little tipsy, and I don't want you to think I'm the kind of guy who would take advantage.

Tink: No need to apologize. I was afraid you'd think I took advantage of you, LOL.

Cruz: I was most definitely a willing participant. I can't stop thinking about it.

Tink: You think about it? I may be blushing right now.

Cruz: It's hard not to. You looked so fucking beautiful.

Tink: Yep, definitely some blushing going on over here.

Cruz: Shit, I'm sorry, Tink. I've gotta go. I'm supposed to pick up Auburn in ten minutes.

Tink: Good luck. He's always a bear when they're getting ready for Fashion Week. Better since he's got Gia now though.

Cruz: For sure. Bye, beautiful. Talk later.

There were a few more texts from the following days, but nothing profound, basically chatting about our days. I hadn't seen her except for a few glimpses through the windows when I'd driven Auburn to and from work. He'd had me busy as hell this week.

I wanted something with Lehra, something lasting, not just a fling so she could get over Dwight and then move on to a serious relationship. I was going to have to find a way to slow things down without making her think I regretted what happened that night.

Because I didn't.

She was special.

She was mine.

And she'd be worth the wait.

CHAPTER 17

"Oh, honeyyyy," my mother cooed, walking around my living room, her eyes taking in everything. "This place is beautiful!" She was wearing black leggings beneath a long T-shirt, and her blonde hair was styled in a cute, curly bob that framed her face.

"Thanks, Mom. I'm so glad you're here."

She wrapped me in a fierce hug that was about the best thing in the world. "I wanted to check on my girl. I know breakups can be hard, and I needed to see you with my own two eyes."

"I'm really okay, I promise. I think it was a long time coming, and it took everything coming to a head to make me realize it."

"I wish you'd told me you were struggling," she said, leaning back and looking up at me, her smile as warm as a fresh cake from the oven. "I could have helped you through it."

"I know, Mom, but you're so busy with work, and I didn't want to worry you. How are things at the hospital, by the way? And how's Dad?"

"Oh, you know," she said, waving a hand at me. "Same old, same old in the emergency department. And your dad is good. He said to tell you he loves you."

A knock at the door interrupted us, and I found Cruz on the other side. "Hey, I ordered some Chinese and wanted to see if you wanted some. I couldn't decide what to get, so I ordered way too—Oh, crap. Sorry, I didn't know you had company."

"I'm Tabitha Kincaid," my mother said, walking over with her hand extended for a shake. "And who might you be?"

"I might be in love," he replied, patting his heart, and my mother let out a girlish giggle. *Good grief!* "Let me guess. You're Lehra's sister?"

"Oh, you! Cut it out," she flirted, swatting his chest. "I'm her mother, and you can call me Tabby."

"Nice to meet you, Tabby. I'm Cruz Estrada, Lehra's neighbor and resident spider killer."

"One time," I shot back, holding a finger in the air, "and he was one of those jumping ones. Scared the hell out of me."

"Well, Cruz sounds like a good man to have around. Did I hear something about Chinese food?" she asked sweetly.

"Yes, ma'am. It should be delivered in about twenty minutes. There's plenty for all of us."

"Ooh, can we eat Chinese, Lehra?" Mom asks me with pleading eyes before turning back to Cruz. "The only delivery we have in our little town is Domino's Pizza. This is all very exciting."

"Sure, Mom," I said with a laugh, "if Cruz doesn't mind."

"Not a bit. I'll just go wait for the food and come back in a few."

"Well, he's a cutie patootie," my mother said when he left, her shrewd eyes narrowing on me. "Boyfriend?"

"Motherrrr," I groaned, "I just got out of a relationship about ten seconds ago." No way in hell was I telling her about the hot tub tryst.

"I think it's smart to wait. It's hard to find your footing after getting out of a long relationship. The next person you date is rarely the one you end up with. I dated the same boy for three years in high school, and when he broke up with me after graduation, I immediately started dating the boy from the farm next door."

"Really?" I asked, settling onto the couch and patting the cushion beside me. I'd never heard this story before.

Mom took her shoes off and sat. "Oh yes, his name was Jimmy. Or was it James?" She drummed her fingers along her jaw as her eyes rose to the corner of the room. "I don't really recall. What I do remember is that he smoked a lot of weed."

I snorted out a laugh. "And what about you? Did you try the Mary J?"

She leveled me with a flat look. "It was the eighties. What do you think?"

"Probably more information than I needed to know."

"You asked," she pointed out.

"Guilty. So what happened with Jimmy James?"

She waved a hand at me. "Oh, he was just a placeholder. Someone to have some fun with until a certain handsome plumber moved into town."

"Dad."

"Yep. Easton Kincaid was a hottie of the first order. And he knew what to do with my pipes, if you know what I'm saying."

I closed my eyes and grimaced. "You could say less right about now."

My mom bellowed out a laugh. "I'm just saying, don't use this Cruz fella for a good time. He seems like he could be a keeper."

"You've talked to him for all of five minutes, Mom."

"I know that, but in my old age, I've developed a good eye. He's polite and funny, as well as a spider assassin." She wiggled her eyebrows. "And not bad to look at."

Cruz arrived with the food before I could reply. She wasn't wrong though. The man looked as good in khaki shorts and a black tee as when he was wearing one of his suits.

"Here we go, ladies. I got Mongolian beef, kung pao chicken, and garlic butter soy prawns." He set down the bags, and the air filled with the scent of spices. "Also got pot stickers and egg rolls."

"Good lord, Cruz! Were you buying for the entire building?" Mom asked.

"It's good to have choices."

I grabbed paper plates, and we settled onto the couch, Cruz in the middle, with me and Mom on either side.

"Tabby, Lehra tells me you're a nurse." He spooned a little of everything onto his plate.

"Yep, for thirty years, the last twenty in the emergency department."

"Bet you've seen a lot," he said, shoveling a shrimp into his mouth with chopsticks.

"A lot of things in people's butts," she replied dryly, and Cruz choked on his food. Mom pounded him on the back. "It's true. People will stick anything up there. We had one last week that had a giant dildo stuck in the backside." She motioned with her hands to show us exactly how giant it was.

"Wow, and it just got stuck in there?"

Mom took a bite of chicken and then pointed at him with her chopsticks. "If you're going to stick something in your anus, the key is to make sure you can get it out, either with a handle of some sort or a wider base. My motto is *flared base for that dark, dark place.*"

"Words we should all live by," Cruz noted with a grin. "What's the weirdest thing anyone's ever stuck in there?"

"Oh, let's see. In the animal category, I'd have to say an eel. Damn thing was seventeen inches long and had bitten through the colon, requiring surgery. The person said they didn't know how it got in there." Mom rolled her eyes. "Most of them either say that or that they accidentally fell on something and it went up their hole."

"And they think the medical staff will believe that? That people are just walking around naked and accidentally falling on things at the perfect angle?"

Mom shrugged. "They're embarrassed that they're having to go to the hospital for such a personal issue. We had one last month with a cell phone in her butt. Damn thing rang every three minutes."

"Gives a whole new meaning to the term butt dialing," Cruz quipped, and Mom and I burst into laughter.

My mother wiped tears of mirth from beneath her eyes. "Okay, enough of all that. Can we watch a movie? I haven't seen *Bridesmaids* in forever."

Even though we'd watched the movie last weekend, Cruz readily agreed. "Sounds great, Tabby. I love Princess Melissa."

"Of the McCarthy Islands," I retorted, and we shared a smile.

After we'd laughed our way through the movie, Mom stood. "I'm going to hit the sack. It's been a long day."

"Mom, I put some earplugs in the bathroom for you. It's much noisier in the city, and it took me a couple months after moving here to be able to sleep well."

"Thanks, honey," she said, kissing me on the top of my head before doing the same to Cruz. "It was so nice meeting you, Cruz. Thank you for dinner."

"Any time, Tabby," he replied, and we watched her head down the short hall and into my bedroom, closing the door behind her. "Your mom is awesome."

"She's the best," I agreed.

He moved closer, eating up the space between us, and took my hand. "Can we talk for a minute, Tink?"

My heart did an entire gymnastics routine in my chest at his proximity, but I nodded. "Sure."

"About last weekend..."

"When I molested you in the hot tub?"

He chuckled. "The way I remember it, it was pretty damn mutual."

"Seemed that way to me too."

"I just want you to know I don't regret it at all."

"Why do I feel a *but* coming?"

His smile was soft as he tucked one of my curls behind my ear. "*But* I think we need to take a step back. Not because I want to," he added quickly, "but because I think it's what's best for you."

"You don't want to see me anymore?" I asked, trying not to let the hurt bleed into my words.

Cruz's head shook side to side. "That's not what I'm saying at all. You're not getting rid of me that easily, Tink." His sweet smile soothed my ruffled feathers. "I still want us to hang out and be... friends. I just think we need to take the sex stuff off the table for a while."

"So friends *without* benefits?"

He laughed and cradled my chin with his hand. "Yes, and I can't tell you how hard it is to say that to you." He leaned forward until his mouth was at my ear, his voice a growling whisper. "Because I *really* enjoyed your benefits."

A shiver ran through my body, but he warmed me by pulling me close until my cheek rested against his shoulder. "I found you quite... beneficial as well," I told him and felt the rumble inside his chest.

"This is an important thing to me, Lehra. I can't lose you, and I don't want to muck things up because you're still trying to heal."

"Cruz..." I started to protest, but he hushed me with a kiss to my temple.

"I know you're feeling relieved right now, but you have to admit that Dwight betrayed your trust with the way he treated you. You have the kindest heart, Tink, and I know deep down inside, there's some hurt there. You need to get that out before you can truly move on."

I literally felt his words inside me, found where the pain was buried, and I knew he was right. "It's not easy to feel second best," I admitted, and he squeezed me tighter.

"You'll never come second with me, Lehra. Never."

I crawled into bed, trying not to wake my mom, but her maternal radar kicked in and she rolled over.

"Good night, Mom."

"What?" she yelled before realizing she had her earplugs in and popped one out. "Sorry, what did you say?"

Stifling my laughter, I kissed her cheek, which smelled like the moisturizer she'd been putting on her face for as long as I could remember. It smelled like comfort and sweet memories.

"I said good night."

"Oh, g'night, honey. Did you have a nice talk with Cruz?"

"I did."

"He likes you, you know."

It was hard to describe how warm those words made me feel inside. "I like him too, but we decided to take things slow since I just broke an engagement."

"That's very smart and mature, Lehra."

She rolled back over and adjusted her pillow before adding, "Though I will say, if he's good with your pipes, I'd be happy to call him my son-in-law."

I managed to sigh and laugh at the same time. *Ladies and gentlemen... meet Tabitha Kincaid, my mother.*

CHAPTER 18

LEHRA BUSTED THROUGH THE door to my apartment like a tornado. "Oh my god. Chloe Bouvier is dead!"

Not even the shock of that statement could take away from the reaction I had to my Tink. The same reaction I had every single time I saw her.

Affection.

Desire.

Love.

Yes, I'd fallen in love with Lehra Kincaid over the past few months, a time period that I liked to call *Cruz's Ultimate Test of Patience.*

Because she hadn't gone through Rebound Guy or Revenge Guy or any of those other fuckers. She hadn't been on a single date since she broke up with dumbass Dwight months ago. Which I'm secretly glad of because if I saw her with another man, I would most likely get arrested.

I was so fucking confused. I wanted to do this right and not be some random rebound guy until she found her happily ever after man. I wanted to *be* that HEA man.

Maybe Curly and all of them were full of shit. Maybe Lehra broke the mold and didn't act like other women. Hell, I had no fucking clue. All I knew was that I wanted her—*needed* her—to be mine. Now.

Looking up at her with her wild, blonde curls and flushed face, I stood to lead her to the couch. "What the hell happened?"

We sat, and Lehra curled her legs beneath her and faced me. She was wearing a red-and-black top and skirt that revealed a Cruz approved amount of thigh in her current position. Luckily I had excellent peripheral vision and could enjoy the view while keeping my eyes on hers.

"It was a car accident outside Atlantic City."

"Wow." I scrubbed a hand over the top of my head. I can't say the news made me sad because I knew entirely too much information about Chloe from Paul. "How did you find out?"

"I called Gianna to check on Janie-Bug."

"Yeah, I talked to Auburn a couple hours ago. He said the surgery went well, and she should be walking soon." I shook my head. "That kid's a warrior."

"She is," Lehra said with a soft smile.

Jane's biological parents had hurt Gianna and Auburn's daughter when she was two, and the little girl had been in a wheelchair ever since. Apparently, Auburn had his cousin, Beau, look into it, and he found out the couple was dead. That was good. Otherwise, I'd be tempted to hunt the fuckers down for hurting that baby girl.

My phone rang, and I snatched it up, seeing that it was Auburn calling. I answered immediately. "Hey, man. I just heard. How are you?"

"I'm okay," he sighed. "It's... weird. I'm not sure how to feel about it. I just got off the phone with Dad a few minutes ago."

Worry rose like a flash in my chest at the mention of his—*our*—father. "How is Paul doing with all this?"

"He seems to be okay. They were going through the divorce when all this happened."

"Anything I can do for you?"

"Actually, yes. We'll be here in Texas for a few more days while Jane recovers enough to fly. My brother, Monty, is taking a commercial flight since we have the private plane to transport Jane. Do you think you could pick him up from the airport?"

My mind reeled. *My other brother is coming, and I get to meet him for the first time.*

"Yes, of course. Send me the details."

"Okay, I'm going to get back in there to Jane."

"Give her a hug from me. Jaxon too."

"I will and, Cruz?"

"Yeah?"

"Thank you. You have no idea how much it means to me that I can always count on you. I feel like... like you're part of my family now."

My heart lodged in my throat. *We are family.*

"What did he say?" Lehra asked as soon as I hung up.

"He, uh, wants me to go pick up his brother."

Her eyes round. "Wow, Monty is coming home? Hasn't he been gone for, like, sixteen years or something?"

"Yeah, about that."

"I wonder what he's like?" she mused.

"I know he's a detective in Florida, and he just solved a big serial killer case." I smiled, oddly proud of the brother I'd never met. "Auburn's been talking about it."

"I saw him on TV. He looks a lot like his brother."

Which one? I wanted to ask.

Averting my eyes so I didn't allow her to see my secrets, I stood. "I'm getting some water. You want anything, Tink?"

"Nope. Just ran home at lunch to change shoes. Tony's got me running around this afternoon, and I needed some flats. Dinner tonight?"

"I'll make burgers."

"Goody. I love your burgers," she said, unfolding herself from the couch and rising onto her tiptoes to press a kiss to my cheek. "See you tonight."

And she was gone, leaving behind the scent of summer and the sweetness of her kiss against my face. I loved how affectionate Lehra had gotten with me. It's the only thing that kept me going.

We ate dinner together several nights a week, and then we'd watch a movie with her snuggled into my side. We'd grown so close, almost like a real couple, minus the sex.

God, how I wanted us to go there. I craved her kisses like I craved my next breath. And not for the first time, I wondered if she would be into the same sexual things I was. She had been pretty adventurous that night in the hot tub, riding my lap in public where anyone could walk in and catch us.

Soooo... maybe?

Pushing those thoughts away, I dialed Paul and was relieved when he answered after the first ring.

"Cruz, hey."

I heard the smile in his voice, even through those two short syllables.

"Hey, Paul. I heard about your... about Chloe, and I just wanted to check on you."

"That was nice of you, but I'm doing okay. Just trying to sort through my feelings. I've despised her for so long, but I can't bring myself to be happy she's dead." A sigh ran down the phone line, and his struggle was evident.

"I understand, but I think it's okay to feel a little relieved that the person who's been blackmailing you is no longer able to do so."

"I think you summed up exactly what I'm feeling. I no longer have all this shit hanging over my head, and I feel... I don't know... free or something."

"That's valid."

There was a short pause. "After the funeral, I'm going to tell your brothers about the things their mother did. I think they have a right to know."

It no longer struck me as weird when he called Auburn and Monty my brothers. The word sounded almost natural to my ears now.

"How deep are you going to go?"

"I actually wanted to talk to you about that. Would you like for me to tell them about you?"

Massaging my forehead with my fingertips, I closed my eyes and contemplated the question. "I'm not sure, Paul. Monty is coming home for the first time in over a decade, and you're already hitting him with a lot."

"A whole fucking lot," he said with a humorless chuckle.

"I mean, you've got blackmail, threats, and the fact that their mother was trying to steal the company from Auburn. To also throw in, '*And hey, guess what? You also have an illegitimate brother. Welcome home, Monty.*' That might be too much right now."

"Cruz," he sighed, "you know I don't think of you like that. You're just as much my son as Auburn and Monty. Maybe you're right about waiting to tell them that part though. It's going to be overwhelming enough."

"I agree."

"Are you worried they won't accept you?"

I chewed on my bottom lip and nodded, even though he couldn't see me. "A little bit."

"Son, I don't think you have to worry about that. You're a good man, and I believe they'll be happy once the shock has worn off."

"Thanks, Paul," I told him my chest tightening at his words.

"I've gotta run. I need to get down to the funeral home."

My brow scrunched, knowing Auburn was out of town and Monty wasn't home yet. "Do you need me to go with you?"

"No, not at all. I've already talked to them and set most everything up. I just need to pay for the services."

"Okay, but I'm here if you change your mind."

"I appreciate it, Cruz. And thank you for calling to check on me."

"No problem. I was worried about you."

His voice sounded thicker when he said, "You're a good son. I'll see you on Monday."

My own words came out hoarse with emotion. "Sounds good. Bye, Paul."

CHAPTER 19

"Fuck, that was intense," Chris said as we stripped out of our gear at the station. "You all right, Estrada?"

"Yeah," I breathed. "I'm okay."

Curly came up and slapped me on the back. "You did a good job tonight, man. You know, with all officer-involved shootings—"

"Yeah, I'll be on leave for a bit during the investigation. I know that's standard," I assured him with a nod.

His face was somber. "It won't be for long, I'm sure. That piece of shit, Cappitani, was on top of an underaged girl when you kicked in the door."

I cringed at the memory. I'd never been more disgusted in my life.

"And he pulled a gun on you," Kai added, giving my shoulder a light shake as I remembered the cold steel rising from beneath the dirty pillow. "You were justified, bro."

"I know. Thanks, guys. I appreciate the support," I told them, clenching my fingers into my palms so no one could see the slight shake there. I was aware it was simply my adrenaline coming down after all the action of the raid. "I'm gonna hit the shower."

"Me too," Jayden said, following me into the tiled room. He didn't speak on the ride back to the station, which was unusual for him. The guy was always joking and carrying on.

"You okay?" I asked him softly. He'd been right behind me when we breached the room where Luca Cappitani was assaulting that poor girl while another cowered in the corner.

His big brown eyes were haunted as he halted and stared across the room. "My twin sisters are seventeen like that girl." I was silent, letting him process. Then his tight face twisted toward me. "I know we're not supposed to say shit like this after a shooting, but I'm glad that sadistic motherfucker is dead."

I placed my hand on his shoulder in what I hoped was a comforting gesture. "That's valid, Jayden. I know we're just supposed to do our jobs and then put it out of our minds, but in real life, that's not how it works. Some of this shit really hits home."

"Yeah," he said quietly, walking into one of the stalls.

Once we were cleaned up and walking out of the shower room with rough white towels around our waists, I forced my tone into something casual.

"You know, they'll probably make me speak to a shrink about this. I haven't killed anyone since my days in the military. I had to wound a guy in the leg once back in Houston, but otherwise, I haven't had to discharge my weapon in a long time."

"Probably," he said, scruffing a hand over his dark curls.

"Do you think you could come with me?" He looked up at me in surprise, and I told a bit of a fib. "I don't want to go by myself, and I think it would help to have one of my brothers there with me."

A hint of a smile passed his lips. "Yeah, okay. I'll go if you need me to."

Maybe he was onto what I was doing, and maybe he wasn't, but at least he was going to go. I was positive he wouldn't take the initiative to seek out the psychological resources we were provided on his own, but I was sure it would do him some good to be able to talk freely about how he was feeling.

As I pulled on a pair of black cargo pants, Jayden said, "Estrada?"

"Yeah?"

His grin was full wattage now. "What's your mom look like?"

"Shut the fuck up, Jay."

I wasn't sure if it was the law enforcement connection or the familial one, but Monty Bouvier and I hit it off instantly. A few days after the funeral, we were at an Irish pub in the East Village, and the talk inevitably turned to women after the waitress flirted with Monty.

"She was totally giving off some fuck me vibes, dude," I said, giving him a light elbow jab to the ribs.

"Not interested," he replied immediately.

"You interested in someone else?" I asked, digging into the mound of Irish nachos on my plate.

"There's someone, but I'm not sure if it's gonna work out."

"Is that someone here in New York?" I suspected it was Kassie Ramirez, his ex-girlfriend Paul had told me about. At least I hoped it was. I'd met her a few times, and she was a strong, beautiful, smart attorney raising her son by herself. She deserved a good man in her life.

He nodded. "How about you? You got a lady?"

I chewed slowly, wavering on how to answer. It didn't seem right to tell him about our night in the hotel hot tub, so I kept it vague. "No, but yes. I really like someone, but I don't know if she likes me, so I guess we're both kinda in the same boat."

"Have you asked her out?"

"No, she gives me signals, but I don't know if she'd be into the same things as me. You know..." I lowered my voice a little, "sexually."

"You into BDSM or something?"

I rimmed the top of my glass of Guinness with my finger. "Not that. Something different. I have trouble finding women who have the same tastes as me."

We talked and ate some more, but when Monty suggested the idea of going to a sex club to find someone that was into my mystery kink, something a guy from my team said a while back popped into my brain. His name was Bryson, and he'd told me about a place he and his wife frequented.

Me and the wifey have been going to keep the spice in our marriage. I could get you a guest pass if you want to come sometime and check it out. They have anything you could want there. Private voyeur rooms—which is what we like—a swingers area, a sex toy store, BDSM stuff. They even have a great shop if you're into role playing.

That last one had sparked my interest, and I hadn't been able to stop thinking about it. Drumming my fingers on the table, I tentatively mentioned it to Monty.

"I have a buddy who goes to one of those clubs. He assures me it's not sleazy or anything. It's really upscale. Just a place to find other people who like what you like."

I definitely didn't want to pick up anyone, and Monty didn't seem to want to either, but we both decided to go one night and see what it was all about.

Because I was intrigued by the thought of that role playing shop. I'd been judged for my kink before, but maybe they'd have some tips on the best way to bring it up to a partner.

I wasn't sure Lehra would be interested in something like that, but then again... what if she was open to trying?

CHAPTER 20

"THIS IS SOOOOO MUCH fun!" I sang, throwing my hands up in that drunk girl dance that made me feel free and happy. Even Nicolette had let her hair down, literally and figuratively. Her dark locks swirled around her as she relaxed into the music.

"I wish Artie could have come," Gianna yelled over the noise. The lights of the dance floor flashed off her gorgeous face, making her smile turn from white to red to green to blue.

For some reason, I found that hilarious, and I pointed. "You have Smurf teeth. And Artie-boy is on a hot date tonight."

"Yay for Artie!" she cheered, swirling her arms above her head and doing a little wiggle.

One song bled into another, and Nicolette said, "Let's go sit and have another drink. These shoes are killing my feet."

"Okay, I'm going to the potty, and I'll meet you up there," I told them as we neared the edge of the dance floor.

Gianna grabbed my hand when I turned to head toward the mile-long line for the restrooms. "Doofus, did you forget we have our own bathroom in the VIP room?"

"It's a whole new experience going to a club with the *Queen of New York City,*" I teased. That's what the tabloids had started calling her since she'd married Auburn. She looked the part of royalty too, though she was the most down-to-earth person ever.

"I hate that nickname," she said, and then her lips rolled into a pretty pout, "but I do miss my king. He's out of town and won't be home till late tonight."

A man in a suit stood beside the private elevator with his hands crossed over his front, and he gave us a respectful nod when we approached. "Mrs. Bouvier, Ms. Kincaid, Ms. Bell." As soon as he pressed the button, the gold doors slid smoothly open.

We stepped inside and were whooshed up to the third floor of the nightclub. The first floor was wild and loud, with a huge light-up dance floor and two bars. The second floor consisted of more bars, some pool tables, and other games.

But the third floor? Just... wow. There was a top shelf bar backlit with ocean blue, a spacious seating area, and five VIP suites, one of which was ours.

And we had our own personal attendant named Lakshmi who greeted us immediately and led us to our suite. "Another round of your favorites?" she asked, her dark braid falling over one shoulder. She was stunning. In fact, everyone who worked at this bar looked like a supermodel.

"Yes, please," I told her before heading to the bathroom, which was larger than my old apartment. The white-and-gold marble shone so brightly I wished I had my sunglasses with me.

I was giggling when I walked back into the main area to find Gianna on the electric-blue leather couch and Nic lounging sideways on the matching chair with her shoes kicked off. It was quieter up here, the booming music from down below a mere throbbing against the floor.

"What's so funny?" Gia asked, sipping her Cosmo, which had been delivered while I was taking care of business.

Sitting beside her, I picked up my lemon drop martini and licked a little of the tangy stuff off the rim. "I was just wondering why there's a shower in there."

"In case someone decides to get *dirty* in the VIP room," she replied, waggling her perfectly arched eyebrows.

I eyed the couch we were sitting on. "You think they disinfect the furniture every night?"

She laughed and nodded her head. "For sure. What are you studying on your phone over there, Nicolette?"

My friend's green eyes were wide and her cheeks were pink when she looked up at us. "Just a, um, a quiz."

Gianna and I shared a smug glance. "Why are you acting so sketch, Nic?" I asked. "Is it a naughty quiz?"

She sighed and rolled her eyes. "Yes, okay? It's a sex quiz from an online magazine." Her nose scrunched up adorably. "The only guys I've really been with are science nerds that I work with, and it's been pretty vanilla. I've never even done it doggy style, so I was just curious."

"Curiosity is healthy. Ain't no shame in that game," Gia assured her. "Send us the link so we can take it too."

Our phones pinged, and I pulled mine from my small white crossbody purse and tapped on the link. The first few questions were basic demographics, and then it got into the meat of the topic. Sex.

I tapped the little boxes, and based on my answers, new sets of questions were generated. *Favorite position? What are you looking for in a partner?*

Then there were a lot of *have you ever* questions and then some *would you like to* ones. I answered them honestly and then heard a little, "Ooh, that sounds fun," from Nicolette and looked up. Her eyes were gleaming at whatever was on her screen, but I didn't ask.

Because then she might ask me about my answers.

When I got to the results page, my eyebrows lifted at the words on my screen.

According to your results, your ideal kink is role playing. It's fun and adventurous, just like you! So get out there and find a partner who matches your daring sexual personality. And remember, there is no shame in enjoying what you like.

One last question for you... what is your ultimate role playing fantasy?

Well, they friggin' nailed me, didn't they? Biting my bottom lip, I typed my answer into the rectangular box just as Gianna groaned beside me.

"This quiz makes me miss Auburn. I'm going to call him."

A few seconds later, she was on a FaceTime call with her husband.

"Hey, baby girl. What are you up to?"

"Still at The Blue with the girls." She turned the phone toward us, and we waved. It looked like his phone was mounted on the dash of his car as he drove.

"Hope you ladies are having fun," Auburn said when Gianna swiveled the phone back to her face.

"We just took a sex quiz," she announced, and I resisted the urge to clamp my hand over her red-glossed lips.

"And what were your results?" Auburn's voice was suddenly deeper, an erotic purr that was a far cry from the brisk tone he used in the office.

"Oh, I think you know," she purred back, and then...

Dear sweet baby Jesus, did she just mouth *Daddy* at him?

Yeah, I did not need to know that little tidbit about my boss.

I attempted to scrub my brain of that knowledge by downing the rest of my drink in one burning gulp as I heard Auburn's car engine rev.

"I'll be home in an hour." His voice was clipped and strained, and I knew Gianna was in for it tonight. *Lucky bitch.* "How are you getting home?"

"We'll walk. It's not that far."

I could literally hear his teeth grinding as his Mr. Bossman persona pushed to the forefront. "No. I'll call Cruz and see if he can come pick you all up."

Even the sound of his name got my gears grinding at full force, and I squeezed my thighs together to try and alleviate the ache I suddenly felt between my legs. I wished he'd be the one to take care of it for me, but I guessed I'd have to once again rely on my very own Seventh Heaven Attachment Head I'd installed a few months ago.

"Auburn, no," Gianna said, scowling at her husband through the phone. "It's his time off. Don't bother him. We'll be—"

"Gianna." The roughness of her name from his lips did nothing to help my needy situation, and I wished I had a certain hunky Latino that would growl my name into my ear like that.

But he hadn't made a move since that night in the hot tub all those months ago. *Months!*

Seriously, what was he waiting for?

That thought was followed by another.

Maybe he's just not into you.

CHAPTER 21

I CHUCKLED INTO MY Jack and Coke before emptying my glass in a long swallow. I'd just watched Monty haul Kassie Ramirez upstairs to the second floor of Club E, the sex club we'd come to tonight.

My suspicions about who he was interested in were obviously correct.

"Another one?" the male bartender asked.

"Nah, I'm driving tonight. I think I'll look around a bit," I told him before paying out my tab. "Can I ask you a question?"

"Of course. Shoot."

"My friend and I just took the tour with Everly, and she said there was a, uh, a role playing shop on the first floor. But I don't see it."

"Oh, sure," he said nonchalantly, slinging a white towel over one shoulder, and I was grateful for his non-judgment. After all, I was sure he'd seen and heard worse here. "It's kinda confusing because you have to go out the front door to get to it. They have it open to the public, unlike the rest of the club, which is members only. People buy Halloween costumes there and everything."

"Cool, thanks," I said, rapping twice on the bar before heading to the front. I found the shop near the discreet entrance to Club E, and when I walked inside, my mouth dropped open. The place was as big as a Walmart.

"Mr. Estrada, hi!" I heard a friendly voice say, and turned to find Everly, the petite blonde who had given us a tour. "Are you into role play?"

"Oh, um..." I pulled at the back of my neck, and Everly patted my arm with a comforting touch.

"It's okay. You don't have to be embarrassed. My husband and I are into it too."

That settled my nerves a bit. "Sorry, I've gotten judged for my preferences before, so it's hard to talk about."

She let out a frustrated noise from the back of her throat and rolled her eyes. "Trust me, I understand. I mean, people accept BDSM and other kinks. So why is it okay for someone to be into impact or breath play, but if I want to dress up like Little Red Riding Hood and let my Big, Bad Wolf devour me, I get the side eye?"

"Exactly," I said, feeling more relaxed by the second.

"Do you have a partner or are you free-ranging it?"

I laughed. "It's complicated. I have a woman I like, but..."

"But you're not sure if she'd be into it, right?" I nodded, and Everly smiled. "I get it. I was so scared to talk to my husband—well, he was my boyfriend then. I was afraid he'd think it was silly or something. Come on. I think I have some resources to help you."

Following her through racks and racks of every costume imaginable, I listened as she pointed to the various sections. "Over there we have anime and cosplay. Then there's your fairytale stuff over on the other wall. In the center, we have occupation-related costumes, such as cops, nurses, your classic French maid, schoolgirls, and military. That's the most popular area for people who are just looking for a Halloween costume or something."

"Wow, you have a little of everything."

"Yep," she agreed, leading me toward the back as she continued pointing around the room. "Over there is historical stuff like Renaissance, Vikings, and pioneer costumes. Animals are near the fairytales. And here," she said as we walked around a corner and found an inconspicuous black door, "is the bookstore."

She opened the door, and I walked inside. It was a small room with only four sets of bookshelves, but they were jam-packed with books.

Everly thumbed over her shoulder. "I've got to stay up front, but you're welcome to browse. That green book on the first set of shelves is the one that really helped me a lot. Take your time and let me know if you have any questions."

"Thanks," I said. "You've been a huge help." When she was gone, I pulled the green book from the shelf and read the title. *Effective Ways to Talk to Your Partner about Role Playing.*

Tucking that one beneath my arm, I checked out the rest of the library. There were books on ideas for scenes, communication, and even a few that gave instructions for do-it-yourself costumes.

My phone rang, and I pulled it from my pocket to see that Auburn was calling, which was weird. He was supposed to be on his way home from upstate after speaking to students at a business college.

"Hey, everything okay?" I answered.

"Yeah, I'm on my way home. Shouldn't be more than an hour. Where are you right now?"

I came to a sex club with our brother, but he's upstairs in a BDSM room with his old flame.

"At a bookstore."

"Listen, I know you're not on duty, but the girls are at a club and saying they plan to walk home."

"Which girls?" I asked, my ears perking up like a dog smelling a steak.

"Gia, Lehra, and... what's the one with glasses?"

"Nicolette."

"Yeah, her."

"I'll go get them. Which club?"

"The Blue in Midtown. Are you sure about this? They looked a little tipsy, and I just worry."

"I don't mind a bit. I'm not far from there."

"Thanks, man. I owe you one."

"Sounds good, and don't worry about the ladies. I'll get them safely home."

"I knew I could count on you, especially if I told you Lehra was there," he teased, seeming to know without me telling him that I had a thing for her.

"Yeah, yeah, shut up," I mumbled, hanging up the phone to the sound of his laughter.

"I'm Mrs. Bouvier's driver," I told the guy at the door, and he nodded his boulder-sized head and pulled back the red rope for me to go through.

I'd passed by this club a few times, but I'd never been inside. It was nice. The air bumped with bass, and the blue furnishings were tasteful and sleek.

Spotting Lehra instantly, I headed toward her position at the bar, where she was seated with a man beside her. Jealousy flared through me, and it quickly turned into anger when I drew close enough to hear Lehra say, "For the hundredth time, no. I do not want you to buy me a drink."

A furious red haze clouded the corners of my vision when he reached out and grabbed her upper arm, and I placed a hand on the asshole's shoulder with an unyielding grip. "The lady said no," I said in a voice just loud enough for him to hear.

"Who the fuck are you?" he sneered, rotating his barstool to face me, his eyes glazed with drunkenness.

"Your worst fucking nightmare," I growled, letting him see the feral glint in my eye.

He paused and seemed to think about that before shrugging. "Yeah, well, I dint want to talk to her anyway," he slurred. "She looks like a bi—"

He stopped talking when I cut off his airway with a firm hand around his throat. "Do you really want to finish that sentence?"

The asshole's eyes bugged out and his face turned puce as he shook his head, and I had to remind myself he was drunk. Not that that was an excuse to harass a woman—*my woman*—but it did keep me from doing what I wanted to do, which was throw him over the bar and into the rows of bottles. Instead, I spun him to face a wide-eyed Lehra and loosened my hand just enough for him to speak.

"Apologize to the lady."

"I-I'm s-sorry," he stuttered out and then, with a flick of my wrist, I tossed him behind me and onto the floor.

Making eye contact with the bartender that rushed over, I jerked my head in the asshole's direction. "Get a bouncer to take out that piece of shit." He didn't even question me, simply nodded and tapped out a message on the phone he pulled from his pocket.

Then I stepped closer to Lehra and ran my fingers gently over the arm he'd grabbed. If I saw even the hint of a mark, I'd rethink my decision, and the man wouldn't be able to walk for a very long time. But he got lucky. The only thing I found were the goosebumps that followed my touch.

"You okay, Tink?" I asked, meeting her astonished gaze.

"Um, yeah, fine. He was just being a jerk."

"He put his hands on you," I growled, and she reached up and touched my face. Her fingers were soft and cool against my heated skin, and I calmed in an instant.

"Thank you, Cruz. That was really sweet... and totally hot." Then she deepened her voice in an approximation of mine and growled, "I'm your worst fucking nightmare."

She was so damn cute, and I laughed, taking both her hands to help her off the stool. "Where are your friends?"

"They were going to the bathroom upstairs. I came down to wait for you."

Scanning the crowd, I saw them winding their way toward us through the crowd. "I see them. You ladies are dressed to kill tonight, aren't you?" I asked the three of them once Nicolette and Gianna reached us. Nic was wearing a black dress with glittery threads running through it, and Gia was in a white minidress made of some kind of shiny material.

But Lehra... *goddamn*. She wore a silver sequin dress that pulled out the sparkles in her gray eyes.

"Thanks," Gianna said, bumping me with her shoulder. "And sorry my husband pulled you away from whatever you were doing tonight."

"No problem at all. I wasn't busy." I gestured toward the front just as two burly men picked up the asshole who had touched Lehra and dragged him away.

"What happened to that guy?" Nicolette asked, glancing back over her shoulder.

I smirked as I walked. "He made bad life choices."

Once I'd gotten Nicolette safely home, I pulled into the underground parking garage and stepped out of the car.

"Alex," I spoke to one of the security guards, "can you escort Mrs. Bouvier up to the penthouse?"

"Certainly," he said, and helped Gianna out of the car before leading her to the elevator.

"Lehra, you ready?" I asked peering into the car, but she was curled up on the backseat, fast asleep. Smiling, I extricated her and cradled her in my arms, hanging her purse over my shoulder. "I'll be back to move the car in a bit," I whispered to the other guard.

"Nah, I'll park it for you, and you can grab the keys in the morning."

I nodded my thanks and carried Lehra up to her apartment. We both had emergency key cards to the other's apartments, so I wrangled mine out of my pocket and unlocked her door.

"Cruz?" she asked sweetly as I hung her purse beside the door and carried her through her darkened apartment and to her bedroom.

"Yeah, Tink?" I asked, setting her on the bed and turning on the bedside lamp.

"Why don't you ever ask me to get in hot tubs with you anymore? I think you're a really good hot tub buddy."

I suppressed a groan at the memories that brought back and smoothed her hair away from her face. "I think you are too, sweetheart."

She grinned crookedly. "Okay, can you get my sleep shirt from the top drawer of my dresser? It's the blue one."

Crossing the room, I pulled open the drawer and froze when I saw the blue shirt. It was one of mine that I'd loaned her when she spilled something on her tank top one night.

"This one?" I croaked, holding it up.

"Uh-huh. I like to sleep in your shirt."

I wasn't sure how I was still standing because every drop of blood in my body migrated directly to my cock. *She sleeps in my shirt?* Somehow I managed to walk to her and place it in her outstretched hand.

"There you go. I'll step out and let you change. Do you..." *Oh Jesus help me.* I swallowed hard. "Do I need to unzip your dress?"

I was flooded with both relief and disappointment when she shook her head. "No, it just pulls off over my head."

Outside her bedroom door, I blew out a few long breaths through pursed lips, giving her a minute before I returned. Lehra was indeed wearing my shirt, lying on her side with a long, tanned leg sticking out from the covers.

"I'll put some water and ibuprofen on your nightstand. Take them as soon as you wake up."

"Okay, Sir," she said, giving me a little salute.

Fuck, did she just call me Sir?

"Anything else you need?"

She smiled up at me through drowsy eyes. "Where's my phone? I need to plug it in and set my alarm."

"I'll get it out of your purse." Backtracking through the apartment, I found her phone in her purse and brought it to the bedroom. "What time do you want your alarm set for?"

Lehra yawned and closed her eyes, curling down deep in the bed. "I'll sleep in, so nine."

I unlocked her phone and sat beside her. As I was about to swipe to the clock app, the words on the screen caught my eye.

According to your results, your ideal kink is role playing. It's fun and adventurous, just like you! So get out there and find a partner who matches your daring sexual personality. And remember, there is no shame in enjoying what you like.

My eyeballs felt like beach balls trying to pop from my eye sockets. I looked from the phone to the woman on the bed, the beautiful, fun woman I loved. My cheeks began to ache, and I realized it was because I was grinning like a loon.

I read the words again—just to be sure—and then stroked Lehra's messy hair until she was deeply asleep. Then I swept my thumb across the screen to set her alarm. But not before I memorized the words at the bottom.

One last question for you... what is your ultimate role playing fantasy?

Response: Viking Warrior

CHAPTER 22

THE NEXT MORNING I awoke with a smile on my face, though I should be exhausted. I'd been like a kid trying to fall asleep on Christmas Eve, the excitement too great to allow my mind to slow down enough to sleep.

After getting dressed, I walked to Lehra's favorite coffee shop and ordered a vanilla bean latte for her and a black coffee for myself. Returning to our building, I retrieved the book from beneath the seat of the Bentley where I'd stashed it last night and headed upstairs.

I stopped by my apartment and gathered a few things from the kitchen before cautiously letting myself into Lehra's place. The shower was running, so I went into the kitchen and began preparing the food.

When I heard her coming down the hallway, I called out, "There's a scary psycho in your kitchen."

"Oh noooo! What should I do?" she mocked, walking into the kitchen. Her hair was twisted up in a towel, and she'd put my shirt back on, the one with USMC across the front. My cock twitched at the sight.

"You should probably sit down and let the intruder serve you brunch." She took one of the barstools, setting her phone on the bar, and I strolled over and kissed the top of her head. "How are you feeling?"

"Pretty good, actually. Thanks for the ibuprofen and water."

"You're welcome. I got you a coffee. It should be cooled enough, just like you like it." I nodded toward the cup in front of her. "And the food is almost done."

"It smells delicious. What is it?"

The timer dinged, and I donned an oven mitt and pulled the tray from the oven. "Nothing fancy. Just Cuban crushed potatoes. I wasn't sure how you would feel, and these are great if you have a queasy stomach."

I sprinkled green onions across the top, plated two for each of us, and sat beside her at the kitchen bar.

Lehra groaned at the first bite. "Oh my damn, these are delicious. How do you make them?"

"Boil them, smash them, brush them with oil, add seasoning, and then broil for about six minutes. My mom used to make them when I was little, and she'd let me smash the potatoes after they were boiled. I thought it was the most fun thing ever."

"Your mom sounds awesome. I'd love to meet her sometime." Then her bare cheeks flushed a pretty rose color. "I mean—"

"I'd love for her to meet you," I broke in. "After all, fair is fair since I met your mom. How is Tabby doing, by the way?"

"Busy as heck. She and my dad are actually going on a cruise next month. Dad is self-employed, so he hardly ever takes time off work."

"My papa was the same."

We talked about our families until we were done eating, and then I took the plates to the sink.

"Just leave those. I can do them since you cooked."

"I got it," I told her, starting to load the dishwasher. When I was done, I turned and leaned my butt against the counter, my hands resting beside my hips. "So, I understand you want to have Viking sex."

Her eyes went comically wide, and she shook her head vigorously from side to side in denial. "N-no I don't. I—" Her eyes flashed to her phone, and she let out a loud groan. "Ohhh, gawd! Stupid quiz."

"I wasn't trying to snoop. I saw it when I was setting your alarm."

Lehra huffed out a breath and stood, stomping toward the living room.

"Where are you going?" I asked, pushing away from the counter.

"To drown myself in the East River," she threw back over her shoulder.

Laughing, I caught her in two strides, looping an arm around her waist and hauling her back to the barstool. "Sit," I ordered, both hating and loving the flush rising up her neck. "Take a look at what's in that bag."

After glaring at me for a long moment, she pulled the book from the bag and stared at the cover. Her eyes blinked and returned to mine, confusion lacing her expression.

"You bought me a book?"

I shook my head. "'No, I bought *myself* a book. I was trying to get some tips on how to talk to you about my... desires."

Her gaze flicked back and forth between the book and me, trying to figure this all out. "So you..." She licked her lips and started again. "You like this?" She lifted the book and waved it at me.

"Yes, I'm into role playing." It felt good to say that out loud and with confidence.

Her eyes narrowed. "Like, what kind of scenarios?"

Here we fucking go. I'm about to tell her something I've never shared with anyone.

"Did you ever see that eighties movie, *Splash*?"

"The one where Daryl Hannah played..." Her eyes widened in realization. "You have a mermaid fantasy?"

"Yes, among others."

"Like what?" she challenged.

I stroked my chin. "Well, very recently, I've had the urge to be a Viking."

Lehra burst into laughter and seemed to relax into the conversation. "Have you role played before?"

"A little, but I've never done the mermaid thing. Hell, I've never even told anyone about it before you. One girlfriend was willing to play around, but she was more into scenarios you'd see in a cheesy porno, like the pizza delivery man or the pool boy."

Her face scrunched up. "I tried to do a *naughty nanny seduces the dad* thing with Dwight, and he accused me of condoning cheating."

I reached out and stroked the backs of my fingers down her cheek. "I'm sorry, Tink. I've gotten judged before and it sucks. Makes it hard to be open and honest about it."

"It makes me feel guilty sometimes because a guy once told me it was disgusting that I wanted to fantasize he was someone else, but that's not it at all," she said, her voice rising.

My heart ached for her because I knew exactly how she was feeling. "Same. It's more about... letting your imagination run wild, both of you falling into a role like an actor or actress. And it's not something I need every time or anything, just enough to make things interesting."

"Me too. And for the record, if there were still real Vikings, I'm pretty sure I wouldn't sleep with one. To be honest, I imagine they wouldn't have very good hygiene."

A low chuckle reverberated in my chest. "I promise to be a very hygienic Viking. I mean, if you want me to."

Lehra's lips twisted to the side, and she looked up at me from beneath her lashes. "You *really* want to be my Viking?"

More than anything, beautiful.

"I do. Would you like to be my mermaid?"

Pulling that full bottom lip between her teeth, she nodded happily. "I've never thought about it before, but it sounds fun."

I was pretty sure I'd never been more excited in my life. Those were the words I'd always wanted to hear but wasn't sure I ever would. Someone willing to step outside the box and let go of their inhibitions.

But with her, I wanted so much more than two fulfilled fantasies, so I decided to lay out the plan I formulated in the wee hours while staring at the shadow of my ceiling fan making quick revolutions above me.

"I was thinking, what if we each wrote down a few things we'd like to try, and then…"

"Fulfill each other's weirdo fantasies?" she finished, and I laughed. Then her expression turned serious. "With no shaming?"

I suddenly felt the need to punch Dwight or anyone else who'd ever made her feel like this. Standing, I gently parted her legs and stepped in between them. It felt like home.

"Absolutely not, Tink, but if either of us doesn't like something, it's okay to say, 'Hey, let's try something besides this.' Everything isn't for everyone, and that's fine." My palms lifted and held her pretty face. "I read that entire book last night when I couldn't fall asleep, and the number one theme was communication without judgment."

"Okay, so I guess we need to talk about ground rules?"

Sliding my hands over her shoulders and down her arms, I linked our fingers together and lowered my voice to a whispery rasp. "Do you like rough sex, Lehra?"

The full body shudder that trembled through her gave me the answer, but she replied verbally anyway. "I do."

Good fucking answer, baby.

I gave her hands an encouraging squeeze. "And what are your sexual limits?"

She tilted her head to the side and thought for a long moment. "I don't want to do a threesome."

"Yeah, not gonna happen," I assured her. If I had my way, no one besides me would ever touch her again.

"This isn't necessarily sexual, but I don't like to be tickled. Actually, I hate it. Dwight used to think it was funny."

Well, Dwight's an asshole.

"No tickling. Got it. What else?"

"I can't think of anything. What are your limits?"

I liked that she asked. Men should have the right to set limits just as much as women. "There's a full list in the back of that book we can go through. Besides agreeing with your no threesomes rule, the only other one I can think of off the top of my head is no pegging."

Her brow creased, and I wondered if that was something she was interested in. Until she asked, "What's pegging?"

With a tiny smirk, I said, "Where you wear a strap-on and…" I lifted my brows, letting the rest linger, and Lehra's mouth popped open.

"Well, darn. Guess I'll strike that from my to-do list then," she teased, her lips turning up at the edges. "This should feel uncomfortable to talk about, but it doesn't with you."

"I feel the same. Anything else we need to discuss?"

She scraped her teeth over her bottom lip a few times. "Are we exclusive during all this?"

"Yes," I said immediately, probably sounding like a possessive asshole but not caring. "Are you on birth control?"

"I have the implant. Are you thinking…"

"I'm thinking a Viking probably wouldn't have a condom in his wallet," I pointed out with a wry lift of my eyebrow, and she giggled.

"I've always used condoms, but I'd be fine with it if we didn't. If that's what you want."

"I always have too, but I don't want to with you," I told her honestly. *And not just because it might take us out of the moment.*

Her smile was tentative and vulnerable as she nodded her assent, and I leaned in for a gentle kiss because I was pretty sure we both needed it. The softness of her lips against mine again was indescribable. I'd wanted this woman for over two years, and now I was finally going to have her.

But how long would it last?

A week later, I was seated in a salon chair with a woman named Cecily running her fingers through my thick, dark hair.

"How blond do you want it?" she asked, her reflection peering intently at mine in the mirror.

"Not like platinum. Maybe a dark blond. And can we do it just temporarily? I really only need it blond for tonight."

"You going to a costume party or somethin'?" she asked in a thick Brooklyn accent.

"Something like that," I mumbled.

"Hmm. Well, your hair is really dark, so I'd have to bleach it, and that's not temporary." One hand slid down and fingered my beard. I hadn't shaved all week, and since my hair grew quickly, it was pretty full. "This too?"

"Yes, please."

Cecily pursed her lips in thought. "Huh. Tell ya what I can do. I'll make you blond today, and then tomorrow afternoon, you can come back, and I'll color it dark again."

"Sounds good."

As she mixed up the foul-smelling stuff in a little bowl, I glanced down at the list on my phone of three role playing fantasies Lehra sent me earlier this week.

I smiled in anticipation of tonight.

Be ready, baby. Your Viking warrior is coming.

CHAPTER 23

I SCROLLED THROUGH MY Instagram feed, stopping to watch a video of a cat named Snoopy and a dog named Garfield. They were snuggled up in a pet bed together, and Garfield had one paw looped protectively over the black-and-white kitty. Snoopy opened one eyelid and gave the blond lab a long, affectionate lick before smacking him in the face.

The caption read, *Snoopy loves her brother.* This was quickly becoming my favorite account on the app. Monty had shown it to Cruz who then shared it with me. We'd spent an entire evening on my couch one night, laughing as we binge watched the adventures of the ill-named duo.

My hand reached into the bag beside me and pulled out a dried banana chip. I crunched on it, wishing I had some *tater twats* instead when my front door burst open.

I leaped off the couch in surprise, spilling banana chips all over as a man stormed into my apartment and kicked the door shut behind him.

Reaching up, I stifled a squeal with my hand. *There's a goddamn Viking in my living room.*

My first thought was that it was Cruz, but fear took over my body when I saw that he had dirty blond hair on his head and face, unlike Cruz's jet-black locks. I took one step back, prepared to run when he gave a quick jerk of his chin and spoke.

"Get over here, woman."

What the actual fuck?

That was definitely Cruz's voice, though it was gruffer than usual. My eyes took him in from head to toe. The Viking wore tight wool trousers, a wide belt, and thick leather body armor, all in a dark brown with gunmetal-gray trim. A tan fur collar draped over his shoulders, and heavy black boots covered his feet.

My gaze went back to his head. *He dyed his hair. For this. For me.*

"I. Said. Come. Here," he grunted, and a tsunami of arousal flooded my white lace panties as he reached for his belt. My feet moved of their own volition at his deep command, and a second before I reached him, I heard the thunk of leather hit the floor.

I let out a little shriek when the Viking spun me around and slammed my back against the door, one hand holding the back of my head to keep me from hitting it. My hands went instantly to his shoulders, fingers sinking into the rough fur.

I couldn't pull my eyes away from him. Cruz looked like a total badass in leather and metal, his normally big body somehow transformed into that of an enormous beast of a man.

Adrenaline coursed through my veins like a potent drug. Excitement mixed with the tiniest shred of fear, which only fueled my desire.

"I'm home to claim my woman," he said in a low voice, and *dear god!* The way he said *my woman* made me want to climb him like a tree.

Then his mouth crashed to mine with bruising force. The kiss wasn't gentle. It was hard... lusty... desperate. And without another word, his lips told me the story.

My warrior had been gone at sea, and he'd returned to make me his. He'd missed me. Craved me with every fiber of his being. He was feral for me and only me, and I closed my eyes and let myself fall into the fantasy.

I moaned into his mouth, and he grunted into mine, our sounds only seeming to push our mutual desire to the next level. As his hot mouth worked its way down my neck, tonguing and sucking my damp flesh, I watched as his fingers undid the ornate silver clasp at his throat, releasing his fur collar onto the floor.

My hands met the warm leather beneath, and I was surprised to find that it wasn't as smooth as I'd thought it would be. Rather, it felt rugged against my fingertips.

"I didn't know if you'd come back to me," I panted, and he lifted his heavy-lidded eyes to mine, the blue there slightly hazy with longing.

"I'll always come back to you, my sweet one."

And then he thrust his tongue roughly into my mouth, his facial hair abrading my skin as he leaned his body into mine, pinning me to the door. My hands found the back of his head, my fingers burying themselves in the coarse strands until I could feel the warmth of his scalp.

He pulled out of the kiss, resting his forehead against mine, and his breaths were ragged beneath the leather covering his chest. Then he opened his eyes and murmured, "I need you."

Those three words were filled with gut-wrenching vulnerability, and at that moment I was pretty sure he'd let a bit of Cruz slip into his Viking persona. But I didn't care. I needed him too.

"Then take me, warrior," I breathed.

His big hands went to my waist to untie my baby-pink robe, but the silky sash had worked its way into a knot. So he did what any horny Viking would do. He ripped it in half with his bare hands. The robe was on the floor a second later, and he let out a feral growl that had my sex trembling. *Trembling, for fuck's sake!* I wasn't sure my pussy had ever trembled for anyone.

"You're wearing my clothing," he stated.

"I sleep in it every night to feel closer to you." That much was true.

His nostrils flared with arousal. He liked that answer. "You look beautiful in it, but you won't be needing it tonight. My woman will be naked beneath me in our bed until I'm done with her."

And I liked *that* answer. Very much. My pussy clenched around nothing as I visualized it. This big, brutal man on top of me, using me until his strong body was weakened from too much pleasure.

He tugged his USMC shirt off over my head in one swipe, and I was left in only my tiny white panties. If the way his blue eyes darkened when he looked down my body was any indication, he didn't seem to mind.

Large hands stroked slowly up and down my sides as if memorizing the feel of my skin before he gathered both my hands in one of his and held them over my head. Then he lowered his mouth to my breast and covered my nipple with his mouth.

"Ohhhh," I whimpered at the first pull, but it didn't deter him. He licked and sucked and bit me without remorse, his eyes closed in apparent ecstasy. Then his free hand cupped that breast as his mouth moved to the other one, and with the pad of his thumb, he massaged the peak he'd hardened only a minute ago.

His blue eyes met my gray ones, as if asking for permission, when his teeth sank lightly into the top of my tit.

"Yes, mark me. Make me yours."

The sharpness of his bite had my back arching off the door and arousal seeping down my thighs. A quick line of desire shot down my torso and straight to my pussy when he sucked until a large purple bruise appeared. He circled the mark with his tongue, and a crude look of triumph lit his eyes when he examined his handiwork.

My hands dropped to his shoulders when he released them, and I went weak as he lowered first to one knee and then the other before me. The Viking's fingers traced delicate lines down my belly, followed by the heat of his mouth. Not an inch of me was left unkissed, like I was the only deity he would ever worship.

He looked so damn hot like this, on his knees, devouring me, and I tipped my head back against the door as I watched him work his way down.

His gaze rose as he reached the apex of my thighs, and I was mesmerized by the ferocity in his glare.

Hooking his thumbs into the sides of my panties, he ripped them off and held them to his nose. His chest expanded with his deep inhale, and I felt my cheeks flush. No one had ever sniffed my panties before. Not in front of me anyway.

"It's time to coat my tongue with my woman," he announced, spreading my legs roughly and hauling one of them over his shoulder. "Every time I went into battle, I pictured your face and imagined the smell of your cunt."

"Oh my god," I breathed when he ran his nose up and down my slit. This was way better than anything I'd ever fantasized about.

"I knew I had to come out alive just so I could do this." He licked me then, a long, wet stroke of velvet against my sensitive tissues, and my supporting leg quivered in its attempt to hold me up. "*You* kept me alive, sweet one, with the promise of your orgasm in my mouth."

I begged him through a series of unintelligible syllables that weren't cohesive enough to form words, but my Viking seemed to understand because he speared me with his tongue.

"Yes!" I managed to say as that thick, rough muscle fucked in and out of me. His face was pressed so far into my pussy, I wasn't sure he'd be able to find his way back out. Not that I wanted him to. I'd be content to ride his face all the way into eternity.

The sounds he was making while he slurped and licked at my sex were so goddamn filthy, and I absolutely loved it. I'd never been devoured by a man so thoroughly, so forcefully, so zealously. It was almost like he was enjoying it as much as I was.

"Fuuuuuck, my woman tastes good," he grunted into me, sliding his tongue forward to lap at my clit. "Did you save this cunt for me?"

"Y-yes," I stammered. "No one has touched me."

"Let me feel for myself." He slid his middle finger inside me and hummed in satisfaction. "Mmmm, that is one tight little pussy. Tell me it will always be mine." His blue eyes blazed up at me, and I could see Cruz inside my Viking.

Is this partly real or completely fantasy? I wondered but brushed that thought away when he worked another finger inside me and snapped, "Tell me, woman!"

"Yes! It will always be yours. Only yours."

He began to finger-fuck me, his eyes focused completely on his task, watching his long, thick fingers stretch me, before taking my clit between his full lips.

I cried out at the delicious burn of his intrusion and the slick slide of his tongue smoothing over my little button. I'd never been more aroused in my life, and as I watched his leather-clad arm bulge with his efforts, I climbed even further.

"Almost… there," I gasped, sinking my fingers into his bleached hair and using the leverage to grind against his face.

His hot tongue laved my pussy. Back and forth, back and forth, in a perfect rhythm that had my head falling back and my eyelids shuttering. And then he stopped.

"Eyes on me when you come," he demanded, and I popped my lids open and stared down at him. With curved fingers, he stroked a spot inside me that made my fingers tighten in his hair.

"Your mouth. Please," I begged, and after a slight smirk, he went back to work.

It didn't take long. The Viking seemed to know exactly how fast to move his tongue, precisely how deep to press his fingers, and just where to touch me to get me… *right… there.*

"I'm c-c-coming," I stuttered as clouds of pure pleasure wrapped around me and blurred my vision. I felt an arm sweep my standing leg out from under me and haul it onto a strong shoulder.

But it didn't matter that my feet were no longer on the ground because I was flying. Soaring into the stratosphere like I had wings formed from long, white feathers.

My eyes and ears seemed to be smothered by the clouds, but I slowly became aware of screaming in the distance. It grew closer, and I realized it was me. I'd never been a screamer before, though I'd also never had an orgasm quite that intense.

The big man kissed his way over my mound and up my belly, leaving damp kiss marks in his wake. I should be embarrassed by how wet his beard and lips were, but I couldn't bring myself to care. I was happy and sated.

Extricating himself from my legs, which had somehow become wrapped around his head, the Viking gently set my feet on the floor. His hands held my waist to steady me for a few seconds, and then he rose to tower over me, an erotic vision in leather and metal.

"Damn, you're loud, woman. Now the entire village knows you've been claimed by me." His half-smile was smug and sexy as all hell. "Though I'm sure they already knew when I got off the ship and headed directly here."

I pictured it in my head. A huge warrior, dwarfing all others as he stomped through a small village, his boots kicking up swirls of dust behind him. Because he couldn't wait to get here. To me.

"And who's claiming you?" I asked saucily.

"You don't need to claim me. I've been yours since the first time I saw you." He took my hand and pressed it over his heart. "This will always belong to you, sweet one."

The beautiful words fluttered through me like a million butterflies as I looked up into his sincere gaze. *Wow. He's either a really good actor or...*

I slid my hand down over the nubbly leather to the front of his trousers. His cock stood straight out from his body, and I wrapped my hand around it over the soft material. It felt like he was going commando.

"And what about this, my Viking? Can I claim this too?" I purred, earning me a sharp thrust of his hips.

"Also yours, but I think I'd like you to claim it anyway."

His fingers deftly loosened the drawstring at his trim waist, and I slipped my hand inside to find him hot and bare in my palm. As I explored him, I found...

Oh my god, he's pierced! Twice! I pulled his pants down until they rested on his hips, and his huge erection sprang free so I could see it. The tip was a deep red color, and I imagined it would be smooth and salty on my tongue.

Both piercings were at the base of his cock, one on top and one on bottom, so no matter if he took me from the front or back, one of them would stimulate my clit when he was fully inserted. My fingers toyed with each of them, and his dick twitched in my palm.

"Fuck," he muttered, slamming his hands onto the door beside my head, effectively caging me in. "Lick my mouth and know that it will be the only one to ever taste you."

I did, lapping up the taste of myself from his lips as I stroked his cock with unhurried precision. He was thick—so damned thick—and pre-ejaculate leaked from his tip and down the length of him.

Beneath his beard, I could see the clenching of his jaw, and I added a little twist of my wrist each time I reached his crown.

"Stop," he panted, his pained face contorted into a grimace, "or I'll come in your hand."

"You don't want to come in my hand?" I teased, giving him another slow stroke and twist.

He yanked my hand away, his grip tight on my wrist. "No. The only place I spill my seed is inside my woman."

Holy hell. That's fucking hot.

Before I could say another word, I was being hoisted up with his hands on my ass and my legs wrapped around him. His cock was hot and heavy against me, and I wriggled against it, needing the friction, despite having just come all over his face a few minutes ago.

"Put me inside you before I die," he rasped, sounding as if he was on the brink of losing his mind.

I wasn't sure how he managed to be so sweet and dirty and possessive all at once, but I loved every second of it. Reaching between us, I maneuvered his cock until the tip was poised at my entrance.

He didn't hesitate for a second, plunging into me in one brutal thrust. I cried out, feeling like he was splitting me in half, but I wouldn't have changed a thing.

"So wet," he groaned, leaning forward for a kiss as he pulsed slowly to let me adjust. "So hot and tight around me. Do you know how long I've waited for this? To make you my fucking woman?"

"Me too. So many months," I exhaled, trying to catch a breath.

His blue gaze met mine. "Try years, sweet one. I've been waiting for you for years." The sincerity and ache in his eyes made me think he was talking about me, Lehra, and not the maiden in this scene. But that couldn't be right.

"You have me now."

The ache in his beautiful eyes dissipated as he pulled back and shoved his rock-hard erection back into me, awakening nerve endings I didn't even know I had. "Say you're mine."

"I'm yours."

Another aggressive thrust. "Say it again."

"I'm yours."

He was literally knocking the words from my mouth with his ferocious fucking. "Again!"

"I'm yours. I promise, I'm only yours," I cried as my arousal flooded his cock. *How the hell am I so turned on by this?*

The Viking pressed deep, grinding the barbell on top of his cock against my clit, and my inner walls fluttered around him. He must have felt it because his lips tipped up into a wicked smile.

"My woman likes taking me inside her pretty cunt, doesn't she?" he growled, working up a fierce cadence that had my eyes rolling back in my head. Our bodies slapped together, the sound echoing around the room as he covered my mouth with his.

The kiss was sweet and slow, so different from the brutal way he was taking me, and my heart melted for him. Cruz was giving me everything I've ever dreamed about and more. I hadn't even given him any details, but somehow he knew I wanted to be so desired that he couldn't help but fuck me like an animal.

Backing out of the kiss, his breath warmed my lips when he whispered, "You are so goddamn beautiful."

Then he reached for one of my legs, unwinding it from his waist and pulling it up and over his shoulder, practically bending me in half. He leaned forward, and the new angle had the head of his cock hitting a spot inside me that was unlike anything I'd ever felt before.

Combined with his piercing rubbing against my swollen clit, something built in my depths. Something foreign. Something powerful. Something a little bit scary, to be honest.

But I didn't care. I wanted it. Whatever *it* was.

I clutched at his shoulders, my fingernails scratching against the leather as my body began to tremble from head to toe. "It's... I can't... it's too much," I jabbered because I didn't know how to explain what was happening to my body.

Looping one strong arm beneath my ass to hold me up, the big Viking used his other hand to tenderly stroke my face. "I know, sweet one. Don't try to fight it. Let go for me."

The words were delivered quietly, still a command but a caring one. So I did what he asked and relaxed into the feeling.

The results were nothing short of magnificent. If I'd thought my first orgasm was akin to soaring like a bird, this one was like I was being rocketed directly into space. Tiny pinpricks of light dotted the periphery of my vision like stars, and I came, and I came, and I came.

A soft beard chafed against the side of my face as a deep, groaning voice growled into my ear. "That's it, baby. Fucking gush around my cock. You're my perfect girl, aren't you?"

Then with three more pumps—each accompanied by a rugged grunt—he held himself deep and filled me. We clung to each other as our heaving chests rubbed together, his covered with leather, and mine bare.

Slowly, I allowed myself to come out of the fantasy and back to real life, and I saw a blond Cruz staring back at me, a look of awe on his handsome face.

We were both perspiring, but his face and body were completely drenched, no doubt from wearing the heavy costume. It was especially damp where we were joined down below. No, not damp. Completely soaked.

Maybe he has a ball sweat issue. Or perhaps he's a cum machine. Hell, I don't give a damn what it is when he can fuck like that.

"Jesus, Lehra. Have you ever squirted before?" Cruz asked, and my eyes widened before moving down. He was still inside me, and the sight of his thickness buried in my sex made me want to take a picture and frame it. But that would be weird. *Right?*

"I squirted?" I asked, returning my gaze to him, and he grinned ruefully.

"Yeah, baby. What did you think all that wetness was? Ball sweat or something?"

"No, of course not," I said a little too quickly. "Are you sure I squirted?"

His lips sucked softly against mine. "Positive."

Embarrassment heated my cheeks. "I've never done that. Did it weird you out?"

He chuckled, shaking his head in amusement as he pulled my leg from his shoulder and back around his middle. "Not even a little bit. It was the hottest thing ever."

"So have you…" I trailed off, not really wanting to hear about it if he'd had the same experience with another woman, but Cruz picked up my vibe.

"No, but I've read a lot about it. The dual stimulation is supposed to help. You know, with me inside and then the piercing on your clit." He took a careful step back, and I realized there was liquid all over the floor beneath us. *Good god! That is a lot of vagina juice.* "Let's take a shower and get cleaned up."

"Why didn't you tell me you have dick piercings?" I asked as he carried me down the hallway.

"When exactly was I supposed to bring it up? I'm not sure of the proper etiquette for that kind of conversation."

I giggled as we entered my bathroom. "Maybe they teach that type of thing at finishing schools."

"I must have been absent that day," he retorted dryly before squeezing my butt with both hands. "Can you stand up?"

"I'm not sure. I think you fucked all the bones out of my body."

He gave me a lascivious grin. "I think you were the one fucking my bone."

I rolled my eyes at his ridiculousness, and as he set me down and began undressing, my mind spun.

I just had sex with Cruz Estrada. The guy I've been crushing on for a long time but who never asked me out.

I was surprised there was no after-sex awkwardness, but there was none at all. We fucked—very well, I might add—and now we were back to our regular teasing selves.

Friends with the best benefit package I'd ever heard of.

As he stripped off his pants, I looked down at his thick, pierced cock. *Benefit package indeed.*

CHAPTER 24

LEHRA RAN HER FINGERS through my slightly damp hair as we lay on her bed facing each other. "I can't believe you dyed your hair blond."

Laughing, I kissed the top of her head. "I wanted to fully commit to the role." *And to you.* "Was it... okay?"

"More than okay. Better than I could have ever imagined." She snuggled closer, and I reveled in holding her warm, naked body against mine. "Thank you," she whispered. "I feel like I should make you some cookies."

Dear god, no.

We'd showered together, and then I cleaned up the, er, evidence from the floor beside the door while she dried her hair.

I'd been rough on her tonight, but she'd taken every bit of me without complaint. My cock hardened against her stomach as I thought about fucking her against that door, the way her body responded to me. She really was the perfect woman.

The room was dark, but I could see her eyes shining silver in the moonlight as they made a quick downward flick. Then she looked back at me and lifted her eyebrows.

"Well, someone woke up to say hello."

Growling, I lowered my voice and yanked her beneath me, covering her with my body. "You didn't think the Viking would be satisfied with fucking his woman only once, did you?"

She grinned as she spread her legs and cradled my hips with her smooth thighs. "Heavens no. My Viking can take me as many times as he wants."

I parted her sex with the head of my cock and slid slowly home. "It's going to be a very long night for you, sweet one."

My phone pinged on the nightstand, and I groaned into the back of Lehra's hair. "Who the fuck is texting me at this ungodly hour?" I slid my hand up and down the curve of her hip. "Grab my phone and see who it is. Then tell them to fuck off till after nine because some crazy woman was on my dick all night, and I need my beauty sleep."

She laughed sleepily and took my phone from the charger before unlocking it. I could feel the instant her body stiffened. "Maybe you should answer this one yourself," she said curtly, handing me the phone and rolling off the bed. "I'll go to the bathroom and give you some privacy."

What the hell is she talking about? Why would I need privacy?

As she went into the bathroom and closed the door, I looked down at the screen.

> **Cecily: I'm so sorry I can't meet you today. I have a stomach bug, and trust me, you don't want me anywhere near you. We can get together next week, if that's okay.**

My eyes went to the white wood of the bathroom door, and I grinned. *I think Tink is jealous.* The thought made me more than a little happy.

When she came out, I was sitting up against the headboard. Her smile was forced, and she had pulled on a T-shirt to cover her nakedness. "I'm just gonna go to the kitchen and make some coffee."

"Come here first, Tink. I've got a problem." Two furrows appeared between her eyes, but she walked slowly toward the bed. As soon as she was within reach, I hauled her over me until she was straddling my lap, earning me a little yelp.

"What are you doing, Cruz?"

"I need your help."

Her lips pinched tightly together. "I'm not sure what I can do."

I took her face in my hand and squeezed her cheeks a few times until the line of her mouth relaxed. Then I kissed her lips with a featherlight touch. "Cecily is a woman I met yesterday."

"Oh. Okay, so you want to... what? Call off our arrangement?"

Damn, she's cute when she's jealous.

Putting her out of her misery, I kissed her palm and then rubbed it over my dark blond beard. "Cecily is the hairdresser who did this to me." Lehra tried to hide her relief, but I felt it in the loosening of her body. "I was supposed to go back for an appointment today to get un-blonded, and now she's canceled."

Her eyes rounded. "And you can't exactly go to work like this on Monday."

"Right. I've driven Gianna a few times to the salon where Cecily works, so that's how I knew about it, but I don't really know where to find someone else. I usually go to a barber."

She tilted her head in thought. "I'm sure the barber could fix this." Her fingers stroked through my hair, and I leaned into the sweet touch.

"He doesn't work on Saturdays. When I need a trim, I go after I drop off Auburn in the morning and don't have anything else to do for a couple hours."

"We'll just find another salon," she reasoned. I totally could have done that myself, but I wanted an excuse to spend more time with Lehra. "I'm sure someone could work you in today."

An hour and a half later, Lehra sighed and dropped her phone on the counter as I walked back into her kitchen. "That one was a no, as well. Apparently there's a huge hair convention in town, and every stylist in New York is attending, and the ones who aren't going are booked. I even checked salons and barber shops in Jersey."

"Shit," I said, handing her the coffee I'd just bought at the local shop. "It should be cool enough for you. By the way, the barista looked at me all weird."

Lehra giggled. "She's probably wondering what the hell happened to your hair." She looked at me over the rim of her cup. "We could shave your facial hair, and that would take care of that, but we have to do something... Hmmm. Do you trust me?"

"Sure."

"Okay, let's go." She took my hand and led me out of the kitchen and toward the front door, obviously on a mission.

"Where are we going?"

"The beauty supply store. I'm going to color your hair myself."

Good lord, I hope she does hair better than she bakes.

"Damn, Tink. That looks really good," I told her, turning my head side to side to survey her work.

"It does," she said proudly before tugging lightly at my beard. "Just have to get rid of this now, though I might kinda miss it."

"I can grow it back anytime you want," I assured her. "This one only took me a few days."

Digging through a drawer, she came out with a slim, pink razor and I scoffed. "Going to need something a little more sturdy to get rid of this." My hand massaged my jaw.

"Ohhh, pardon me for insulting your very manly beard."

"Damn straight this beard is manly." I tugged on her curly ponytail. "Let's go to my place to finish this mission."

While we walked down the hallway to my apartment, she asked, "How is the investigation at work going? After the shooting during the Cappitani raid?"

"It's over now, and I'm being reinstated as of next weekend." One of my shoulders lifted into a shrug as I unlocked my door. "I mean, I had no doubt about it, but I'm glad it's over."

She stalled me with a soft grasp of my hand once we were inside and pulled me around to face her. Her pretty eyes glistened in the dim light. "And you're okay?"

I loved her empathetic heart. "I'm okay, Tink. I promise." My lips pressed a soft kiss to her forehead.

"Did your appointment go well with the psychologist?" Before I could answer, her face scrunched. "Sorry, that was too personal."

Nothing is too personal with you, sweetheart.

"Not at all. And it was fine. I know a lot of officers grumble about doing that, but it's a good idea to talk it out." I tugged her along with me and headed to my bathroom. "We're taught as humans to value other human lives, so it gets all jumbled up in your head when someone as evil as Luca Cappitani dies. It's hard to muster any sympathy at all for the man."

"Understandable. I've been watching on the news, and I'm not even sure that horrible man could be considered human. Have they found the son yet?"

"Nope. He wasn't there or at his home when the raids took place. He's disappeared just like his brother."

"Brother?" she asked, confused. "I thought there was just one Cappitani son."

"He had a younger brother that vanished years ago. Probably pissed off his psycho father and is now resting at the bottom of the Atlantic."

I rummaged through my middle drawer and came out with my clippers and my green-and-black razor. Lehra picked up the latter and studied it.

"This looks like it could cut through the Amazonian jungles," she mused.

"Yes, well, that's my face. Take it or leave it."

She patted my cheek. "I think I'll take it. I kinda like this face."

An almost unbearable warmth spread through my chest, and I dropped a kiss on her nose before handing her the clippers. "You want to do the honors of de-bearding the Viking? Then you can shave me."

"Seriously?" she squealed. "You'll let me?"

Honey, when you smile like that, I'd let you shave my entire body.

"Of course," I said, grabbing a chair and sitting so she could reach me.

Lehra's face was a mask of concentration, her small pink tongue between her teeth as she ran the clippers over my jaw. Then a look of amusement curled her lips upward, and I asked, "What are you smiling about?"

She stepped back and allowed me to look in the mirror at the very long sideburns she'd left me. "You look like Elvis," she giggled.

I immediately stood and pulled her into my arms, swiveling my hips into hers as I did my best impersonation of the King of Rock and Roll while singing about being a hunka hunka burning love.

We laughed as I twirled her around the spacious bathroom, and I was sure I'd never had as much fun with a woman. Lehra Kincaid was everything I'd ever wanted.

"You're getting your man hairs all over me," she complained lightly, and I bobbed my eyebrows up and down as I gave one more Elvis-like thrust of my hips.

"Then we'll just have to take another shower together, won't we?"

She stood on her tiptoes and kissed my lips. "I love your voice. Can you sing something else for me?"

Pulling her even closer, I chose another Elvis tune, this one much slower, and her face burrowed into my neck as I sang, "Can't Help Falling in Love." Our arms were wound tightly around each other, and we swayed in place on the marble tiled floor. I hummed the few lyrics I didn't know, though she didn't seem to mind.

When I was done, she kissed the side of my neck but didn't pull away. "I think that's the most beautiful song ever."

My hands stroked up and down her back as I inhaled her sunny scent.

Because you're the most beautiful woman ever.

Chapter 25

I WAS ASLEEP IN my bed when my phone rang in the middle of the night. "Hello," I answered groggily.

"Hey, it's me," Lehra's voice said quietly.

I popped up, immediately alert, and turned on my bedside lamp. "What's wrong?"

"It's me inside your apartment. Don't attack me or anything." Then she hung up.

Rubbing at my left eye, I blinked down at my phone. *What the...*

That's when I heard footsteps in my hallway and stood, anxiety spearing through me. She pushed open my door and strode in like she owned the place. The black pencil skirt she wore rode high on her thighs—mouth-wateringly high—and her black jacket was fitted. A crimson tie draped down across the white top covering her breasts, and I was amazed she could walk in those damn patent-leather heels she was wearing. She'd tamed her curly hair into a prim bun on top of her head.

"Lehra, why are you—" I was about to ask her why she was fully dressed while I was standing here in my underwear, but she cut me off.

"Shut your mouth, prisoner." That's when I noticed the police baton she was pointing at me. "Back on the bed."

Ahhh, one of the role playing fantasies I'd written down for her. This one had been tough for me because I liked to be in control, and this would leave me as the vulnerable one. I'd debated having her as the prisoner and me the warden, but at the last minute, I'd changed my mind, curious as to what she would do in this scenario.

So far, she's fucking killing it. My cock is already interested.

I sat on my bed, and she walked toward me, her expression hard. "Do you know who I am?"

"Yes."

"Yes, what?" she barked, tapping the T hard at the end.

"Yes, ma'am," I answered dutifully, trying to fight my smile. "You're the warden."

"Very good, prisoner sixty-nine." I chuckled at that, and she narrowed her eyes, causing me to school my features and mutter an apology. Lifting the baton, she placed the end of it against my chest and pressed. "Lie back and keep your hands to yourself. Don't give me a reason to hurt you."

"Of course, ma'am. Whatever you say."

Every one of my reservations about being the vulnerable one fled from my brain in an instant. This was fucking hot. *She* was fucking hot.

She dragged the tip of the baton down my abdomen, watching as it bumped over each of my abs before reaching my crotch. She prodded it and purred, "I've been watching you on the cameras in the shower room. Verrrrrry impressive, prisoner."

I widened my eyes in faux outrage. "You can't do that. It's an invasion of my privacy."

The warden lifted her eyebrows, unimpressed with my complaint. "Let me make one thing clear. This is *my* prison, and *I'm* in charge here. Am I understood?" She placed the baton between my legs and pressed upward, not hard enough to hurt, but definitely enough to get her point across.

"Y-yes, ma'am." I didn't even have to fake the stammer because she was holding a big black stick against my junk. Strangely enough, my cock decided he liked being threatened by a gorgeous woman and thickened behind my heather-gray briefs. *What the fuck, dude?*

She pulled back and traced the outline of my dick with the baton. "Why aren't you wearing your uniform, prisoner sixty-nine?"

"I get hot when I sleep."

"Hmm," she mused, still looking at the erection that was growing by the second. "You've been here a while. I'd think you'd know the rules by now. What do you think we should do about this breach in protocol?"

"Let it slide?" I asked hopefully, and she shook her head.

"Oh, I don't think so." She slid the stick up until it was beneath my chin. "I think you need to be properly punished."

"Whatever you think, Warden Kincaid. I could wash your car or something."

Her beautiful lips curled into a catlike smile. "Oh, I'm sure we could come up with something better than that." Placing the baton on the bedside table, she removed her suit jacket, revealing that the white shirt beneath it was sleeveless.

"This seems highly inappropriate, Warden," I commented, and her eyes held mine as she slowly untied the crimson tie.

"Remind me again... who's in charge here?" Her voice was saccharine sweet.

"You are."

"Good. Now put your hands above your head and hold on to the rail."

I did, wondering what the hell she was up to, but I didn't have to wonder long. The warden hitched up her skirt and straddled my chest, using the tie to bind me to my wooden headboard.

I knew the instant her wet pussy made contact with my chest that she wasn't wearing panties, and my cock throbbed a hard beat of approval in my underwear. She was as aroused as I was, her divine scent reaching my nostrils and making me groan.

"What?" she asked with a sigh as she scooted back until she was sitting on my aching cock.

"Are you going to force me to eat your pussy, ma'am?"

Please say yes. Please, for the love of god, say yes.

She scooped up the wetness she'd left on my chest and scowled at me. "If you are a *very* good boy while I'm getting myself off on this magnificent cock," she swiveled her hips, and I almost came on the spot, "then I might allow you to lick your cum from my very tasty cunt."

Then she stuck her finger into my mouth and ordered, "Clean me."

Holy fucking shit. She is going hardcore with this little fantasy, and I'm loving every second of it.

Locking my eyes with hers, I rolled my tongue around and around her finger, savoring every drop and relishing the desire that darkened her eyes.

Her soft hands slid down my abs as she shimmied backward until her knees were on either side of my shins. Hooking her fingers into the waistband of my briefs, she slid them down to my thighs, smiling when my dick came into view, fully erect against my stomach.

Her thumbs smoothed against the front of my hip bones as she lowered her head and licked a hot trail up my length.

"Fuuuuck," I hissed.

"I've never had a cock this big in my mouth. Do you think I can take it?"

I gave her a lazy smirk. "I'm sure you're a woman of many talents, Warden."

Her cheeks twitched with a restrained smile before she lifted my dick and wrapped her lips around the head. When her gray eyes met mine, she sank her sweet mouth slowly down onto me until I touched the back of her throat.

"Oh my fucking god," I cried out, my hips lifting from the bed and shoving my cock down her throat. She gagged, pulled back a little, and then deepthroated me again. My breaths were coming in harsh pants as she began bobbing her head up and down my shaft, her movements slow and tortuous.

She had the absolute hottest mouth I'd ever been in. Tight lips. Constantly moving tongue. And just the barest hint of teeth.

I was gritting my molars to maintain my composure when the warden lifted her head and took my length in her small hand as she tasted my balls, first one and then the other. Every lash of her tongue brought me higher and higher, closer to that peak that I knew would undo me as she stroked me with hard, fast pumps.

"Your mouth is perfect," I groaned as she took my dick back inside that warm cavern. "I like watching your lips stretch around my cock."

She hummed when a gush of pre-ejaculate dripped onto her tongue, and then she really went to town on me. I lifted my hips, fucking up into her mouth, and she stopped.

"Be. Still," she commanded.

Fuck. "Sorry, Warden. You just suck my dick so good."

She held my hips down with two hands and went back to work. As she sped up, my back strained off the mattress and my arms tugged at the restraint holding me to the headboard. I could have easily snapped the damn thing, rolled her over, and fucked her mouth until I came, but I was trying my best to give her the lead.

It was hard to give up control, but it was also exhilarating as hell watching her confidence in this scene. My head pressed hard into the pillow, and my jaw tightened so brutally, I was afraid I'd snap a tendon.

"I'm about to come," I gritted out, my entire body shaking with effort to hold back. She was so damned good at this.

The warden pulled back to the tip, swirling her velvety tongue around the head a few times before releasing me with an audible pop. "Not yet," she cooed, rising up onto her knees and unbuttoning her shirt.

My eyes followed every movement as I inhaled lungfuls of air. I'd never been this fucking turned on in my life. She shrugged off her shirt, and my eyes traced a line between her hard nipples.

"Your tits are so fucking pretty, but I bet that cunt would be even prettier swallowing my cock," I told her boldly.

She crawled up my body, dragging her wet pussy over my length as her mouth hovered over mine. "You've got an awfully dirty mouth, prisoner. If I were wearing panties, I'd stuff them in there to shut you up."

"Next time," I suggested, and her lips arched into a coy smile. "Will you untie me so I can touch you?"

"Ohhh, I don't think so," she purred, licking at my lips. As soon as I lifted my head to kiss her, she pulled away and grinded down onto my throbbing erection. "It would be a shame to let a big, hard dick like this go to waste."

"Such a shame," I agreed, my voice gritty with desperation.

Straightening at the knees and hips, she took me in her hand and positioned herself on my tip. With our eyes locked together, she spread her legs and sank down on me in one unhurried motion. We both moaned our pleasure.

"Mmmm, you are a big boy, aren't you?"

"And you're a very sexy girl. Let your hair down for me."

She was sheathing me so tightly, holding herself still as she reached up and released her bun. A riot of blonde curls draped down over her shoulders, taking her from sleek prison warden to sex kitten in about five seconds.

"That's it, pretty girl. Now ride this cock like you own it."

Her gray irises flared with mischief. "I do own it."

Goddamn right you do.

She began to move, and her motions were so fluid, so sensual, I had to bite down on my inner cheek to keep from coming just from watching her. Sliding her hands up her stomach, she gripped her breasts, rolling those rosy nipples as her head tilted back and her cunt slid up and down my thick length.

I couldn't take my eyes off her. She was so fucking beautiful, lips parted and eyes closed as she rode me slowly. Her hip movements were nothing short of erotic, rotating in a deliberate swivel on every downstroke.

My hands itched to touch her, but I didn't want to ruin this perfect moment as she lost herself in the carnal act of fucking. Shoving my own desires to the wayside, I clenched my ass muscles, raising my hips a few inches off the bed and letting her use me for her own pleasure.

"God, yes!" Her cry was deep and throaty as she dropped her hands to my abs and grinded her clit against my piercing. Her rhythm picked up a notch, her head tilting back to form the most tempting arch of her neck. I wanted to sink my teeth into that soft spot on the left side, the one I'd found when we'd spent the night together a couple weeks ago. The one that made her go wild.

The tightness of her pussy increased to the point where I was pretty sure she was going to break my cock. And then she came. It was absolutely breathtaking. The air stalled in my windpipe, and I watched in awe as her body trembled above me, her cries of pleasure filling the room.

When her orgasm began to fade away, I let out a loud exhale when her sated gaze met mine. A slow, sexy grin draped itself across her lips, and she leaned over me to untie my hands. I took full advantage of the tits hanging right over my face and lapped at one rock-hard nipple. She let out a little whimper and shimmied back down my body.

"It's your turn," she whispered, rolling her hips and resting her nose against mine. I didn't waste a second, sliding one hand to her round ass and one into her hair to pull her lips to mine. Then I thrust upward as our tongues tangled together.

My burning needs hit front and center, my entire body demanding a hard, fast climax. Over and over, I shoved my cock crudely up into her, our bodies slamming together with loud clapping sounds that rocked the entire bed.

I came only a minute later, roaring my release into her mouth. Her pussy walls were clenching rhythmically around me, telling me she was about to come again, but my erection was deflating like a balloon after that epic orgasm. *Fuck, gotta take care of my girl.*

Before I'd even caught my breath, I hauled her off my dick and up my body until her knees rested on either side of my face. Then I slipped two fingers into her wetness and devoured her clit with long laps, hard sucks, and tiny bites.

She pressed her hands against the wall and rode my face and my fingers, once again losing herself in the pleasure. I could feel my own release inside her, could taste the mingling of us dripping out onto my tongue. She was the only woman I'd ever come in, so this was the first time I was experiencing it. I found it sexy as hell.

"Fuck. Coming," she panted, clamping down around my fingers and letting out a scream. She shuddered, dropping her head down and breathing heavily as she rode the last flutters of her orgasm away.

I tugged her gently until she was lying beside me, engulfed in my arms and covered with my kisses. "You were such a badass, Lehra." Nuzzling her ear, I nipped at the lobe. "So fucking hot."

She seemed to love my praise, her lips curved into a satisfied smile. Her hand made slow circles on my ass, and then she gave me a light smack. "Next time maybe I'll spank you."

A chuckle escaped my throat. "Maybe I'll let you." There was no maybe about it. Any dirty and depraved thing this woman wanted, I would do. I was so in love with her.

A few minutes later, she rose from the bed and went to the en suite bathroom. I heard the toilet flush and the water running, and then she returned with a cloth in her hand. She proceeded to remove my underwear the rest of the way and clean me up before telling me she'd be right back. Tugging her skirt down and pulling on her shirt, she left the room. When she came back, she handed me a bottle of water and ordered me to drink while she gently rubbed my hair.

I was blown away. Was she giving... aftercare? To me? I'd always thought the guy should be the one to do that, but... damn. She *had* been the one in charge tonight. And I couldn't deny it made me feel cared for and special.

With a coy smile, she took my discarded boxer briefs and informed me, "I'm keeping these."

Bellowing out a laugh, I said, "Okay, Warden." When she turned to leave, my eyebrows furrowed. "Where are you going?"

"To my office," she said, taking on her Warden Kincaid posture once again. "And prisoner?" she asked as she reached the door to my bedroom.

"Yeah?"

"You can wash my car tomorrow."

And she strutted out, leaving me stunned but with a big grin on my face.

CHAPTER 26

I SLEPT IN ON Saturday, and as soon as my eyes opened, I closed them again and buried my face in my pillow.

"God, what was I thinking?" I groaned into my pillow, the words muffled against the fluff as I remembered going to Cruz's apartment in the middle of the night. "I was like a crazy person."

Maybe I could smother myself with this pillow, I thought before deciding against it. I needed to get my hair color touched up before I could die. No one wanted to be lying in a casket while the funeral attendees lamented about the state of the deceased's roots.

Rolling onto my back, I stared at nothing and did a quick playback of my middle-of-the-night sneak visit. Then I started overthinking. *Was the baton thing too much?* He'd looked surprised, though he did get hard. Very hard.

No, he definitely enjoyed the scene. The sight of his veins popping out the side of his neck while I was going down on him would live rent free in my brain forever. A smile pushed my cheeks upward. *It was a pretty damn good blow job, if I do say so myself.*

I'd felt confident and alive last night, though acting like a bossy bitch was way far out of my comfort zone. But that's what role playing was all about, right? To do things you wouldn't normally do. Like fucking a Viking.

I wasn't sure what had come over me; it could've had something to do with the liquid courage—in the form of one of those small bottles of Fireball they display on the counter at the liquor store—I'd shot before walking down the hallway to Cruz's.

Adjusting the pillow beneath my head, I giggled at the ceiling. I'd even tied him to his bed, which was completely unplanned.

Suddenly I sat bolt upright, reaching for my phone as a thought occurred to me. "No. No, no, no." I searched my email and found the document Cruz had sent me. After our initial discussion about our arrangement, he'd sent me an extremely detailed list of limits we could both fill out. I'd read his over after he sent it, but I thought I remembered...

Scrolling down the list, I found the item I was looking for:

Are you okay with being tied down? Answer: No.

"Fuck!" I squeaked out. "Noooooo."

The number one rule when playing sexual games of any kind was to respect each other's clear boundaries, and I'd obliterated this one last night. How could he ever trust me again?"

I ran through the memory once more in my head, cringing when I thought of sitting on top of Cruz and binding his hands to the bed frame with my tie. It had felt like such a sexy thing to do at the time.

He hadn't said anything. *Why hadn't he said anything? Shit!*

My fingernails drummed against my lips as I paced back and forth. What should I do? What if he'd had some kind of traumatic experience while he was in the Marine Corps and that's why he didn't want to be tied up? Maybe he'd been captured or something and... *Oh god, this is a nightmare.*

I had to go check on him to make sure he was okay. Clipping my hair on top of my head, I quickly showered, brushed my teeth, and got dressed in a purple workout set. Then I walked to his apartment and knocked.

No answer. *Shit.* Just to make sure he wasn't lying on his bed in a traumatic ball, I used my key card to open his door. After a quick search of the apartment, I determined he wasn't there.

He wasn't resuming work until next week, so maybe he'd gone out to run errands or for an early lunch. *Might as well get your workout done to burn off some of this nervous energy, you rule-breaking perv.*

Our apartment building was swanky as hell and had a workout room on each level, designated only for the residents of that floor. It was nice not to have to battle for machines with everyone in the building. Walking to the end of the hallway, I pushed open the glass doors and stepped into the small foyer. As I rounded the corner into the main room, which was beautifully done with hardwood floors and mirrored walls, I froze.

Cruz Estrada was in the weight room on the far side of the gym. He had a bar laden with what looked like a couple tons of weights across his shoulders, and he was doing squats.

I'm not ashamed to say that I gawked. His thigh muscles were thick and moved like fluid beneath his caramel skin. The black tank he wore covered what I knew was a strong back, and his ass? Have mercy! It was like God and Satan had joined forces to sculpt Cruz's behind. Beauty and temptation combined to form two very fine gluteus maximus muscles that perfectly filled out his tight black shorts.

Oh, and to top it all off, he had his hat on backward. *My damn weakness.*

I was happy to see I wasn't the only one staring. The poor woman running on the treadmill in the main room was ogling so hard, she lost her footing and had to grab onto the handles to keep from falling off the machine. She was dressed in beige-colored shorts and a matching sports bra, giving the impression that she was working out naked.

My attention went back to Cruz. He seemed okay, but the gym wasn't the best place to have the kind of serious discussion I needed to have with him. Not with someone else present anyway.

Go away, lady. You're hot enough already.

She didn't heed my silent plea, instead choosing to shut down the tread-mill and head to one of the machines that I didn't know the name of. It did involve a lot of leg spreading though as she kept her gaze trained on the glassed-in weight room.

A frisson of jealousy arced through my chest. Naked girl was definitely interested. But hells bells, who wouldn't be?

Cruz finished his set and wiped down with a plush dove-gray towel before exiting the small room with the weights. I pulled back, finding his reflection in one of the mirrored walls. He climbed on one of the treadmills and worked up a nice jog while watching his phone and laughing at whatever he saw there.

Okay, he doesn't seem to be traumatized, I noted with relief, though I still wanted to talk to him about last night. My phone rang in my pocket, and I stifled a surprised scream. Ducking quickly out into the corridor, I answered in a rush.

"Hello?"

"Hey, girl! Still on for lunch today?" Nicolette's cheery voice asked.

"Lunch? Today?" I asked breathlessly, running to my apartment like I'd been caught doing something illegal.

"Um, yes. We're meeting Artie at that breakfast shop he's been wanting to try. Are you okay? You sound out of breath."

"Just left the workout room," I panted as I entered my living room and flopped onto the couch. It wasn't technically a lie.

"Okay, I'll let you get cleaned up. See you in an hour."

"Seriously, it was the most uninspiring sexual experience of my life," Nicolette complained, sipping on her mimosa. "And I've had some boring sex in my days."

Artie and I shared a glance. We'd heard similar stories from Nic for years.

"And where did you meet this lousy lay?" Artie asked.

Our friend lets out a long sigh. "At a convention."

"Therein lies the problem," I commented. "You need to have smexy times with someone other than other scientists."

"And the people said *Amen*," Artie sang, raising his own champagne glass in the air. "You need to get you a big, hairy biker dude, honey."

Nicolette looked appalled. "Not my type."

"Ohhh, that's right. Your type is men who don't know what to do with their penises," Artie said a bit too loudly. Two women who appeared to be in their eighties gasped as they passed our table, and Artie gave them an overexaggerated smile and a sarcastic twiddle of his fingers.

"I like clean-cut guys. I just want a *dirty* clean-cut guy," Nicolette clarified.

"Clean-cut doesn't necessarily mean a science nerd," I mused. "What about, like, an accountant or something?"

Nic gave me a droll roll of her green eyes. "The only accountant I know is my own. His name is Earl, and he sucks his teeth while he talks." In demonstration, she placed her tongue against her top teeth and emitted a long sucking noise.

Giggling, I mouthed a *thank you* to the server, who was dropping off our breakfast sandwiches. I was feeling a little better after seeing that Cruz looked okay today at the gym and now that I was with my crazy friends.

"What about work? How are things in the lab?" I queried, changing the subject.

Her nose scrunched. "My boss is a bitchy, micro-managing, shrew who is driving me cuckoo pants. Last week she told me she wanted to observe me running an HPLC assay to make sure I was doing it correctly. I mean really! A first-year grad student could do that, and I have two doctorate degrees." She held up two fingers to prove her point.

"The, um, H-L-what?" I asked. Sometimes I wasn't sure Nicolette was actually speaking English.

"HPLC," she corrected. "It's a reversed-phase high-performance liquid chromatograph, and I've been running them for over a decade." She waved a hand at Artie, whose mouth was gaping so wide, a piece of egg fell out and onto his lap. "Hell, even he could do it."

Artie closed his mouth and lifted a doubtful eyebrow. "Yes, well, I think I'll pass on running the chromosome-o-graph of asses or whatever. I wouldn't want to embarrass the other scientists."

Nicolette giggled. "Chromatography assays, and my boss isn't even a scientist. She has a bachelor's degree in women's studies."

Artie and I shared a stunned expression. "How the hell is she running that lab then?" I asked. Nicolette had a PhD in biochemistry, an MD with a residency in dermatology, and a master's in microbiology. I couldn't imagine anyone being more qualified than her.

"Oh, she's not. I run the entire lab, but she has the title—and the corresponding salary—because she's the CEO's favorite niece. The other day she asked what I was doing, and I told her I was checking a sample for mercury. She asked what a planet had to do with cosmetics."

I pressed my forehead against my palm and shook my head. "Please tell me that's not true."

"It's the god's honest truth, and I'm not sure how much more of this shit I can take." She pushed her glasses up her nose and took a bite of her bacon, egg, and cheese croissant.

"What are you going to do?" Artie asked.

Nic's pretty face contorted into a wince. "I've put in an application with Hale Cosmetics."

"That's the one in Houston?" I could feel my heart dripping with sadness. Of course I wanted my friend to do what was best for her career, but I'd miss her if she was all the way in Texas.

She gave me a gloomy smile. "I don't want to move, but cosmetic research and development is my jam, and they're supposed to have the best in-house lab in the country."

I put on my brave face and my best smile for her sake. "Then you did the right thing. I'll keep my fingers crossed for you."

"Fingers and toes," Artie added, and we each reached across the table to squeeze one of Nicolette's hands.

"Hey, what are you wearing to the party?" Gianna asked down the phone line as I walked home from the restaurant.

"Oh, uh, hmmm." To be honest, I'd forgotten Gia had invited me to a party tonight at Monty Bouvier's apartment. Her brother-in-law had just moved into our building this week. "Not sure. Maybe my gold off-the-shoulder top?"

Which happens to be at the dry cleaner's, I remembered, doing a U-turn in the middle of the sidewalk to go pick it up.

"Ooooh yes! That looks so pretty on you."

"Should I wear a skirt or pants?" I asked, mentally flicking through my wardrobe.

"I'm wearing jeans. It's really casual, mostly family."

"Okay, gold top, jeans, and my gold gladiator sandals."

"Sounds great," she replied. "I think I'll wear that red shirt with the little ruffles on the shoulders."

"That would be cute with your red kitten heels."

"Boom. Decided. Thanks, girl. I'll see you tonight."

"See ya."

As I approached the dry cleaner's, I remembered that I'd thrown out my gold sandals when one of the straps broke, so after picking up my top, I sought out a shoe store. Then I decided to pick up a housewarming gift for Monty, grabbing a bottle of wine before heading home.

I spent the rest of the day taking a long, hot bath to rid myself of the soreness from last night's activities and primping myself for the party.

Because Cruz was good friends with Monty, and I was pretty sure he'd be there tonight.

CHAPTER 27

KASSIE RAMIREZ GREETED ME at the door to Monty's new apartment, which was a couple floors above mine. The gorgeous Latina woman was dressed in dark-wash jeans that fit her curves perfectly and a cream-colored asymmetrical-hem top that set off her dark hair and eyes.

I didn't know all the details of hers and Monty's past, but what I did know was tragic. My heart was so happy they'd reconnected and seemed to be getting their second chance at love.

Walking into the apartment, the first thing I noticed was the eggplant-colored sectional couch that took up half the living room. Or rather, the man that was standing from said couch with a shy smile on his face.

Our eyes locked, and it took all my strength not to blurt out something stupid in front of the entire party. *Hey, Cruz. I'm so sorry I tied you to your bed last night when I snuck in and pretended you were my prisoner. I know when we started our sexual arrangement, you indicated that was a limit for you, and I apologize for crossing the line. I hope your fine ass still wants to fuck me because you're, hands down, the best sex of my life. And also, I might be falling for you.*

"Hi, Lehra," he said, his gaze running up and down my body.

A blush rose to my cheeks. "Hi, Cruz." And then I high tailed it after Kassie to put the wine in the kitchen, waving a hello at Monty as we passed him.

"You could have stayed out there and talked to your friend," Kassie commented as we entered the kitchen. It was homey and modern, with dark-green countertops, fancy appliances, and frosted-glass-fronted cabinets.

"He's not my friend," I said quickly before amending that. "I mean, he is my friend, but only my friend. That's all." *Yeah, that sounded convincing.*

Gianna strolled into the room, wine glass in hand. "What's up? Are we talking about why Cruz was literally panting after Lehra?"

"He was not!" I protested, and Gianna rolled her eyes toward the other woman for confirmation.

"Kassie?"

"Oh, he was definitely feeling you," she said, grinning as she located the wine fridge on the counter and put the bottle on the top rack.

"Come on, Lehra, don't you think Cruz is hot as fuck?" Gia cajoled.

I folded my lips between my teeth before finally admitting, "Okay, he's nice to look at." They teased me for a couple more minutes until I changed the subject. "Let's talk about how Monty looked like he was about to gobble Kassie up in a single bite."

We stayed in the kitchen for almost an hour, laughing, talking, and sipping wine. I hadn't spent much time with Kassie before this but found that I really liked the sweet, funny attorney.

At one point, Cruz and Monty came into the kitchen to replenish the food tables in the living room, and my heart rate sped up when Cruz gave me a sexy smile that would melt butter.

"Uh, no sir, dear brother-in-law," Gianna said, smacking Monty's hand when he reached for the tray of shrimp toast on the center island. "We've claimed these for ourselves."

"You ever noticed how much Cruz and Monty look alike?" Kassie asked after the guys left.

I nodded, comparing their similar faces and builds in my mind. "They do, though, of course, Cruz's skin tone is darker."

"And they and Auburn all have those amazing blue eyes," Gianna said, nibbling on a piece of the delicious shrimp toast. "Hey, we should have a girls' night at my house next weekend."

"That sounds fun," Kassie said, and I nodded my agreement. Cruz would be working, so I knew we wouldn't be doing any of our role playing scenes. *That is, if he even still wants to.*

"Good. See if Artie wants to come. I miss his face," Gia said.

"Let me text him." I pulled out my phone and sent him a message, receiving an instant reply. Laughing, I met Gianna's eyes. "He said he's in as long as Auburn will be there. Shirtless."

"Tell him he can look at my man candy, but no touching," she replied with a cheeky grin, rising from her plush barstool. "I need to go check on the kids."

"I'll go with you. I want to check on Sully too," Kass said.

"I'm going to get another glass of wine," I told them as they left the kitchen. Going to the small wine fridge, I pulled out the bottle, almost dropping it when a pair of hands landed on the counter on either side of me.

The sultry scent I knew so well surrounded me as firm lips lightly grazed my neck. "Were you a dominatrix in a former life, Tink?" Cruz asked, and a shiver passed down my spine at the sound of his husky, deep voice.

Setting down the wine, I turned to face him, and he took the opportunity to step even closer, plastering his front against mine.

"I'm so sorry about last night," I blurted, and his sexy smirk morphed into a frown.

"What are you sorry for?"

"I tied you up, and you didn't want to be tied up. I read your list, I really did, but I guess I just got caught up in the moment, and then I remembered this morning, and I freaked out and came to your apartment, but you weren't there, and I'm so sorry." I realized I was talking in one long, run-on sentence, but I was unable to stop myself.

Cruz stopped me though. With gentle hands on my face and a not-so-gentle kiss against my lips. "Shut up, Lehra."

"I... what?" I was feeling a bit dazed from the kiss.

"I liked it. I liked everything you did last night. In fact, if you want to tie me up and have your filthy way with me every fucking day, I'm down for it."

My eyes searched his. "Y-you're not mad at me?"

Those panty-dropping dimples appeared alongside his slow smile. "I'm not mad, sweetheart. I put no on that question because I didn't think it was something I'd be into. I was wrong. If I didn't like it, I would have told you."

My entire body melted with relief, like a chocolate bar left in the sun. "Okay, good. I got in my head and freaked out."

His thumbs brushed lazy circles on my cheeks. "You know you can always talk to me, right?" I nodded, my lips parting when he lowered his mouth to mine. Diving in with his tongue, Cruz ran a hand beneath my curls to grip the hair at the base of my neck. The kiss was deep and perfect, his fingers massaging lightly against my scalp.

When he pulled back, his thumb dusted over my bottom lip. "I think—"

"Does she have food on her face?"

We jerked apart as soon as we heard the small voice. Kassie's little boy was standing only a few feet away, looking curiously up at us.

"Sully, my dude," Cruz said, with faux cheerfulness, taking another step back. "Yeah, uh, Lehra had something on her mouth."

Uh-huh. Your mouth.

"You have to do it like this," the boy said, licking his thumb and miming rubbing something from an imaginary face. "That's what my mom does." His cute nose wrinkled as his voice lowered. "With spit."

"Oh, good tip," Cruz replied, fighting a grin.

"Monty says Mommy spits on him sometimes," the kid said conversationally, and poor Cruz fake-coughed to cover up his laughter. Then he squatted to Sully's level and ruffled his sandy-brown hair while I covered my smile with my fingertips.

"Did you need something, bud?"

The kid's eyes darted around the room. "Some more of those piggies-in-a-blanket," he whispered, and I wondered if maybe Kassie had told him he couldn't have any more.

Cruz took the boy's little hand in his big one, and my core clenched at the sight. He was always so sweet and gentle with kids. "Let's go, Sul. I could use some of those myself."

Then he turned and gave me a questioning look, asking me with his eyes if I was okay. When I nodded, he gave me a wink before herding Sully from the kitchen. Of course I was okay. I was convinced that man's kisses could bring about world peace.

Over the next six weeks, Cruz and I did two more role playing scenes. Mine was an adventurous Bonnie and Clyde theme, and we had dressed the part in vintage clothing. Cruz took me on a tour of an old-fashioned bank that had been closed for years, and afterward, we went to a cool-as-hell speakeasy for dinner and drinks. Then we'd had sex in the back of the vintage car he'd rented.

His fantasy had been hitchhiker themed. After driving us upstate, Cruz had pretended to "pick me up" on the side of the road. With a few *casual* brushes of his hand against my leg, and some extremely dirty innuendos, I found myself in a field, spread across the hood of the car with a big, sexy man between my legs.

But in between those times, we spent more and more time together. Cruz Estrada was everything I wanted in a man: fun, attentive, respectful, and affectionate. He was my best friend in the world.

And I was irrevocably in love with him.

CHAPTER 28

I STEPPED INTO MY darkened apartment and heard a crunch beneath my black lace-up boots. "What the hell is that?" I muttered, flicking on the living room light.

A small, beige seashell lay crushed on the floor. Another lay a couple feet in front of it. My gaze traced the floor, finding a trail of seashells winding through my living room and toward the hall.

My lips turned up into a grin. *Lehra.* Stripping off my black backpack, I hung it on the hook beside the door and removed my boots before following the path all the way through my bedroom and to the closed door of my bathroom.

Excitement traveled through my body, making my toes and fingers tingle in anticipation as I pushed open the door. She was in my round, sunken bathtub. *My mermaid.*

Lehra's hair was different tonight. Instead of her usual curls, she was sporting beachy waves that flowed over her shoulders like a blonde water-fall. Her bikini top was encrusted with rhinestones in sea hues... a mixture of blues, greens, and corals.

And on her bottom half, she was wearing a gorgeous multicolored tail. The top was pink, which faded into purple, then blue, and finally into aqua at the fin. The scales had a metallic sheen to them and glistened beneath the water.

"Who the hell are you?" I asked, putting on a show of indignance.

The mermaid cowered, bringing her knees up in front of her chest. "I-I'm Coraline."

"Well, Coraline," I sneered, "why the hell are you in my bathtub? And what is..." I waved my hand at her fin. "That?"

"I needed to be in water. And that's... my tail." Her teeth sank into her bottom lip as she looked up at me with pleading eyes.

"Don't be ridiculous," I scoffed. "People don't have tails."

"I'm not a people. I'm..." She hesitated, and I fought a grin, waiting to see where her story took us.

"You're what?" I prodded.

"We've been called many things. Water nymphs, sirens, Oceanids, sea-maidens. But the one you're probably most familiar with is... mermaid."

I rolled my eyes. "You're trying to make me believe you're a mermaid?"

One eyebrow lifted as she retorted, "Helloooo? I have a tail." To emphasize her point, she lifted the fin end in the air and wiggled it.

The tip of my tongue slid against the scar on my bottom lip as I stifled my smile. "Great. I've got a smartass mermaid in my tub."

A small giggle escaped her. "You can come closer and touch my tail if you want."

"Words every man wants to hear," I shot back with a lascivious smirk on my face.

Stepping to the edge of the tub, I kneeled on the plush white rug and reached my hand down into the warm water, stroking up and down the coarse tail. Of course, I had to reach around and cop a feel of her ass. Her eyes twinkled playfully at me.

"Are you convinced?"

I huffed out a sigh. "I guess, but you still didn't answer the question of what you're doing in my apartment."

"I'm... well, you see... my father sent me."

"Your father?"

"Yes, he's high up in our government."

"There's a mermaid government?"

"Technically, he's a merman, but yes. And there's a war starting beneath the sea. The octopuses are just being completely unreasonable." She rolled her eyes, and I cleared my throat to keep from laughing. *How is she so fucking cute?*

"That sounds terrible."

"It is. There were threats made against my life because of who my father is, so he sent me to live up here. On land."

"How did you get up here to my apartment if you can't walk?"

"Oh, I have legs during the day so I can walk about, but at night, I turn back into a mermaid."

I was loving this little story she'd concocted. "That means you have to stay in water when the sun goes down?" She nodded, and I raised a skeptical eyebrow. "So, you think I'll let you use my bathtub every night?"

She dragged a finger over the curved surface of the tub, her eyes following the movement. "Well, it is very nice in here, but actually, I was hoping you'd help me with something else." Her mischievous gaze slid back to mine. "I want to become human, but the only way I can do that is if I... mate with a human male."

I widened my eyes. "Really?"

Coraline nodded earnestly. "Yes, it's the only way. Do you know how to mate? I've never done that before."

My lips twitched. "I'm familiar with the procedure."

Drifting seductive fingers down my arm, she lifted my hand to her mouth and asked, "So you'll help me?" Then she gave my ring and middle finger a long suck, and I was fucking done.

Rising swiftly to my feet, I stripped off my black T-shirt, feeling her hot, heavy gaze on my body as I unbuckled my belt and unfastened my pants.

My cock was already raring to go, popping free with relief as soon as I shoved my pants and briefs down.

I held her hands to scoot her forward enough that I could settle in the tub behind her. Scooping her blonde waves over one shoulder, I nibbled up and down her neck, my teeth reddening the delicate skin there.

"You are so beautiful," I murmured, sliding my hands up and down her body before finally cupping her breasts in the rhinestone swim top. She moaned, a soft, wanting sound, when I slid the straps down her arms and bared her pretty tits for my hands.

"Th-that feels good," she stammered as my fingers and thumbs rolled her nipples into tight beads. My erection was hard and thick between us, and she pressed her back against it, giving me the friction I craved.

"God I want you so much, Coraline," I groaned into her ear, tugging her nipples until her back arched.

Her tail made a light splashing noise when she rolled to her stomach, her gray eyes twinkling up at me as she slid her body back until her face was right above my cock. The breath stalled in my lungs when she submerged her head and took me into her mouth.

"Fuuuuck," I breathed out, watching her hair floating around her as she gave me an underwater blow job. Her mouth seemed infinitely hotter than the surrounding bath water, and I stroked my fingers through her wet strands.

Coraline took me deeper, and my head tilted back against the rim of the bathtub. She came up for air a few times before returning her attention to my throbbing dick. It was incredible, watching this gorgeous woman fucking me with her mouth, long, slow pulls that had me right on the edge of sanity.

Winding my hands into her hair, I pulled her up, my breaths shallow and ragged. "Stop, sweetheart, or this will be over before it starts." The upward tilt of her lips told me she was pleased with herself. *I know I'm sure as hell pleased with her.* "How did you know how to do that?" I asked.

"I've been going to the library during the day. I found something called the internet."

I chuckled and kissed her hard, our mouths curving into mutual smiles. "Get on your knees for me and hold onto the rim of the tub."

She did, and I positioned myself behind her, finding the zippered hole I'd noticed earlier and unzipping it. My tub was deep, so her hips rested just below the waterline. Much as she had, I submerged my face in the water and found her pussy through the opening. It was pink and swollen, and I blew a stream of bubbles directly onto her clit.

Even below the water, I could hear her wanton cry, and I lapped at the little bundle until I had to come up for air. Then I went right back to licking her sweet cunt, feeling the water churning around me as she rocked back and forth, grinding herself against my mouth.

She was close, and when I pushed a finger inside her and felt her clenching around it, I lifted my head. Dragging air into my lungs, I rose onto my knees and kissed up her spine before nudging the tip of my cock against her entrance.

"Are you ready, Coraline?"

"Yes," she hissed, shoving her hips back and taking the first inch of me. "Oh god, that feels so good. Give me more."

I took my time working myself into her tight sheath, gritting my teeth against the need to come. This wasn't going to last long. She was already squeezing me with her inner walls, and I wrapped my hands around her hips and sank in to the hilt.

Rolling my back, I slid out and back in, my strokes long and measured as the water swirled around us. Her legs were bound together by the tail, so she felt extra tight around my plunging cock.

I braced my hands on the rim of the tub beside hers and covered her back with my body, softly kissing the side of her face. "Coraline?" She turned her head and looked at me questioningly. "Do mermaids mate for life?" I asked.

Her eyes widened for a second, and then her face broke into a shy smile. "They do."

"Then you're mine," I stated, reaching one hand up to cup the back of her head as I took her mouth in a searing kiss.

As my tongue slipped deeply into her mouth, Coraline lifted her fin from the water and pressed it against my ass, urging me to take her harder and faster.

I gave in to the animal urge to rut, to claim her, and the crown of my erection found that spot inside her that made her knuckles white. She bucked against me, sending water splashing onto the floor as we devoured each other's moans of pure bliss.

Please come, I silently begged her as my balls tightened up against my body, and as if she heard my unspoken plea, she cried out into my mouth. As a shudder shook through her frame, I twisted my fingers in her hair and finally allowed myself to release inside her.

Later that night, we'd just finished round two, this time in my bed and without the tail. Lehra's body was plastered to mine, her neck buried in the crook of my neck.

Gently, I tugged her hair until her face was visible in the soft moonlight streaming through the cracks in the blinds. "Sweetheart, can I talk to you for a second?"

Her lips pressed together, and she nodded. "Is something wrong?"

I kissed her forehead, my hand sliding soothingly up and down her spine. "Nothing's wrong. I just..." A heavy weight settled on my shoulders. The next role playing fantasy would be hers, and then our little agreement would be done.

"What is it, Cruz?" she asked, tracing her fingers along my cheek.

"It's about your next fantasy."

"Oh." Her chin dipped, and I could feel her body stiffen against me. "If it's not something you're comfortable with, I can choose something else."

A smile played across my lips as I tilted her face back up to mine. "No way. I'm looking forward to that one." Her body relaxed in my arms. "I don't want it to be our last time, Lehra."

My heart thumped so hard, I was surprised it wasn't shaking the bed as she processed my words. "You have another fantasy you want to try?"

"No, I mean, yes," I fumbled. "I have lots of them, but..." My inhale cut through my windpipe before I finally said, "I want us to last beyond the role playing thing. I want us to be together for real."

She gnawed on the corner of her lip. "Like a couple?"

"Yes. We can still play any time you want, but I want a real relationship with you. I'm..." I almost blurted out that I was in love with her, but she would probably think I was crazy. "You've become my best friend the past couple of years, and I've developed more feelings for you, deeper feelings."

Her answering smile stilled my heart with hope, as did her next words. "I have too. I didn't want to say anything in case you just viewed this as a sex thing."

My heartrate galloped a hard cadence in my chest. "I love what we have, but it's more than that to me, Lehra. I'm crazy about you. I really want to try and make this work between us. Is... is that what you want?"

She snuggled her face back into my neck, and I could feel her lips tilt up into a smile. Then she spoke a single word that was like a beam of sunshine, lighting my entire world.

"Yes."

CHAPTER 29

"Hey, Mama."

My mother's face brightened as soon as she answered my FaceTime call. "Mi hijo! I've missed talking to you."

I grinned at her. "We literally talked two days ago, Mama."

Her soft brown eyes rolled. "Pshhh. What have I told you about teasing your mother?"

Leaning back on my couch, I rested my phone on my abdomen. "It's my favorite pastime. Don't try and take away my joy."

"If teasing me is your favorite pastime, you need to get out more. Are you dating anyone?" she asked with hope lilting her voice.

For once, I had the answer she wanted to hear. "Actually, yes. I've met a woman I like a lot." *Love a lot.*

Mama's eyes danced with delight as she started her maternal inquisition. "What is she like? Is she pretty? Where did you meet her? Are you being polite and respectful? You better be opening her door and treating her like a lady, or I'll come up there and throw a shoe at you." Her questions and comments came like rapid machine-gun fire, and I couldn't help but laugh.

"Mama, you raised me right and taught me how to treat a woman, so no need for any shoe throwing. And yes, she's beautiful. Her name is Lehra, and she has blonde hair and the prettiest gray eyes." I let out a soft sigh.

"She's so sweet and funny, Mama. There's just something so vibrant about her. Everyone at work loves her."

It had been a while since I'd seen my mother smile this big. "Oh, so you met her at work. Which job? Your security one or your police work?"

"The security one. She's a receptionist, but she's training for an executive position."

"Oooh, ambitious. I like that," Mama crooned. "Have you met her parents?"

"I met her mom when she came up for a visit. Tabby is a nurse, and I really liked her a lot. I haven't met her dad yet. He's a plumber with his own business, so you know how that is."

"Yes, your father worked so hard, but he always made time for family. You need to remember that when you start your own family, mi hijo. You're working two jobs, and I worry about that."

"I know, but you don't have to worry. I'm making time for some fun. My security job pays the bills, but I really enjoy being on the force, even part-time."

"You've always been a protector," she said, her voice soft with pride. "I never had to worry about Quintessa or Eli because I knew big brother would look after them."

"Always," I confirmed. "How is Eli, by the way?"

"Oh, that boy! You and Quinnie were always so ambitious, and he's just... not. He wants to stay tied to my apron strings all the time."

I frowned. I didn't want my brother to end up like Dwight. "I know he's the baby of the family, but you need to be firm with him, Mama, like you were with us. Don't get soft in—" I cut myself off.

"In what?" Mama asked, her eyes narrowing.

Well, I've really gotten myself into a pickle here. "In, um, now that Papa's not around to back you up."

Her lips quirked up on one side in amusement. "Nice save. For a second there, I thought you were about to call me old."

"Never," I chuckled. "You don't age, Mama. You're as beautiful as when I was a kid." I wasn't even schmoozing with that comment. My mother barely had a wrinkle on her lovely face.

She ran a hand through the hair over her ear, fingering the few gray strands that had started appearing there in the past couple years. "Except for these," she stated flatly.

"I like them. They show you've lived."

"They show I'm a worrywart," she retorted on a laugh. "And I'm handling your brother. I've started making him go to the P.I. office with me, and he's actually doing a good job as an investigator. He's got a sharp mind; he just has to put it to use on something other than those stupid video games."

"That's good, Mama. Maybe he can take over the business one day and you can finally retire."

"Won't that be the day," she sighed. "Now, how are your jobs going? You never talk much about whatever you do in the security business."

I tried not to let the stress of what I was hiding show on my face. "It's just basic personal security for a corporate executive. He's... in the clothing industry." I wanted to tell her that I was working for Auburn Bouvier, but I didn't want to do it over the phone. This was a conversation best had in person. "Tell you what. Why don't you come for a visit, and I'll tell you all about it. Maybe you could ride with me for a couple days."

"I could use a little vacation," she said thoughtfully. "And I'd love to see mi nieta in person. Noelle is getting so big, and I'm a little jealous you get to see her all the time. Quinnie said you babysit quite often to give her a break."

"She's such a doll, Mama. She has Quinnie's sweet personality, but she's a little sassy too."

"Oh, corazón mío," she said, patting her chest.

"So you'll come?" I had the sudden urge to spill my guts to my mother about everything. Working with Auburn. Meeting my biological dad. Everything.

I'd been upset about her hiding my paternity when I first found out, but after reading the letters and my long talks with Paul, I understood that she was only doing what she thought was right. But I wanted—*needed*—to clear the air.

"I'll see when I can get away," she promised. "Te amo, my hijo."

"Te amo también, mamá."

I'd organized the letters between Papa and Paul, arranging them chronologically and reading them like a conversation between the two men. With one of them in my pocket, I entered the restaurant and found our usual table at the back.

"Son, how are you?" Paul asked, rising and giving me a hug, which I returned. It was becoming easier and easier to relate to this man, and I enjoyed our weekly dinners as much as he seemed to. We no longer focused on what happened all those years ago, and instead, we just talked. Like a normal father and son would do.

Paul had served as my sounding board regarding my feelings for Lehra. While he initially agreed that I should give her time, after a few months, he pointed out that maybe she was waiting on me to make a move. I think his exact words were, "Cruz, you need to either shit or get off the pot."

Then I'd seen her quiz results on her phone and knew he was right. Knew Lehra and I would be perfect together. *Like I didn't already feel that with every fiber of my soul.*

"I'm good. How is your week going?"

"Very well. I was glad to see you at Monty's get-together. You two seem to get along well." He smiled. "That makes me so happy."

"Me too. He's a good friend." The server brought our drinks and took our food orders before I continued. "I think I'm feeling better about telling them. I just... I don't know... I wanted them to get to know me as a person before we tell them I'm their brother."

Paul's smile and nod were filled with compassion. "I understand where you're coming from on that. Whenever you're ready, we'll tell them."

"Thanks," I said with gratitude for his patience. "I talked with Mama today, and I'm trying to talk her into coming up for a visit."

His breaths visibly quickened, and I wondered, not for the first time, if he still had feelings for my mom. He always spoke about her with something like reverence. "So you can talk to her about everything? I know you said that you wanted to talk to her face-to-face."

"I do, and after I get the whole story from her point of view, I think I'd feel more comfortable talking to Monty and Auburn."

Paul was quiet for a moment. "After you speak with Stella, would you ask her if she'd be willing to meet with me? If it would make her uncomfortable, I completely understand, but I'd like the opportunity to ask her what Chloe said to her when she fired her. And to apologize and let her know I knew nothing about it until she didn't come to work the next week."

"I'll ask her. Hopefully, after all these years, she'll be okay with it."

"Thank you, Cruz. How are things going with Lehra?"

We chatted about that for a few minutes, and after Kenzie brought our food, I pulled the letter from my pocket and handed it over. "I was wondering if you could tell me more about this letter. It's the only one I've seen that was a bit hostile between you two."

Paul opened it and smiled after reading. "Yes, Benjamin was quite annoyed at me." He laid down the letter, forked up a bite of his salmon and chewed slowly. "This was shortly after I found out about you. I'd agreed to step back since you were obviously in good hands with your parents, but

I still wanted to support you financially. I called Ben and made an offer to him."

"Oh, like child support?"

"Yes, initially, but... well, he took offense to that. Said he was perfectly capable of supporting his family."

"I can imagine. Papa was very proud."

Paul chuckled and tapped the sheet of paper with his knuckle. "He was indeed. He sent me this letter to let me know what I could do with my money. I gave him time to cool off and called him again a few weeks later."

"I'm guessing you two worked things out?"

"We did. I came up with another proposition that was more... palatable to him. See, at that time, your papa was a private investigator at a firm, working for someone else. The guy he worked for was a bit of an ass. He grossly underpaid and overworked his employees, so I offered to start a corporation with Ben as the CEO. He would have full control over all the operations, though I would provide the office space and any necessities."

Taking a bite of my chicken, I scraped through my memories. "I don't remember Papa working for another firm."

"You were probably too young. Anyway, my proposal would give him the opportunity to work for himself, and then, after seven years, I would sign over the entire corporation to him. Of course, as you know, Benjamin's business flourished, and he did very well for himself."

I smiled across the table at him. "So you gave Papa autonomy, but you were still able to help out financially without making him feel like he was taking a handout." Paul was a damn smart man.

"All I did was give him the opportunity. He's the one who did all the work and turned Estrada Investigations into a booming business."

I knew he was just being modest. Paul had been the catalyst behind Papa's success while still allowing him to maintain his pride. Something twisted in my stomach, but it wasn't unpleasant at all. It took me a minute to realize what it was.

Love for Paul.

The man who'd seen someone struggling and helped in the best way he could. The man who'd sacrificed his own wants and happiness to do what he thought was best for his child.

Benjamin Estrada loved and raised me, and I absolutely loved him with all my heart. He was my papa. But that didn't mean that I couldn't make room for someone else inside my heart.

My chest felt like it was expanding, forming a new and open space, and for the first time, I truly saw Paul Bouvier for what he was.

My dad.

CHAPTER 30

"Ms. Kincaid, we have a delivery for you," the concierge for my apartment building said. "Would you like me to have someone bring it up to you?"

"No, that's okay. I'll come down and get it."

A few minutes later, I walked back into my apartment with a huge white box adorned with a bright red bow. "What the hell?" I asked the box, but it didn't answer.

Placing it on my couch, I opened it, my eyes bulging when I pulled back the tissue paper to find a glittery emerald-green dress and a shoebox with strappy black stilettos. A small velvet bag held pretty silver jewelry dotted with dark-green stones.

A grin crept over my lips when I saw the cream envelope with my name on the front in Cruz's handwriting. I impatiently opened it and read the card.

Meet me at the bar in the King Nelson hotel tonight at 7:00. Sit at the bar and wait for a stranger to make contact.

I'm looking forward to seeing how beautiful you will look.

Yours, Cruz

P.S. Don't you dare wear panties.

I was positively giddy. We must be doing the final role playing scene on my list... a one-night stand with a dark and dangerous stranger.

I'd never had a one-night stand in my life, but it made me hot as hell when I read about them in books. And tonight, I knew Cruz would fulfill my fantasy.

Entering the upscale space, I walked straight for the bar, keeping my eyes forward. Everything was done in dark woods and greens, and the lighting was dim. I'd wanted to be someone totally different tonight, the kind of woman who would go home with a complete stranger, so I straightened my hair and fashioned it into a high, sleek ponytail with a thick strand wrapped around the base. My makeup was more dramatic than I usually wore, my eyes smoky and my lips a sparkling copper.

As instructed, I took a seat at the bar and hung my small black purse on the hook underneath. A bartender approached immediately, his gaze dropping to the ample amount of cleavage on display in this green dress.

"What can I get you?"

"Top shelf margarita on the rocks, please," I ordered.

The man was back in a few minutes, placing the icy drink in front of me and waving me off when I pulled out my wallet.

"Your drink has been taken care of by the gentleman in the back corner," he informed me, inclining his head to a spot behind and to the right of me.

Hmmm, he's already here?

Picking up my drink, I took a leisurely sip before swiveling my chair to find the "stranger." And sweet baby Jesus, I almost choked on my drink. Cruz Estrada was seated in a round booth, looking like a sin I'd like to commit.

He was dressed in solid black, from his pants to his suit jacket to his button-down shirt, which had three buttons open. I noted a gold cross on a thin chain around his neck, and it hung directly against his muscular chest. His hair was slicked back tonight, giving him a dark and dangerous vibe.

Going for aloof, I lifted my glass in thanks before turning back to face the bar. From that angle, I could only see a sliver of him in the mirrored back wall, but each time I turned slightly to cast a glance at him, his full attention was focused on me.

My heart galloped with anticipation. This was as exciting as I'd hoped.

As soon as I finished my drink, the bartender set another one in front of me. "Oh, I didn't order this," I told him.

He smirked. "Your admirer sent this one as well."

"Hmmm, that was sweet." Rotating my stool a few degrees, I met Cruz's fiery blue eyes and gave him a coquettish smile over my shoulder before mouthing, *Thank you.*

He gave a sharp jerk of his chin, as if to tell me to come over there, but I simply lifted an unimpressed eyebrow at him.

Gotta work for it, buddy. We're strangers, remember?

A slow, sexy smile pulled one corner of his lips up, giving me a glimpse of that dimple and telling me he accepted my challenge. He rose from the booth, straightening his jacket before prowling across the room toward me.

When he stood, I got a good look at his entire body, and my mouth went dry, all the moisture heading south. Cruz's pants hugged all the right things. Thick thighs. Tapered waist. And... gulp... that prominent bulge. The man was sex in a suit, moving with the raw grace of a cheetah, despite his size.

God, how is he so damn smooth?

I turned all the way around to face him and slowly crossed one leg over the other. His hungry eyes followed the movement, and heat scorched my bare legs as he openly stared. Then those heavy-lidded azure eyes lifted to my face. The look he gave me told me he had one thing on his mind. Well, maybe several things, but they were all related to a whole lot of nakedness.

"Thank you for the drinks," I said, holding out one hand for a shake. "My name is Lena."

He took my hand but didn't shake it, and my breath snagged in my trachea when he brought it to his lips and tasted me with the very tip of his tongue. It was a small, quick circle, and then he was simply kissing the back of my hand like a gentleman. Though the smug expression on his face told a different story.

"You're very welcome," he said in a low, smooth voice. *Holy hell, he's going to wreck me tonight.* "I couldn't help but notice how beautiful you are."

Leaning closer, I caught a whiff of his masculine scent, and a wave of dizziness threatened my ability to stay upright on the stool. But I did my best to play it cool. "Does that line work on all the women?" I whispered.

His fingers drew a mesmerizing path up my forearm, raising a line of goosebumps in their wake. "All that matters is whether or not it's working on *you*."

"Maybe," I replied airily.

He turned my hand over and pressed his pillowy lips against the sensitive pulse point of my wrist, his eyes holding mine prisoner. "I would be honored if you'd join me at my table."

"Okay," I breathed, unable to resist his obvious seduction.

His hand was gentle as he helped me stand, wrapping possessively around my smaller one before landing on the small of my back as I grabbed my purse. My skin was exposed there, thanks to the low dip of the fabric, and the simple touch was intoxicating.

I paused beside his table and looked up at him. "I don't even know your name."

A glint of mischief sparkled in his blue eyes. "Rider."

"Nice name," I replied, sliding into the booth.

He followed, leaving about six inches between us, and then set my drink in front of me. I'd been so entranced, I hadn't even realized he'd picked it up.

"Would you like anything to eat, Lena?"

You. I'd like to gobble you up.

"Maybe just something small," I suggested and then had to clench my fingers around the smooth edge of the booth seat to keep from visibly shivering when Rider dragged his knuckles down my upper arm. I'd never been with a man whose touch affected me so completely.

"Would you like to share something with me, pretty girl?"

Good grief! It wasn't a complicated question, but the way he purred the words made them rife with innuendo.

So I innuendo-ed right back. "I'd love to share with you, Rider. Anything you choose."

His tongue slipped out and toyed with the little scar on his lower lip. "I'm going to assume you mean food. For now." Then he leaned forward until his mouth brushed my ear. "But later, I'm going to happily misinterpret that statement."

I wasn't sure how I was still able to form actual thoughts with his delicious scent, deep voice, and warm breath surrounding me, but I managed to sound semi-cool when I said, "We'll see."

He chuckled darkly and traced a single finger up and down my throat several times, his eyes following the movement. "You have a beautiful neck, Lena. I'd like to see how it looks with my hand wrapped around it."

Oh holy hand necklace! This man...

After a final brush of his finger against my suddenly damp skin, Rider turned and nodded to a server, like he hadn't just obliterated my vagina with his seemingly offhand comment.

A short, thin man approached a moment later, his eyes flicking between us before landing on my cleavage. "Hi, guys. I'm Charles. What can I get for you?"

Is he asking my boobs? Maybe I should order them a margarita.

Rider casually draped his arm over the back of the booth, not quite touching me, though I was exceedingly aware of the possessive nature of the motion.

"We'll have an order of patatas bravas," Rider said, dropping the tips of his fingers to my bare shoulder.

Charles smiled over at me. "And for the lady?"

"*My lady* will be sharing with me," Rider replied coolly, though his eyes were anything but. The side of his large body was suddenly pressed directly against mine, and his fingers wrapped around my shoulder.

As soon as a chastised Charles scurried off to the kitchen, I lifted an eyebrow at the man beside me. "Your lady?"

"While you're with me, you are mine, and I don't tolerate other men leering at what's mine."

"Awfully presumptuous of you," I suggested. "What if I don't want to be yours?"

"Then you wouldn't be sitting in this booth with me right now," he replied with another of those cute but smug half-smiles.

Keeping my tone noncommittal, I hummed and changed the subject. "What do you do for a living, Rider?"

He took a sip of whatever clear liquid he was drinking, his blue gaze holding mine over the rim of the short glass. "I'm in the family business."

"And what business is that?"

"We provide... goods and services. How about you?"

"I actually have two jobs. During the day, I write fortunes for fortune cookies."

He grinned. "Oh really? Let me guess. You write sappy ones about secret admirers or dreams coming true."

"Nope. I try to make people think with my fortunes. I did one last week that read, *That wasn't chicken.*"

Rider barked out a laugh. "Definitely thought provoking. Tell me another one."

Tapping my chin, I thought about it for a second. "This is one of my favorites. *Help! I am being held prisoner in a fortune cookie factory.*"

Shaking his head in amusement, he remarked, "I'm a little afraid to ask what your night job is."

"I'm a professional cuddler," I informed him, barely able to keep a straight face.

"That's not a real job," he scoffed.

"It is. Look it up."

Rider's lips curled upward before he took another drink. "And what, pray tell, does a professional cuddler do?"

"People hire me if they've had some past trauma or suffer from depression. Proper cuddling can solve a myriad of problems. It's a type of therapy," I said breezily.

"And you think you're a good cuddler?" He allowed a bit of skepticism to color his words.

Taking a drink of my margarita, I flashed him a cheeky grin. "Oh, I know I am. Care for a demonstration?"

He smirked. "Depends. How much is it going to cost me?"

"I think I can give you a freebie since you've bought my drinks." I took one of his hands between both of mine. "First of all, tell me what kind of trauma you're dealing with."

His lips twisted to the side. "Let's see... when I was five, my goldfish escaped."

I burst into giggles. "Escaped?"

He shrugged. "That's what my parents told me when I came home and he was gone. They said he went to the ocean to be with all the other fish."

"Ah. I can see where an escaped goldfish would be traumatic. How have you even functioned in adulthood?"

Rider smiled sadly. "It's not been easy. So do you think you can help me?"

"Oh, I have just the cuddle for you." Shifting my body to face him, I wrapped one arm around his shoulder and the other around his waist. "Now do the same to me," I instructed.

I was in his arms before my next breath, his head buried in my neck. "I think you might be right. I'm feeling soothed already."

"Yes, well, the direction your right hand is moving is against the professional cuddler's code of ethics," I said, referring to the hand that was about a half inch from a full-on ass grab.

"But it's helping my trauma," he argued. "I have to admit, you're very good at this."

"Told you," I said smartly, lightly brushing the back of his neck with my fingertips.

Rider dragged his nose up and down my neck. "I've almost totally forgotten about Fido already."

"Fido?"

"My goldfish," he explained. "Maybe I'll just hire you full-time as my own personal cuddler."

"You couldn't afford me."

He chuckled. "Sweetheart, I assure you I could." Then he softly bit my earlobe, sending a delicious shiver down my spine. "Can I tell you something?"

"Yes." The single word sounded husky.

"I've never wanted to kiss a stranger as much as I want to kiss you," he said, the low timbre of his voice vibrating against my neck.

"Then why don't you?"

He didn't waste any time, dragging his nose along my cheek until it brushed mine. Our eyes met and then closed simultaneously as his lips took mine.

I was being seared, burned alive by the complete possession of his mouth and the boldness of his tongue. This was no *let's work up to the good stuff* kiss. No, Rider started with the good stuff. Deep and slow, tasting every inch of my mouth with his greedy tongue.

That hand that had been almost grabbing my ass earlier was now fully committed to the task, kneading the globe like he owned the damn thing. His other hand was cupping the back of my neck, one lazy thumb trailing up and down my jugular vein.

His mouth held the smooth taste of expensive vodka as we kissed until my toes were practically curling in my heels. He pulled back with soft sucks, and my eyelids seemed to weigh a ton when I finally dragged them open. Rider looked me dead in the eye while giving my butt a final squeeze.

"All I can think about is holding this firm ass while you're on all fours in front of me."

The images that brought to mind were beautifully vulgar, and a moan escaped before I could stop it. Rider's warm laugh gusted against my face as his lips dusted soft kisses over my mouth.

"I have a room upstairs," he whispered, and I restrained myself from dragging him immediately out of the booth and upstairs.

"Really?" I sang. "Does it have a bed?"

"No, I requested they remove it so I could fuck you on the floor," he shot back.

"Who said you'll be fucking me?" I asked, going for indignant. And probably failing.

"I did," he replied with all the confidence in the world.

I rolled my eyes, "I don't sleep with men I just met."

"Okay." His tone was easy and a little too light. "We won't sleep then. I'll just fuck you till dawn. Unless you're a prude," he goaded.

"I'm not a prude."

He kissed my temple and let his mouth linger there. "Are you a good girl, Lena?" The curve of his smile against my skin told me he didn't miss the tremble that ran down my back. "Ahhh, someone likes being called a good girl."

"I do not," I protested weakly, and then air made a sharp entrance into my lungs when he yanked my leg over his, binding it between his thick thighs.

"I know a way to find out." His short fingernails scratched deliberate lines up the inside of my thigh until he reached my pantiless sex. He taunted me with raised eyebrows. "Well, well, well. What do we have here?"

"If you don't know, maybe you should have paid better attention in anatomy class," I told him cheekily, barely holding onto my sanity because Rider was stroking one thick finger up and down my slit.

His laugh was like a midnight sky with no stars, dark and foreboding. "Trust me, Lena. I specialize in the female anatomy. Clit." He flicked my bundle of nerves, and I almost flew off the seat. "Cunt." Two fingers pushed deeply into me. "G-spot." Those fingers curled forward, sure and precise, and my damn eyes crossed until I saw double.

"Oh my god," I whimpered, grasping the edge of the table with both hands as he stroked that sensitive spot inside me.

"Hmmmm," Rider hummed in my ear. "Maybe you're a bad girl after all, Lena. I don't think good girls allow themselves to get finger-fucked beneath a table in a public place. And by a stranger, no less."

Holy hell! This is even hotter than anything I could have imagined.

He picked up my margarita with his free hand and held it to my lips, allowing me to lick salt from the rim before tipping a small drink into my mouth. All the while, he continued the sweet assault between my spread legs. *Thank god this place has long tablecloths.*

"I'm... I'm close," I panted, closing my eyes as I felt the familiar tightening inside me.

Then his fingers were gone, and I snapped my lids open to see Rider's fingers a couple inches from my face. They were embarrassingly wet with my arousal. With a wicked grin, he dipped them into his glass, turning the clear contents slightly cloudy as the ice tinkled against the sides.

Holding my eyes, he sucked them clean before downing his drink in one go with a long groan. *Did he just...* Before I could say anything, the server approached with our food. Rider's thighs tightened around my slimmer one, holding it hostage when I attempted to close my legs.

"Here we go. One order of patatas bravas," Charles informed us, setting the plate down, and I wondered if I looked as flustered as I felt. "Can I get you anything else?"

"Another vodka on the rocks," Rider said coolly. "That was the best-tasting one I've ever had."

Lord have mercy! No he did not just say that. I was sure my cheeks were the color of ripe cherries as the server scurried away.

For the next hour, I was a ball of electricity contained in skin, bones, and lust. Rider fed me crispy potatoes dipped in the creamy sauce. He purposely smeared the sauce on my lips, my cheek, my shoulder, and then proceeded to lick it off.

All the while, he edged me with tortuous fingers between my legs, pumping in and out, stroking all the places I needed to be touched, but never letting me come. By the time he licked his fingers clean of... me... and paid the bill, I wasn't even pretending to be demure anymore.

Hell, I was so eager to get upstairs with him, I almost forgot my purse. Rider pulled it from the seat and tucked it beneath his arm, a smug-as-fuck look on his face as he placed his hand on my lower back and led me from the bar.

Why is it so hot when a man is secure enough in his masculinity to carry your purse?

I somehow managed to walk calmly toward the elevator bank rather than sprinting like my poor vagina was urging me to do. Rider dipped his head toward me at the same time his finger hit the call button. "Are you ready to come?"

The words had barely left his lips before I barked out, "Yes!"

He chuckled and led me into the elevator, crowding me until my face was inches from the glass back wall. His voice was an octave lower as he dipped his head and spoke his demand in my ear.

"Put your hands on the rail and spread your legs."

Chapter 31

THE ELEVATOR WAS COMPLETELY glass except for the metal doors. I was currently staring at the inside of the elevator shaft, but I knew once we rose above the ground floor, I would have a clear view of the lobby.

And anyone there would have a clear view of me. Excitement infiltrated my every cell.

Surely he didn't plan to fuck me in here where anyone would be able to watch. Right?

Doing as I was told, I wrapped my fingers around the metal bar that was waist height for me and spread my legs. "Wider," Rider growled, nudging my legs obscenely wide with his knee. As the elevator began to rise, he placed one hand on my hip and slid the other up the inside of my thigh from behind. "Very messy down here, Lena." His voice was stern, which only made me messier.

"Your fault, Rider," I returned as he pushed two fingers inside me.

Oh shit! There was a large group of people in formal wear milling about in the lobby. I could see them clearly, which meant they could also see me. Glancing down, I was relieved that my dress covered my bare pussy from the front.

With his mouth at my ear, Rider began to finger-fuck me with ruthless efficiency. I was so keyed up when we left the bar, I was sure I would come as soon as he touched me again. *But with all those people down there. I can't...*

"Get out of your head, pretty girl. My room is on the fifty-fifth floor, and you have until then to come all over my fucking hand. Or else."

"Or else what?" I squeaked as his ring finger reached forward to give my clit some attention.

"You don't want to know," he replied ominously, only ramping up the thrills running up and down my legs. My pussy tightened around his invading fingers as he sped up his movements. "Fuck, you hear that, baby? You hear the sounds your cunt is making for me? Such a nice, wet, tight, little pussy. It's crying for my touch, isn't it?"

"Y-yes," I stammered, my breath forming a circle of steam on the glass in front of me. The sounds of wetness filled the elevator car with every in and out movement of his thick fingers.

"You're going to come right here like a good fucking girl, and then, when we get to my room, I'm going to make you choke out my name around my cock while you suck me off."

Good fucking hell!

He continued spewing pure filth into my ear, his skilled fingers never stopping between my legs. "I want you to drink me down, and if you spill a single drop, I'll spank your pussy until it's bright red and swollen. And then I'll fuck it till you're raw."

His words ignited me, and my sex clenched hard around his roughly plunging fingers. "God, I'm..."

All movement and speech ceased when the elevator stopped on the twelfth floor. *Shit, shit, shit!* Rider quickly stepped closer to me, but didn't remove his damn hand from beneath my dress. I could only hope his body blocked my bare ass from view as I heard two women enter the car, their voices chattering happily.

"Which floor are the guys on?" one asked.

"Seventeen. They're so effing hot," the other giggled.

Rider leaned forward, his voice a hissing whisper. "I feel you pulsing around my fingers, cariño. You have to hold on for five floors. Don't come until they get out of this elevator, or I'll bend you over and fuck your ass in front of them."

My hands clasped the rail so hard they cramped as his fingertips massaged my G-spot, not enough to make me come, but enough to keep my impending orgasm from fading completely away. He did seem to be quite well versed with how the female anatomy worked, as he'd mentioned back in the bar.

I listened to the beeps that indicated the floors passing and decided this must be the slowest damn elevator in the entire world. A whimper of frustration escaped my lips, and in the next second, Rider's wet fingers left my pussy and pressed against my lips.

"Be quiet and suck," he demanded softly. When he pressed both digits inside my mouth, I rolled my tongue around and around them, tasting myself as he nudged his hard-on against my ass.

I almost collapsed with relief when we reached seventeen and the women disembarked. Rider pulled his fingers from my mouth, dragging my saliva down my chin before returning to his previously scheduled activity, destroying my vagina with his touch.

His movements were fast and savage, hitting all the right places as he grunted directions at me. "Look down at all those people. You're going to come for them, Lena."

"I... I..."

"Let them see how beautiful you are when you lose control. I guarantee every man down there wishes he was the one fingering this hot little cunt. And every woman wishes her man wanted her so much, he would make her orgasm in an elevator, even with everyone watching."

My head thunked forward against the glass as the car rose. I could no longer make out individual faces, but I imagined all those people looking up and watching me get finger-fucked. The thought was exhilarating.

Rider's mouth sucked the side of my neck, and his erection throbbed hot and heavy against my hip. I focused my gaze on his reflection in the glass. His eyes were closed, lips parted against my neck, and he appeared to be in ecstasy, simply from pleasuring me.

And that, as much as anything, tipped me over the edge. "I'm... coming," I panted, barely able to force the words out as the orgasm swelled inside me and broke like a wave crashing against the shore. "Yes, god, yes!" I cried out, my knees weakening to the consistency of cooked noodles.

Rider wrapped a thick arm around my waist, taking my weight so I didn't collapse into a puddle on the floor. "That's it, baby. You're my good girl, aren't you? So beautiful when you come all over my hand."

If I hadn't already suspected I had a praise kink, I was fully aware now. His adoring words extended my climax beyond what I thought was humanly possible. He tilted my face toward his and gave me a series of soft kisses before pulling his other hand from beneath my dress.

Then he smeared both our lips with my arousal and kissed me again, our tongues lapping at each other's mouths. It was perhaps the most intimate thing I'd ever done.

Through my blissful haze, I was confused when the floor felt weird beneath my feet. That's when I realized the elevator was coming to a stop.

"I'm not sure I can walk," I announced, only half joking, and Rider immediately swept me into his arms, carrying me out into the hallway. About halfway down, two men walked toward us, their eyes fixed on my limp form. *Oh my god, how embarrassing.*

"My girlfriend had too many margaritas at the bar," Rider explained, giving them a wink as we passed. I could hear their knowing chuckles as they continued on toward the elevators.

Once inside the room, he set me on my feet and steadied me with firm hands on my waist. "Go to the bathroom, my messy Lena. Do you need help?"

"No," I assured him, though I walked slowly in the high heels. Nothing killed sexy vibes quicker than a broken ankle. After cleaning myself and using the restroom, I emerged into the room. It was a suite with a large sitting room in front of floor-to-ceiling windows and a door off to the side that I assumed was the bedroom.

But the focal point of the space was the man sitting with widely spread legs in a roomy navy-blue armchair. He'd untucked and unbuttoned his shirt, giving me a view of the prime real estate that was Rider's torso.

His gaze was focused intently on me, the eyes of an animal ready to rut, and one hand rested on his crotch. As soon as he saw me, his fingers curled around the thick rod in his pants, making the outline of his cock visibly apparent.

My freshly cleaned pussy dripped at the sight. He looked so fucking dark and dominant, and my steps faltered when he held a hand up in a *stop* gesture.

"Undress for me, querida." The demand was delivered quietly, but it was a demand nonetheless. So I did.

"Eres tan jodidamente hermosa," he said in a sexy Spanish accent—which made me want to kiss the hell out of those full lips—before translating. "So fucking beautiful. Now I want to see how you look on your knees for me."

His hungry eyes roved up and down my naked body as I lowered myself to my knees. "Fuck," he ground out through clenched teeth. "Crawl to me, Lena."

Sweet baby Jesus in a manger! This was some next level shit. I'd read about this in romance novels, but it had never turned me on when a man asked a woman to crawl to him. But from the mouth of this man? It was a different story altogether.

So I dropped to all fours and crawled across the plush, carpeted floor until I was directly in front of the imposing man. His hand reached out and stroked my cheek, and I tilted into the affectionate touch.

"Thank you, sweetheart. You're my good girl."

My cheeks heated at his praise, and my chin dipped demurely. "Thank you, Rider."

With two fingers beneath my chin, he lifted my face and leaned forward for a tender kiss. "Sacame la verga." I blinked at him, not understanding. I'd had three years of Spanish in high school, but I wasn't familiar with that phrase. "Take my cock out," he explained, leaning back and looking arrogant as hell as he waited for me to follow his order.

I did it gladly, unbuckling his black leather belt with meticulous fingers before undoing the button at his waist. When I lowered his zipper tooth by tooth, I raised my eyes to his. A tightness strained his jaw, and I was afraid he'd snap a tendon when I reached into his underwear and pulled out his dripping cock.

"Devórame por completo," he groaned, and I didn't need a translation for that. He wanted me to devour him completely.

And I would. But first... My tongue looped around and around his mushroom head, licking up his arousal before cleaning his shaft with long, slow licks.

"Mmmm, you taste good. Is all this for me?" I teased, stroking the hard length of him before wrapping my lips around his crown.

"Hell yes, baby. All for you. Suck me down. Please." His voice trembled around the plea, and I'd never felt more powerful. Yes, maybe I crawled across the floor for this man, but now I had him begging for my mouth.

I lowered down onto him, inch by inch, my lips stretching around his girth. One of his hands wrapped several times around my long blonde ponytail, and the other gripped my throat as I bobbed up and down on him.

"Joder, sí. Me chupas la polla muy bien, bebe. Tu boca es tan caliente, tan perfecta." I caught enough of that to know he was still praising me. But to be honest, it didn't matter what he said when he spoke in Spanish to me. He could have been saying he likes piña coladas and getting caught in the rain, and it would have sounded sexy.

His fingers tightened slightly around the sides of my neck. "Tell me whose cock is stuffed in your mouth, Lena. Choke out my fucking name."

I did, though he was filling every inch of my mouth with his thrusts, and it came out more like "Wy-wer."

Rider dropped his head back against the chair, his moans becoming louder as he abused my mouth in the very best way. I'd orgasmed in the elevator less than fifteen minutes ago, but the sensuality of this situation had me wanting more.

Twisting my ponytail, he controlled the movements of my head as he lifted his fine ass from the chair and fucked up into my mouth. He was so long and thick, causing saliva to drip down my chin.

"Fuck, I'm about to blow in your pretty mouth, Lena. Can you take it?"

I nodded, wanting it all, and took his length as far as I could down my throat, doing my best to suppress my gag reflex. The first spurt was huge, and I clung to his thick thighs, drinking him down as he bit out a mixture of English and Spanish curse words.

When his body finally sagged deeply into the chair, I smiled around my mouthful before releasing him and kissing up his torso. He pulled me into his lap, his face the picture of serenity when he traced my face with his fingers.

"Dios, woman. You blew my damn mind."

"That's not all I blew," I reminded him, earning me a chuckle before his face turned serious.

"You were perfect, cariño." Eyes the color of the ocean locked on mine as he used his thumb to gently clean around my mouth.

"What is cariño?"

"It's a term of endearment. Like sweetheart or honey or baby. Do you like when I talk to you in Spanish, or is it too confusing?"

"Does this answer your question?" Taking his hand, I guided it between my legs to feel how soaked I was. His cocky smile spread slowly across his face as he fondled me almost lazily. "And I understand some of it, but they didn't teach the dirty words at my high school."

"Too bad. Those are the most fun," he said, holding my chin. "I want to taste myself in your mouth. Quiero saborearme en tu boca." Then he kissed me until my toes curled.

When we finally came up for air, I glanced down and then back up, lifting an impressed eyebrow as his dick twitched beneath my butt. "Glad to see the old boy is showing some signs of life. I was afraid I'd killed him."

He laughed and gave my clit a flick. "He'll always resurrect when you're around." His finger slipped along my crack until he reached my back hole. "You up for some ass play tonight, Lena?"

"Yes," I said with a nod, and in the next second, Rider was standing with me cradled in his arms. I ran my hands over his muscular biceps and shoulders, loving that he could carry me like I weighed nothing.

Dipping his head, he sucked one of my nipples into his mouth as he kicked the door to the bedroom open. Then he moved to my other breast, his tongue circling it before nipping it with his teeth. I closed my eyes and buried my hands in his hair while his mouth worked up over my neck and to my jaw.

"Open your eyes for me, Lehra." I did, surprised that he'd used my real name during our role playing. He settled on the edge of the bed with me in his lap. Our eyes met, and we were no longer Lena and Rider. We were Lehra and Cruz. "I have so many things I want to do to you, but I never want to hurt you, okay?"

"Okay."

His big hand cupped my cheek. "I'm going to be rough with you, but if I do anything you don't like, just tell me, and I'll stop. Would you like a safe word?"

I shook my head. "No, I trust you to stop if I ask you to."

"Good girl," he said, pulling me forward for a tender kiss. Then he stood and tossed me on the bed. "Spread your legs, Lena. I want to look at your little pink pussy while I undress."

Sliding back into my Lena role, I did as he told me, lying back on my elbows and spreading my legs wide while I watched him watching me. There was only a lamp on beside the bed, but his tattoos popped in the dim light when he shrugged out of his shirt.

This man was so damn fine, rocking muscles on top of muscles. His chest and shoulders were broad and covered with taut bronze skin, and his torso tapered to a lean waist that I wanted to wrap my legs around.

And the bottom half? *Dayum!* His thighs were thick, his ass was a perfect bubble, and his cock was long and heavy.

With both hands, he reached for my waist and flipped me over with little effort before slapping my ass. "Up on all fours," he snapped, and I immediately complied. My eyes widened when he went to the nightstand and pulled out a pink rose toy, a bottle of lube, and a silver anal plug that scared the bejeezus out of me. He tossed them all on the bed.

"I'm not sure what you think you're going to do with that thing," I commented, biting my lower lip and nodding to the plug.

He laughed. "I think you know exactly what I'm going to do with it. It's going in that tight ass of yours. The one I've been thinking about fucking all night."

Eek!

The bed dipped behind me, and warm hands massaged the globes of my butt as he pressed wet kisses down my spine. "Put your chest on the mattress, Lena," he demanded quietly.

I lowered myself until my breasts touched the fluffy white duvet, a smile crossing my lips when Rider playfully bit each ass cheek.

"Quiero follarte por detrás. I want to fuck you just like this, from behind. But first..." I yelped when Rider buried his face in my pussy and began eating me like a man who just got out of prison and was presented with a nice, juicy steak.

Smooshing my face into the covers, I rocked back against his hot mouth, loving the burn of his scruff against my sensitive tissues. "That... feels... so good," I panted, my voice slightly muffled.

"Mmmm, me encanta tu fragancia," he groaned, using his nose to rub against my clit. "I want to bathe in the scent of you." Then his tongue circled my back hole, and I squeaked in surprise. No one had ever put their mouth on me *back there*.

Rider wrapped his arms around my thighs and pulled me tightly against his face as he lapped at my ass. I could feel the heat in my face, probably from embarrassment because I liked the forbidden act more than I should have. When the tip of his tongue slid inside and his thumb massaged my clit, I moaned into the mattress.

"Fuck me. Please fuck me," I begged.

Rising up on his knees, he spread my ass cheeks apart and spat. His warm saliva landed directly on my back hole, and I whimpered when I felt something touch me there. His voice turned soft and soothing. "Just my finger, baby. For now."

For the next few minutes, he worked one and then two fingers into my backside, adding lube as he patiently prepared me. Then he reached for the plug. "I'm going to put this inside you and then I'm going to fuck your pussy until you come."

"Okay," I breathed. I'd never been more turned on in my life, though the size of that damn thing filled me with a sense of trepidation. But also excitement. Rider rolled the metal plug up and down my back, and I stammered, "W-what are you doing?"

"Warming it up," he replied, and I noticed that the cool metal was indeed warming from being rubbed against my skin.

I tensed when he placed the tip of it against my asshole, but he stroked my lower back and spoke quietly. "Shhh, relax, baby. I'll go slow." And he did, taking his time and distracting me with firm, skilled fingers on my clit. He worked the toy in and out of me, occasionally stopping to add more lube, before finally saying, "It's all in, Lena. Are you okay?" My head twisted around to find him staring down at me with concern.

"It's all the way in?" He nodded. "It doesn't even hurt," I replied.

Rider chuckled at the surprise in my voice. "It's not supposed to. I want to make you feel good, not hurt you." He leaned over my back and pressed his lips to mine. "I need to be inside you, bebe. Can you handle both your ass and your cunt being filled?"

His fingers were still circling my clit, keeping me on edge, and I felt like I was about to go crazy. "I'll give it a damn good try," I replied, wiggling my butt playfully.

After one final kiss, he rose up behind me, spanking my ass on each side and causing my tiny hole to clench around the plug. "Hold on tight, cariño. You're mine tonight, and I'm going to fuck you bare."

Those dirty words only added to the sense of danger of this scene. I was about to let a very possessive stranger screw me in his hotel room without a condom.

"Yes. Please," I begged, curling my fingers into the covers as I felt the head of his cock at my pussy. He eased in a couple inches, and the feeling of fullness overwhelmed me. "Fuck, go slow."

Grasping my hips in both hands, Rider held me steady as he pumped shallowly, letting me adjust to having both holes filled. "So fucking tight, Lena," he gritted out. "Your sweet pussy is strangling my cock."

"It feels good," I whimpered. "I can take more."

"Jesus fucking Christ, woman." His fingers were going to leave bruises where he was grasping my hips as he slid all the way home. He held himself deep, and I could hear his harsh, heavy breaths between his words. "You're so goddamn sexy."

I eased my hips forward and then back a few times, fucking myself on his dick and causing us both to moan our pleasure. The piercing on the bottom of his penis stimulated my clit when he was balls deep, and I knew it wouldn't take long before I was coming all over him.

"Fuck me. Please. Hard and fast."

Rider pulled back and slammed into me, jolting the plug in my backside. Bursts of erotic sensations flickered outward from my center as he let out a masculine grunt. And then for the next few minutes, he showed off his stamina. He fucked me relentlessly with sharp snaps of his hips, the sounds of our flesh smacking together joining with the sound of the headboard banging against the wall.

The sex was hard and fast, just like I'd asked for, and the smells and noises of fierce fucking filled the room. My entire body tingled with my oncoming orgasm, and when Rider placed his hand on the back of my neck and held me down...

I shattered.

CHAPTER 32

WATCHING LEHRA FALL APART was the hottest thing I'd ever seen. And yes, she was my Lehra, not Lena right now. I wanted to give her this fantasy, and I was definitely letting a darker side of myself show, but in my head I knew I couldn't think of her like some random stranger I'd picked up in a bar.

She was the woman I loved, and I had to keep my wits about me and make sure not to hurt her. Because it would be so easy to lose control, especially given what we were about to do.

Lehra told me once she wasn't very experienced with anal but that she wanted to try it with me. I'd never betray that trust, so I had to make this good for her.

Though she was the most important thing, my motivations weren't entirely selfless. I was hoping that if she enjoyed having my cock inside her ass, she would let me do it again in the future. Because, dear god, I knew she was going to feel amazing around me. She had the tightest little hole I'd ever felt, and there's no way I wouldn't be addicted once I'd had her.

My dick protested when I withdrew from her and rolled her over onto her back. Her pretty eyes were drowsy, lips curved into a sated smile. Despite the mess I'd made of her makeup and the strands that had escaped from her sleek ponytail, she was still the most gorgeous thing I'd ever seen.

I pushed a sweaty lock of hair from her neck. "You were amazing, sweetheart. Do you need a break?"

She bit her bottom lip and shook her head. "No, I need to make you feel good."

Popping one eyebrow, I wryly replied, "You sucked my brains out through my dick earlier, Lena. Anything else is just icing on the cake."

She giggled, the happy sound making me smile. "Do you still want to… you know…"

"Fuck your pretty ass?" I inquired bluntly, and she nodded. "I'm going to assume that was a rhetorical question."

"Do you want me to turn over?"

I stroked my hands up and down her thighs and shook my head. "No, we'll do it like this so I can watch your face."

She reached up and cupped my cheeks, her thumbs rubbing over my dimples. "I want to watch your face too. I kinda like it."

Dammit, the feelings this woman gave me were like nothing I'd ever experienced. My chest felt full and light at the same time. Reaching for the bottle, I lubed up my erection as she watched. Then I reached for the plug, looping my finger in the handle.

"Take a deep breath and then let it out." As soon as she exhaled, I pulled the toy out and tossed it aside. Hopefully it had stretched her out enough to take me, though I was a couple inches longer. Grabbing a couple pillows, I wedged them beneath her lower back and butt to adjust her to the perfect angle. "Pull your knees back against your chest," I ordered, and she did. "Have you ever done it like this before?"

"No, just from behind."

"I think you'll like this position because I can do this." I picked up the rose-shaped clit stimulator and licked it, coating the ruffled surface with my saliva before holding it against her pussy. When I turned on the suction feature and moved it around until I found the perfect spot, she gasped at the sensation.

"That's... ohmygoddd," she moaned, drawing out the last word.

Holding the pink toy against her clit, I fisted my cock with my other hand and brought the head to her tiny back hole. "Relax for me, cariño." Then I pushed forward until my tip was inside her, holding still when she winced. My thumb hit the rose's button to increase the suction, and Lehra's mouth dropped open.

"Ohhh, that's good."

I took more and more of her with slow, gentle movements, pausing occasionally to give her time to adjust. Finally, I was all the way inside, and the feeling was fucking exquisite. She was squeezing me so tightly, I wasn't sure how much longer I could hold on.

Tipping my head back, I groaned, "Ahhh, qué rica, mami."

"God, you're sexy," she croaked out, sliding a hand up and over my abs. "This feels really good."

My eyes dropped to where we were joined, and the sight of her asshole stretched around my girth had me gritting my teeth so hard, they would probably be mere nubs tomorrow.

Look away before you nut ten seconds into this, dumbass. I lifted my gaze to her face and was mesmerized by the raw ecstasy I saw there. Lehra stretched one arm over her head, clutching the covers in her fist as she began to pump her hips.

"You like having my thick cock up your ass, don't you, bebe?"

"Yesssss. You're so big, but I love it." Her pretty pink lips parted as she pressed her head back into the pillow, exposing her slender neck, and I bent to run my tongue up one side and down the other. "Rider," she whimpered, "I never knew it could feel this good."

"Fuck, sweetheart. That makes two of us."

Working my way down her chest, I took one of her rosy nipples between my lips and sucked. Her back lifted off the bed and she clutched at my hair, holding me to her when I switched to the other.

"Suck me harder," she begged, twisting her fingers in my hair. I applied more suction and allowed my teeth to graze across the diamond-hard peak, smiling around her tit when she groaned her approval.

I felt like a professional multitasker with my cock in her ass, my lips around her nipple, and my hand holding the rose between her legs. But to see her like this, in the throes of ecstasy, I would have grown more hands if I could.

Her overstimulated body writhed beneath mine, thighs trembling as she neared her completion.

"Does it feel good baby? Do you like me filling that ass up?"

She nodded, tugging on me until I pressed my lips to hers. She was bent completely in half as I held myself up on one arm and plunged in and out of her, feeling my own orgasm approach.

Flicking the sucking toy up another level, I mumbled against her lips, "Come for me, mami. Let me feel you clamp down around my dick."

In the next second, I lost the ability to breathe when Lehra cried out my name, my *real name*. "I'm coming, Cruz. Oh god, so hard."

My balls cinched up against my body, and I buried my face in the pillow beneath her to muffle my roar. After one more hard thrust, I found my own release, spilling myself inside her warmth. I pulled the rose toy away and dropped to both forearms, my muscles weak from exhaustion and the intensity of my orgasm.

When air finally found its way back into my lungs, I pressed my forehead against hers. "I know this was supposed to be a one-night stand, but I think I might just keep you, Lena."

She smiled, and it practically lit up the dim room. "I might just let you."

We sat in the long white bathtub, facing each other with Lehra's legs draped over mine. "You okay, baby?" I asked, massaging one of her feet.

"Mmmm, yes, especially with you rubbing my feet like that," she groaned, staring up at the ceiling with a satisfied smile on her swollen lips. "They're sore from those damn shoes."

I kissed the spot just beneath her toes. "Why did you wear them? It wouldn't have hurt my feelings if you'd worn something more comfortable instead of the ones I sent you."

"Because they were so pretty," she gushed and then waved a dismissive hand at me. "It's a girl thing."

I dug my thumb into the arch of her foot, and she let out a low, sultry hum, making me have some pretty unsavory thoughts, even though my penis should be satisfied for at least a week after tonight. But that shady bastard was apparently greedy, especially where Lehra was concerned.

"Well, I wouldn't have cared if you walked around barefoot."

She laughed, scooped up a mound of bubbles in her hand, and blew them at me. "I can't believe you like bubble baths."

"Correction: I like a bubble bath with a gorgeous woman."

"You do this often? Bathe with your lovers?"

"Actually, you're the first."

"Bullshit," she retorted. "Why?"

I leaned forward and kissed her ankles before starting on her calves. "I didn't want to. I've showered with women, but I've never taken a bath with anyone until the mermaid thing with you."

Lehra tickled my ribs with her toes. "Awww, I popped Cruz's bathtub cherry. They say you never forget your first."

Laughing, I tugged her until she was straddling my lap. "I don't think we have to worry about that, Tink."

Her hands cradled my face as we stared at each other. "Your eyes are so pretty. Do your siblings have blue eyes too?"

Talk about a complicated question. And answer...

"Actually, I've been wanting to talk to you about that."

"About your eyes?" Lehra asked, eyebrows inching together.

"About... some things." I'd spoken with Paul about this, and he was totally fine with me sharing my parentage with Lehra.

"Okay." She kissed my lips softly. "You can tell me anything."

The blood hummed in my veins, a combination of nerves and relief at finally telling someone my secret. "Okay, here goes," I rushed out. "I found out after Papa died that... he's not my biological father."

Lehra's eyes popped wide, and she instantly wrapped me in a hug that I wanted to last forever. "Oh, sweetie. That must have been so hard to find out." Her soft hands stroking my neck calmed me, making it easier for me to spill the story.

"That's the reason I came to New York. I found some letters between my father and... my other father."

She sat up, keeping her hands on the back of my neck as her gray eyes searched mine. "They knew each other?"

"After the fact. Many years ago, my mother worked here in New York and got pregnant. I don't know all the details because I haven't spoken with her about it yet. I've just pieced together details from the letters and from talking to my biological dad."

"You found him?" her voice was incredulous.

"Yes, it's... Paul Bouvier."

A myriad of expressions flashed across Lehra's face. "Oh my... your eyes... and his eyes. And that means... oh my god. Auburn. And Monty. And holy shit. They're your brothers!"

I couldn't help but laugh at the choppy expression of her realization. "They are."

"Wh-what do they think about it?"

My face creased into a wince. "We haven't told them."

Anger colored Lehra's cheeks. "Is Paul trying to keep you hidden from them?"

"No, no, not at all," I assured her, rubbing my hands up and down her back. "He wanted to tell them immediately, but I've been reluctant. So much shit has gone down in the past couple years. I didn't want to add to the drama."

"And you're worried how they might react," she said—a statement not a question.

The corner of my lips twitched. "Yeah, maybe a little. We've decided to tell them after Kassie and Monty get married."

Her face softened. "I'm so happy for those two. It was cool getting to watch him propose to her after so many years." She leaned forward and pressed her lips to the spot just in front of my ear. "You are an amazing man, Cruz. Monty and Auburn would be honored to have you as their brother. Don't be afraid."

God, I fucking love this woman. Her incredibly sweet heart, her compassion, the way she knew what I needed to hear before I even realized it.

"Thank you, Tink. I think it will be okay."

"It will be more than okay," she whispered, nuzzling into my neck and warming me from the inside out. "You and Monty are already like brothers, and you seem close with Auburn too."

I chuckled. "Yeah, he was a harder nut to crack, but he does already treat me like part of his family."

She leaned back so she could look at me, and I immediately missed the closeness. "So how exactly did this happen? Your mom getting pregnant by Paul Bouvier?"

I raised one eyebrow. "Well, you see, little Lehra. When two people really, really like each other, they lie down in a bed, and the man puts his—"

"Stop it!" she giggled, smacking the back of my head. "You know what I mean."

"I do. So my mom was the nanny for the Bouvier family. Apparently, Chloe Bouvier was a… not very nice person even back then. She left town when Evie was a baby, and Paul ended up filing for divorce. He'd started developing feelings for my mother."

"So Monty wasn't born yet," Lehra mused.

"Right. Chloe was pregnant with him when she left, but Paul didn't know that. And he made sure to let me know that he filed for divorce *before* he and my mother… got together."

"But why didn't you know about Paul until you were grown?"

"This part is kind of convoluted. Chloe came back and told Paul she was pregnant. She threatened to take the kids to Europe to live with her family if he went through with the divorce, so he was torn. He really loved my mom, but he couldn't lose his kids either."

"Oh my god, that witch!"

"Exactly. And back then, custody usually went to the mother, so he was pretty much screwed. He went to my mom's apartment to tell her about everything, but when he arrived, her cousin who lived next door told him Chloe had fired her, and she left town."

Lehra covered her mouth with her hand. "Did she know she was pregnant with you?"

I shook my head. "No, this was literally days after Mama and Paul were together."

"Your poor mom," she said, her eyes thoughtful. "Do you think Chloe threatened her or something and that's why she never told Paul she was pregnant?"

"Probably. My dad told Paul that she wouldn't talk about it, but she seemed scared of *that evil woman*."

"And how did your fathers get in contact with each other?"

"Paul hired a private investigator to find my mother, and then he showed up at our house. And there was this little blue-eyed boy staring back at him."

"Wow, that must have been a shock. How old were you?"

"Six. My mother told him to go the hell away, but he and my dad stayed in contact." I told her about the letters and how Paul stayed in my life from afar.

Lehra's eyes filled with tears. "That's such a sacrifice he made."

I nodded my agreement. "We've grown really close the past couple years. Paul is an amazing man. Like I said, he wants to shout it from the rooftops that I'm his son. I've been the reluctant one."

"Now that Chloe's dead, what's the harm?"

"That's my thought too. We'll wait till after the wedding, and also I want to talk to my mother about it."

"How do you feel about her keeping your paternity a secret all these years?"

"I was... not really angry. More disappointed that she lied. But as I talked more with Paul, I understand better now. She was doing what she had to do, and she and Papa were wonderful parents."

"They must have been to raise such a good man." She wiggled her eyebrows at me. "Who happens to be pretty hot too."

My cock perked up in interest when Lehra pressed her tits against my chest. "Well, enough about all that," I told her, standing with her legs wrapped around my waist. "If I only have one night with the beautiful Lena, I don't want to waste any more time."

I didn't even bother drying us off, instead lying her on the bathmat and making love to her wet body until we were both spent.

Chapter 33

I HEARD A KNOCK on my door and could literally feel my face brighten. It was probably Cruz stopping by before I left for Kassie's, and his presence always made me positively giddy.

We spent most nights together, alternating between my apartment and his. Both felt equally like home to me.

After he'd told me about his paternity secret a month ago, it seemed like we'd grown closer than ever. I loved the trust we had in each other. And, well, I loved *him*.

Not even checking the peephole, I swung the door open and grinned. "Hey, sexy!" But it wasn't my hunky Cuban on the other side of the door.

No, it was Dwight.

Fuck.

My former fiancé's eyes flashed with surprise at my enthusiastic greeting that hadn't been meant for him. At all.

"Well hey, beautiful." He pulled me into a hug, and I gave him a little pat on the back before quickly extracting myself from his arms.

Doing my best to keep my tone neutral, I asked, "What are you doing here?"

He grinned winningly. "I worked some things out and got transferred to New York."

What in the fucking fuck?

"Oh. Well. That's... something," I hedged, unable to think of anything else to say.

"Great, right?" he asked, face beaming.

Not exactly the adjective I was thinking of.

I stared at the man I'd been prepared to marry and felt... nothing. So much nothing. How was that even possible?

How was it that the feelings I'd had for Dwight seemed like strings while my feelings for Cruz were like strong ropes? The kind sailors used on ships, hardy and powerful and all-binding.

"Lehhhhraaaa," Dwight sang, waving a hand in front of my face with a chuckle. "Big surprise, right?"

"The biggest," I muttered. "So what are you doing here?"

His brow creased at my less-than-thrilled tone. "I just told you, I got transferred to New York."

"Yes, but what are you doing *here*, specifically?" I pointed at the floor. "At my apartment?"

"You'd put me on your visitor's list, so the concierge let me up. I came to see you," he returned, like I was mentally challenged for even asking. "So we can give this another shot."

"No." The word wasn't shouted, but it was no less emphatic, and he took a step back.

"What do you mean no?"

"It's a two-letter word, Dwight. It's not that difficult."

He managed to widen his eyes and scrunch his eyebrows at the same time, a hybrid expression of shock and hurt.

"But I-I moved here for you."

I let out a sigh, showing a hint of the exasperation I was feeling. "That wasn't a very smart thing to do Dwight, you moved here without even talking to me first?"

"But I was trying to do one of those..." he circled his hand a few times trying to think of the phrase, "one of those grand gesture things."

Jesus help me.

Putting on my most patient smile, I said, "I don't need grand gestures, Dwight. I need the small things. The daily things that tell a person you care." My mind went to Cruz, the king of the small but sweet gestures. "I need a man who cools my coffee off before he brings it to me because he knows I don't like it super-hot. I need a man who rubs my feet after I wear heels. I need a man who tells me every day with his actions and his words that I am his priority."

Dwight rubbed the lines between his eyebrows. "But I can do that, Lehra. I want to try again with us. I promise you'll be my number one priority from now on."

I shook my head slowly from side to side. "It's too late for that, and to be honest, I'm not sure we were ever right for each other."

He tossed his hands up and let them fall to his sides. "What am I supposed to do now?"

"You're supposed to get on with your life just like I have."

"But—"

My voice was firm when I interrupted him. "No, Dwight, it's not going to happen."

His shoulders deflated like a popped balloon. "Can I at least stay here until I figure out what I want to do?"

"There are plenty of hotels in New York."

He stared at me for a long moment and shook his head. "Are you sure about this?"

I had never been more sure about anything in my life, and I gave him a slow nod. I almost felt a little bit sorry for him, the big dummy, so I had a modicum of pity on him.

"I have to leave in a few minutes, but I'll let you come inside so you can find a hotel room. Where's your luggage?"

He pouted like a big baby and mumbled, "I left it downstairs with your concierge. They said they would bring it up for me."

"I'll call down and tell them to hold onto it." His face fell almost to his feet, and I stepped back, gesturing for him to come in and settle on the couch. I spouted off the names of a few hotels, and he opened the browser on his phone and began tapping away, his face forming an irritated scowl.

"Okay," he finally said, "I booked a room for the next two nights until I can figure out if I want to stay here or go back to Michigan." His jaw muscles tightened. "I mean, I already took the job, but now I don't know if I want to stay here."

"I'm sure you'll figure it out. I have somewhere I have to be, so…" I bobbed my head toward the door."

Dwight's eyes widened. "You're kicking me out? But I can't check into the hotel until two. It's not even noon. I have seven suitcases and nowhere to go."

I puffed out a sigh and gritted my teeth. I had to get to Kassie's and didn't have time to stay here and babysit his dumb ass.

"Fine. You can stay here until 1:30. Like I said, I have somewhere to be, so just close the door behind you. It's self-locking."

Grabbing my purse, I hooked it over my shoulder, and Dwight's forehead crinkled once again. He was going to have major wrinkles if he kept this up. "You're leaving right now?" he asked, seeming offended that I wasn't going to stay here and entertain him.

God, how did I ever tolerate this big man-baby?

"I am," I said, backing away when he rose and tried to hug me, instead offering him a sad smile. "I hope you find what you're looking for Dwight."

His eyes filled with tears. "I already did, but I lost her."

I wanted to tell him that he'd had ample chance to fix things, and he chose to put me second every single time. But he already knew that, even if he wasn't quite ready to admit it to himself.

On my way upstairs, I called the building's concierge and informed them I'd be at Monty Bouvier's apartment and that my "guest" would be gone by two. And to remove him from my approved visitors list.

Dwight Jones was a manipulative prick, and I didn't trust him as far as I could throw him.

"Thank you for coming over and helping me today," Kassie said. "Doing wedding stuff is so much more fun with friends here."

"And champagne," Gianna said, lifting her glass in a salute before going back to tying little ribbons around party favors.

Kassie and Monty's wedding was six weeks away, but Kassie had a big case coming up and was trying to get as much done early as possible.

The bride nudged me with her shoulder. "How are things going with you and Cruz?" she sang.

I couldn't help the smile that broke across my face. "So good. He's just the perfect man."

"He's a sweetheart," Gianna agreed. "So much better than the last one."

I laughed. "Speaking of him, you'll never guess who showed up at my apartment today."

"No!" Gianna practically shouted. "Did you punch him in the face?"

Taking a sip of my champagne, I shook my head. "No. I should have though. He said he moved here so we could try again."

"Oh, puh-leeze," Gianna groaned, scrunching her nose up. "Like you would give up a man like Cruz Estrada for the titty-sucking mama's boy. I mean, Cruz absolutely adores you."

That made my heart so happy. "He does," I agree.

"He has for a while, obviously."

"You think?"

"Oh, for sure," Gia replied, tugging at a very crooked bow before untying it and trying again. "I've known ever since he arranged for Auburn to help you out with the apartment."

Hold on... he...

"What?" I screeched.

Kassie's eyes were as big as bowling balls and bounced between us.

Gianna bit her bottom lip and muttered, "Um, oops. You didn't know that?"

"No," I said weakly, pressing my hand against my chest as I thought back. That had been right around the time I had told Cruz that I was being kicked out of my apartment. "You have to tell me everything right now, Gianna Bouvier."

She rolled her pretty green eyes. "Fine, but you didn't hear this from me. Cruz called Auburn and told him that you were having housing issues and needed a new place. He wanted to see if there was any availability here in our building. He even offered to pay for it."

"He did not!" I exclaimed before downing a big slug of champagne.

"Oh yes, ma'am, he did," Gia drawled. "Auburn had already decided to offer you a raise so he thought he would see if you wanted the apartment as part of your salary. But Cruz was definitely the catalyst behind it. Auburn never would have known you needed a place if he hadn't told him."

"Awww," Kassie cooed, "that's really sweet."

"Well, now I feel bad," I lamented. "Did Auburn just give me the apartment because he felt sorry for me?"

"Not at all," Gianna said, shaking her head vehemently. "I swear he had already talked to me about giving you a raise. He wanted to make sure I was okay with you being his assistant after my dad retired."

"Awww," Kassie said again. "That was really thoughtful of him to consider your feelings about it, Gia."

"It was, but of course I told him I had no problem with it, even though Lehra is freaking gorgeous."

"Well, thank you," I told her, "but trust me. The man only has eyes for you."

Her green eyes sparkled with mischief. "His eyes and every other part of him belong to me. Including his big—"

She stopped talking when three little ones entered the room.

"Mommy, we're done with the menu for the wedding," Kassie's son, Sully, said, handing her a sheet of paper with boxes check marked in blue crayon. Gianna and Auburn's twins, Jaxon and Jane, followed with proud smiles on their faces.

"She let the kids pick the menu for the wedding?" I asked Gianna from the corner of my mouth.

"Just the kid food," she whispered back.

"Let's see what we've got," Kassie said, feigning shock at the first item. "Oh, big surprise. Pigs in a blanket."

The kids all giggled. "That was Sully's choice," Jane said, pointing a finger at her cousin. "I picked the sliders."

"But with fancy cheese," Jaxon added with a wise nod of his little head.

"Fancy cheese, huh?" Kassie asked with a smile.

"Yeah, Buddha cheese," he informed us, and Gianna and I had to cover our mouths to hide our snickers.

Janie sighed and rolled her eyes like a teenager. "It's called *gouda* cheese, Jaxon. Not Buddha cheese."

"Well, that's weird," Jaxon said before poking at the paper. "I wrote mine at the bottom."

"Oh, um." Kassie tilted her head and squinted at the scrawled words. "Does this say pickle... dar?"

"Pickle *bar*," Jaxon corrected. "Mom and Dad took us to a pickle store and they had like one million different kinds of pickles or something like that. I thought it would be really cool if we had a pickle bar at yours and Uncle Monty's wedding. That way people could choose which kind they want on their sliders, or they could just eat 'em because pickles are awesome."

"Soooo, you didn't like the mini pizza idea?" she cajoled.

Jaxon's adorable nose crinkled. "Aunt Kassie, mini pizzas would be okay, but they're a little basic. A pickle bar would be freaking epic."

Gianna let out a snort, and I elbowed her.

Kassie's lips twitched at the corners, but she gave each kid a hug and a kiss on the head. "I think these are all great ideas. Thank you all for helping. I'll talk to Uncle Monty about the pickle bar since that wasn't on the caterer's list."

Jaxon wiggled on the spot. "He'll definitely say yes."

"I'm sure he will," I whispered to Gia. "Monty would have a petting zoo at the wedding if his son or his niece and nephew requested it."

She widened her eyes at me and hissed, "Don't give them any more ideas."

"Why don't you guys go play for a while," Kassie told the little ones. Both boys took Jane's hands and walked slowly since she was still adjusting after her surgery. They were so freaking sweet I wanted to cry.

"Well," Kass said, settling back on the eggplant-colored couch. "This is shaping up to be quite the classy affair."

Gianna and I were unable to hold in our laughter for another second, falling over and holding our stomachs. "Oh my god, I almost busted a gut when Jaxon said he wanted a pickle bar," Gia gasped.

Kassie caught the giggles too. "You know, maybe we can make it work. Put the pickles in pretty little bowls, and maybe add in some olives too. Then we can put meats, cheeses, and fruits nearby, and everyone will think it's a charcuterie table."

"That's not a bad idea, but don't think you have to do it, Kass. I'll get Auburn to explain to Jax that maybe a pickle bar isn't appropriate for a wedding reception."

"And end up with something *basic* like mini pizzas?" Kassie scoffed with a big grin on her face.

As I continued filling the small white bags, my mind drifted to the metaphorical ropes analogy from earlier, the ropes binding me to Cruz, and I finally understood. He had woven those ropes for me, first with his friendship and then with his... *love*. Realization hit me, not like a ton of bricks but like a gentle rainfall.

Cruz Estrada loves me.

As I took the elevator down to my floor a few hours later, I decided I was ready to hear him say it, and a plan developed.

When Cruz got home from work with the SWAT team tonight, I was going to ride that man until he admitted it.

Chapter 34

I checked my pockets to make sure I had everything before leaving my apartment on Saturday afternoon, when I saw a man exiting Lehra's apartment.

"Can I help you?" I asked and then almost keeled over when I saw who it was. *Dwight fucking Jones.* "What are you doing here?"

"Oh hey! Cruz, right?" He gave me a smug smile. "I live here now."

My fists balled up at my sides as I tried to control my anger. "What do you mean you live here?"

"I just moved here. I got transferred by my architectural firm."

"Lehra..." I said but was unable to form any other words.

"Yeah, I talked to her a couple hours ago."

No way. No fucking way.

Unable to even look at him, I stormed off down the corridor to the elevator bank, stabbing the button so hard I cracked my fingernail.

I was absolutely furious but also hurt, as though someone was stabbing a white-hot poker directly into my chest. *There's no way she's going back to him, right?* She said she wanted to be in a relationship with me. She said she wanted to make this work.

When I walked into the station, I didn't even remember how I got there. My brain was going ninety miles an hour while my heart was cracked into pieces in my chest.

"Look alive today, guys," Curly told us. "There's a big political rally downtown, and we have to make sure everyone plays nice."

We made it through the workday with only a couple small skirmishes, which we dealt with quickly. But it had been enough to keep me distracted for a bit.

As I stripped off my gear, I heard my phone ping. Checking it, I found a message from Lehra.

Tink: Hey, I was wondering if I could come over tonight.

Shit. I couldn't deal with her breaking up with me right now. I needed time to process, so I replied back.

Cruz: Not tonight. I'm not feeling great.

Tink: Oh no! Do you need me to come take care of you?

What the hell is she playing at?

Cruz: Just need some rest. We'll talk tomorrow.

Tomorrow came approximately one million hours later. At least that's what it seemed like while I ran every horrible scenario over and over in my head.

I trudged to the kitchen and put on some coffee. I had to be at work again in a couple hours, and I needed to get my mind clear.

As soon as I took my first sip, I heard my front door open.

"Cruz?" a soft voice called out, and my heart rate doubled, both in excitement to see her and fear of what she was going to say.

"In the kitchen," I replied, hearing the tremble in my own voice.

Her sweet smile was coated with sympathy when she walked in, and it almost killed me. She was about to do it. She was going to ruin my life.

"Are you okay?" she asked, walking toward me and pressing a cool hand against my forehead. "You don't feel like you have a fever." I hated that I still craved her sweet touch. This was going to kill me.

"I'm fine," I replied curtly.

"What was wrong with you? Was it your stomach?"

No, my heart, I thought.

"Did you need something, Lehra?"

Her eyebrows knitted together in confusion at the ice in my voice. "I just wanted to check on you. I was worried."

"I told you I was fine."

"Cruz, what's wrong?" she asked.

I was unable to keep the bitterness from my tone. "I saw Dwight, Lehra. He told me he moved in."

She stared at me for a long moment. "Moved in where?"

"With you."

"What?" she shrieked so loudly my ears rang. "And you actually believed him?"

"I, uh..."

She stood toe-to-toe with me and glared up into my face. "You big idiot."

I blinked at her. "I'm the idiot?"

She rolled her eyes and planted her hands on her hips. "If you think I would ever go back with Dwight Jones, then yes, you're a complete moron. He did show up at my apartment to tell me he'd moved to New York, but he's certainly not moving into my apartment."

"He said... the way he said it..." I shook my head in confusion. "I saw him coming out of your apartment while you were at Kassie's. That's when he told me, and I quote, *I live here now.*"

"Ohhh, I'm just sure he did," she fumed. "The jerk showed up without calling and announced that he was here so we could get back together. Like I would take his sorry ass back." Lehra flailed her arms and stomped around the kitchen. "And he brought all his things, thinking I was going to let him move in here, I guess. Well, I informed him that he could take a damn hike."

Every organ in my body seemed to melt with relief.

"So you're not back together with Dwight?" I asked, just to confirm.

She whirled on me, looking even more beautiful in her fierceness. "Absolutely not. He was in my apartment because I told him he could stay until his hotel was ready. *While I was not there,*" she emphasized. "Now I wish I'd kicked his ass out onto the street with all his luggage."

I scruffed a hand up and down my face. "Oh my god, Lehra. I was freaking out all day yesterday and all night. I thought you were leaving me."

Her face softened, and she took my cup of coffee and set it down before climbing me like a tree. I instantly gripped her butt to hold her up as her legs wrapped around my waist and her arms wound around my shoulders.

"I adore you, you big jealous doof."

Feeling like an ass, I leaned my forehead against hers. "I adore you too, Tink. I'm so sorry I jumped to conclusions."

"Well, I'm pretty sure dipshit Dwight knew you'd interpret it that way."

"Where is he staying?" I growled. "I want to punch him in the face."

"I have no idea. I didn't ask. and I don't want to know." Any remaining tension I may have held dissipated in an instant. "Is this why you didn't want me to come over last night?"

"Yes," I admitted. "I feel so stupid for buying into that. I'm really sorry, Lehra."

Her soft hands stroked my messy hair. "Stop apologizing. We've got it all straightened out now. You know I'm not going back with mama's boy, and I'm now aware that you have a jealous streak a mile wide."

"It was more than jealousy," I whispered, giving her a soft kiss on the lips. "I was devastated."

"Baby," she crooned, pressing kisses all over my face. "How about if I'm waiting in your bed when you get home tonight? And I'll show you how I feel about you."

I placed my woman on the counter and slid my fingers into the waistband of her shorts. "How about I give you an apology right now? Kinda like an appetizer before the main course tonight."

"Don't you have to go to work?"

"I always have time to get you off, Tink."

She giggled as I worked her shorts and panties down her legs. "You do have quite the uncanny knack for that."

I sank to my knees and gave her my best apology. Twice.

"What are your plans for the day?" I asked as we walked hand-in-hand out my front door sixty minutes later, my heart lighter than it had been in the past twenty-four hours.

"I'm going to Two Rivers Mall. They have that new sporting goods store, and I wanted to get some new workout gear."

"Okay baby," I said, giving her another kiss when we stopped beside her door.

"Mmmm," she hummed, licking her lips. "You taste like me."

I grin down at her. "You're my favorite flavor, Tink. If I could get Ben & Jerry's to make—"

She stopped me with a hand over my mouth. "Please don't say anymore."

We were three hours into our shift when Chris leaned his head back against the wall of the armored vehicle we were riding in. "Been a slow day today," he commented.

Maverick punched him in the arm. "Shut the hell up, dude. You're gonna jinx us."

Five minutes later, Mav's prediction was proven correct when we heard the words *active shooter* over the radio.

"Shit," Curly muttered. "What's the location?"

My blood froze in my veins when the voice said those three little words. The most horrifying words I'd heard since I learned my father had died.

Two Rivers Mall.

CHAPTER 35

"WE'RE ON IT," CURLY replied. "We're less than five minutes from there."

It was the longest five minutes of my life. Fully armed and armored, we were met outside by the head of security, a guy named Carter, who debriefed us.

"The bastard started out on the first floor," he reported, leading us through a side door and into the security office. "Two civilians have been injured, and he took out three of my guards. One is dead and two are alive but have gunshot wounds."

"Where is he now?" I asked quickly, a red haze curtaining the edges of my vision.

Carter pointed to a monitor with a map on it. "Last spotted on the second floor. The first floor has been cleared of all shoppers and employees except for the injured."

My eyes instantly went to the largest store on floor two, the one dead center. Dewitt Sporting Goods.

Fuck me.

"Are you sure it's a single shooter?" Curly asked.

"Yep, a guy with a long brown ponytail. He's in full body armor, including a helmet, so if you want to take him out, it's got to be a headshot from the front."

"Who were the civilians?" I asked. Carter looked questioningly at me, and I specified with a bark. "Men or women?"

"One man, one woman," he answered.

I cleared my throat, preparing for the answer to my next question. "What did the woman look like?"

"Um." Carter glanced around at our group before landing back on me, probably trying to figure out what the hell was going on. "She has blue hair, shaved on one side."

I guessed Curly saw my shoulders sag with relief, and he stepped directly into my space and snapped, "What the hell is going on, Estrada?"

"My girl is here. In this mall," I admitted.

"Fuck," he bit out, massaging the spot between his eyebrows. "Do you need to sit this one out Estrada? I really can't afford to lose anyone. We need all hands on deck, and the next team is at least twenty minutes out."

"No, I swear to god, I can do it. Please." Desperation wrapped around every word like a vine.

His eyes narrowed on me. "Fuck almighty," he mumbled. "I'm trusting you, Estrada. Your priority here is to do your fucking job. You are not a boyfriend right now; you're a machine. Understood?"

"I've got this, Curly."

"Christ, don't make me regret this." He swiveled and began barking out orders. Chris was to stay on the first floor to provide protection for the medical first responders who were coming in to help the victims. Kai, the best sharpshooter, was sent to the third floor so he would have an elevated position and the best chance to take the guy out.

Me, Curly, Maverick, Jayden, and a guy called Radar were sent to the second floor. I didn't know Radar all that well because he didn't hang out with us after work, but he was a damn good teammate.

Carter was synced to our comms so he could keep us updated if he spotted the shooter on camera. The suspect was apparently using the employee hallways behind the stores to travel between locations because security cameras were sparse back there.

The entire debrief and Curly's orders took less than four minutes, and then we were storming the second floor from all directions. Curly and I took the central stairs, our heads on a swivel and our eyes taking in every detail.

As we encountered civilians, we quietly hissed orders to them to head downstairs and out the main door, where they would be met by uniformed officers and any necessary medical personnel.

I counted at least fifty that made it safely down the stairs behind us, but none were a curly blonde with gray eyes. *Jesus, where are you, baby?*

With my H&K MP-5 held confidently in my hands, I motioned to Curly that we should enter the sporting goods store first, and he nodded. We entered, him going left and me going right to cover more ground.

Fuck, this store is huge. The space seemed empty, hopefully because all the customers and employees had gotten out safely.

Taking cover behind a free-standing wall with athletic shoes lining the shelves, I peeked around the corner and almost fell to my knees when I spotted a blonde head poke out from a circular rack of athletic pants.

Lehra!

It was as if she could hear my silent scream, and our gazes locked. The fear in hers broke me, and I started to step around the wall and go to her when a movement from my right caught my eye. With a quick flick of my hand, I motioned for her to hide, and she immediately pulled her head back into the rack of clothes, concealing herself once again.

Good girl.

The shooter was making his way across the floor at an angle.

Motherfucker. He's right between us. Stay hidden, Lehra. Please, for the love of god, do not move an inch.

I prayed she was somehow catching my silent messages.

The suspect was going from rack to rack, separating the clothes with the barrel of his Uzi, looking for... what? Survivors? Someone else to kill?

God no. Please keep her safe.

He was dressed all in black, much like our team, complete with Kevlar vest and helmet. My mind assessed the situation. His back was to me, so any shot I took wouldn't do any damage to his body armor. I was a damn good shot, but if I missed, a stray bullet could hit Lehra, who was hiding just on the other side of the fucker.

Not an option.

He was two racks away from her now, and I glanced at Curly—who was hidden behind another wall to my left—in a panic. He nodded and pointed up and behind him, indicating that he'd notified Kai of the shooter's location.

"I need him to turn around," Kai's soft voice said through the earpiece in my left ear. *Right. He needed to see his face to get a clear shot since the guy was wearing an armored helmet.*

The suspect was now one rack from the one Lehra was hiding in. She had only seconds before he would find her.

Fuck no. Not going to happen.

Stepping out from behind the wall, I yelled, "Drop your weapon!"

The man whirled around, pointing his Uzi at me, and I saw brown eyes widen behind his black ski mask. Then he opened fire on me.

A split second before I was knocked onto my back, I saw a small red circle appear on his forehead.

And Kai instantly became my favorite teammate.

I blinked through the haze floating through my brain.

My first thought was: *get to Lehra.*

And my second thought was: *ow, fuck.*

I grunted through the pain—because even while wearing a bulletproof vest, getting shot fucking hurts—as I rolled over and army crawled toward the clothes rack.

My beautiful Tink busted out, scattering clothes everywhere as she ran to me and dropped to her knees. I'd never been so grateful to see anyone in my entire life.

"Cruz!" she screamed.

Hauling her beneath me, I covered her body with my own and glanced over to where Curly was kneeling beside what I hoped was a corpse. "Curly?"

"Dead," he replied, giving me a curt nod.

"You sure?"

"He's missing the back of his head, so yeah. Pretty sure."

My adrenaline was so thick in my veins I was surprised they weren't all hemorrhaging. I focused my attention back on the woman beneath me, clenching my teeth when I saw the tears streaming down her face.

"Are you okay, Lehra?"

"He shot you!"

"I'm wearing a vest. Are you okay?" I enunciated the question, syllable by syllable.

"I'm... not hurt. Just freaked the fuck out."

Now that I knew she wasn't physically injured, there was only one thing on my mind. The words were practically burning a hole in my tongue in their effort to escape my mouth.

"I love you," I blurted out. "I have for a while, and I should have told you before, but I love the fuck out of you, Lehra Kincaid."

Her tears came even faster, wetting her face and dripping down into her hair. "I love you too, Cruz Estrada."

The absolute sweetest words I'd ever heard.

My vision blurred with my own tears at her admission. "You love me?" I asked, because I wanted to make sure I'd heard her correctly.

"Of course I do. God, I was so scared I'd lost you."

"I'm right here, baby. Not going anywhere."

And then I kissed the ever-loving shit out of her. As our tongues twisted together, I could practically feel our hearts binding themselves to each other as well.

Her mouth was warm and delicious as our lips moved slowly, trying to get their fill of each other. My hands cupped her face, and I deepened the kiss, wanting to remove the ugliness of the afternoon for Lehra and replace it with my love for her.

She let out a little moan, and I pulled back with a soft suck. "Please stop making those sexy noises or you're going to give me a boner while I'm at work."

"You're killing me with the romantic talk, Estrada," she giggled.

"What do you mean? I talked about my boner after professing my love for you on the floor of a sporting goods store, after we'd both had about ten years frightened out of us." *Not to mention we're next to a dead body*, I wisely refrained from saying.

"If this was supposed to be one of your role playing scenes, it was a tad too extravagant for my tastes," she informed me, lifting an eyebrow.

I laughed and kissed the tip of her nose. "Absolutely not." The gravity of what had happened was finally sinking in, and I rested my forehead against hers. "I've never been more scared in my life."

Lehra's chin trembled. "You saved me."

I stroked my thumbs over her cheeks, wiping away the fresh round of tears. "Always, Tink. I'll always protect the woman I love. I couldn't live without you."

And then I kissed her again for good measure, losing myself in her. Until...

"Jesus Christ, is Estrada mauling a civilian?"

I heard Curly's low chuckle. "Don't worry about it, Jayden. She's *his* civilian."

Damn right she is.

"Cruz, I told you, I'm fine. There's no need—"

I shut my woman up with a hard stare. There wasn't a single thing in the entire world that she could ask for that I wouldn't give her, but I was absolutely adamant about this one thing.

Softening my glare with a kiss to her forehead, I dialed a number and pressed the phone to my ear, tucking her into my side with my free arm as the chaos of police and paramedics surrounded us.

"Dude, are you seeing this shit at the mall?" Monty asked in the way of a greeting.

"I'm here."

He let out a harsh breath. "Shit. You okay, man? Are you hurt?"

"I'm fine. Lehra was in the store where... where it all went down."

"Oh my fucking god. Please tell me she's—" His voice broke before he could finish.

"She's safe, but I don't want her to be alone. It will be a few hours till I get out of here."

"I'm on my way. I'll stay with her until you get home. I won't leave her for a second."

Relief flooded my body. Other than myself, there was no one I trusted to take care of Lehra more than... my brother.

CHAPTER 36

I WAS SANDWICHED BETWEEN Monty and his soon-to-be-wife, Kassie, on Cruz's couch. They'd fed me, given me wine, and completely smothered me since Monty had picked me up at the mall after I'd given my statement to the police.

"That chicken noodle soup was so good," I said, glancing at the door for approximately the thousandth time in the past hour. Cruz should be here soon.

The couple shared a look over me that seemed to tell a story. "It's from the deli around the corner," Kass informed me. "Monty brought me some when I was sick."

I was surprised his pupils weren't shaped like little hearts when he looked at his bride. "Well, it was my fault you were sick, Kasserole." I loved when he called her that. It was so cute.

Kassie bit her bottom lip as they stared at each other. Were they about to start making out with me right in the middle?

Pushing off the couch before I got stuck in the midst of a hot and heavy makeout sesh, I felt the nerves of the day settle in my stomach. *Oh crap. Literally.*

As I made my way to the bathroom in Cruz's room, I felt Monty's presence behind me, and I turned. "I'm just going to the bathroom, Mont."

He nodded. "Okay, I'll wait right outside the door."

"Monty," I said bluntly, crossing my arms over my chest, "I need to poop, and I'd rather you not be within listening distance."

His face turned a hundred shades of red. "Oh. Yeah, right. Okay. Um, do you want Kassie to wait by the door?"

I fought a smile. He was taking his orders from Cruz seriously, not letting me out of his sight for even a second since we'd gotten here.

"I don't particularly want Kassie hearing my digestive noises either," I told him, giving his thick arm a squeeze. "I'm okay. I promise. I might take a shower too, so don't call in the National Guard if I'm more than a couple minutes."

He chuckled. "Sorry if I'm being a little over the top. We just want you to know you're not alone."

Tears threatened the rims of my eyelids, but I managed to hold onto them as I gave him a big hug. "Thank you. I know you two are trying to finalize wedding stuff, but I appreciate you being here for me."

"You feeling safe is the most important thing to both of us right now," he said sweetly, kissing the top of my head before pulling back and giving me a gentle shove between my shoulders. "Go do your business, and we'll turn the TV up loud."

I laughed as I went into the bedroom and closed the door. I really liked those two, and I hoped that one day, I'd be lucky enough to call them my in-laws.

"He's on his way up," Monty informed me thirty minutes later, setting down his phone and standing. He seemed to have as much nervous energy as I did.

My hair was still damp from my shower, and I had donned my most comfortable lazy day clothes, a pair of Lululemon leggings and one of Cruz's sweatshirts that swallowed me whole. I'd stolen a lot of his shirts over the past few months, and after every laundry day, I'd make him wear them for a while so they'd smell like him when I wore them.

There was nothing better than smelling your man on your comfort clothes.

Monty crossed to the door and opened it, standing beneath the door frame with his fingers drumming anxiously against his thighs until we heard heavy footsteps in the hallway outside. Cruz appeared, and the two men stared at each other for a beat before Monty grabbed him in a fierce hug.

I heard low murmurs but couldn't make out what they were saying, but it was obviously an emotional moment.

"Oh my god," Kassie breathed, clutching my hand. "They are so cute. Almost like brothers."

Kass, you have no idea.

When the guys broke apart, we heard Cruz say, "I promise I'm okay, Mont."

Kassie stepped forward, and Cruz enveloped her in a hug. "Thanks for coming over, Kass. I know you being here helped a lot."

She sniffled and nodded.

A second after he released Kassie, I was being lifted off the ground by Cruz's strong arms and carried swiftly down the hallway. "Thanks for everything guys," he shouted, keeping his eyes firmly on my face, "but... you know..."

"We'll see ourselves out," Monty said with a knowing chuckle.

And then it was just us. Me and the man I loved with all my heart.

He lowered me gently to my feet and cupped my face with his big, warm hands. "I've been so worried about you," he murmured. "How are you feeling?"

"Like I want you."

His exhale brushed against my lips. "I want you too, but I was afraid you'd be too upset or something." Blue eyes searched my gray ones, looking for any sign that I wasn't okay.

"I'm not. I need it. I need you."

"Thank Christ," he said, his lips quirking up on one side. "I love seeing you in my clothes, Tink, but I need to have you naked so I can feel your skin, warm and… alive." His voice cracked a little at the end, and I buried my face in his neck and inhaled. He smelled like sweat and man, and it was about the best scent ever.

We held each other for a long moment before I backed up and pulled the shirt off over my head and removed my leggings. "I'm here, Cruz. I'm here, and I'm alive, thanks to you."

Cruz dropped to his knees and moved his hands reverently over every inch of my body, following each path with tender kisses. Tears streamed down my face. I'd never felt more adored.

His own eyes were suspiciously moist when he looked up and rasped, "I love you, Lehra. Every beat of my heart belongs to you."

The sight of Cruz on his knees with tears in his eyes made my legs weak. The man looked like a complete badass in a very tight, black, microfiber tee and black cargo pants. The bulge of his biceps threatened the seams, and his tats peeked out from beneath the sleeves.

In a word, he looked invincible. But I loved the way he showed me his softness, the way he shared his vulnerable side with me.

"I love you too, Cruz. Everything about you except for one thing."

He rose to his feet, eyebrows inching together as he towered over me. "What's that?"

I dragged my fingers up and down his thick, veiny forearms. "You're wearing too many clothes right now."

His smile was devastating, full of affection and dimples. "We can fix that. Why don't you get in bed, and I'll go take a shower right quick?"

"No," I said, clinging to his arms and resting my nose against his chest. "I like how you smell after work. It's sexy."

"Baby, I sweat a lot in the body armor," he warned, but I shook my head and lowered my hands to the hem of his shirt.

"You smell like a man," I whispered, earning me a low growl from him as I inhaled the salty scent of him. Raising the shirt, I didn't miss the wince when he lifted his arms above his head. As I revealed his skin, I saw why. "You're hurt," I cried, brushing my fingers oh so gently over the deep purple bruises dotting his torso.

"It's okay, Tink. It's from the impact of the..." He hesitated.

"The bullets?" I asked, horrified by what I was seeing. "You got shot because of me, and now look at you. You're... oh my god!" I was nearing hysteria levels, and Cruz took my shoulders and squeezed, urging me to look up at him.

"Lehra, listen. It's fine. The vest protected me. I don't have a single gunshot wound, only a few bruises. It happens."

"It happens? You look like you've been beaten with a baseball bat. You could have broken ribs or something."

He sighed. "The paramedics think a couple are cracked. It's definitely not the worst that could have happened." The implication of that settled deep into my gut, and everything inside me twisted.

I leaned down and kissed each circular bruise. Slowly. Softly. "We don't have to do anything tonight," I whispered against his warm skin.

Cruz gently cupped my chin and lifted my face. "If you think for one minute that I'm not going to make love to you tonight, Lehra, you don't know me very well."

I was officially a puddle.

"If it hurts, promise me you'll stop."

His thumb dusted along my bottom lip before he kissed me firmly. "God you're so fucking sweet."

"Promise me," I repeated, and he smiled.

"I promise, but if I'm inside you, the last thing I'll be thinking about is a few little bruises."

I didn't argue the *little bruises* part, though some of them were the size of my fist. I simply crawled onto the bed and beneath the crisp white sheets before he could try to lift me. Again.

Cruz shucked the rest of his clothes, and I gawked at him without an ounce of shame. Despite his injuries, he was still the most beautiful man in existence, all tanned skin, hard angles, and lean muscles. His cock was already fully erect, the tip glistening with his desire.

Slipping beneath the covers with me, he pulled me into his arms and lowered his mouth to mine. The kiss was laden with promises of forever, and I wound my arms around his neck, pressing my body to his.

The skin-to-skin contact was precisely what I needed, and I relaxed into his caresses as we made out until our lips were sore.

"Do you want me to be on top?" I asked, still concerned about his ribs.

"No," he assured me, his voice gritty with need when he pushed me to my back and covered my body with his. "I need it like this tonight, mi amor."

His erection was hot and hard, and he slid the length of himself between the lips of my sex. Back and forth, back and forth, until I was dripping with need for him.

"Please, Cruz," I whimpered, desperate for him to be inside me.

The head of his dick found my entrance, and he paused there, looking down into my eyes. Time seemed to stand still around us like we were in our own little bubble.

"I love you," I told him, holding his perfect face and rubbing my thumbs against the slight stubble on his jaw. "I've never loved anyone like this."

Cruz's eyes swam with emotion when he pushed in the first inch. "I love you too, Lehra. You're my forever." He slipped his arms beneath me, binding our bodies together as he entered me fully with aching slowness.

We moved together, our hips rocking in a sublime rhythm that had the bedsprings creaking like a love song beneath us. He covered my mouth with his own, and our tongues joined the band, circling and tasting as he moved between my thighs.

His large body pressed me into the mattress, and I rested my ankles against the backs of his thighs, urging him deeper.

"I can't get enough of you," I panted when he kissed across my cheek and to my ear.

"Mi alma ha estado buscando la tuya desde siempre," he whispered against my damp flesh before translating. "My soul has been searching for yours forever."

They were the most beautiful words I'd ever heard.

As fat tears streamed from my eyes, Cruz reached for my hands and pulled them over my head, linking our fingers. He still moved slowly on top of me, though there was a desperate edge to our lovemaking now. Like we were attempting to crawl inside one another.

His eyes were liquid blue pools, locked on mine as he tunneled in and out of me, hitting all my perfect spots. When my need coiled like a compressed spring, he seemed to sense it, his cock swelling inside me.

"Together," he gritted out as my inner walls began to pulse around him.

"Together," I repeated, squeezing his hands hard when he held me down and angled his hips to grind the smooth head of his erection over my G-spot. The piercing on the top of his dick rubbed against my clit, the dual stimulation overwhelming me in the very best of ways.

"God, baby," Cruz groaned, his thrusts growing erratic. "You're so tight around me. So beautiful when you come for me."

His mouth closed over mine and dominated it as the orgasm took over my body. A series of incomplete words garbled from my mouth and into his, and I arched my hips up for more. I was on fire, the inferno starting at my groin and eating up every inch of my bare flesh.

Cruz's slick body trembled over mine, his low grunts vibrating the back of my throat as he spilled into me. He released my hands, dragging his fingers down my arms until he was caressing my cheeks. "Love you, baby," he murmured, sounding as exhausted as I felt.

"Love you too," replied, my voice thick with satiation.

As we began to come down, he kissed me again, making love to my mouth with his tongue, sweet and unhurried.

"You okay?" I asked him, stroking tenderly along his ribcage when he finally ended the kiss.

"Yeah, I'm good." Though he groaned when he rolled off me and onto his back. Less than a minute later, he was sleeping soundly, one forearm draped across his middle.

I propped up on my elbow and watched him for the longest time, running my fingers through his hair as he slept. Cruz Estrada was truly a gorgeous man.

And he loved *me*.

I was the luckiest woman in the world.

"When is your mom arriving?" I asked as Cruz moved me smoothly around the dance floor at Monty and Kassie's wedding reception.

He smiled down at me, looking like the most delicious man alive in his tuxedo. "Next week. I can't wait for you to meet her."

"You think she'll like me?"

"I think she'll adore you almost as much as I do," he assured me.

We passed beneath a string of purple flowers wrapped with fairy lights. "That was such a beautiful wedding," I sighed.

"It was, and Sully was so cute." Cruz glanced over to where Kassie was doing something that looked suspiciously like the funky chicken with her son, and his face softened.

"Do you want kids?" I asked, and he returned his attention to me.

"I do. How about you?"

My head bobbed up and down. "I'd love more than one. There are some benefits to being an only child, but I always wanted a sibling."

I laughed at Kass and Sully, who were now doing the Cupid shuffle, even though the band was playing a waltz.

"Do you want to marry me?"

My head whipped around, and I was surprised spit didn't fly out of my mouth as I gaped at Cruz. He was smiling but didn't seem like he was joking in the least.

"Are you proposing?"

He pressed a kiss to my lips. "Sweetheart, when I propose, you'll know it. Right now, I'm just having a conversation."

"I would marry you in a heartbeat," I told him, not even having to think about it.

"Good," he said when the song ended. His eyes focused across the room and then brightened. "Hey, is that a pickle bar?"

CHAPTER 37

"Mama!" I called when I spotted her entering baggage claim at the airport. Her eyes lit up, and I jogged to her, picking her up and spinning her around.

"Ay dios mio! You're going to make me dizzy," she complained, but she was laughing that sweet, warm laugh that always made me think of home.

"I'm just so happy you're here," I told her, setting her back on her feet. "I wish you could have come for Christmas."

"Where's Lehra?" she asked, eyes darting around like my girlfriend was going to pop up from behind a planter.

"She's at my apartment cooking dinner."

"Oooh, she cooks?" Mama sounded pleased and pinched my cheek. "I like that she can keep my big, handsome son fed."

"I'm perfectly capable of feeding myself," I said with a chuckle. "I haven't starved to death yet."

My mother's eyes turned sharp, and she wagged her finger at me. "You make sure you do your share too. I taught you to cook, so you make your lady a special meal sometimes. Women shouldn't be the only ones in the kitchen."

I kissed the top of her head. "I know, Mama, and I do cook for her. I made her your Cuban crushed potatoes for breakfast one morning, and she loved them. Most of the time, we cook together."

Mama beamed. "That is so special, mi hijo. Families should do things together."

"We're not a family… yet." My mother literally vibrated with excitement when I tacked on that last word. "Don't start talking about marriage and babies the second you see her."

Like I had room to talk. I'd blurted out some kind of pre-proposal thing at the wedding reception just last week. But I hadn't been able to help myself. I chalked it up to love being in the air.

My mom waved a hand at me. "Psssh, it's all good, homie."

I groaned. "Mama, please don't use Eli's slang."

I needn't have worried about Mama and Lehra getting along. They hit it off the instant they met, and I was on cloud fucking nine. They chattered during the entire meal, and I wasn't sure I'd even gotten ten words into the conversation.

Not that I cared about that. I loved seeing two of my favorite women enjoying themselves and each other. My heart was so damned full.

"That was delicious," my mother said, dabbing at her mouth with her napkin. "Would you share your chicken and dumplings recipe with me, Lehra dear?"

"Of course, Mrs. Estrada." She lowered her voice conspiratorially. "I had to work today and didn't have time to make the dough from scratch like I normally do, so I used canned biscuits. It's much better when everything is homemade."

Mama patted her hand. "I understand. I'm a working woman too. We do what we can. And stop calling me Mrs. Estrada. I'm Stella." Her eyes glinted with mischief. "Or you're welcome to call me Mama."

Yep, heart is bursting right now.

"I thought it was delicious," I said, interrupting before my mom could start offering Lehra the pearl wedding necklace she wore when she married my papa. I was happy though because she was treating Lehra like a future mother-in-law should treat the woman her son loves. *Unlike Bambi fucking Jones.* "The cornbread was outstanding, babe."

She pointed at me. "Now *that* was homemade. My granny's recipe. It doesn't take much longer to mix those ingredients up than the stuff from a box."

My mother clapped. "Oooh, I need to give you my recipe for Mexican cornbread. Cruz loves it with chili."

"I'd love that. I can make it for the Super Bowl," Lehra said, beaming.

"Gee thanks, Mama," I said wryly. "You wouldn't even give *me* that recipe. You guard it like a mama dragon protecting her eggs."

She swished her hand at me. "Oh, that was my way of making sure you came to visit often." Turning her warm brown gaze to Lehra, she smiled. "Now I know you have someone who can make it for you when Mama isn't around."

I stood and kissed each of them on the head. "I'll do the dishes while my favorite ladies relax." Mama beamed with pride like I just said I was going to solve world hunger.

"Actually," Lehra said, rising from her chair, "I was going to make those cookies you like."

Dear god.

"You don't have to—"

"I'll help," Mama interrupted. "I love baking."

Well, this oughta be interesting.

A few minutes later, I was loading the dishwasher while the women mixed up ingredients. "Wait, why are you adding so much flour, mija?"

Lehra paused with a cup full of flour. "That's what the recipe says. Three cups."

Mama squinted at the small, handwritten card. "No, this says two cups. It's kind of smudged, but that's definitely a two."

"It's really old. It was my grandmother's," Lehra said, peering at the card. "Oh my gosh! I think you're right. That is a two."

"Three cups would make them very dry," my mother commented.

Lehra scrunched her nose. "They are always dry, but Cruz seems to like them, so I keep making them."

I turned my head to hide my grin, but I could feel the weight of Mama's gaze on me. She knew exactly what I'd been doing, eating the cookies because Lehra made them, not because I actually liked them. I could somehow feel her pride from across the room.

The results were amazing, the cookies moist and absolutely delicious. "I can't believe I've been making them wrong all this time," Lehra said, eating her fourth one. "Why didn't you tell me, Cruz?"

"I thought they were supposed to be like that," I hedged. "I ate them with a glass of milk, and they were fine." *More like a half gallon of milk, but that's just semantics, right?*

I reached for the last cookie, but my mother snatched it off the platter before I could snag it. Crossing my arms, I pretended to pout. She grinned wickedly and stuffed the entire thing into her mouth.

"Well, it's been a long day with travel and everything. I think I'll hit the hay," she said after swallowing the yummy confection. She rose and gave Lehra a long hug. "I'm so pleased to get to know you, mija. Will I see you tomorrow?"

"Oh, well, I thought you two were going out for dinner with Quinnie and her family."

Mama placed her hand affectionately on Lehra's cheek. "You'll come. You're family now."

I'll be honest, my vision got a little hazy from the tears, and I noticed my girl biting the inside of her cheek. Maybe she was thinking about how differently she was being treated as compared to Dwight's mom. There was no *you're not invited because you're not family yet.*

There was only love and acceptance. And that was exactly how it should be.

Tossing Lehra a wink, I led Mama to her room. "I put your suitcase over there in the sitting area, and there's an en suite here, so you'll have your own bathroom," I told her, pointing to the door on the left. "My room is just down the hall if you need anything."

"You're not staying at Lehra's?" she asked curiously.

I hesitated. This would be the first night I'd spend without her in my bed, but we'd talked about it before Mama's arrival. My mother was going to stay at Quinnie's home for a couple days later this week, so I told Lehra we could make up for lost time then.

"Not while you're here," I replied.

Mama rolled her eyes. "Oh, please. I'm going to call your brother to check on him and then go straight to sleep. There's no reason you shouldn't stay with your beautiful woman." She stood on her tiptoes and kissed my cheek. "I can already tell she's the one for you, my hijo. She's going to be your wife one day, and your wife should always come first."

Dammit to hell. Is someone cutting onions in here?

I wrapped my mother in my arms and swayed us back and forth. "I love her so much, Mama. I never knew it would feel like this."

She sniffled against my chest. "I'm so happy for you. She's a beautiful person, inside and out. I felt it from the first time I saw her." She gave me one last squeeze before releasing me. "Now get out of here. I saw some chorizo and eggs in the fridge, so I'll make breakfast. Just text me when you two lovebirds wake up, and I'll get started."

"You don't have to cook while you're here, Mama."

"I want to," she insisted and then pushed at my shoulder. "Now scoot. We'll spend the day together tomorrow. All three of us. I need to get to know my future daughter better."

I gave her one last kiss and left the room with a grin on my face. There was absolutely no way I could love my mother any more.

Saturday had gone perfectly. Lehra and I showed Mama the sights of New York City, doing all the touristy stuff as well as showing her our favorite local places for gelato and bagels.

We had dinner with Quinnie, Flynn, and Noelle in the evening. The Italian restaurant was boisterous and fun, exactly like my family, and Noelle had eaten her entire spaghetti meal sitting on her grandmother's lap, which thrilled Mama.

Of course, Lehra fit right in with everyone, which thrilled me.

"I'm stuffed," Mama lamented, leaning back in her chair and toying with Noelle's pretty little curls. "But I still think my favorite thing I've tried today was that bagel. I'd pack up and move here for the bagels alone."

Quinnie's eyes met mine before she turned back to our mother. "You should move here, Mama. Flynn was offered a position at the hospital once he finishes his residency, so we'll be staying here."

Jumping in, I said, "You could bring Eli, or he could stay back and run the private investigation business since you said he's been working there."

"Oh, he's nowhere ready for that," Mama demurred. "I'll hand it over to Phil when I retire. He was with your father almost from the beginning, and he was invaluable to me when I was getting my license. His wife, Trina, took over my job as office manager when I stepped into my investigator role."

"Are you thinking about retiring, Stella?" Flynn asked, voicing the question that had risen in my own mind. She'd never seriously mentioned retirement before.

"Always in the back of my mind. It would be nice to slow down and enjoy my family instead of working six days a week. This has been the first time I've relaxed in years. I'm rather enjoying it."

Lehra, who was sitting beside my mother, reached for her hand. "It would be so nice to have you around all the time. I'd love to spend more time with you."

We ended the dinner with my mother announcing, "I'll think about it."

Chapter 38

On Sunday, I told Mama I wanted to spend some time alone with her. I needed to have the difficult conversation with her about my paternity.

"This is the nicest parking garage I've ever seen," she exclaimed, eyes wide as we passed the glassed-in security booth in our apartment building. "So well lit."

I waved to the two guards, and they returned the gesture. "Over here, Mama," I said, leading her to Auburn's black Bentley, which had a prime parking space since the man owned the whole damn building.

"What a snazzy car!"

"It's my boss's. He has a few, so he lets me drive this one for errands on the weekends."

"How fancy of you," she teased, sliding into the front seat when I held the door open for her.

"I wanted to show you where I work," I told her once I was seated behind the steering wheel. My nerves were buzzing, making the tips of my fingers and toes a little numb, and I prayed she didn't freak the fuck out.

It only took a few minutes to arrive at the office, and I parked at the curb in front of the black stone building with *BOUVIER* stamped in bold, blood-red letters.

"This is where I work, Mama," I told her quietly. *Shit. Here it comes.*

Her eyes rose, taking in the name above a set of dark-tinted glass doors. She was quiet for a long moment before turning to me, and was that... *amusement* on her face?

"Auburn's certainly done well for himself." There wasn't an ounce of surprise in her voice.

My mouth dropped open as my mind worked to play catch up. "You... you knew?"

"Mi hijo, I worked in your father's investigation office for over twenty years, and now I'm a licensed investigator. Did you honestly think I didn't know where my son was working?"

"But..." I scrambled to think of what to say next. "But you never said anything."

"You're a grown man, Cruz, and you know I want you to live your own life. I didn't pry into any of your personal affairs, but I did run a background check for your places of employment and your residence to make sure everything was on the up and up. I'm a mother, after all, and no matter how old you get, I still worry about you."

"Okay, wow." My head felt like that brain-exploding emoji, and I massaged my temple. "I wasn't sure how you were going to take all this."

"As soon as I saw where you were working, I knew it couldn't be a coincidence." Mama reached over and placed her hand on top of mine on the steering wheel. "I'm assuming you've met Paul?"

"I have." I turned my hand over until my palm met hers and wrapped my fingers around her small hand. "Are you mad at me, Mama?"

She answered my question with a question, her soft eyes intent on mine. "Are you mad at me for keeping that secret from you for all these years?"

"I'm not mad. I was really confused at first, and I wanted answers."

She nodded. "That's fair. You deserve answers. You know you could have talked to me about it."

My chest felt tight, and I realized I hadn't taken a deep breath since we'd arrived. Remedying that, I sucked in some air and blew it out. "It was so soon after Papa died, and I didn't want to upset you. I found some letters beneath the hot water heater that he was obviously hiding from you, so I guess I decided to do my own investigation."

"Hmm, I always wondered where he was keeping the letters."

If my mother had told me she was actually Gisele Bundchen in disguise, I wouldn't have been more surprised. "You knew about the letters?"

She rolled her eyes. "I was the office manager. I saw the bills for the post office box he rented and figured out that was how Benjamin and Paul must be communicating."

"And you never said anything?"

"I trusted your father to handle it. He was the peacemaker while I was the person who would throw shoes."

I laughed at that. "I can't believe you knew all this time."

"I don't know any of the details, and I had no idea what was in the letters. Paul showed up at the house when you were six, and your father and I stayed up all night, worrying he would take you from us. The next evening, Benjamin told me he'd handled it and that I shouldn't worry. He slept like a baby that night, so I took his word for it." Her bottom lip trembled. "Maybe I was afraid to know. One of the most important things in a marriage is trust, and I trusted your papa to take that burden from my heart."

"Paul didn't want to take me away, Mama," I said gently.

Her eyes met mine, and she looked nervous. "So you talked to him about all this?"

"We actually have dinner together every week." Her eyes widened in shock. "I'm surprised you didn't know that, Miss Investigator," I teased, and she broke into a laugh.

"I told you, I just checked the basics. I wasn't keeping tabs on you." Dipping her gaze, she asked, "How is Paul?"

"Paul is…" I huffed out a sigh. "I don't think Paul has been okay for a very long time, but he seems to be doing better. His son Monty is back in his life, and he has grandchildren now."

"I saw on TV that Monty just got married."

"He did. Kassie is a great woman. They're actually on their honeymoon right now."

"I never met him. Only Auburn and Evie." Her lips turned down, and her eyes filled with tears. "I do miss them very much. I still say prayers from time to time for that sweet girl. I can't imagine my child going missing and never knowing what happened to them."

"It's a horrible situation. I can see the sadness all over Paul's face when he speaks of her."

"Evelyn was always a daddy's girl," my mother said fondly. "What do Monty and Auburn think about having a brother they never knew about?"

I cringed. "We haven't told them yet. I've been apprehensive, especially at first. Then so many things happened in their lives, and I didn't want to add more drama," I told her and then quickly added, "Paul wants to tell them. He's not ashamed of me or anything."

Mama's eyes flashed with indignation. "Of course he's not! There's nothing to be ashamed of. You're a wonderful man, Cruz."

"Thank you, Mama," I said softly because I needed to hear that.

No matter what, there was always the stigma of me being the secret illegitimate son of a billionaire. Paul did everything in his power to not make me feel like that, but my perception of it was hard to shake completely.

I swiveled a little in my seat. "Will you tell me your side of what happened all those years ago? Why you left New York and didn't tell Paul he had another son?"

Mama's face tightened, but she nodded her head. "First of all, I want you to know that leaving wasn't my choice." Then she went silent for a long time, her eyes following the passersby on the sidewalk. When she spoke again, her voice was low and raspy. "Lying was though. I wouldn't blame you if you hated me."

A single tear made its way down her face, and it cut right through me. I lifted her hand and kissed the back of it with all the affection and love I felt for my mother.

"I could never hate you, Mama. We all have things we haven't been honest about. You, me, and Paul, and I don't think any of those lies were malicious." I thought of my own secret that I'd been keeping from Monty and Auburn, and I decided it was finally time to tell them, come what may.

As though her eyes were melting, a torrent of tears slid down Stella Estrada's face, the softness giving way to a fierce determination. "I would do it again for you. I would sell my soul to the devil to protect my children."

I took Mama gently in my arms, and her body trembled like a feather in a windstorm as she finally let loose. "I was so young and so afraid," she cried, pressing her face against my shirt, her sadness soaking the fabric.

I patted her back and kissed the top of her head, allowing this strong woman her moment of fragility. She didn't show it often. When her sobs slowed, I said, "It's okay, Mama. You don't have to talk about it."

"I really do. You deserve to know." She sighed heavily and lifted her head, swiping vigorously at the wet spot she'd left on my shirt. It was such a *mom thing* for her to do, and I almost smiled.

"When you're ready."

She stopped wiping at my shirt and raised her chin, her tenacity returning with the simple movement. "I'm ready. I haven't talked about this in years. It was a very painful time in my life, and..." I could see the apprehension warring with determination in her eyes. "Do you think Paul would come over some time so I can talk to both of you and not have to tell it more than once?"

"Of course. He's mentioned he was interested in talking to you."

She cringed. "Does he absolutely hate me? Do you think he just wants to yell at me?"

I let out a half-laugh half-scoff noise. "Not at all, Mama, and if he does, I'll set him straight," I told her, teasingly punching my palm with my fist. "Paul's out of town for a few days, but I'll text him and see if we can get together when he gets home."

"Well, that's my new favorite way to wake up," I groaned as Lehra rolled her hips one last time. She was on top of me, and I was still inside her after some sexy morning lovemaking.

"My grandmother always said there's nothing better than a morning ride, and I have to agree," she said, shoving a wild chunk of curly hair behind her ear.

I put on my best scandalized face. "Your grandmother said that?"

She shrugged and flashed me a playful smile. "She grew up on a horse farm, so in all honesty, she was probably talking about her morning jaunts on her mare, Becky." Lehra bent down and bit my bottom lip before sucking it into her mouth and releasing it with a pop. "I personally prefer a morning ride on a stallion."

Growling, I rolled us over until I was on top. "Stop tempting me, Tink, or I'll spend all day in this bed with you."

"I'd like that, but you can't. Paul will be at your apartment in an hour." Her voice softened, and she held my cheek. "Are you nervous about him and Stella meeting for the first time in so many years?"

I reluctantly withdrew from Lehra's warm pussy and stretched out beside her so we were facing each other. "Maybe a little. Hopefully it won't be World War Three. I'm not sure I could deal with that."

"I'm sure it will be fine. Mr. Paul always seems so mellow." She gave me a smack on the butt. "Plus, I bought bagels for you to use to pacify them if things get heated."

Lifting up on one elbow, I popped my eyes wide. "You got bagels? From Bagley's? Woman of my dreams!"

Lehra laughed and drawled, "Yeah, yeah, whatever. Gianna and I dropped some off at Kassie and Monty's yesterday before they got home from the honeymoon. They were planning to sleep for a full day because of the jet lag. Since they've been gone for a few weeks, we figured they didn't have much food in the house and wanted them to have something to eat when they woke up."

"Yeah, I got a text from Monty that basically said, *We're home. Don't call us unless you want to die.*" Her nose crinkled, and I frowned in question. "What's wrong?"

"I'm lying in a wet spot now."

I kissed her ear before rolling off the bed. "I'll get you a towel, but next time, maybe you'll think of that before you decide to treat me as your own personal stallion."

"Like you were complaining," she retorted at my back, and I laughed.

Lehra's eyes scraped up and down my naked body when I returned. "What's that look?"

Her grin was wicked. "We should do a horseback riding instructor role play. I was picturing you in riding clothes." She fanned herself. "Totally hot."

Slipping the towel beneath her, I kissed a circle around her belly button. "I'll try to find somewhere upstate where we can rent some horses. Maybe we can spend a weekend up there when it warms up."

She tugged my hair until I looked up at her. "Don't forget the jodhpurs."

My mother was a ball of nervous energy. I'd thoroughly cleaned my apartment before she came last week, but so far today, she'd dusted the baseboards, cleaned the oven, and changed all the sheets—even though I hadn't slept on mine at all.

"Do I need to give you a shot of vodka and a Valium?" I asked when I caught her trying to stand on the bed to clean the ceiling fan.

"You have some?" she asked so quickly I almost laughed.

"I have some whipped cream vodka, but no Valium. Though this is New York City. I could probably find some within half a block."

Mama's eyes almost ballooned out of her head. "You're not buying drugs off the street are you, Cruz? Do you have any idea how dangerous that is? Haven't you heard about fentanyl?"

I let her rant on for a couple minutes before assuring her I was not taking any sort of street drugs. At least when she was nagging me, she wasn't cleaning anything.

She let out a little squeak when the knock came on the door, and I gripped her hand. "Mama, it's okay."

"You're right," she said, nodding vigorously as I led her back to the living room.

After a reassuring squeeze, I released her hand and walked to the door, swinging it open. Paul looked a little nervous as well, but he wrapped me in a hug like he usually did, though this time he held on for a few extra seconds.

"Good to see you, son."

"You too, Paul." I stepped back to let him in, and his eyes went directly to the woman standing beside the couch with her hands twisted at her waist.

They stared at each other, and something electrified the air in my apartment as I closed the door, observing them. My mother took a tentative step forward, and Paul closed the rest of the distance, reaching for both her hands.

"Star," he breathed, and a shy smile curled across her lips.

Star? I'd never heard anyone call my mother Star before. *And is she blushing?*

"You look wonderful, Paul."

"And you're as stunning as ever, Star."

What the hell is happening right now? And why are they still holding hands?

Shaking my head, I attempted to clear away the very confused cobwebs forming in my brain. I was well aware that Paul and my mother had been... *intimate*. I was exhibit freaking A. But it had always been some vague notion in my head.

Not anymore. Now it was slapping me directly in the face, and the attraction—or whatever you wanted to call it—was palpable in the room. I wasn't sure how to feel about that.

Mama was the first to break away, stepping back and gesturing toward the couch. They sat, no longer staring, but certainly casting frequent glances at each other.

I couldn't help but think it was kinda cute.

"Lehra got bagels," I announced. "What would you two like to drink?" Both requested orange juice, and I headed to the kitchen. While warming the bagels, I arranged a tray, poured the juice, and added a shot of vodka to mine. Yeah, it was only ten in the morning, but I was going to need liquid fortification to get through this.

At least they're not fighting, I told myself, carrying the food and drinks into the living room. Mama and Paul were chatting easily, showing each other pictures of their grandchildren on their phones.

After we'd all prepared our bagels how we liked them, Paul took a small nibble of his before huffing out a loud sigh and then letting his words come out in a rush. "Stella, first of all, I want you to know that I don't blame you for leaving all those years ago. I was angry at first, but I finally came to the realization that you probably had no choice, due to... certain influences."

Also known as Chloe Bouvier.

My mother seemed taken aback by his statement, but her shoulders visibly relaxed. "Thank you for saying that, Paul."

Then he launched into the story I'd heard several times, and Mama listened aghast. "So Chloe threatened to take Auburn and Evie and leave the country? But she rarely had anything to do with those babies."

"I know. And she announced she was pregnant again," Paul said. "I couldn't let her take my kids, but I also couldn't lose you. I planned to talk to you about it so you could help me figure out what to do, but you didn't show up for work on Monday."

My mother looked horrified. "She fired me and told me to leave the state."

Paul cringed. "I didn't know Chloe fired you until I talked to your cousin, but by then, you were already gone. Believe me, Stella, I had no clue, and there's no way I would have allowed it."

She stared at him in that way she had. My mom had been like a human lie detector when I was a teenager, and she was using her superpower on Paul. "You really didn't know."

He shook his head. "I didn't. All I knew was that I was being coerced into staying with a woman I despised in order to keep my kids. If I'd known you were carrying my son..." His words trailed off when he turned his sad eyes toward me.

I'd planned to keep my mouth shut and let these two talk it out, but he looked so damn miserable. "There was no way you could have known, Paul, and it wouldn't have changed anything. Chloe was trying to take your children, and she threatened to expose your relationship with Mama to the press and drag her name through the mud."

Mama muttered, "Esa perra," calling Chloe a bitch under her breath.

"Agreed," Paul replied with the hint of a smile before glancing back at me. "I would have done anything to have kept you two in my life if I'd known. I could have... I don't know... hired a hitman or something."

"Dios mio!" Mama exclaimed, smacking him on the arm. "Don't make me take my shoe off, Paul Bouvier. Don't even speak of such things."

He shrugged wryly. "You live with that evil woman for almost forty years and then tell me you wouldn't have some dark thoughts." With a small smile, he changed the subject. "I really liked Benjamin, and I'm so sorry for your loss, Stella."

She dipped her chin and nodded. "Thank you. He was a wonderful husband and father and treated Cruz like he was his own."

"I know he did. How did you two get together? I tried not to pry too much regarding you because I didn't want Ben to feel any more uncomfortable than he already did by talking to me. We mostly spoke about Cruz."

Mama laughed softly and took a drink of her juice. "My mother was scandalized when she found out I was pregnant out of wedlock. She insisted I call the father immediately and get married, but I told her that was impossible." She puffed out a breath and shook her head. "She made it her mission to find me a husband."

I took a bite of my cinnamon bagel and listened with rapt ears. Of course I'd never heard this before. Mama and Papa always told us they met at church.

My mother took a nibble of her bagel before replacing it on her plate. "Apparently, Benjamin Estrada had a crush on me during high school. I was not that interested in boys back then, so I never noticed. But my mother did. When she learned he had moved back to town after college, she decided to play matchmaker."

She chuckled and shook her head, lost in her memories. "I was having morning sickness all day every day, and to be honest, I was tired of hearing her yap about me being an unwed mother all the time. About what the people at church would think. So I agreed to marry him, mostly so I could get out of that house."

Mama glanced up and seemed almost surprised that we were still there. "I hate to admit it, but I was terrible to Benjamin after we got married. Refused to share a bed with him, spoke only when necessary." She threaded the paper napkin between her fingers. "It wasn't until Cruz was born and I watched how he treated my baby that I finally saw him for the man he was."

A tear snaked down her cheek, and Paul reached up and swiped it away as if it were the most natural thing in the world. "I'm sorry you lost him, Star. And I'm so grateful for Benjamin. For your sake and for Cruz's. He loved his family very much."

And that's when the dam broke. A torrent of tears washed down my mother's face, and I stood in a rush to get to her, but Paul beat me to it. He pulled her to him, his touch gentle and somehow familiar as he stroked her dark hair and let her cry against his shoulder. I settled back in my chair, feeling kinda like an intruder.

"I'm so sorry, Paul. How can you not hate me for taking your son away?" Her words were barely audible through her sobs. "I've carried this guilt for so many years about it. I'm such a horrible person for doing that to you."

He clutched her more tightly before pulling back and lifting her chin with his fingers. "Don't say that, Star. I never hated you. Was I angry at you for leaving? Yes, but I could never hate you. My heart wouldn't allow it."

My hand covered my mouth to contain my gasp as I realized the truth. *Paul Bouvier still loves my mother. Even after all these years.*

And I couldn't even muster any negative feelings about that because her sobs subsided at his softly spoken words.

"You don't hate me?" she asked on a hiccup.

He shook his head. "Not at all. I regret not being able to be closer to my son as he grew up, but I know you were only doing what you thought was right." Smoothing a strand of her hair behind one ear, he asked. "Can you tell me why you never told me the truth? We could have worked something out. You didn't have to be afraid of me."

"I wasn't afraid of you. It was... *her*."

"Chloe," he gritted out through his teeth, and Mama nodded.

"She told me you wanted me to leave. She said you were excited about the new baby and wanted me gone so you two could work things out."

Paul stood abruptly and moved behind the couch where my mother sat, pacing back and forth as he ran both hands through his hair. "When was this?"

"That Friday after we were together. She came home and surprised me. About noon, I think."

He whirled to face her, the fingers of his left hand flexing. "I hadn't even spoken to Chloe at that time. I didn't even know she'd come home from her trip."

"So... you didn't..."

"Shit," Paul cursed, shaking out that same hand. "I never said that, Star. What else did she say?"

"Sh-she said you were only playing around with me, and I was a dumb girl for thinking a man like you would ever have a real relationship with *the help*. Then she stuffed some money in my purse and said it was from you. I'd never felt so... cheap."

I could hear Paul's teeth grinding together. "That fucking bitch," he snapped. "I wish she was still alive so I could strangle the life from her. She brought nothing but misery to everyone who knew her. She—"

He grunted and coughed a couple times, as if he were in pain. As soon as he clutched at his left shoulder, my medical training kicked in and I shot from my chair. "Paul, does your shoulder hurt?"

He sucked in a few breaths, very shallow ones, as I rounded the couch. "Just... probably... pulled something." His hand slid to his chest, fingers working back and forth. "Just some... tightness."

Fuck, fuck, fuck.

In the calmest voice I could muster, I shot a sharp look over my shoulder. "Mama, call an ambulance. He's having a heart attack."

She let out a squeak of fear at the same time Paul emitted a grunt of protest. "I'm... fine."

And then he collapsed in my arms.

I could hear Mama on the phone as I laid him out on the floor and checked him over. His pulse was thready, and his face blanched of color. He was conscious and still breathing—barely—so I didn't need to start chest compressions. We just needed to get him to the hospital as soon as fucking possible.

"Cruz." The single word was so weak and yet said so much. It was round and full of love.

Tears welled in my eyes when his eyelids closed, and I clutched his face in my hands in a panic. "Dad, wake up. Please, Dad."

His eyes popped back open in surprise, and his lips tipped up in a small smile. "Y-you called me Dad."

It was the first time I'd ever said it to him, and that burned my cheeks with shame.

"Because that's what you are. I'll say it every day if you'll just stay with me."

Tears dripped from my eyes and landed on his chin and neck. His face was ashen and sweaty, and I needed a goddamn ambulance *right fucking now*.

His breathing became more labored, and he reached up to cup my wet cheek. "S'okay, Cruz."

My chest hurt like I was having a heart attack of my own, though I knew it was something else causing my pain. I'd held this man at arm's length for years, feeling like it would be disloyal to the man who raised me if I let Paul in. But I knew now that love was bigger than that. There were no limits on how many people you could love. It was infinite.

So I leaned down and pressed a firm kiss to his damp forehead and whispered the words I should have said long ago.

"I love you, Dad."

CHAPTER 39

"So your mom just pushed you out of the way and climbed into the ambulance with Paul?" Lehra asked with a hint of amusement.

I confirmed with a nod. "She did." I'd immediately called Lehra after the ambulance arrived, and she sprinted over and insisted on riding to the hospital with me. Grateful for her presence, I'd held her hand the few minutes to the hospital and the entire time the doctor was explaining that my dad had indeed had a heart attack.

She snuggled beneath my arm, and I inhaled the fresh scent of her hair, so grateful for this amazing woman. "He's going to be okay. The cardiologist said the stent surgery was quite routine."

"I know." Staring at the wooden door to the hospital room, I willed it to open.

"And they put him in a regular room on the cardiac floor, so that's a good sign. He's not in the intensive care unit."

"True." I moved us forward to get out of the way of a gurney holding an elderly man that was being pushed down the corridor. "Thank you for being here. You make me feel... comforted."

"That's me. Lehra the comfortable," she chirped, kissing my chest. "How are you feeling about everything that happened? It had to be strange seeing your biological parents in the same room for the first time."

"It was, but it wasn't bad or anything. Their connection was just... there. Staring me right in the face. I didn't expect that."

Lehra gripped my chin and turned my face toward hers. "It's okay to feel conflicted about it. You've only ever seen your mom with your papa. I felt really weird when I looked at my dad's old yearbook and saw him escorting the homecoming queen—who was not my mother. I'd never even thought of him with someone else because them as a couple is all I've ever known. But we have to remember that our parents had a whole life before we came along."

My eyes went to the door again. "I think he still loves her, and I'm surprisingly okay with that."

"Love doesn't have to be diluted by more love. Sometimes it makes it grow."

"When did you get so wise?" I asked, smiling for what seemed like the first time in hours.

Before she could answer, the door swung open, and a nurse emerged. She was smiling. "You can go on in. Just don't give Mr. Bouvier anything else to eat or drink because he'll have surgery in a few hours." She patted my arm. "He's perfectly stable now."

Lehra and I entered to find my mother fussing with the blankets on the bed. "Not even tucked properly," she muttered, pulling the bottom of the sheet free before tucking it back *properly*. "There. How's a patient supposed to be comfortable if the sheets are all willy nilly?"

I tutted from inside the door. "A man can't even have a decent heart attack in peace in a place like this."

Mama flashed me a fake glare before hugging me and Lehra. "Always with the smart mouth, this one," she complained, patting my cheek.

Paul Bouvier was slightly reclined on the bed, and I was thrilled to see that the color had returned to his skin. Crossing to him, I sat on the edge of the bed and pressed a kiss to his warm cheek. "You look better, Dad."

The last word rolled off my tongue as naturally as if I'd been calling him that for my entire life.

"It's the hospital gown," he said, pinching the neckline of the gray patterned garment. "It does wonders for the complexion."

Lehra sat on the other side of him, and they shared a warm hug before she teased, "I'm going to tell Devereaux you're not wearing a Bouvier hospital gown."

My father chuckled. "He'll be trembling in fury. Maybe I'll talk to Monty about designing a new line." He patted her hand and turned back to me. "Did you call your brothers?"

My brothers. I actually liked the sound of that now.

"I called Auburn. He and Monty should be here any minute."

Lehra stood and looped her arm with my mother's. "Stella and I will go get a coffee and maybe hit the gift shop for a while."

Mama didn't move to hug Paul, but she placed a hand on his shin and met his eye. "I'll be back." He nodded, and once again, I was struck by the visceral feeling of their connection.

Once the ladies were gone, I rounded the bed and took the chair beside my dad. "How are you?"

"I'm good, son." His blue eyes seemed full of life when he smiled. "Thank you for saving my life."

"I didn't do anything. Just had Mama call the ambulance."

"You were there. That's all I needed," he replied, voice thick with emotion. Before he could say anything else, the door swung open and my brothers entered. Monty waved and I flashed him a small smile, my anxiety ratcheting up a couple notches. I prayed this went well... that they would accept me.

"Boys! I'm glad to see you. I'm sorry to have interrupted your Saturday," Dad said.

"Hush up, young man," Monty said before pressing a kiss against his forehead.

They talked for a few moments, Paul filling them in on the surgery he was about to have.

"That's good. We'll be here the whole time," Monty assured him, resting a hand on his shoulder.

Our father passed a look between his two oldest children. "I wanted to talk to you about something before they put me under. I was going to tell you the day after Chloe's funeral, but I thought I'd dropped enough on you for one afternoon."

He smiled weakly before continuing. "And then it never seemed to be quite the right time. Monty, you moved back, there was all the wedding planning, and then our sweet Janie started walking. I didn't want to over-shadow all that."

"Well, now we're focused on you, Dad," Auburn said softly. "What do you need to talk to us about?"

"I'm just going to say it." His eyes scanned all three of us this time, holding on me for a long beat.

"Auburn, Monty..." Dad took a deep breath, and I could sense his nerves, so I reached out and gripped his hand.

After a long pause, he finally said it.

"Cruz is your brother."

There was no yelling. No accusatory looks. No demands for proof. I'm not sure what I expected, but it sure as hell wasn't this.

Monty blinked in confusion, but he didn't look mad at all. Auburn didn't either, though he crossed his arms over his chest and stared at me with... was that *smugness*?

I wasn't sure what to make of his reaction. The oldest Bouvier brother was a bit of an enigma, a much tougher nut to crack. Monty was the one I was most worried about because he'd become one of my best friends since he moved back here last year, and I feared this would drive a wedge between us.

Our father spoke up to try and clear up the confusion. "You remember that I told you I separated from Chloe all those years ago? And that I fell in love with Auburn and Evie's nanny?"

Monty's eyes narrowed and then widened as he put the pieces together like one big, familial puzzle. "That was before I was born, so you and, um…"

"Estrella," Auburn filled in, his gaze intent on mine. I still wasn't sure how to read him.

Our other brother snapped his fingers. "That's right, and then she left town because the evil egg donor fired her."

I spoke up for the first time. "And threatened her."

Monty's top lip curled. "God Chloe was such a bitch."

I couldn't disagree. "I can fill you in more on that later, but that topic is what landed, um, our d-dad in here." I stumbled over the word, unsure how my brothers would react to it, but neither flinched. In fact, Monty grinned and rose from his chair before coming around to the side of the bed where I was sitting in a vinyl chair.

Standing to face him, I released Dad's hand a second before Monty pulled me into a hug. Not one of those half-ass bro hugs, but a real one with both arms. "This is so fucking cool," he rasped, and I chuckled out a laugh when we finally released each other.

"Sorry, I wasn't sure what y'all's reaction would be, but it wasn't that."

"Why not?" he asked, playfully slapping my arm. "We hit it off from the first minute you picked me up from the airport. Now I know why. We're brothers."

I hadn't realized I'd been hunching my shoulders with worry until relief lowered them a few inches. "I'll be happy to take a DNA test or whatever," I assured them. "I don't want anything. I just came to New York for answers."

Auburn nodded sagely. "Makes sense. Your father had just died, and you didn't want to question your grieving mother about something so sensitive."

"Yes," I breathed, as more of the tension left my body. "You don't seem very surprised by all this."

He smirked at me. "I had my suspicions." At the lift of my eyebrows, he explained. "When I was reading over your personnel file during employee assessments at the end of the year, I noticed your mother's name was Estrella, and I remembered the story Dad told us. Then, with your blue eyes and the way you look so much like Monty…" His eyes moved between us. "It just clicked."

"Oh. Wow." I couldn't think of much else to say.

"And don't start that DNA bullshit. If Dad says you're his son, we accept that." His eyes shifted to Monty for confirmation, which he gave with a firm nod.

"Right."

The air in my lungs shuddered out, and my father met my gaze, his telling me *I told you so.*

"Is that why you gave me that absolutely ridiculous raise?" I asked Auburn, and he chuckled.

"No, I did that because my wife told me to." And to my utter shock, my oldest brother stood and pulled me into a hug, his voice low near my ear. "Even before I suspected you might actually be related, you'd already become like family to me, Gianna, and the kids."

Auburn pounded me a couple times on the back before releasing me and reverting to his gruff demeanor, his eyes shifting between me and Monty. Auburn was the tallest, but Mont and I were much broader than him.

"Would you two hulks sit down and relax?" he grumbled before settling on the bed beside our father again. "Little brothers are so annoying, Dad. Can we sell them or something?"

Paul Bouvier's eyes shone with tears, and yet the man—our father—looked happier than I'd seen him since the first time I met him. I said a silent prayer for my father and the medical staff that was about to do surgery on his heart.

He had to be okay. He just had to.

Six weeks later, I was on a fancy golf course with my two brothers and our dad. Paul and Auburn were awesome at the sport. Monty and me? Not so much. But we were having fun.

All three of us had gone to our father's last cardiology appointment with him, where we'd listened intently to the doctor's instructions. When Paul asked about golfing, Dr. Leeman told him it would be excellent exercise for him but to use a golf cart between holes.

Monty, Auburn, and I walked toward the sixteenth hole, all of us keeping an eye on our dad in the golf cart in front of us. He stopped to talk to someone he knew, and we paused.

Monty nudged me with his elbow. "Hey, you know that Instagram account we follow, The Adventures of Garfield and Snoopy?" I nodded. "The owner of the account sent me a DM and said they're making a trip to New York. We're going to meet up."

"Oh, that's cool. It will be like meeting a couple celebrities."

He laughed. "Right? You're welcome to go with me and Kass."

"Yeah, that sounds like fun." I hesitated before asking, "Can I ask you guys a serious question?"

"You should ask me," Auburn said firmly. "Monty will probably give you a stupid answer."

"Says the man in the sweater vest," our brother retorted.

"You're just jealous you can't pull off this look."

He was right. Monty and I would look like apes playing dress up in the forest-green vest over an ivory shirt. Auburn, of course, looked like he'd just stepped off the pages of *Golf Digest*.

"Ohhh nooo," Monty cried dramatically. "The hottest brothers aren't able to look like pompous assholes."

"Hottest brothers, my ass," Auburn mumbled, and I laughed. These two killed me with their banter. As we traversed our way through this whole new family situation, they were starting to include me in their teasing. "Cruz, what was your question?"

"I want to propose to Lehra. Do you think it's too soon?"

The other two looked at each other and burst into laughter. "The Bouvier men aren't known for their patience when they find what they want. I know you're keeping your last name," Monty explained, "but you're no less a Bouvier." My heart warmed at his unfettered acceptance.

"It's just... well, something is happening in New York next month, kind of a once in a lifetime thing, and I want to take advantage of it and ask her then." I explained my idea to them, and they shared an amused look.

"That's certainly an... unconventional way to propose to a woman," Auburn said cautiously.

I chewed my bottom lip before blurting, "We're into role playing."

"Okay, that's cool," Monty encouraged. "Like the naughty nurse thing? I think lots of couples do that."

"Yeah, like that, but sometimes more elaborate. Though we did do a nurse thing last month when I had a cold." My mouth went slack as the memories came back to me, and I stared off across the bright green grass. "The way Lehra took my temperature..."

Auburn snapped his fingers in front of my face. "Focus, you horny bastard. Tell us more about the role playing. I think Gianna might like to try something like that."

I filled them in on the costume shop and a couple of the scenes we'd tried. Without going into too much detail, of course.

"I bet you were hot as a Viking," Monty said with a nod.

"You know, I think you and Kass should try some new stuff to keep things fresh," Auburn said thoughtfully, a glint of mischief in his eye. "Kassie could be a Domme, strap you down, and whoop your bad little ass."

I barked out a laugh at that visual as Monty scowled at him. "So do you guys think it's a good idea?" I pressed. "My proposal idea?"

"I think it sounds fun," Monty said. "I'm in."

"Me too," Auburn agreed.

Paul circled back and pulled up beside us with the man he'd been talking to in the passenger seat. "Monty, Auburn, you remember George Pepperfield." They all nodded and shook, and my father climbed out of the cart and looped an arm around my shoulders. "George, this is my other son, Cruz Estrada."

The man's eyes went as round as golf balls. "Oh, I guess I didn't realize you had another son."

"I do," he said firmly and without further explanation. "Would you take a picture of us? I need a photo with all three of my sons."

The way those words hit me...

George climbed out of the golf cart and posed us in front of the lush green backdrop before snapping a few pictures.

"Okay," Dad announced. "Now I'd like a pic with my *favorite* son."

None of us moved a damn muscle for a long moment, and then we all burst into laughter with George snapping away.

A few days later, when Paul presented us each with a print of his three "favorite" sons surrounding him, our mouths open in laughter, I framed it and displayed it on the mantel above my fireplace.

With pride.

CHAPTER 40

"THIS IS SO EXCITING," Jane Bouvier said, sitting sweetly like a little princess in the back of the huge stretch limo Auburn had rented to accommodate all of us. Beside her, Sully and Jaxon were pretending to slap fight. Loudly.

"Boys," Auburn said through gritted teeth. "If you don't cut it out, you're riding in the trunk."

"That's child abuse, Uncle Auburn," Sully informed him.

The man lifted an eyebrow. "You wanna try me and find out?"

"Trust me, when he says that, you don't," Gianna said from beside me before whispering cheekily in my ear, "but I do it anyway. Every chance I get."

The warning worked, and the little ones calmed down, though now they were alternating sticking their tongues out, trying to make the other laugh.

"It's a shame Cruz couldn't come today," Kassie said from across the car.

"I know. He would have loved this, but he got called into work with the response team today," I lamented, looking out the window. "Oooh, we're here!" I sounded as excited as the kids.

The vehicle pulled up to the pier, and we all piled out... me, the Bouvier brothers, their wives and kids, Paul, Stella—who was, *ahem*, visiting again—Gianna's dad, Tony, and his partner, Tora.

Gianna passed out tickets to each person as they emerged, and I let my eyes rise to the giant pirate ship docked in the harbor. This was so freaking cool.

Our entire group trooped across the gangplank and onto the ship, flashing our tickets at the young woman dressed in tan and brown. The creamy sails were artfully dingey, billowing with sharp snaps in the wind above us.

"Helloooo," a man drawled in a fair approximation of Johnny Depp a la Captain Jack Sparrow. He stood on a wooden deck above us, leaning on the elaborate railing with a bottle of what looked like rum held loosely in one hand. "My name is Captain Hummingbird."

Everyone in the crowd responded with laughter and applause as the guy swaggered back and forth in a fake stumble.

"Welcome to the Trinidad, my ship, *hic*. It's a replica of one of Magellan's ships." The pirate sighed dramatically and lifted his eyes to the sky. "Ahhh, Magellan! How I do miss that rogue."

Everyone laughed and he continued, swinging one leg over the other as he walked back and forth, addressing his rapt audience.

"My lovely maidens are circulating with a souvenir for our younger savages. But don't you think for one moment that wearing them will make you the captain. I'm the boss on this glorious vessel." He lifted his chin at a haughty angle and added, "And I'm obviously the best looking."

That was met with a few good-natured jeers, and the man stuck out his tongue and blew a raspberry at the audience. Women in costume circulated around and handed out fabric pirate hats to the kids.

"This is so cute," I squealed quietly to Gianna, and she nodded with a grin before helping Jane adjust her hat.

Captain Hummingbird lifted his bottle and slurred, "I'm in need of a saucy wench to help me with something. Are there any saucy wenches in this crew?" There was a titter of amusement, and a few women in the audience readily raised their hands. "Tell you what, everyone take a look at the back of your ticket. If you see a gold star there, raise your hand."

Checking the back of mine, I nudged Monty beside me. "Mine has a star. Does yours?"

He shook his head and then pushed me toward the front of the crowd, calling out, "This wench has a star."

I snorted out a laugh and smacked at Monty, but when I looked back up at the pirate, he wiggled his eyebrows at me and crooked a jaunty finger. Rolling my eyes, I made my way up the wooden steps to the next level to much cheering from the people in our party. The man snapped his fingers and called, "Maidens! See if you can find this woman something decent to wear."

Two smiling women immediately surrounded me and led me through an oak door, introducing themselves as Amy and Melanie. "What the hell is going on?" I asked with a giggle.

"You're going to help with the show. It'll be fun," Amy informed me, holding out a pair of chocolate-brown breeches for me to step into. She pulled them up over my leggings and tied them at the waistband.

Melanie handed me a cream shirt with puffy sleeves and ruffles on the chest. "Now put this on." Then they turned their backs while I changed.

"I'm done." They turned around and held up a brown leather vest that I stuck my arms into. "What am I supposed to do?"

"Just play along," one of them said as she began lacing up the corset top. The other bent and changed my loafers out for pirate boots. When they were done, they tied a dark-red scarf over my hair and expertly knotted it on the side. "There ya go. All done."

The whole dressing thing only took a couple minutes, and then they were pushing me back out the door and onto the raised deck. I took a little bow when the audience cheered, and my eyes met Gianna's when she let out a loud wolf whistle.

And then my eyes narrowed on a young man in a red ball cap, holding a little girl wearing a pirate hat. *Is that...*

The thought was interrupted when something swung down from above and landed with a thud in front of me. Okay, more of a some*one*, really. Letting out a squeak of surprise, I stumbled back a step before he caught me by the shoulders.

"Careful, Tink."

"Cruz!" I shrieked in delight. "What are... I thought you were at work!"

My boyfriend was decked out in full pirate regalia, looking sexy as hell in the dark leather costume. He hadn't shaved, and his scruff added to the rakish look. "I came to save my wench," he told me with a wink.

"Well, well, if it isn't Captain Raven," the Johnny Depp lookalike drawled, sauntering toward us.

Cruz, or apparently *Captain Raven*, turned and squared off with the other pirate. "Hummingbird, you old drunk. I heard you're kidnapping women again."

"Yeah, *hic*," he retorted with a hiccup, "what are you gonna do about it?"

Cruz put one finger on the man's forehead and pushed with little effort, causing Hummingbird to fall comically to the ground, much to the hilarity of the crowd. Then a thick arm looped around my waist, binding me to my man.

"Hey, Tink." His blue eyes sparkled down at me.

I was smiling so big my cheeks hurt. "What is all this? And how did you pull it off? And also, I may be crazy, but I'm pretty sure I just saw your brother Eli holding Noelle."

"You're not crazy; Eli's here," he assured me.

My eyes scanned the crowd, searching for the guy in the red cap again, but froze when they fell on a grinning couple near the front. "Mom! Dad!" They waved, and my mother dabbed at her eyes as my mouth gaped open. I turned back to Cruz. "Why are my parents here?"

"I asked them to come," he said simply, a smirk on his handsome face.

"But... why... and how did you get my dad out of Missouri?" My head shook side to side in confusion.

"Because I told him he definitely wouldn't want to miss this," Cruz said, dropping to one knee in front of me.

Oh. My. God.

Not even both hands covering my mouth could hide my smile. Unlike when whatshisface had proposed, I had no reservations about what was happening here. I was absolutely, one hundred percent, all in.

"Yes," I shouted, and the entire crowd laughed, including Cruz, who was now holding a black velvet ring box.

Cruz's dimples popped out on either side of his brilliant smile even as he rolled his eyes. "Would you let me ask the question first, please?"

"Okay, but then I'm going to say yes."

"Good to know," he chuckled before taking my hand and kissing my knuckles. "Lehra, the very first time I met you, when you called my lips pretty pillows and told me about puke coming out of your nose, I think I started falling in love with you."

My cheeks flushed, and I. Could. Not. Stop. Smiling.

"But it was more than just your charming conversation that drew me to you," he said with a wicked grin.

The happiest tears in the world slid down my face. My man was so sweet and funny. And hot. *Good god, he's friggin' hot.*

Cruz closed his eyes and rested his forehead against the back of my hand as his chest heaved with emotion. When he raised his eyelids again, his eyes were swimming with unshed tears.

"Lehra, you became my best friend, and that's what you'll always be. But I love you more than my own life, and I hope you'll also do me the honor of being my wife."

He lifted his brows, and I whispered, "Can I say it now?"

"Please."

"Yes!" I shouted for the whole damn world to hear, causing raucous cheering from the crowd.

With a smile that could light up Manhattan, Cruz popped open the box. The ring was a halo style in a rose gold setting, and I'd never seen anything more beautiful in my life. Sliding it onto my finger, my fiancé stood and swept me up into his arms, twirling me around and around as we kissed.

My tears mingled with his, but they were tears of pure joy. Because I was marrying my best friend... the man of my dreams.

"Damn, bro. I'm glad your wench said yes since you rented out this entire restaurant," Monty quipped. "This could have been a really awkward meal."

"Would you stop calling me a wench," I complained, hip-checking my future brother-in-law.

"Meh, probably not."

We were at a fish and chips restaurant near the pier where the pirate ship had been docked. All our family and friends were with us to celebrate.

"That was the coolest proposal ever," Artie said. "How the heck did you get a pirate ship to come to New York?" I'd been so flabbergasted to see my parents, and then with the whole proposal thing, I hadn't even seen him and Nicolette in the crowd. But of course they were there.

"Actually, it was already scheduled to be here for the week," Cruz explained. "I just contacted them and asked if I could hijack the proceedings for a bit today. When I told them how many tickets I was buying, they were more than happy to play along." We looked around at the huge group of people mingling around the restaurant.

"It was fun. Thanks for letting us be a part of your special day," Captain Hummingbird said. We'd learned his real name was Bruce, and he had a thick Jersey accent when he wasn't playing the role of a rogue pirate.

"We appreciate it," I told him. "You were fantastic."

He took a dramatic bow and then wandered off to take pictures with the other partygoers, with Artie hot on his heels. I think my friend had a bit of a crush on the pirate.

"Champagne?" a server asked, walking by with a tray laden with tall flutes of sparkling liquid.

"Yes, please," I said, taking a glass for Cruz and myself.

"Could you bring my wife a sparkling water?" Auburn asked the woman in a low voice, and she nodded. I eyed Gianna, who avoided my gaze.

The woman smiled and held out the tray toward Monty and Kass. "None for us," he said. "Could we get a couple Sprites?"

She headed off, and I raised a hand, palm out. "Wait a minute. I've never seen you two pass up champagne."

"Oh, well, I just... I decided I needed to drink more water," Gia rambled.

Kassie's brown eyes were wide and nervous. "And Monty and I decided we should start, you know, drinking more, ummm, Sprite," she said lamely, looking at her husband who just smirked down at her.

Come to think of it, Monty and Auburn both looked a bit smug. Like...

"Are you two pregnant?" I hissed. They looked at me and then at each other in startled realization.

"Are you?" Kassie asked, and Gianna nodded.

"Are you?"

Kass's cheeks flushed pink. "Yes."

"Oh my god!" I squealed, doing a little happy dance. "I'm so excited for you both."

Auburn pulled his wife closer and looked down at her like she was the sun, moon, and stars, all wrapped up in one. "We were going to tell everyone, but then Cruz told us about his plans, and we didn't want to steal your thunder."

"Same," Kassie said as Monty rested a hand on her flat stomach.

I shook my head. "That was really thoughtful of you, but this only makes our day better." Setting down my drink, I pulled both of my future sisters-in-law into a group hug, squeezing them tight as the men all did the hand slap, bro hug, *congrats on having good swimmers* thing. "I promise, we don't mind if you want to tell everyone."

When we broke apart, Cruz pulled my back against his front and kissed the top of my head. "Lehra's right. The more people to love, the better."

Emotion swam in Gianna's green eyes as she looked around our little circle. "Our family just keeps growing, and I love it."

Monty smirked over at my new fiancé. "You're behind, little brother. You and Lehra better get to work."

Cruz's lips twisted to the side, and he eyed Monty speculatively before nodding. "You know what? I think you're right." Then he lifted me, tossed me unceremoniously over his shoulder, and smacked me right on the ass.

"What are you doing?" I squeaked.

He started striding toward the restaurant's front door with me hanging upside down, much to the amusement of everyone in attendance. "We're getting started. Now. I may be the youngest brother, but I guarantee my sperm game is on point. Your eggs won't know what hit 'em."

My stomach hurt from laughing so hard, and I chastised him through my giggles. "Put me down, you lunatic. We're not even married yet."

He stopped in a little alcove, away from the view of everyone else, and set me gently on my feet before cupping my face. "I love you so much, Tink. You've made me the happiest man in the universe, and I can't wait to marry you."

I covered his hands with my own as tears of unadulterated joy filled my eyes. "I love you too. And I loved the proposal. It was so... *us*."

"I was worried you'd think it was too soon," he said, concern clouding his blue eyes. "But when I saw that a real pirate ship was making a stop in New York, I couldn't help myself."

"It was perfect. *You're* perfect."

"I don't want you to think I'm rushing you. I want you to take your time and plan the wedding of your dreams. I thought we could get married in your hometown church in Missouri."

Tears flooded my cheeks and he kissed them each away with tender brushes of his lips. "Thank you, Cruz." He pulled me close, and I felt a familiar bulge throbbing against my stomach. "Good grief, tell your little swimmers to take a chill pill."

He chuckled and copped a feel of my ass through my leggings. "Whenever you're ready, my boys will be waiting."

Looking up at him, I dragged my tongue along the small scar on his bottom lip and felt his cock jerk hard. "You looked really hot as a pirate. The costumes... um, did you borrow those..."

I let the implication hang in the air, and he picked up on it immediately, his grin nothing short of rakish.

"I bought them. They're in the trunk of the car."

Heat flooded my nether regions, and I grabbed his hand, tugging him toward the exit. "On second thought, let's leave now."

He pulled me back with a laugh. "Be patient, cariño. We have family here we need to entertain, but later tonight, Captain Raven is all yours."

As we walked hand-in-hand back to the party, I looked up at the man who knew me better than anyone—the man who loved me better than anyone—and my heart was incredibly full.

"Tell me your happy thing," I requested, and his blue eyes lowered to mine as his lips curved into a sweet smile.

"You, Tink. It's always you."

And so the roguish pirate and the saucy wench lived happily ever after.

Epilogue

I strolled through Central Park with Monty and Kassie, who was now several months pregnant. I swear, my brother's face turned to mush every time he looked at his wife's round belly.

It was a Saturday, and the sun beamed high in the sky, the leaves casting dappled shadows on the ground.

"How's the new job going, Cruz?" Kassie asked.

"It's good, actually. I work pretty much nine to five now and only get called to the building at night or weekends in case of an emergency, which is rare."

"I'm glad you took the job, Chief," Monty added, referring to my new position as Chief of Security for *Bouvier, Inc.*

"I am too. I miss the excitement of the response team, but I'm going to be a married man soon, and I don't want to work seven days a week anymore."

"That's right. You need to spend time with your bride." Kass bumped me with her elbow. "And your kids when you two decide it's time."

"Yeah, SWAT work is difficult on a family life. Most—though not all—of my former teammates are bachelors or divorced. Lehra and I talked about it, and she said she'd support me in whatever I chose to do. That only made my decision easier. I chose spending time with her."

Monty smirked. "And it's not like you have to work two jobs for financial reasons now."

I shot him a glare. He'd been witness to the only real fight between Auburn and me. My oldest brother wanted me to take a share of *Bouvier*'s annual profits, and I not-so-politely declined. In my mind, it wasn't my company.

Our grandfather Bouvier had built it into the fashion empire it was today, but I'd never even met the man. Monty and Auburn had grown up in the industry with our dad at the helm, so I didn't feel like I had any right to the company's profits.

Auburn wanted me to be an equal recipient since I was a Bouvier brother, and while I appreciated the sentiment, I didn't feel comfortable doing so. There was a lot of yelling, stomping, pouting, and table banging, but we'd finally reached a compromise with Monty serving as referee.

I accepted the position as Chief, along with an absolutely ridiculous salary that I had no idea what to do with. I'd thought my pay from being Auburn's driver and personal security guard was exorbitant, but the money I was making now as an "executive" member of the staff was mind-boggling.

Once my hot-headed brother accepted that I was just as stubborn as he was and calmed down, he hooked me up with his financial advisor and also some worthy charities he thought I might like to help manage my newfound wealth.

"When are your mom and Eli moving here?" Monty asked, changing the subject.

"Next month. Mama is wrapping up things with the security business and handing over the reins to Phil. He was Papa's right-hand man for years, so he's the right choice. They're planning a buyout plan, so the lawyers are hammering that out."

Kassie smiled sympathetically. "Is it hard seeing your father's business change hands?"

I rubbed at my forehead. "It is, but I can't expect Mama to run it forever. She's worked her ass off for years, and I'm glad she's finally taking time for herself. The important thing is that she and Eli are moving to New York, so we'll all be together."

"I know she wants to be close to you and Quinnie, but I think a certain blue-eyed silver fox may have had a little bit to do with her decision to move here," Kass said, her brown eyes sparkling.

It was hard to contain my smile. Paul Bouvier and Stella Estrada were officially dating. He flew down to Texas to see her every weekend, and I hadn't seen my mother smile so much since before Papa died. Any weirdness at seeing her with another man—albeit my biological father—went up in a cloud of smoke each time I witnessed them together. They were like moony-eyed teenagers, and to be honest, it was pretty fucking beautiful. I was happy that they were happy.

"I've been meaning to talk to you about something, Mont. Mama told me that Eli has been taking art and design classes at the local community college. We thought he was just wasting his life away with video games and shit, but apparently, he applied for a scholarship, got it, and has been studying in secret for the past year."

Monty nodded. "Dad told me. He said Eli showed him his sketches from his fashion design class, and he was impressed. Said the kid's got some talent. I'll check them out when he gets here and take him under my wing. If he's as good as Dad says, we can find him a job at *Bouvier* whenever he gets his degree."

"Thanks, man. I was hoping you'd say that."

"No prob. Any brother of my brother is a brother of mine. Or something like that." We shared a laugh before he turned his attention to his wife. "Need to sit for a few minutes, baby?"

"Can we? Carrying your daughter is hard work. How about over there in the shade of that tree? It's hot as Hades out here."

"Sounds good."

"Are you guys more excited to meet Snoopy or Garfield?" Kassie asked as Monty held her hands while she sat on a colorful wooden bench. We were meeting the stars of our favorite Instagram page today, as well as their owner.

"Garfield," Monty answered instantly. He sat on one side of his wife while I took the other. "He seems like such a chill dog."

"Same," I agreed. "I'm thinking of getting Lehra a puppy. She had dogs growing up in Missouri, and I think she misses having a pet."

"You should," Kass agreed. "I'm looking forward to meeting Snoopy the cat. She reminds me of my husband, grumpy and cute."

Monty rolled his eyes and grumbled, "I'll give you grumpy when we get home tonight."

"How about you get me a bottle of water for now," she suggested, batting her eyelashes at him.

Of course, he hopped off the bench like his pants were on fire. "There's a cart right over there. You stay here with Cruz." Then he kissed her lips, followed by a sweet kiss to her protruding belly over her pink maternity shirt.

"He's such a sucker for you," I commented with a huge grin on my face.

"I know," she said without shame, her eyes following her husband's huge frame across the grass. "But you have no room to talk. Lehra could crook her finger, and you'd come running. And I guarantee you'll be ten times worse once you knock her up."

"No lies detected," I confirmed. I'd seriously burn down the world for my woman. "How is Sully handling the situation of being a big brother?"

"Oh, he's so excited. We know that can change as soon as this little one is born because babies need so much time and attention. Monty has ordered twelve books on helping kids cope with a new baby in the house." She laughed. "He's studying those books like a college student during finals week."

"That's pretty damn awesome. I mean, completely over the top, but I love how he treats Sully as his own."

She bit her bottom lip, eyes still trained on her husband. "Sully and I hit the jackpot for sure. I tried to be both mother and father for years, but Monty stepped in like it was second nature to him. He takes Sul to ball games, teaches him how to be a little man, everything a boy needs from a daddy. I seriously can't touch a door handle anymore or my son berates me because Monty taught him that he should always open doors for ladies."

"You did a wonderful job with Sully, Kass. He's a great kid, so don't sell yourself short. But I know what you mean. My papa stepped up and raised me like his own as well. I never even suspected that he wasn't my biological father."

"You were lucky to have him, and you're lucky to have Paul as well." Her eyes flashed to the side and widened. "Oh, look! There're Snoopy and Garfield." Kass pushed to her feet and shimmied her shoulders with excitement.

I stood too and shielded my eyes with one hand, training my gaze in the direction she was pointing to find the fluffy blond lab on a leash being held by a woman with a dark pixie haircut. A black-and-white cat was being pushed in a baby stroller by a man with raven hair. They were just beyond where Monty was standing in a long line for refreshments.

"I think Mont spotted them too," I said, watching as he got out of line and walked slowly in their direction. The woman handed off the leash to the man and crossed a patch of grass, hands clasped in front of her waist. *She looks nervous*, I thought vaguely.

My brother's steps faltered, and all of a sudden, he took off at a dead run toward the woman. "What the hell is he doing?" I muttered, seeing the pets' owner running toward him as well. As soon as they neared each other, she jumped, and Monty caught her. The woman's legs wrapped around his waist, and my hackles instantly rose.

"Oh my god," Kassie whispered beside me.

"What the fuck?" I barked, anger spiking inside me as Monty spun the woman around and embraced her. Had he been having some kind of online affair with this woman or something? No, surely not. He adored his wife.

But this shit was difficult to watch, especially when Kassie sank to her knees in the grass, wailing like someone had just died. I fell onto the cool grass beside her, wrapping myself around her and pressing her face against my shoulder so she didn't have to witness... whatever this bullshit was.

But she fought me, yanking her head back to stare at the spectacle across the way as tears streamed down her face and landed with wet plops against her pink top. It broke my heart to see.

"Kass, sweetheart, just don't look. I don't know what's going on, but I'm about to kick my brother's ass all over this park for treating you like this."

"No," she croaked. "No."

"Shhh," I soothed, trying to keep my fury at bay for the time. *Who is that woman? Some old girlfriend or something?* "Let me get you home. I'll call Lehra to come sit with you, and then I'll take care of it."

I had no idea what I was going to do besides punch Monty Bouvier right in the mouth. How fucking dare he do this in front of his pregnant wife?

"No," Kass said again, her voice stronger this time. "You don't understand."

Well, that's the fucking understatement of the century.

"Explain it to me. Do you... do you know that woman?"

She nodded, focusing her gaze on the hugging duo. Then Kassie bowed forward, her body curling over her pregnant belly as she wept.

"That's his..."

I couldn't understand the last part of that through her heart-rending sobs.

At a loss, I rubbed a hand up and down her back, attempting to soothe her. "Who, Kassie? I'm sorry, I can't hear you."

She lifted her reddened eyes to mine, tears streaming down her face as her lips curved into the hint of a sad smile.

"That's his sister." As I attempted to process her words, she turned her attention back to the pair and lifted a shaky hand to point. Her next words were clear as day and shook me to my core.

"Evie Bouvier is alive."

NOT QUITE THE END

Well, well, fucking well...

If you're not dancing in a circle with your arms in the air, yelling, "She's alive! She's alive! Evie Bouvier's alive!" like Kathy Bates in that movie *Misery*, then you need to up your game.

For all of you who have messaged and emailed, asking where Evie was... if she was still alive... if we were going to find out what happened to her... now you know.

And I promise, all your questions will be answered in **Book Four: Love Without Control.**

Flip to the next page for the prologue to this compelling and heartbreaking story.

And I promise... this will be the last full book in this series. Still thinking about a couple spinoff novellas though. (Paul and Stella, anyone?)

EXCITING NEWS: I've got a new series in the works, and Lehra's friend, Nicolette, will be the main character in Book One! This series will follow the family who owns Hale Cosmetics in Houston. Flip over a couple pages to read the blurb for **Hale Yes: Book One in the Highway to Hale series**. It's available now on Amazon.

Prologue to Love Without Control

Evie Bouvier

I WALK TOWARD THE man I haven't seen in years, my heart hammering in my chest. My brother, Monty Bouvier.

God, he's gotten big. Which is a silly thought because he's a grown-ass man now, and the last time I saw him in person, he was only seventeen.

He stares at me with confusion on his face, and I see the moment he recognizes me. We simultaneously break into a run, our arms entwining around each other when our bodies crash together. He's so strong now, lifting me from my feet with ease as my legs wrap around his waist.

Tears. Nothing exists except for the tears of sorrow and regret that stream down my face and soak his shirt. I can feel his grief dripping down my neck.

We say nothing for the longest time, aside from murmuring each other's names, his with question marks behind each word, as if to assure himself that it's really me.

"Evie?"

"Monty."

"Evie?"

We go back and forth like that until he finally pulls his head from my neck and searches my face. His blue eyes mirror my own, blue and extremely wet.

"It's you." His tone is awestruck and raspy as he touches my face and swipes at my tears. "It's really you." My brother's voice is so damn deep now, but there are cracks between each word that I know match the cracks in his heart.

Because of me.

"It's really me," I promise him.

Monty shakes his head back and forth, his expression a jumble of wonder and confusion.

"Where have you been all this time? What the hell happened to you, Evie?"

Well, here the fuck we go.

I heaved out a long breath and spit it out. "I was kidnapped."

My brother's face transforms into one of rage, one of the protective big brother, even though he's a year younger than me. "By whom?" he grits out.

I glance over my shoulder at the man standing nervously near a tree about twenty yards away, his face a mask of apprehension as our eyes meet.

Dear god, Monty is going to kill him.

But I can't let that happen. Because while Dane is the man who took me away from my family, the man who was my captor...

He is also the man I love.

Love Without Control is available now on Amazon, or you can order signed paperbacks on my website: www.jadedollston.com

Sneak Peek of Hale Yes

My name is Nicolette Bell, and I spend more time with microscopes than men. I've got the doctorate degrees, the lab coat, and the resume that all scream "boss babe scientist."

But what I don't have is a love life. I've only dated other scientists in the past, and let's just say my Bunsen burner is not being properly lit.

I hate my current job at a large cosmetics company in New York, so when I make the move to Houston, Texas, to work at Hale Cosmetics, I make a solemn vow to myself: Absolutely no more science nerds in my bed.

Zero. Zilch. Nada.

And then I meet the scientist in charge of the lab, Dr. Helix Hale. Tall and handsome, he's got dreamy eyes and a jaw that would make a Renaissance statue green with envy.

Did I mention he wears glasses? And would you like to venture a guess as to who is a sucker for a man in glasses? If you guessed me, here's your gold star.

But no. I've sworn off science guys forever.

Until we begin this crazy fake dating scheme for a wedding and have to share a room. And let me tell you, the things this man is hiding beneath those starched clothes and suspenders would have any woman doing a triple take.

I swear, Helix Hale is like Superman in a lab coat.

Despite my best efforts, I find my resolve wavering, and after a steamy night ends with me bent over a lab table, all I can say is...

Hale Yes.

Also by Jade

Bouvier Family Saga
Love Without Numbers Auburn and Gianna
Love Without Influence Monty and Kassie
Love Without Demands Cruz and Lehra
Love Without Control Evie and ???

The Fierce Protectors Series
Features six super-hot, possessive, growly former Navy SEALs who live to love and protect their women. They're all available on Amazon.
Dauntless Protector- Grumpy/Sunshine, Nanny Romance
Devoted Protector – Love After Loss
Deadly Protector – Second Chance Romance
Disgruntled Protector – Enemies to Lovers
Determined Protector – Single Parents
Damaged Protector – Age-Gap Forbidden Romance

You can also check out **Young Protector –** Deadly Protector Prequel Novella

Standalones

The (Kinda) Secret Pineapple Island Swingers' Resort *If you love laugh-out-loud rom-coms, vacation flings gone rogue, and a hero who definitely knows how to handle his (hockey) stick, The "Kinda" Secret Pineapple Island Swingers' Resort is your next must-read.*
Rating the Book Boyfriend – Hilarious Holiday Rom-Com
Delay of Game – Angsty, funny sports romance
I Dream of Johnny – Genie Rom-Com

Highway to Hale Series
Coming in 2025

Follow the Hale Family, owners of Hale Cosmetics, in their amusing and dramatic search for love.

Book 1: Hale Yes

Book 2: Hale No

Book 3: Hale Damage

Book 4: All Hale the Queen

(Titles and order of books subject to change.)

Make sure to follow me on my social media accounts or visit my semi-neglected website www.jadedollston.com There's a link there to buy signed paperbacks of any of my books.

facebook.com/profile.php?id=100081302873689

instagram.com/author.jade.dollston/

tiktok.com/@author.jade.dollston?lang=en

One of the best ways you can help indie authors is to leave a review on Amazon, so please hop on over and do that now.

AUDIOBOOK NEWS!

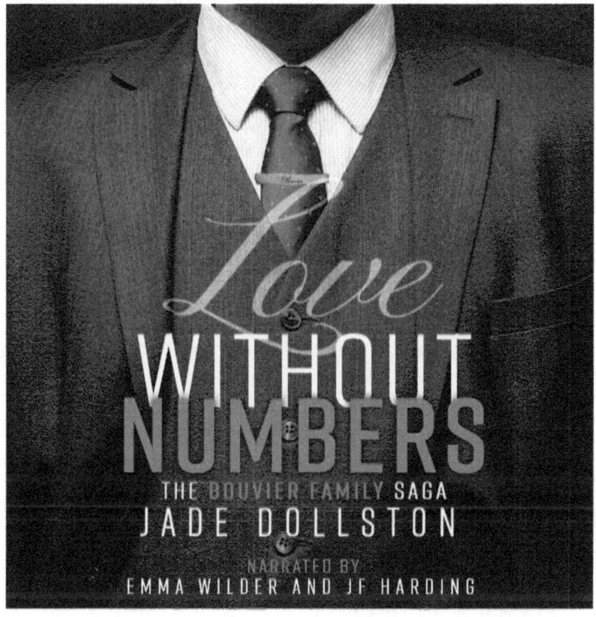

AUBURN AND GIANNA FROM **Love Without Numbers** are now available on audiobook! You can find them exclusively on Audible and Amazon. If you'd like a spicy little sample, type this into your internet browser: https://dl.bookfunnel.com/5o2s834noh.

Book Boyfriend Builders

What happens when four friends drink way too much one night and *accidentally* start a man training business?

They run with it, of course.

After all, who better to build the perfect book boyfriend than a group of romance authors? But it's not all sunshine and roses when the men you're dealing with prove to be impossible to train.

Stubborn, enigmatic, grumpy, annoying, deceptive... you name it, and we've got a guy.

In the midst of teaching the art of listening to your woman, the famous door frame lean, and how to properly growl that she's *such a good girl*, things begin to happen between us and our clients. Things that aren't exactly professional.

So grab a cocktail and relax as we share our stories. We are Gemma, JoJo, Ava, and Libby, and we're...

The Book Boyfriend Builders.

This rom-com collaboration is brought to you by authors L.A. Ferro, Carolina Jax, AK Landow, and Jade Dollston.

Acknowledgements

First of all, thank you so much to my **readers**. It means so much that you took a chance on an indie author, and I appreciate the time you took to read **Love Without Demands.** I love when readers reach out to me while they're reading, so feel free to do so on my social media platforms that are listed on the "Also by Jade" page.

To the fabulous TL Swan: Thank you so much for your encouragement, advice, and humor. If it weren't for you, my stories would still be collecting virtual cobwebs on my computer.

To my beta readers: You chickies are amazing! Lakshmi, Mindy, Thorunn, Brittany, and Amanda, thank you for being absolutely the BEST team I could hope for, even when you possessive bishes argue for hours over the men. I adore each of you - thank you so much for always keeping me on my toes. Your insights are invaluable, and I couldn't do this without you. A special thanks to Amanda for being my Spanish translator. Your knowledge of dirty Spanish words is unrivaled!

AK Landow: You're my sister from another mister. My book signing roomie. My book bestie. My bath buddy. (Wait, what!?) You're an amazing author, and you inspire me every day with your brilliance. Thanks for hashing out every single detail that goes into publishing a book with me. (But seriously, do you really like the L in this font, or should I switch to another one?) You're also a kick-ass alpha reader, and you ALWAYS make my books better – THANK YOU!

Carolina Jax, and LA Ferro: Thank you both for being such wonderful and supportive friends. It's so awesome to have people who will tell you like it is while always having your back.

Chrisandra: You are the most amazing editor in the history of ever. Thank you for the REAL TALK and for your confidence in me and my writing. I'm also so happy to be your fave – but don't worry... I won't tell the others!

Chanel, Becca, and Kalie of Good Girls PA services: Wow! I am so freaking lucky I've found you ladies. Thank you for handling business like boss bitches so that I can spend more time writing. Your support means everything to me.

To my ARC and Street Teams: I honestly couldn't do this without you! I love getting to know all of you in the groups, and I just want you to know that I think you're the most amazing, beautiful, fun, book-pimping people on Earth. So keep pimping! Mama's got new cover ideas.

ABOUT THE AUTHOR

JADE DOLLSTON IS A Texas author who loves reading, Doritos, and rum. She is married to her high school sweetheart, and they have one amazing daughter.

Her love of reading all things smutty has turned into a love of writing all things smutty. She enjoys a diverse selection of romance, and this is reflected in her writing style. Be prepared to laugh, cry, cringe, and fan your face, possibly all in a single chapter.

Jade is so excited to share her work with the world and hopes that you enjoy reading the words from her heart.